Jason Dean was born in South London in 1966. He spent many years as a graphic designer before turning his talent to writing and deciding to write the kind of American thrillers he'd always loved to read. He lives in Thailand with his wife.

Praise for Jason Dean:

'*The Wrong Man* is a fantastic debut novel . . . An adrenaline fuelled thriller . . . Prison Break meets The Fugitive with Mission Impossible, in book form!'
Tesco Book Blog

'Slickly written, cleverly plotted and hugely entertaining . . . an action-packed thriller'
Chris Ewan

'*The Wrong Man* is a roller coaster of a ride with a superhero at the helm. Doesn't miss a beat'
Thrillers4u

'Tough, intelligent, driven, Bishop is a thinking reader's action hero'
Matt Hilton

'The central fellow, former Marine James Bishop, is a great character launching a really pacy new series – excellent stuff'
Bookseller

'A thrilling debut from an author who has the necessary skills to entertain readers for many years to come'
CrimeSquad

'A classy thriller'
Lancashire Evening Post

By Jason Dean and available from Headline

The Wrong Man
Backtrack
The Hunter's Oath
The Outsider

Exclusive Digital Short Stories

One Good Turn
The Last Quarter
The Right Way
The Hardest Part

JASON DEAN
THE
OUTSIDER

headline

First published in 2015 by
HEADLINE PUBLISHING GROUP

1

Cataloguing in Publication Data is available from the British Library

ISBN 978 1 4722 1265 8

Typeset in Adobe Garamond by Palimpsest Book Production Limited,
Falkirk, Stirlingshire
Printed and bound in Great Britain by Clays Ltd, St Ives plc

HEADLINE PUBLISHING GROUP
An Hachette UK Company
Carmelite House
50 Victoria Embankment
London EC4Y 0DZ

www.headline.co.uk
www.hachette.co.uk

To my brother, Stuart

ONE

James Bishop spotted movement on the other side of the street and pressed his eye to the scope for a better look. But it was just one of the male tenants at number forty-five, locking the front door behind him as he left for the day. Bishop already knew that particular townhouse had been converted into separate apartments, and that all of them were currently rented out. But he wasn't interested in that house. He was interested in the neighbours at number forty-seven.

It was 11.43 on a cold Friday morning in early November, and he was sitting by the window of a dingy, stale-smelling studio apartment on Stenlake Drive in Bethesda, Maryland, about ten miles north-west of Washington DC. The apartment had little in the way of furnishings. Three empty wooden crates set against one wall. Another one by the window that he was using as a seat. The tripod-mounted Zeiss spotting scope. A knapsack on the floor containing his lunch, a flask of coffee and a few other essentials. That was about it.

But what the place lacked in amenities and creature comforts, it more than made up for in location. Stenlake Drive was a fairly upmarket street made up of quite expensive townhouses, and the one Bishop was here to observe was directly opposite this apartment. The house was owned by the manager of a popular sports bar in town, and he lived there with his girlfriend, a woman named Amelia Parrish.

Currently, Bishop was waiting for Amelia to show herself.

The reason he was there at all was because he occasionally did contract work for Equal Aid, a small non-profit set-up that specialized in supplying financial aid to victims of domestic violence. A week ago his contact there, Ed Giordano, had called him and said there was a woman at the small offices in Brooklyn who might need more than financial help, and was he free?

Since it had been over a month since he'd said yes to a job, Bishop said he was and made his way over from his place on Staten Island to the offices to meet Amelia Parrish face to face.

She was in her late thirties and would have been attractive if not for the excessive amount of make-up she was wearing. Bishop could guess the reason for it. The story was familiar. After years of physical and mental abuse Amelia wanted to escape and start afresh someplace else while she was still young, and since the boyfriend didn't allow her to leave the house alone she'd taken a real risk driving from Maryland to Brooklyn. Naturally, she was afraid to go to the cops for fear of what he would to do her once he was back on the streets. And Bishop knew he would be. Guys like that always managed to get out somehow.

And next time she'd end up in hospital. Or worse.

So he was currently checking her story out. As a first step Bishop always undertook close surveillance of the client's home circumstances himself. He'd learned the value of on-the-spot reconnaissance from his time back in the Corps, where accurate intel could mean the difference between life and death. Even more so when he'd entered the close protection business a couple of years after his discharge.

Old habits died hard. Especially the ones that worked.

In Amelia's case, before he could set events in motion he needed to be absolutely sure everything she'd told him was on the level. So far it looked like it was. The boyfriend had left for the bar at 07.15 that morning and had returned again at 11.37.

It was 11.48 when Bishop saw him emerge from the front door with Amelia close behind. Bishop lowered his eye to the scope and adjusted the magnification. Amelia was wearing smart, casual clothes that emphasized her trim figure. Looked like the guy was treating her to lunch somewhere, just like a regular boyfriend. Except Amelia was wearing sunglasses on an overcast day, while a scarf partially obscured her face. She waited and looked around the street as the guy locked the door behind them.

Bishop rotated the eyepiece to its maximum zoom setting. Amelia's nose filled the lens and he gripped the tripod lever and panned it slowly across her face. She was wearing even more make-up than when he'd first met her, but it wasn't helping much. This time the facial bruises were dark enough to show through.

There were a lot of them. Much more than last time. The boyfriend had probably found out about her unauthorized trip to New York and decided to punish her for her mistake.

Bishop followed her with the scope as they both turned left and walked down the street. Once they were gone, he leaned back on the crate and stared at a large discoloured water stain on the ceiling. This was only a preliminary recon, but it looked like the woman could genuinely use some help. In addition, the guy would need to be persuaded how unhealthy it could be to try seeking her out once she was gone.

He was thinking of how to do this when he heard a knock at the apartment door.

Which was puzzling, especially as nobody other than the landlord knew he was there. And with the landlord more than happy with the cash arrangements for the week-long rental, it was unlikely to be him.

Bishop ignored it and continued thinking on the problem at hand until the person knocked again. This time it was accompanied by a muffled female voice, saying, 'I know you're in there, Bishop. Come on, open up.'

Frowning, Bishop slowly got to his feet. That voice, muffled though it was, had sounded familiar. He was still trying to place it when he unlatched the lock and pulled open the door.

And came face to face with the one woman he'd never expected to see again.

TWO

Supervisory Deputy US Marshal Angela Delaney stared back at him with a faint smile on her lips. 'Hello, Bishop,' she said, glancing at the bare apartment behind him. 'It's been a while. So are you planning on inviting me in or what?'

'Sure, come in.' Bishop took a step back to let her enter, then watched her walk over to his place by the window. It had been a couple of years so she had to be in her mid-forties now, but as before she looked a decade younger. She was still attractive and her face still had that stern quality he remembered so well, with those pronounced cheekbones and the large, dark brown eyes that missed nothing. Her shoulder-length blond hair was also tied back in the usual ponytail. Today she was wearing a smart navy-blue pantsuit that emphasized her trim, athletic figure. He also noticed the discreet bulge under her right armpit.

She bent down and took a quick peek through the scope, then turned to him. 'If I asked what you were doing here, would you tell me?'

'I'm working. And I notice you're packing. Does that mean this is an official visit?'

'No. Far from it.'

'In that case, take a seat.'

Delaney smiled and lowered herself onto the crate and crossed her legs. She looked around the bare apartment again. 'Real nice place you got here, Bishop. Spacious.'

'I've stayed in worse.' Bishop grabbed one of the other crates from against the wall and set it down opposite her. Sitting, he said, 'I wasn't expecting visitors, but I've got a flask of cool coffee if you want, or there's tap water.'

'I'll pass, thanks. You look about the same, Bishop. Still in shape,

4

I see, and still cutting your hair to within an inch of its life.' She narrowed her eyes. 'Hey, do I see a couple of grey ones in there?'

Bishop brushed a palm over his buzz cut and said, 'Trick of the light, probably. So, you mind telling me how you found me?'

'Finding people is a big part of what I do, remember? And blame it on your cell phone. It's amazing what you can find out these days, given the right equipment.'

'It's a brave new world, that's for sure.' He really needed to start using only pay-as-you-go cell phones from now on. Nothing was untraceable these days, but they came pretty close. 'So suppose you tell me why you're here.'

'Okay, I came to ask for your help.'

Bishop stared at her. '*You* want *my* help.'

'In a way.'

'They got you chasing another fugitive, Delaney? Maybe a guilty one this time?'

She smiled, clearly remembering their past associations. The first time had been three years before when Bishop, having been framed for murder and handed a life sentence, made a solo prison escape and hit the streets of New York in an attempt to uncover the guilty party, while Delaney used every available resource to try and track Bishop down and put him safely back behind bars again. And though the situation had ultimately ended satisfactorily in his favour, he had to admit she'd gotten very close a number of times. Very, *very* close.

A year later, Bishop was a free man with all that behind him when he suddenly got a call from Delaney, completely out of the blue. She was on leave and wondered if she could buy him a coffee and pick his brains regarding the methods he'd used to remain on the loose for so long. For future reference, she said. He'd accepted and they'd met at a Starbucks and talked over coffee. Once Delaney had gotten the information she wanted, the conversation gradually moved onto other subjects and they soon discovered they not only respected each other, but actually liked each other too. Things had progressed very quickly from there, and the following fortnight had been a pretty physical one for the both of them. Not to mention just plain fun, which was something that had been lacking in Bishop's life at that point. And while he still occasionally looked back on that period with fondness, he'd never really expected to ever see Delaney again.

Yet here she was, sitting right across from him.

'Chasing fugitives isn't *all* we do, you know,' she said. 'We have other duties.'

'So I gather that means you're currently on a protective detail for an important somebody or other, right? Either a federal witness or a member of the judiciary, probably. And since I couldn't care less if a judge gets offed or not, I'm guessing the first one.'

'That's correct.'

'So who's the principal?'

'I can't say at this point.'

'Okay. Male or female?'

'Male. Although we're looking after his son too.'

'And who's this guy testifying against?'

'Again, I can't say.'

Bishop smiled. 'So what *can* you tell me?'

Delaney went over to the window and looked out. 'Okay, this is what it is,' she said, turning to him. 'I'm currently the replacement team leader for a special protection detail responsible for a witness who's due to testify in a murder trial on . . . well, very soon. His real name's being kept a secret until the day of the trial, while the man he's testifying against is . . . let's just say he's a very bad man who's not short of influence or money. If he wants something or somebody bad enough, he can usually get it.'

'Okay.'

Delaney sighed. 'So a short while ago this guy somehow found out my witness's identity and location and sent in a professional to kill him. And even though the assassin ultimately failed in her task, she ended up killing the witness's wife instead.'

That got Bishop's attention. 'I'm assuming this wasn't on your watch?'

'God, no. I was called in to take over the moment my predecessor screwed up.'

'When and where was this?'

'Two weeks ago, in Apple Valley, California.'

'All right, I admit it. I'm intrigued now. So how did it all go down?'

Delaney sat back down on the crate. 'The way I understand it, the only outside party my predecessor – let's call him Connors – allowed into the safe house was this cleaning woman who came once a week. Connors got her from this company we've used before and vetted her completely, and she never saw the witness or his family at any time, either. So everything's fine and dandy until she has to fly back to Mexico for a sudden family emergency. Another cleaning girl shows up at the appointed time, a Desdemona Alvarado, and before Connors lets her in he gets the office to do an immediate check on her, which comes out fine. Connors also gets the owner of the cleaning company on the line to describe her in detail. He does and she checks out, so Connors lets her in.'

'He didn't search her?'

'He couldn't without blowing their cover.'

'Which was?'

'They were supposed to be a low-budget movie production company scouting locations for a future project. But they had a metal detector disguised as a movie prop just inside the front door and that gave her an all-clear, so Connors let her get to work.

'The way Connors explained it, Alvarado must have hidden some electrical wire in her hair that she was planning to use as a garrotte. Somehow, don't ask me how since we're still not clear on this, Alvarado got into the witness's bedroom and saw him dozing on the bed. She was creeping up on the guy, ready to do the deed, when the wife came in and saw her and shrieked. Alvarado got her right in the throat with one of those lethal karate kicks and broke the poor woman's neck, and she was just turning her attention to the witness himself when Connors burst in and put her down with a head shot. Naturally, all hell broke loose after that and as soon as the director heard what happened, he ordered me to go in and take control of the situation, including getting the witness and his boy out of there and somewhere safe. Which is what I did.'

'FUBAR,' Bishop said.

'That's one way of putting it. Then once we got resettled I had to use some pull to arrange a very private cremation service for the wife, which was a logistical nightmare, but the witness insisted on it and I couldn't really blame him. And now we're all just holding our breath and staying away from the neon lights until the day our guy's set to testify, which he's *still* prepared to do, believe it or not. If all goes to plan, once the trial's over we'll bury him and his boy in WitSec and nobody will hear of them again, at least not under their present names.' She puffed out her cheeks. '*If* all goes to plan.'

'Things rarely do.'

'Agreed.'

'You said California before. Is that where the trial's being held?'

Delaney gave a faint smile. 'Not even close, Bishop. With secret witnesses we often go the low-key route by taking them completely off the grid and sticking them in the boondocks far away from prying eyes, and flying them in and out when necessary.'

Bishop rubbed a palm over his scalp again. 'So the owner of the cleaning company who endorsed this Alvarado woman. What did he have to say for himself?'

'Not a whole lot. The sheriff's department found him in his office with his throat slit from ear to ear. Alvarado must have had a backup stay with him and make sure he said all the right things when Connors called him. Then he gets quickly disposed of and there are no more loose ends.'

'Professional.'

'Definitely.'

Bishop thought it all over for a few moments. The story had a familiar ring to it, based on his own past experiences. 'You know it's a leak from inside, don't you? Possibly somebody on your own team.'

'To be honest, I don't know anything for sure at this stage, but I'm leaning heavily towards that conclusion, yeah. That's why I'm here. Now I've made thorough checks on all the team members since the attack, and from there all the way up the chain of command, but nothing's flagged up as even remotely suspicious. And I can't simply request a whole new team without *some* kind of evidence to back me up, since that would only put a black mark against all our names for years to come. I've cut out all unnecessary links in the communication chain, though, just to be on the safe side, and currently I'm reporting directly to Director Christiansen and nobody else. So outside of my team, he's the only one who knows our current location.'

Bishop smiled. 'Plus whoever else he decides to tell. His deputy, possibly. His secretary, almost certainly.'

Delaney smiled too. 'A cynic.'

'No, a realist. I know how government agencies operate. So back to this witness. What is he, a disgruntled relative, an ex-employee, a John Q Public, what?'

Delaney paused, then said, 'He's just a normal guy off the street, Bishop. Nothing more than that, really. Just a normal guy with a really nice wife and a great kid. Except the wife's now gone, and it's just him and his boy.'

'And he's still willing to testify? That's pretty impressive.'

'Yeah, I know. And the worst thing is this could have all been avoided if he hadn't gotten cold feet the day he was originally set to testify.'

'Really?'

'Yeah, a case of nerves or something. The DA did some fast talking, though, and convinced the judge to postpone the trial date that time. Then after the murder of the witness's wife the judge *had* to authorize a second continuance, but he's made it clear to the DA that he won't postpone again under any circumstances. This time my guy either gets on the witness stand on . . . on the day he's supposed to, or the case gets dismissed and the accused gets to walk out a free man. Which, believe me, would be very bad all round.'

'So if your guy wants to get on the stand now, what's the problem?'

'The problem is, my gut's telling me there's going to be another attempt on his life before the trial date. I can feel it in my bones.'

Bishop nodded. He could understand that. He'd learned long ago that you ignored your instincts at your own peril, especially in the close-protection business. 'Okay.'

'But now I find myself in a position where I can no longer trust my own team, and that's not a good place to be. I'm in a Catch-22 situation here, Bishop. One of them could well be the leak, but I can't have them all replaced at this late stage without more proof than I've got. Which is zilch.'

'And somehow this all leads you to my door.'

'Right. Now what I want is to bring in an extra person, an experienced professional from the outside with no connection to the Marshals Service or any other law enforcement agency, and therefore no hidden agendas. See, I need somebody I can trust, Bishop. I'd want them to point out anything I might have missed, and I'd also want them to watch the other team members very carefully and tell me anytime they spot any suspicious behaviour.'

Bishop stared at her. 'And this somebody. That would be me, right?'

Delaney smiled back. 'Can you think of anyone better?'

THREE

Bishop thought for a moment, then said, 'For how long?'

Delaney paused. She obviously knew that the more she told Bishop, the easier it would be for him to find out which high-profile murder trial she was talking about. There were only so many. Finally, she said, 'A week, maybe. Ten days tops.'

'A week to ten days,' he said, then shook his head. 'I still don't get it.'

'Don't get what?'

'There's no shortage of decent talent out there, Delaney, and any one of them would be more than happy to take you up on an offer like this. So why come to me?'

'Well, there's another big problem, which is this has to be completely off the books. And that means I can't get official authorization to pay a professional close protection officer the going rate. What I *can* do is fudge my expenses and pay him out of that, but it wouldn't be much. I could probably go to eight or nine hundred, but that's about it. How many of your old colleagues at RoyseCorp would agree to that kind of reduction in pay?'

'Not many. More to the point, why would I?' Bishop stood up and walked over to the window. 'Out of interest, how exactly would you explain this new addition to the rest of your team? Without getting lynched, I mean.'

'That's all been arranged. Once I told the principal what I had in mind and how it might cause problems, he understood and said I can tell my team that he's given me an ultimatum, that after what happened to his wife, either I bring in an outside agent to help or he takes his son and walks. They won't be happy, but they'll accept that.'

'Sure about that?'

'About as sure as I am about anything.'

Bishop looked out the window again. The sky was overcast with dark grey clouds coming in from the east. Looked like more bad weather was on the way, or worse weather.

After a few more moments spent thinking to himself, he turned back to Delaney and said, 'Sorry, Delaney, but I don't think I can help you.'

'Really? Care to give me a reason?'

'I can give you plenty. I've been out of the close protection game far too long, and I'm too rusty. That's one. And I also stopped taking orders a long time ago. That's another. I can roll off some more if you want, but the end result will be the same.'

'Come on, Bishop, I can be pretty diplomatic when I want to be. I can suggest without ordering. And I already know your record back to front so it wouldn't be hard for me to look upon you as an equal. In fact, I'd value any advice you had on possible weak spots in our defences. And I don't believe you're *that* rusty. So what other objections have you got?'

He stood up and sighed. 'Okay. Here's a big one. *Why* should I? And don't bring up the money again. I'm not that desperate.'

'Well, in that case, maybe you should cast your mind back to the first time we encountered each other. I seem to recall I played a sizeable part in getting you off the hook, in more ways than one. Or have you forgotten?'

'I rarely forget anything.'

'I know. Eidetic memory, according to your high-school teachers.'

'So what's your point?'

'My point is you owe me one.'

Bishop shook his head. 'I don't see it that way, Delaney. While chasing me you came across evidence that confirmed I wasn't quite as guilty as you'd been led to believe, which you then passed on to the relevant people. As far as I'm concerned you were simply a professional doing her job. And doing it well, I might add. I wish there were more cops around with your work ethic, but don't start thinking I owe you any favours, because I don't.'

She looked at him. 'You're a hard man, Bishop.'

'That's the second time you've said that to me. Maybe you should have thought about that before making this trip.'

'And I can't exploit any personal feelings you may have for me at all? We did share some pleasant moments together a couple of years back, or am I misremembering?'

'No, you're not, but we were just ships passing in the night, that was all. It was fun, but after two weeks I came out of it knowing as much about you as when I went in.'

She paused for a moment, frowning. 'Okay, how about this for an idea? Come in with me, and after all this is over I'll owe you a favour. A *professional* favour.'

He raised both eyebrows. 'You mean like a get out of jail free card?'

'My influence doesn't run that far, Bishop. But if you ever get yourself in a bad scrape, I might – repeat, *might* – be able to get you out of it. And that's not an offer I make lightly. In fact, I almost regret making it now. So what do you say?'

Bishop smoothed his hand back and forth over his scalp. 'That's a very tempting offer, Delaney. You don't know how tempting, but it's still a no. Sorry.'

He walked over to the front door, pulled it open and waited.

Delaney got to her feet and used a hand to carefully smooth out the creases in her trousers. She went over to Bishop and stopped just before the doorway. 'Meeting's over, is it? Just like that?'

'I think we've pretty much exhausted the subject, don't you?'

'And I can't say anything else to change your mind?'

Bishop shook his head. 'I can't think of anything else I want.'

'In that case, I'm sorry to have wasted your time.' She nodded grimly at him before walking out and down the hallway towards the stairs.

Bishop watched her go, then gently closed the door.

FOUR

Angela Delaney hated Mondays as a rule of thumb, but this particular Monday morning was turning into a real peach and it wasn't even ten yet. They'd been ensconced at this new safe house in this remote section of North Vegas for almost a fortnight now without too many problems, so John Strickland decided today was the day to abandon all caution and screw with the routine, just so he could take in some fresh air. He currently had her cornered in the kitchen. She'd only come in to get a coffee refill, and now this.

'Come on, Delaney,' he said, 'I need fresh air. We both do. Barn and me have been cooped up here for two weeks now and we're going stir crazy. At least I am. I need a cigar and I need to feel the sun on my face. Just for a few minutes, that's all I'm asking.'

'Look, you can suck it up for just a few more days, can't you?' she said for about the twentieth time. 'Then once this is all over you can have all the fresh air you want.'

'Hey, we got desert all around us, for Christ's sake. Who's gonna see?' He motioned to Deputy Marshal Reiseker, standing by the sliding glass doors at the other end of the room, watching them both. 'Your man's right there, keeping watch on the rear. He hasn't seen anything. None of the others have spotted anything either. Just let me out in the backyard there for a few minutes. I mean, what can it hurt?'

'I'd prefer not to find that out the hard way.'

Delaney took a sip of her coffee and watched him exhale loudly, trying to calm himself. She realized he was greying at the temples, and wondered why she hadn't noticed before. Or maybe it was a recent thing. She studied the handsome, tanned face and saw it also contained lines she hadn't seen before. Strickland had always looked younger than his forty-five years, but now he seemed to be aging before her eyes. Not too surprising, though, after what he'd been through. As annoying as he was being today, she still felt sorry for the guy.

Strickland went over to the kitchen island, perched on one of the breakfast bar-stools and in a calm voice said, 'Listen, Delaney, in all the time we've been here I haven't asked for much, but I want this and I'm not gonna take no for an answer anymore. Now anybody else would have told the DA to get screwed after Carrie . . . after Carrie got killed by that bitch, but I'm still sticking to the plan like I said I would, even though it was *your* people who screwed up in the first place. So it comes down to this. I'll get up there and do my thing when the time comes, but only if you let me have some time in the open air right now. That's the deal.'

'And if I refuse?'

'Then I don't testify.'

'Are you serious?'

'I've never been more serious. I'm not bluffing, either. Try me and you'll see.'

Delaney sighed and wondered if it was worth the risk. He looked as though he really meant it, though. And as much as she hated to admit it, he did have a point. He *had* been a good boy so far, despite having every reason not to be. She knew she was just being stubborn. And a few minutes of fresh air wasn't an unreasonable request. But only after a few precautions were taken first. She wasn't about to start getting careless now.

'Okay,' she said finally, 'against my better judgement you can get your fresh air, but you follow my instructions to the letter and only one at a time. Agreed?'

'Now *that's* what I'm talking about,' he said, grinning. 'You're okay, Delaney. Let me go tell Barney while I get my cigar.'

As he trotted off to his room, Delaney said, 'Reiseker, go get the camera.'

'Right, boss.' The deputy moved off down another corridor towards his room, where both cameras were kept.

Delaney stepped over to the rear doors, made a gap in the shutters and looked out onto the large, empty, north-facing backyard and the desert beyond. This wasn't anywhere near as good a spot as the one in Apple Valley, but it had been the best she could come up with on such short notice.

They were on Gulliver Street, in the sparsely populated north-eastern tip of Las Vegas. All the houses around here were set on large plots with plenty of space separating them. The streets at the front and sides were also quiet enough that strangers could be spotted immediately. The biggest downside was the flat desert beyond the rear fence back there. It was totally open, or almost. The unlit Las Vegas Beltway cut across the landscape two hundred yards to the north. But beyond that, nothing. That was why she'd also brought the thermal imaging cameras along. Day or night, they could pick out any life form within a five-hundred-yard radius.

Reiseker came back in holding the ATN thermal eye monocular scope. He slid the rear door open, stepped outside and kept going until he reached the wooden fence. It only reached his chest. She watched him bring the scope up and make a slow arc from west to east. Then back again. Then again. Finally, he lowered the scope and in her earpiece Delaney heard, 'A few cars whizzing by on the Beltway, boss. Otherwise, nothing out here at all. Not even a road runner.'

'Fine,' she said into the wrist mic. 'Stay there and keep scanning. Hammond, Lomax, I need you both at the rear kitchen doors. The principals are going to take a little fresh air. Alpha One will be going first.'

Both men acknowledged. They arrived in the kitchen area at the same time as Strickland, who had an unlit corona in one hand and a book of matches in the other.

Swallowing her misgivings, Delaney motioned to Lomax and Hammond, who both nodded back. Lomax, the larger of the two, went out first. There were three lawn chairs stacked up against the left-hand fence and he brought one over and set it down five feet from the rear doors. Then he came back and stood by the door, waiting.

'I don't like that low fence back there,' Delaney said, 'so do your smoking sitting down, okay? I'll give you ten minutes to finish your smoke and then you get back in here.'

Strickland nodded and stepped outside with Reiseker and Hammond on either side of him. Then he just stood there for a moment, breathing in like a man just released from prison. 'Man, air never tasted so good,' he said, raising the cigar to his lips.

Delaney strode over to him and hissed, 'Sit *down*, I said.'

She was in the act of placing a hand on his left shoulder when Strickland's head suddenly snapped round violently to the left and a sharp crack echoed through the air.

Delaney had just enough time to see a blood-red dot appear on Strickland's left temple before he dropped to the ground like wet cardboard.

FIVE

The shooter watched from his hiding place as the four deputies moved in a blur of motion around the fallen target. He smiled. His patience had been rewarded. As he knew it would be. Almost thirty hours in this same spot, but it had been worth it. He knew there would be at least one opportunity, however minimal, but that's all he needed. All he'd ever needed.

He watched the woman immediately dive to the ground and cover the victim with her body. The others had already pulled their pieces and were scanning their designated areas like they'd been trained. The one with the thermal scope kept the device at his eye and swept the desert again, frantically searching for him.

Yeah, good luck with that, the shooter thought.

He was currently in a shallow trench of seven feet by three feet, about three hundred yards away from the rear fence. It had taken twenty minutes of intensive digging the night before last. Then he'd placed his equipment, rations and water supplies in there, laid himself down and carefully covered himself in the thick foil thermal sheet he'd brought along. He'd taken great care to camouflage it so it would be indistinguishable from the rest of the desert. At least when seen from a distance.

The marshals were very disciplined in their movements. Calm and collected. None of them panicked. The second man was covering the west side, while the other took the east. Impressive. They'd obviously gone through enough drills to ensure every movement counted. For all the good it would do them.

Three seconds had passed already.

The shooter slowly brought his left hand away from the trigger and, without looking, slid it along the dirt to the cell phone he knew was there. He felt along the keypad and pressed a single button and waited. In his earpiece, he heard the familiar ringing tone begin.

Through the rifle's viewfinder, he watched the magnified face of the woman as she frantically gave orders to her people. He saw her look down at the principal under her as she talked. Then she frowned and said something else. Looked like she was shouting. She got to her knees and pulled the principal onto his back. The shooter noticed the principal's hands seemed to be moving. The female deputy reached into her inside jacket pocket and pulled out a cell phone. She looked at the screen before bringing it to her ear, looking in every direction.

'Who's this?' she said into his earpiece.

'The guy who just took out your witness,' Bishop said. 'I think I just found one of those weak spots you talked about.'

SIX

Bishop slowly got to his knees and let the thermal blanket slide off his back. He felt like he'd aged twenty years overnight. His leg muscles were almost totally numb, which wasn't too surprising after spending over thirty hours in one position.

He slowly arched his back muscles, then raised his hands and clasped them behind his head. And kept them there. He sat with his legs folded under him. Pointless trying to stand. It would be a few more minutes before the blood started circulating down there again. Besides, it was safer this way. Two of the deputies were sprinting towards him, handguns at the ready. About fifty feet away and closing. One was shouting, '*Down on your stomach. On your stomach. Do it NOW.*'

The guy's voice sounded a little shaky, which was understandable under the circumstances. So Bishop carefully lowered himself onto his stomach again. When they reached him, the one who'd been yelling pressed his gun barrel hard against the back of Bishop's head and said, 'Don't move.'

Bishop wasn't sure he could even if he wanted to. His hands were pulled behind his back and cuffed. There were pretty rough about it, but that was okay. Bishop understood. They'd just been made to look bad and needed to assert their authority again.

After giving a complete body search, they pulled him to his feet and silently marched him back to the house, keeping him upright whenever he stumbled. Which was often. Delaney was waiting by a door-sized gap in the fence and shaking her head. She looked as angry as her colleagues. Bishop didn't blame her. Nobody liked being made a fool of.

His two guards brought him to a stop a couple of feet away from her. One of them passed Delaney the RAP4 T68 sniper paintball rifle.

The other one handed over the camo sheet Bishop had brought with him from New York.

'You know, I'm seriously considering having you placed under arrest,' she said. 'Or shot. Of all the arrogant, thoughtless, *idiotic—*'

'It could have been much worse,' Bishop said, 'don't you think?'

Delaney blew air out of her cheeks and said nothing. She studied the two items in her hands, still shaking her head. Bishop glanced past her shoulder and saw the principal sitting on the ground by the rear doors with two more deputies around him. One was offering him a glass of water. The principal had a hand pressed to his left temple, but otherwise didn't look too bad for a dead man. Better than he had any right to be. His son was there, too. He was saying something to his father while staring hard at Bishop.

'Where did you get this thing?' Delaney asked, inspecting the rifle.

'A specialist paintball store just off the Strip,' Bishop said. 'Even second-hand those things aren't cheap. I kept the receipt, though. You can put it on your expenses.'

'Yeah, right. And this thermal sheet?'

'That's my own property.'

'How the hell did you even find us?'

'How long are you planning to keep me tied up?'

Delaney rolled her eyes and said, 'Okay, Lomax, you can uncuff him.'

'You sure, boss?' asked a voice behind him.

'Yeah. This is the same guy I went to see on Friday. Go ahead, take them off.'

The cuffs were removed and Bishop brought his hands round and rubbed his wrists.

'Now answer the question,' Delaney said. 'How did you find this place?'

'Well, all I had to go on was neon.' Delaney winced slightly, no doubt remembering her little slip back at the Maryland apartment, and Bishop went on quickly, 'So I played a hunch it wouldn't be too far from your last place, and Vegas fit the bill nicely. I also scanned the news sites until I found a story about a shooting in a house in Apple Valley, then did a little research until I found the house in question and the name of the person who rented it. Turns out a Simon Garrett signed the papers for that place on September seventeenth. Then it was a case of calling every realty agent in Vegas to see who'd rented houses on the day of the murder. You know, it's amazing how most people on the phone believe you're a cop if you simply say you are.'

Bishop saw the principal was watching their impromptu gathering. He got to his feet and looked about to walk over, but the other deputies quickly got him and the boy inside, then slid the doors closed.

'And?' Delaney prompted.

'And,' Bishop continued, 'it turns out there was a Stephen Garland who rented a one-storey house in a fairly remote part of North Vegas on that day. If your guy's going to change his name, Delaney, tell him to change the initials too. It's a common mistake. Anyway, I flew over here to check the place out from a distance and it didn't take long to discover I'd hit pay dirt. Your guy sitting on the chaise longue in the front yard, under the big umbrella. That's a really nice touch. He looks very natural sipping from his endless supply of beers, lazily watching the day go by as he listens to the radio. What's he really drinking?'

'Iced tea.'

'Any spares in that cooler of his? All I've been drinking for the last thirty hours is stale water.'

Delaney studied him. 'You've been waiting out there since the night before last?'

Bishop shrugged. 'I've been stuck in worse locations, and for far longer. Course I was a lot younger, too. Still, I figured you'd allow your principal some fresh air at some point, even if it was for a few minutes. It was worth a shot. And one was all I needed.'

Delaney looked skyward and quietly said, 'I knew I shouldn't have given in.'

'If it's any consolation, I was watching your guys' reactions and I couldn't see any weak areas there. Of course, that would have all been academic had I been the real deal.'

'Wonderful,' a second voice said from behind him. 'So if this guy found us, that means we're compromised again, right?'

'Not necessarily,' Delaney said.

'She's right,' Bishop said, turning briefly to the two men. 'I was privy to certain information nobody else would have known. At least in theory.' He turned back and added, 'But I *would* suggest no more smoking breaks for your boy from now on.'

'So you plan to stay the course, then?'

'If the door's still open. I'm thinking of that special favour clause, in particular.'

'It's still open. But what's changed since we last spoke?'

'You're a good-looking woman. I realized I like being around you, that's all.'

Delaney gave a faint smile in return.

'I could also really do with a shower. And maybe a change of clothes if one of your deputies can oblige. I didn't pack any extras with me.'

'I'm sure we can arrange something. Lomax, Hammond, go and collect the rest of his stuff. Bishop, come on inside and I'll introduce you to everybody.'

SEVEN

The principal was leaning on the counter of the kitchen island and wincing as he touched the darkening bruise on his left temple. He was about five-ten, stocky, dark complexion, with thick longish black hair that was greying at the sides, and a symmetrical face with dark eyes set far apart and deep creases running from the sides of his nose to his mouth. Bishop put him somewhere in his late forties.

Next to him, his son was carefully cutting two strips from a roll of Elastoplast. He was a slim, good-looking boy with dark blond hair cut very short, dark blue eyes and skin a lot fairer than his father's. So he probably took after his mother, at least physically. He wore blue jeans and a black T-shirt with a huge white barcode on the front. Bishop put his age at somewhere between twelve and thirteen.

As Delaney led Bishop over to them, the man said, 'So you're the son of a bitch who shot me. I'll have this stinking headache for the rest of the day, thanks to you.'

Bishop shrugged. 'Better than being dead, wouldn't you say?'

'Yeah, well, I don't take kindly to being made a target, even if it's just a paint pellet. You can believe if Barn wasn't in the room I'd lay you out right now.'

'Maybe once this is all over, you can give it your best try.'

The man nodded slowly. 'Maybe I will at that. It'll give me something to look forward to.'

Bishop smiled. It seemed they'd already gotten off to the best possible start, and he had to admit the guy had some balls. He kind of reminded Bishop of a compadre from his old Bravo Company called Hurley who'd always been quick off the mark to right any and all perceived wrongs to his honour. Especially in front of witnesses. The two men even shared the same body shape.

24

Delaney introduced Bishop by name, and added, 'So you've met our witness, John Strickland, and this is his son, Barney.'

'Hello, Barney,' Bishop said. But the boy just gave a curt nod as he fitted an Elastoplast to his father's temple.

Strickland winced. 'Jesus, I feel like I've walked head first into a cannonball.'

'There's an old quote that goes *"Pain is just weakness leaving the body,"*' Bishop said. 'If that helps.'

'It doesn't. And I bet whoever said it never had some idiot shooting at them.'

'Actually, it came from the mouth of a Marine Corps general, so he probably did have some experience there.'

'Yeah?' Barney said. 'What was his name then?'

Bishop turned to the boy. 'Who, the general?'

'Yeah, what was his name? Bet you don't know.'

'I do actually. His name was Lewis Puller.'

The boy gave a snort. 'Yeah, sure. Probably just pulled his name out of a hat to make yourself look smarter.'

Bishop smiled at the kid. 'That's right. You've seen right through me.'

Barney gave him his best sneer back. 'So you know any others? *Real* ones, I mean. Not made up, like that one.'

'One or two. There's an old Chinese one that goes *"It is good to strike the serpent's head with your enemy's hand."* You ever hear that one before?'

Barney paused for a moment, appearing deep in thought. Then he said, 'Oh yeah, yesterday morning on *Sesame Street*, Burt said it when Big Bird took a dump on Ernie's head.'

Bishop's smile widened. He couldn't help it. The kid was quick on the draw, no doubt about it. He reminded Bishop of himself as a boy. Combative, always questioning, never accepting, always answering his elders back. Even though they'd only just met, he had a feeling he and Barney were going to get along just fine.

Strickland, looking at his son with unconcealed pride, said, 'Don't ever try and match wits with my boy, Bishop. You'll come off second best every single time.'

'I'm beginning to see that.'

'Well, *you* sure know how to make a first impression on people,' Delaney told Bishop. 'Maybe now would be a good time to give you the ten-cent tour.'

'Good idea.' He nodded once at Barney, and let Delaney lead him out of the room.

The single-storey house was twice as wide as it was deep. Around a hundred and twenty feet by sixty, Bishop estimated. The interior layout was simple enough. Upon leaving the kitchen and dining area, he and Delaney entered a short hallway with a bathroom on the left and a narrow utility room on the right. This room also allowed direct access to the garage via another door at the end. Then it was mostly open-plan at the front of the house, while the bedrooms continued along the rear. Delaney's room was followed by the Stricklands' room, then two shared bedrooms, and finally another short hallway with another bathroom on the left and the door to a fifth, front-facing bedroom directly opposite.

On the right was a large recreation room with a pool table, with the huge main living area taking up the space on the other side of the house. The front door was located halfway down, with two long wooden divider shelves serving as a makeshift entrance hall.

Bishop made mental notes of everything, especially the Stricklands' room, looking for weak spots. He could probably have written a book, there were that many. But then no location was ever perfect. It was impossible. All you could do was make sure the weak areas were covered adequately.

He also met two more marshals; Reiseker had been the one in the kitchen, and another, Jiminez, had been watching the street from one of the windows in the living room. Neither man acted pleased to see him, but that was okay. Bishop was here to do a job. As long as they did theirs, everything else was secondary. Delaney said another marshal, Sweeney, was currently resting in his room.

She finally led him back to the utility room and opened the connecting door to the garage. She turned on the lights and Bishop saw spaces for three vehicles. Only two bays were currently in use. The nearest one held a five-year-old silver Ford Taurus. The middle bay was left empty, while the far bay held a large black Toyota Highlander SUV.

'The Ford we use for day-to-day stuff,' Delaney said. 'Food shopping, and the like. The SUV's solely for transporting the Stricklands to and from whatever airfield we decide to use. Both vehicles have also got police scanners, tuned to the local police frequency.'

'Both fully armoured?' Bishop asked.

'The SUV only. The body's bolstered with steel plates, ballistic nylon and Kevlar. Ballistic nylon in the floor and ceiling. Windows are half-inch-thick polycarbonate mixed with leaded glass.'

'What about tyres?'

'We've got polymer run-flats clamped around the wheel's centreline. They're good for fifty or sixty miles of driving even after being shot out.'

'Yeah, I've used them before. Don't these vehicles also have built-in GPS trackers?'

Delaney nodded. 'Hidden in the armrest on the driver's side.'

'Uh-huh. And the keys are kept where?'

'One key in the ignition at all times, the spares I keep in my pocket.'

'Good,' Bishop said. Straight out of the manual. He walked to the front of the garage and checked the three wooden doors. They were single-panel overheads, operated both manually and remotely from the looks of things. Bishop looked to his left and saw a slit of a window at the side of the garage that looked out onto the front yard. He went over and peered through and saw the same deputy as before, lazing on the chaise longue.

'That's Gordon,' Delaney said. 'Goes out at eight every morning and comes back in at six. Any longer would bring unwanted attention from the neighbours. As it is, he's just another deadbeat drinking his days away.'

'What about when he has to go?'

'He always warns us before he needs a bathroom break. Don't worry, there's always somebody watching the front. Same for the back.'

Bishop turned to her. 'Not always.'

Delaney grimaced. 'Yeah, that's right. What time was it when you dug your nest?'

'About three a.m. I worked fast using that thermal sheet as a windbreak, but one of your men should have spotted movement out there.

But I'm aware that looking through those thermal imagers can really screw with your eyes after a while, so maybe you should split the night watch so that they change over every couple of hours.'

'Will do. Any other suggestions?'

Instead of answering, Bishop slapped a palm against the nearest wall. The sound of flesh hitting clapboard sidings echoed through the room.

'Yeah, I know,' she said with a sigh. 'A stucco or adobe house would have been ideal, but I was short on time and there were none on the rental market. At least not any this size. This was the only one that came close to what I needed, especially in this area.'

'It's a problem,' Bishop said and looked out the window again. 'On top of which, these are all large plots around here. Each house is surrounded by masses of open space, including this one. Especially at the sides. And no boundary walls, either. Only the concrete one out front, and at three feet high that's not much good for anything. I know there's no such thing as a perfect safe house, but I'm seeing more cons than pros with this one. If you really believe there's going to be another attempt on Strickland's life, I'd recommend you find somewhere else to hole up till Thursday morning.'

'Thursday?' Delaney narrowed her eyes. 'Where did that come from? I didn't give you any specific dates.'

Bishop gave her a look. 'I don't make a habit of going into situations blind, Delaney. You should know that. And from the minimal information you gave me in DC, it didn't take me long to discover that of all the major murder trials in the news at the moment, only one has been postponed twice for unspecified reasons. We're talking about the Felix Hartnell trial, right?'

Delaney shrugged. 'Yeah, that's right.'

Bishop nodded. He'd made it his business to find out all about Felix Hartnell. The Coke King of America, according to the popular media, at least on the distribution side of things. But always with an *alleged* before it. Because nobody had ever been able to touch him for spitting on the sidewalk in over twenty years. His record was spotless. According to legend, he was the ultimate paranoid and never spoke to anybody outside a small circle of trusted lieutenants and never

28

talked on the phone. At the same time he made large donations to all the right charities and institutions, and made a habit of being seen with all the right movers and shakers. The man just seemed to have a natural talent for doing everything right.

'So once you learned he was involved,' Delaney said, 'is that what changed your mind about joining us?'

'Let's just say I'm surprised you didn't bring his name up when you came to see me last Friday. It might have simplified things.'

'Or complicated them. You have to understand I couldn't take the risk of giving out too much information without knowing for sure you'd say yes at the end of it and, let's face it, you can be . . . well, unpredictable.'

Bishop smiled. 'Thanks. So assuming the media stories are accurate, our guy in the next room actually witnessed Hartnell execute an undercover DEA agent by the name of Salvador Ferrera in Columbus, Ohio, three months ago?'

'That's correct.'

'How?'

'By being in the right place at the right time, I guess.'

'I doubt he sees it that way, not after what it's cost him. But I'm still curious as to how an apparent law-abiding citizen happened to witness a major paranoid like Hartnell actually pull the trigger on somebody. And not just somebody, but a cop, no less. I mean, what are the chances?'

'Don't read too much into it, Bishop. Apparently, Strickland's car simply died on him when he was driving home from work in the early hours of the morning. With his cell phone battery dead, he started searching on foot for a nearby gas station or a phone box to get help. He was taking a short cut across an old abandoned industrial area when he witnessed the shooting in question, then waited until Hartnell and his guy had left before getting the hell out of there and pretending nothing had happened. Then when he saw Hartnell's face in the paper a week later, he and his wife had a long discussion about what to do and they finally agreed to do the right thing and take it to the feds. And so here we are.'

Bishop thought there had to be more to it, but now wasn't really the time. They had other problems. 'So back to the subject at hand. What are your thoughts on another move?'

'The problem is each move we make leaves an additional paper trail that the enemy can pick up on. You're evidence of that. I know that slip I made back in DC gave you your starting point, but who's to say Hartnell's people aren't already refocusing their efforts on this section of the country? One more move from us could be just the break they need. That bastard's got almost unlimited resources, don't forget.'

It was a reasonable argument. But Bishop already knew what he'd do if he was in charge. Only he wasn't.

'Okay,' he said, watching the street outside through the narrow window. 'It's your call. So give me a breakdown of what constitutes a typical day around here. What time the mail comes, that kind of thing.'

Delaney paused. 'Well . . . the mailman usually comes at around eight fifteen every morning except Sunday. He doesn't deviate much. Let's see, before that we get a school bus that starts its route here at seven fifteen every weekday morning. It passes by outside, but doesn't stop. Its first pick-up is a girl in the next street across. There's also a Fat Daddy's ice-cream truck that does a tour around here every weekday at about five p.m. Not always at the same time, though. It stops on this street for about three or four minutes.'

'What about garbage pick-ups? How regular are they?'

'Every Monday and Thursday morning.' She looked at her watch. 'It's now ten forty-five. Today's pick-up should be at around eleven.'

'Okay.' Bishop turned from the window and went back through the house with Delaney following behind. He opened the door to Strickland's room and they both went inside. It was at least twice the size of the other bedrooms, more a suite, with a separate living area with its own couch and TV and an en-suite bathroom. Two shuttered windows looked out onto the rear of the backyard and the desert beyond.

'This here's my biggest concern,' he said. 'If I'd brought a rocket launcher with me, I could have taken the two of them out easily from my position. It's a shame there isn't another room like the utility room we just passed through, but bigger. It's the best room in the house by far. No windows. Centrally located. A projectile would have to pass through at least two walls to reach its intended target.'

'And it's not much bigger than a broom closet. Strickland would never agree to move there.'

'I wouldn't expect him to. Two in a room that size would be impossible. However, I do have an idea, although it'll mean digging into your expenses.'

'The federal government's got large pockets, Bishop. As long as I can present them with receipts. What do you have in mind?'

Bishop brought out his cell phone. 'Just let me make a call first to see if it's possible, then I'll tell you all about it.'

EIGHT

Bishop scratched his cheek as he looked out the side window at the Mojave Mountains in the distance. Or looked in their direction. He didn't really see them. What he was doing was thinking about further preventative measures he could take to secure the house, or at least recommend. He also thought about possible methods the enemy might use to try to get to Strickland a second time. Because he agreed with Delaney. Hartnell would make another attempt before Thursday. If he found them once, he'd find them again, especially if there *was* a leak from within the team itself. All Bishop could do was help prepare for the worst.

Hence, this road trip.

Deputy Marshal Frank Lomax was driving. They were in the SUV, heading west on Interstate 15 and making pretty good time. They'd been driving for the last two and a half hours, having crossed the California state line ninety minutes before. It was now almost two thirty in the afternoon. Traffic was light for the most part, and not a cloud in the sky. Perfect driving weather. That was one of the good things about being on the West Coast. Other than the colder nights, January weather wasn't much different from June weather.

Bishop faced front and saw a sign up ahead that showed they were twenty miles from Barstow. He made a quick mental calculation and said, 'There should be a turn-off about a mile and a half ahead on the right. You'll want to take that and keep going until you see a gas station on the left.'

Lomax nodded. 'And your guy's waiting for us there?'

'If he's not, we'll wait for him.'

The car was quiet again as they both looked for the turn-off.

When it came, Lomax slowed and took the turn, then kept going at a steady forty. There were a few lone warehouse-type structures in the distance, plus a few clapboard houses here and there. If they constituted a town, then it was one without a name, at least not one printed on any map Bishop had ever seen. But it did have a combo gas station and auto shop. Bishop could see it about two hundred yards up ahead. He'd stopped there once before, a long time ago. And since it was equidistant between North Vegas and Bakersfield, California, he'd decided it would make the perfect meeting point for today's business.

As they got closer, Bishop could see the place hadn't changed much. It was one of those basic, old-style gas stations you don't see much of anymore. There was a rusted APCO sign out by the road, then a dirt forecourt with a single set of pumps. Further back was a low grey clapboard building with two overhead garage doors and an office on the right. One of the garage doors was open. The front of an old Ford jutted out. A man wearing dark overalls was leaning over the open hood, doing something to the engine. To the left of the building, under a long wooden lean-to, were several vehicles in various states of disrepair.

The mechanic saw them turn in and strolled over to the pumps to meet them. Bishop lowered the window and the man, a grizzled guy in his fifties, raised the visor of his cap and said, 'Fill her up?'

'Yeah, unleaded,' Bishop said, 'and a couple of Cokes if you got 'em.'

'Can do,' the man said and went to the rear of the vehicle. He opened the gas cap, placed the pump inside, then went over to the office and came back out with the two sodas.

Bishop took the bottles and handed one to Lomax, and said, 'Okay if we stick around for a while to drink these? We're waiting for somebody.'

The man shrugged. 'No skin off my nose.'

Once the guy had filled the tank, Lomax paid him, got his receipt, then drove over to the lean-to. He parked the SUV next to an old Plymouth and switched off the engine. Bishop took a slug of his soda and watched as the mechanic went back to work on the Ford.

Lomax said, 'So tell me, Bishop. Just what makes you so damn special?'

Bishop almost smiled. He'd been waiting for the simmering resentment to show itself and here it was. Finally out in the open. 'You tell me,' he said.

Lomax gave a snort. 'I wish I could, but all I see is another wannabe from the private sector looking to put something cool on his resumé, that's all. But when the principal decided he didn't fully trust us anymore and demanded my boss bring in a body from the outside, Delaney picked you out specifically. And I'd like to know why.'

'Delaney seems fairly approachable for a team leader. Why don't you ask her?'

'I'm asking you.'

'Maybe she just likes my company. She's chased after me before, you know.'

'I'm serious.'

'So am I.'

''Cause I gotta tell you you're screwing up the dynamic just by being here, man. The way we see it our team's like a well-oiled engine and we're just clicking along nicely, then you come along like a loose screw rattling around the carburettor, ready to block the fuel line and screw up the whole works. I don't like that. The team don't like that.'

Bishop sighed. 'Look, I've headed up protection teams before and I know how it works. Anybody from the outside tries to mess with the inner workings is classified as an enemy and is immediately repelled. I get it. But I'm not here to step on anyone's toes, Lomax. All I'm doing is helping fill a few gaps here and there. That's all. You do your jobs and I'll do mine. We don't have to like each other, but I'm sure we can all get along for a few more days.' He looked at Lomax. '*Are* we going to get along?'

'I'll let you know,' Lomax said, and picked up his Coke and took a swallow.

Bishop decided to let it go. He understood it was nothing personal. He might have felt the same in Lomax's shoes, back when he was in the game. But now he was out of that life it all seemed a little dumb and petty to him, like dogs pissing on the ground to mark their territories.

Bishop decided to clear the air and move the subject to something else. He noticed the man's wedding ring and said, 'Been married long?'

'Almost seven years. Why?'

'Just curious. Never got round to it myself. You got kids?'

Lomax shook his head. 'Got a dog, though, which is almost the same thing.' He smiled faintly to himself, obviously visualizing his pet, and said, 'You like dogs?'

'Who doesn't? What kind is he?'

'German shepherd. Four years old. Here, I got a photo.' Lomax reached into his jacket pocket and pulled out his wallet. He slid out a four-by-six photo, folded down the middle, and showed it to Bishop.

Bishop saw it had been taken in somebody's backyard. In the forefront, a friendly-looking German shepherd panted at the camera, while just behind, tickling his ears was the wife in question. With her sharp cheekbones and large eyes, she was extremely good-looking, which was surprising only because Lomax was so plain. In Bishop's experience, like generally attracted like, at least in physical terms. Or maybe he just had hidden talents.

'Beautiful dog,' Bishop said. 'And a stunning wife. You're a lucky man.'

'Yeah, you don't need to remind me,' he said, and took the photo out of Bishop's hand and stuffed it back in the wallet.

'So you live around these parts?'

'No, I'm from back East.'

'New York?'

He sighed and turned to Bishop. 'No, a little place called Bloomington, Indiana. Believe it or not, New York isn't the centre of *all* life on this planet. Anything else you wanna know about me, like what kind of grades I got in high school, maybe? My favourite football team? The chest measurements of my first date?'

Bishop could see the conversation had quickly soured for whatever reason, and said nothing else. The car interior was filled with silence again, which was perfectly fine with Bishop. Silence was his favourite sound.

After three more minutes, he noticed movement in the side mirror. A black panel van was slowing as it approached the station.

'Here we go,' he said.

NINE

Bishop got out and adjusted his suit jacket as he leaned against the SUV. Back at the house Hammond had loaned him a spare suit and shirt, since they were about the same size. But no tie. That was taking things too far.

He watched as the van slowed and turned in. There was a tasteful shield logo on the side with the words DALY DESIGNATED DEFENSE in silver next to it. Underneath was a Bakersfield, CA, address and a toll-free number. The windows were tinted. The driver paused, then steered the van in Bishop's direction before coming to a stop beside their SUV.

The driver's door opened and a smiling black man in his thirties got out and stretched his arms out. He had close-cropped hair and wore tan chinos and a tight black T-shirt that emphasized his muscular physique.

'Bishop,' he said, holding out his hand. 'Long time, man.'

'Long time, Nels,' Bishop said, shaking the hand. The man's grip was as strong as ever. 'I was expecting somebody else to make the actual run, or does the CEO of a major supply company have nothing better to do than play delivery boy these days?'

Nelson Daly shrugged. 'Hey, I just decided this'd be a good chance to see how my old sergeant was doing. I could have flown in on the company jet, man, but I'm in cloak-and-dagger meetings in Mexico City for the next couple of days and I figured this'd be my last chance to see daylight for a while. So, you been waiting long?'

'Not long.'

'Cool. So based on your request, am I to assume you're still in the close protection racket?'

'No, I got forced out of that a few years back. This is just a one-off deal.'

'Something special, huh? I can dig that.' Nelson looked over at Lomax getting out the other side and said, 'Who's the square-head?'

'A federal marshal by the name of Lomax. So you made your first billion yet?'

'In my tax bracket? Forget about it. I sure ain't starving, though. Man, private security's a field where you have to work real hard *not* make a fortune these days. You should really come and see me, Bishop. I could always use a man like you. And I'll make you a millionaire in less than six months, guaranteed.'

'There's more to life than money, Nels, but thanks for the offer. So have you got the stuff I asked for?'

Nelson smiled. 'Yeah, I got it all in the back. Come with me.'

At the rear of the van Nelson unlocked and opened the double doors. Completely filling the interior were two dozen large flat boxes, all stacked against each other.

'All four by two,' Nelson said, 'except for the three extra pieces measuring seven by two. Those are the dimensions you wanted, right?'

'Perfect,' Bishop said. 'Let's get them loaded. Better lower the seats in the back.'

'Right.' Lomax opened the rear door of the SUV and went about making room.

While he was occupied, Nelson said, 'Those extra *extra* items you asked for,' and handed Bishop a snub-nosed Taurus .38 Special in a horsehide pocket holster, along with two speed loaders.

'Thanks. This thing traceable?'

Nelson smirked. 'You need to ask?'

'Guess not.' Bishop pocketed the gun and ammo.

'And you can take this, too.' Nelson handed Bishop a business card with just Nelson's name on it and two phone numbers. 'For future reference. My private *private* numbers, only available to the chosen few. I'm incommunicado for the next couple of days, but after that either of those numbers will go straight through to me, without fail.'

'I'm honoured.' Bishop nodded his thanks and pocketed the card.

Then both men began removing the boxes one at a time and stacking them next to the SUV for Lomax to load. At a hundred and twenty pounds per box, it took a while. It was almost fifteen minutes before the three of them had finished transferring everything over.

Nelson locked his rear doors and said, 'So who's paying for all this, Bish? You?'

'No, Uncle Sam,' Bishop motioned towards Lomax, 'in the shape of this guy here. All right, pay the man.'

Lomax pulled out his wallet. 'You got a total for me?'

Nelson opened the driver's door and from the passenger seat grabbed an invoice he'd obviously printed out earlier. He handed it to Lomax and said, 'Including sales tax, the grand total comes to exactly thirty-seven thousand, four hundred dollars.'

Lomax's eyes went wide. 'Thirty-seven *thou*–?'

'But since Bishop and me go way back,' Nelson interrupted, 'I can do you a twenty per cent discount, which brings it down to a nice round thirty thousand. How's that for customer service?'

Lomax still didn't look too sure. Bishop said, 'Just pay the man. Delaney's already authorized it.'

The deputy mumbled something, then handed Nelson a credit card. Nelson grabbed a portable wireless credit card processor from the passenger seat. He swiped the card and said, 'So, you keep in touch with any of the other guys at all?'

Bishop knew Nelson was talking specifically about the other members of their old FAST unit. He shook his head. 'I'm not too good at that kind of thing. One of my many shortcomings. How about you?'

'A couple.' Nelson handed the machine over so Lomax could key in the PIN. 'Burrows, Hastings. Remember them? Oh, yeah, Jeffries, too. Funnily enough, your name often crops up in our conversations.'

'In a good way or a bad way?'

Nelson took back the machine and said, 'You never ordered us to do anything you weren't willing to do yourself, man. And you never left anybody behind. They've always been major virtues in my book. And believe it or not, I learned a hell of a lot about leadership from you. I know the others all feel the same way.'

'I'll take that as a compliment.'

'You should.' Nelson printed off a receipt and handed it to Lomax. 'Okay, we're all squared away here. Thanks for your business, Mr G-man. Maybe you could put in a good word in with your boss about the discount, huh? I always say a growing business can never have too many government contracts.'

Lomax gave a vague nod and went round the other side of the SUV and got back in.

Nelson was still smiling. 'I don't think he likes me.'

'I don't think he likes anyone,' Bishop said. 'Well, I better get going, Nels. Thanks for delivering on such short notice. I appreciate it.'

'Hey, glad to help out. And just between you and me, if I thought the money was coming out of your pocket I would have handed this stuff over gratis. But since the government are paying . . .'

Bishop nodded. 'I don't blame you.'

'You have a safe drive back, okay, man? And try and stay in touch from here on in.'

Bishop smiled as he opened his door and got in. 'Maybe I will at that,' he said.

TEN

Back at the house, it took less than three minutes to transfer all the boxes from the garage to the Stricklands' room. Five men were doing the carrying this time, though. Strickland and Barney both sat on the main bed, watching the activity. Once the boxes were all stacked against the wall and the deputies had returned to their posts, Bishop glanced at his Seiko diver's watch and saw it was only 16.27.

Good. They still had plenty of daylight left.

Bishop used a small kitchen knife to cut through the packing tape on the nearest box and then opened the flap. Barney got off the bed and came over to join him.

'So is this stuff any good?' he asked.

'Better than good,' Bishop said, hauling the rectangular four-by-three bullet-resistant fibreglass panel out and resting it against the box. It was about one and a half inches thick and had a crochet-ribbed design across its rough surface. 'Since we don't have a safe room in this house, fortifying this room is the next best thing, and these panels will do that.'

Barney felt along the side of one. 'Pretty thick,' he said.

'It's got a level eight protection rating, which means it'll stop anything up to and including a .762 lead core full metal jacket. I've tested it myself. It's serious stuff.'

'What are these things here?' Barney asked, feeling the thick, stubby fibreglass rods that protruded all the way down one side of the panel.

'Built-in dowel joints,' Bishop said, 'so each panel can connect up to its brother to form one long unbroken shield. See the corresponding holes in the other side here? Each panel's the same. Easy to assemble. Even easier to take apart. No drilling necessary.'

'So what's your plan, Bishop?' Strickland said. 'You going to cover this room from top to bottom and lock the two of us inside?'

Ignoring the sarcasm, Bishop said, 'Not quite. These plates will cover the bottom four feet. Anything larger, there's too much danger of the dowel joints coming apart and causing a breach in the defence. For the windows over there, I've got three taller panels that'll cover them up entirely, but that's it.'

Strickland frowned. 'Four feet? So we just duck-walk everywhere?'

'You'll be either sitting or sleeping in here most of the time anyway. This is just an extra level of defence, that's all. If the worst happens you all dive to the floor and stay there. This stuff will stop anything short of a frag grenade. And even then it'll minimize the intensity of the blast by roughly seventy per cent.'

'So you agree with Delaney?' Strickland said. 'You think they'll try again?'

'We have to be prepared for the possibility. And to paraphrase Ben Franklin, I've always believed an ounce of prevention is worth a pound of cure.'

Delaney entered the room at that point and glanced at the large packages leaning against the wall. 'Your pal came through for you, then.'

Bishop nodded. 'He always has done.'

'Need any help putting it all up?'

'No, I can probably do this solo. If I can't, maybe Barney here can lend a hand, right?'

Barney shrugged his shoulders. 'I guess.'

'Good,' Bishop said. 'In that case, you can make a start by opening these other boxes for me. Want this kitchen knife?'

'Nah,' Barney said, and pulled out a miniature multi-tool on a keychain from his front jeans pocket. 'I'll use mine.'

ELEVEN

Bishop had almost finished assembling his improvised safe room by 17.55, yet while Nelson had included some panels with dowel corner joints to ensure no gaps, there was still one gap he couldn't avoid. The door. Despite what he'd told Barney, Bishop had to drill a single panel onto it and hope nothing got through the unprotected spaces on either side. It looked as though he'd have one corner panel left over once he was done, too, which suggested he'd either miscalculated or Nelson had been in something of a rush when packing the van.

As he worked on the last two panels, he glanced over at Barney. It was just the two of them now, Strickland having left shortly after he'd started work. Barney had stayed quiet through most of it, occasionally watching Bishop assemble the inner wall while he quietly played a video game on his pocket console.

'What you playing over there, Barn?' Bishop asked. 'A shoot-'em-up or something?'

'Uh-uh. Tetris.'

'Tetris?' Bishop smiled as he worked. 'They still producing that old thing? I used to love that game.'

The boy looked up at him. '*You* used to play Tetris? But you're too old.'

'I'm not *that* old. Back when I was in uniform, a guy in my squadron would always bring one of the very first Gameboys with him on manoeuvres and any down time we had, we'd take turns on Tetris. Everybody in our squad was addicted to it.'

'Yeah? So what was your record for clearing lines in a single game?'

'Five thousand, seven hundred and forty-six.'

'No *way*. Seriously?'

'But I paused the game a lot during that one, and I never played it again afterwards. I'd gotten it out of my system by that point. How about you? What's your record?'

'I haven't got past five thousand lines yet. But, you know, I don't really care about it too much these days, not after . . . not after what happened with . . . you know, Mom.'

Bishop looked over at the boy. His head was down and his shoulders were jerking a little, but if he was crying he was doing it silently.

'No, I guess you wouldn't,' Bishop said. 'I'm sorry about your mom, Barney. I know what you're going through, and I know there's nothing I can say that will—'

'You *don't* know,' Barney said, glaring at Bishop, his red-rimmed eyes flashing angrily. 'You don't know *anything*.'

'You're wrong, Barney,' Bishop said calmly. 'When I was about your age I lost both my parents, so I know exactly what you're going through.'

Barney paused and gaped at him, his anger gone. 'You did? What happened?'

'Auto accident one foggy night on the New Jersey Turnpike. It was rush hour and there was a major pile-up and six people died in the wreckage, including my folks. It was my tenth birthday too.'

'*Jeez*, your birthday.' He shook his head. 'So does it . . . does it ever stop hurting?'

'Eventually. Like everything. Your grief's at its absolute worst right now, but as the weeks and months go by it'll gradually taper off until it becomes just a dull ache. But that ache'll always be there and you'll never want it to completely go away anyway. At least, I don't. To me, it always acts as a reminder.'

'Good, 'cause I don't ever want to forget Mom. She was the greatest mom ever, you know? I really really miss her.'

'I know you do.' Bishop suddenly had an idea to take the boy's mind off the subject for an hour or two. 'Look, Barney, I've been thinking that it might be an idea to run through one or two worst-case scenarios with you, if you're up for it, that is.'

'What, you mean like role-playing?'

'Yeah, kind of. For example, you've been taken hostage by unspecified hostiles and somehow you've got to find a way of getting word to the outside. Like that.'

Barney nodded, smiling. 'Yeah, that sounds kind of cool. We could do that.'

'Good. I'll work out something for later, then.'

Bishop finally finished connecting the last two fibreglass panels together and stood up and inspected his work. 'There. So what do you think?'

'Not bad,' Barney said, studying all four walls. 'You do good work, Bishop.'

'Well, it's not perfect, but it should hold. Assuming the worst happens. Hopefully, it won't.'

'Do you always do that?' Barney asked.

'Do what?'

'Assume the worst.'

Bishop smiled. 'When I'm on the job. I wouldn't be much good if I didn't, would I?'

The boy gave a shrug. 'I guess.'

'Well, I've got to go now, but I'll see you later, okay?'

''Kay,' Barney said, and went back to his game.

Out in the hallway, Bishop was shutting the bedroom door behind him when he saw Delaney approaching from the living-room area.

'All finished?' she asked.

'I've done as much as I can. Now if it's all right with you I'd like to borrow the Ford and cruise the surrounding streets while there's still some light left. I always like to get a feel of the area whenever I'm on the job.'

'Good idea.' Lowering her voice, she said, 'Look, Bishop, we haven't discussed weapons. I can loan you a backup piece, but I'll have to deputize you first. As a supervisory deputy marshal I have that authority, although I've never had a reason to do it before now.'

'You mean turn me into a cop? You sure know how to scare a guy, Delaney.' He shook his head. 'Don't worry about me. I'll be fine.'

'And what does that mean?'

'It means what you don't know can't hurt you.'

Delaney's eyebrows came together. 'I'm not sure I like the sound of that. Are you telling me you're already armed?'

'You said I'd be assuming an independent role while I was here. Is that true or not?'

'To a point.'

'Well, then, this is me being independent. Ask me no questions, I'll tell you no lies.'

'I get it. Rules are fine for other people, just not you?'

'Nothing wrong with rules if they're sensible. But sometimes even the sensible ones can get in the way.' He paused. 'Look, maybe we should talk about something else.'

She studied him for a moment, then shrugged and said, 'So what do you think of our principals so far?'

'They're better than most. Barney's a smart kid, and Strickland seems reasonably intelligent, although I imagine he's hard work in large doses. At least he's not actively working against you, though, like some people I've protected.'

'Yeah, I know what you mean.' She stared at him quietly for a few moments then said, 'Look, Bishop, I've been thinking . . .' She paused.

'Yeah?'

She gave an embarrassed shrug. 'Nothing. I'm just glad you changed your mind is all.'

'Just don't forget that favour you promised me.'

'I won't forget. Just as long as you don't use it as a licence to get yourself into hot water unnecessarily.'

'I never do anything unnecessarily, Delaney. You know that.'

'There's a first time for everything,' she said, smiling. Then she turned away back to the living-room area.

Bishop watched her back, faintly curious as to what she'd really wanted to say, but hadn't. He still liked her a lot, he knew that. And not just for her looks either. She knew when to bend and when not to, which showed very good judgement for somebody in her position. Yeah, Delaney was all right for a cop. Better than all right, in fact.

Smiling absently to himself, Bishop entered the utility room and made for the garage.

TWELVE

The cell phone on the kitchen table started ringing at 22.17, and Bishop took the call. Delaney and Strickland were also sitting at the table, watching Bishop with interest.

Bishop put the phone on speaker and said, 'Hello?'

'We've got the boy,' a slightly muffled male voice said. 'Do what we say and you'll get him back unharmed, understand?'

'I understand. But before we do anything else I need to talk to him.'

'Naturally,' the voice said. 'He's right here. You've got thirty seconds, so don't make any stupid mistakes.'

After a brief pause Barney's voice came on the line. 'Bishop, is that you?'

'It's me. Are you all right, Barney? How are they treating you?'

'Not too bad. I, uh . . . I just wish I could see you, though. I was real scared a while back, but then I remembered those two breathing exercises you taught me and I'm kind of okay now.'

'That's good, Barney. Try not to worry too much. We'll get you back. Best thing for you right now is to keep your mind occupied as much as possible. You still got your pocket games console with you, I hope.'

'Yeah, I still got it.'

'That's something, at least. Got any decent games on it?'

'Uh . . . yeah, the same two as before, Tetris and Dragon Ball. I always keep them on there.'

'That's fine. Play one of those, then. Now have they given you anything—'

'All right,' the male voice from before said, 'that's enough. You've had more than enough time to get reacquainted.'

47

'That wasn't thirty seconds,' Bishop said.

'So sue me. Next time you'll hear from us will be exactly one hour from now, so keep that phone handy.'

The line went dead.

Bishop put the phone down on the table and nodded at Delaney, who called out, 'Okay, you guys can come on out now.'

'Well, *that* was pointless,' Strickland said. 'They didn't give you anything like enough time.'

Bishop watched the door to the utility room open and Barney and two of the marshals, Reiseker and Hammond, came out. Both men were wearing bandanas over the bottom parts of their faces to represent ski masks. They could have been villains in an old Western, although the suits kind of ruined the effect. While they removed their minimal stage gear, Barney came over to the table and said, 'How did I do?'

'Not bad at all, Barn,' Bishop said. 'I'm impressed.'

'Huh?' Strickland was frowning. 'What conversation were *you* listening to?'

'The one underneath,' Bishop said. 'During those few seconds Barney managed to pass on some useful nuggets of information.'

'Like what?'

'Well, first he told me he was being kept in a room with no windows: *I wish I could see you.* When he mentioned the two breathing exercises, he was telling me there were two exits. That's what we agreed on before. First talk about the windows, then the doors.'

Strickland smiled at his son. 'There. Told you, didn't I, Bishop? Smart as a whip.'

Delaney said, 'And I assume the video game part of the conversation was about more than just playing Tetris.'

'Correct,' Bishop said. 'When he said he had two games on his system, he was telling me that there were two men assigned to him.'

'And the *I always keep them on there* line?'

'That meant his two guards are always watching him. He's never allowed to be on his own.'

Barney was smiling proudly. 'I was trying to think how to tell you that they were both wearing masks, but Marshal Hammond cut me off before the thirty seconds were up.'

48

'Just as a real kidnapper might have done,' Bishop said. 'Things don't always go to plan in real life, but you still did real good with the time you had. You kept the conversation totally natural too, which is the most important thing. Never let them think you're trying to outsmart them.'

'All right,' Delaney said to the two men, 'you've had your fun playing bad guys, now back to your posts.'

The two men left the kitchen and Barney sat down next to Bishop.

'I still don't see the point of all this,' Strickland said. 'Kidnapping's not really Hartnell's style, and even if it did happen, what good's knowing how many windows Barney's room has, or how many exits?'

'It might make all the difference in the world,' Bishop said. 'In these kinds of situations all information is useful information, even if it might not seem so at first glance. And I know kidnapping's not exactly Hartnell's MO, but if the opportunity presented itself to get at Barney he sure wouldn't turn it down, would he?'

'Can't fault that kind of thinking,' Delaney said, getting up and taking her coffee cup to the sink. 'It's always best to prepare for the worst. That's why Bishop's here, after all.'

'Well, I still don't know,' Strickland said. He turned to his son. 'Not freaking you out at all, is it, Barn? All this talk of kidnapping?'

'I'm cool, Dad. Really. And it's good to be prepared if something does happen.'

'As long as you're sure.' Strickland stood up from his seat with a hand against his forehead. 'Man, this damn headache's really getting to me. I think I'll take some more Advil and see if I can grab some sleep.' He kissed his son on the top of his head. 'Don't stay up too late, huh?'

'Sure, Dad. Hope you feel better.'

Once he and Delaney had both left the kitchen, Barney said, 'I'm gonna keep my console in my pants pocket from now on, Bishop. *And* an adapter in the other one so I can always charge it.'

Bishop smiled. 'Good idea. Always be prepared. That's the key.'

'So what else have you got for me?'

'Not much else, Barney, except to emphasize that you should always try and keep your cool in a hostage situation, and always stay positive, no matter how hard it might seem. And don't ever grovel or beg, either. That kind of behaviour usually works against you, both in the short term and the long term. And while you shouldn't ever challenge your captor or play the smartass, it's a good idea to speak your mind occasionally and try and show your captor that you're a human being worthy of respect.'

Barney made a face. 'No way would I *ever* cry in front of a stranger. Even if I wanted to, I just couldn't do it.'

'Good for you. Well, I think that's about it. Maybe we should call it a night for now, Barney. You get some rest.'

'What are *you* gonna do?'

'Well, I've only got the living-room couch to look forward to,' Bishop said, rising, 'so I think I'll take another walk around the neighbourhood before calling it a day.'

THIRTEEN

Bishop woke up to the sound of muted conversation from somewhere behind him. Or one side of a conversation, at least. He kept his eyes closed and listened. A man's voice, just above a whisper. Tense-sounding. It seemed like he was on the phone to somebody. Bishop could only make out a few words. One was *Karen*, soon followed by *Forget it*.

He sat up on the couch and turned round to see Lomax sitting at the table at the rear of the living room with a cell phone pressed to his ear. He noticed Bishop watching, then muttered something else before pocketing the phone and disappearing into the connecting hallway.

Bishop remembered how quickly the conversation had turned sour yesterday after he'd commented on the wife's looks. Presumably, the wife's name was Karen. If so it sounded like there was some kind of marital strife going on there. Or maybe something else? Delaney had asked him to keep a lookout for any kind of odd behaviour from members of her team. He'd have to mention it to her later.

According to his Seiko it was 06.23. It was still dark outside. Another quarter of an hour before sunrise. Light spill from the central hallway behind him allowed him to spot Sweeney sitting at the window, keeping an eye on the front until Gordon went out to his post on the chaise longue in a couple of hours' time.

Bishop opened up his knapsack and pulled out the double-pack of boxer shorts and the toothbrush he'd bought yesterday. Then he took them with him to a free bathroom and brought himself to full consciousness with a long cool shower.

It was 06.48 when he emerged, wearing the same shirt and pants he'd slept in. They were a little crumpled, but presentable enough.

Back in the living room he saw the dawn light peeking through the shutters at the front windows. Delaney was already up and about, too. Assuming she'd slept. She was sipping from a mug as she spoke with Sweeney. He was also drinking from a cup and glared at Bishop when he saw him approaching. The strong aroma of freshly ground coffee beans filled the room.

Delaney saw Bishop and said, 'Well, you look a whole lot better than I feel. Was the couch okay?'

'I've got no complaints. That coffee smells great, by the way.'

'I just finished brewing some. Let's go to the kitchen. I need a second helping.'

As they walked through the house, he said, 'So, you're on the home stretch now. The final forty-eight hours, or close to it. Nervous?'

'Mildly apprehensive, maybe. But then, that's my usual state. Comes with the job.'

'Yeah, I remember the feeling clearly.'

In the kitchen, Delaney took the half-full carafe and poured fresh coffee into a spare mug, then refilled her own mug. Bishop took a sip of his and nodded his approval. It tasted as good as it smelled. Nice and fresh. Strong flavour.

'Out of interest, who signed the rental papers for this place?' Bishop asked. 'One of your team?'

She nodded. 'Sweeney. And for the other place too.'

'And is he part of your regular protection crew?'

'We don't have regular crews in the Marshals Service, Bishop. This isn't the private sector where we can choose favourites. We take what we're given.'

'Okay, but have you worked with Sweeney before?'

'No. Why?'

'Just curious,' he said. 'You told me to keep an eye on everybody, so that's what I'm doing. And on that subject, Lomax was on his cell phone as I was waking up, talking in hushed tones to somebody named Karen. Is that his wife?'

'Yeah. And she's a real looker, too. I'm no expert on relationships, but I have to say marrying her probably wasn't the wisest decision he's ever made.'

'Why? Does she fool around?'

'I don't think so, but Lomax just naturally assumes she does. The jealous type, you know? I do know he's always calling her, making sure she's exactly where she's supposed to be. To be honest, I really can't see the marriage lasting much longer with that kind of attitude, but what do I know? And it's none of my business anyway.'

'Fair enough,' he said. 'Just thought I'd mention it.'

'I'm glad you did. I need to know anything out of the ordinary, but I'm afraid in that particular case it's simply business as usual.'

He took another sip of his coffee and said, 'What about you?'

'What *about* me?'

'No desire to settle down at all?'

She made a harsh sound through her nose. 'The demands of this job aren't exactly conducive to long-term relationships, Bishop. Have you got any idea what the divorce rate is for people in law enforcement?'

'Around the seventy per cent mark, I read somewhere.'

'And you can probably add on another ten per cent for US marshals. I rarely know where I'm going to be from one week to the next in this job, and I've seen too many of my colleagues' marriages go down the crapper to want to make the same mistake they made. In my line, an undemanding casual relationship is about as much as I can handle.'

'And are you in one now?'

She tilted her head at him. 'Not right at this moment, no. What about you? You ready to settle down at all?'

'Not me. I find female companionship nice for a while, and then . . .' He waggled his hand from side to side.

'And then you start getting antsy,' she finished for him.

He shrugged. 'It seems to get worse as I get older. I think I'm destined to die alone.'

'We all die alone, Bishop, but let's just hope that's all in the far distant future. For both of us.'

'Amen to that.'

Delaney watched him for a moment, then said, 'You know, I'm due some vacation time after this assignment. Three weeks at least, by my reckoning. And I think I'll need it too.'

'You can fit in a lot in three weeks. Got any plans?'

'A few ideas, but nothing set in stone yet. It all comes down to whether I want to spend it solo or not.'

'Uh-huh. You got anybody in particular in mind?'

She looked at him again and gave a small shrug. 'I've got a germ of an idea rolling around my head, but I'm not completely sure yet. I'll have to give it some more thought.'

Bishop thought it best to say nothing at this stage. It was an interesting little conversation with plenty of possibilities beckoning, but there was no point in rushing anything. They took their coffees back to the living room.

Sweeney was still standing at the window, looking at something to his right. Bishop went over and made a small gap in the shutters and looked in the same direction. He saw a yellow school bus parked in the street at the front, almost at the next house along. It was one of the traditional models with the engine out in front of the windshield, and the entrance door just behind the front wheels. It was empty except for the driver. Bishop checked his watch and saw it was 07.06. A little early today.

'School bus outside,' he said, and Delaney came over to see for herself.

'It was juddering some before it stopped,' Sweeney said. 'I think the engine died.'

Delaney looked at him. 'Really?'

Then they all watched as the driver opened the front door of the bus and stepped down onto the sidewalk. He was dressed in the requisite bus driver's uniform of grey pants, navy-blue jacket and navy-blue cap. He opened the hood and studied the engine.

Bishop said, 'Is that the usual driver?'

'It's the same one as yesterday,' Sweeney said. 'Different guy before that.'

Bishop turned to Delaney. 'You like it?'

'Not too much.'

'Me, neither. Well, it looks like I'm the one wearing the red shirt today.'

'Huh? How'd you figure?'

'I'm the extra man, aren't I?' Bishop went over to the couch and slipped his suit jacket on. 'Plus I know a little about engines. I don't mind checking it out.'

'We'll be watching,' Delaney said, raising her wrist mic to her mouth. Probably to make sure everybody was up and on their toes, just in case.

Bishop headed towards the front door. Once he was out of their view, he pulled the small .38 Special from the horsehide holster in his pants pocket. When he quietly flipped open the cylinder he saw the same six .9 mm shells in there. He closed it again and slipped it back into the holster.

Hope for the best, but always prepare for the worst. The key to successful living.

He opened the front door and walked out of the house.

FOURTEEN

Bishop moved down the gravel driveway towards the bus. He could see the driver shaking his head at the engine as he pulled a cell phone from his jacket pocket. The guy looked truly pissed off. Or was it just an act? That was something that needed answering, and fast.

The guy was still scrolling through his contact list when he looked up to see Bishop a few feet away. 'Oh, hey,' he said. 'Can you believe it? Engine trouble.'

'I noticed. You all right? You seem a little nervous.'

'Nervous?' The man tried to laugh and failed. 'Why would I be nervous? I mean this is only my second day, and now this shit happens. The engine started stuttering about half a mile back. I kept hoping it'd kick in again, but then it just went and died on me.' He went back to his contact list. 'Now I gotta call my supervisor back at the depot and tell him to send out another bus. And to bring a mechanic out, too. Christ.'

'Before you do that, why don't I take a look first? It's probably something simple.'

The driver brought his brows together. 'Hey, you don't have to—'

'It's no trouble,' Bishop interrupted and came over to join him at the engine. He saw it was a typical twenty-four-valve diesel. Probably about ten or fifteen years old. Looked like it hadn't been cleaned in a while. There was oil everywhere. 'You want to go and try the ignition again for me?'

The driver pocketed his cell. 'Okay, sure. Why not.'

He got in the driver's seat and inserted the key. Bishop leaned in and heard the sound of the armature rotating as the engine tried to turn over. The driver kept at it for a few more rotations before giving up. He came back down and said, 'Man, this bus is screwed seven ways from Sunday.'

'Well, you can hear the starter motor's not catching,' Bishop said. 'But I don't think that's the problem, not if the engine was stuttering before. You could have a leak in the fuel hose, maybe, or a faulty clutch, or even just a warped flywheel. Don't you make a check of the vehicle before each run?'

'Well, I'm supposed to, but I guess I forgot today.'

'Have you got your toolkit handy?'

'Uh, I don't think we got one.'

'You kidding me? All buses have toolboxes somewhere for emergencies. It's regulations. Let's go check the luggage bay, there's bound to be one there.' Bishop didn't know the first thing about city regulations for school buses. He just wanted to check the hold. His internal radar had been pinging since the bus had come to a halt outside the house and one way or the other he wanted to make it stop.

Bishop kept his left hand in his pocket as they walked back along the side of the bus facing the house. The driver knelt down and used a special key to open up the outer flange near the rear. Bishop took a look inside the compartment. It was over six feet long. Easily room for two people in there, but this one was empty. Except further in, Bishop spotted a faded red plastic carrying case lying on a dirty rag. *How about that?*

He reached in and pulled the case out. It was heavy. Metallic items rattled around inside. 'Your toolkit,' he said, handing it to the driver.

Back at the front Bishop said, 'Let me try the engine one more time. You got the keys?'

'Hey, I don't know . . .'

'Don't worry, you'll get them back.' The driver chewed his lip and handed them over grudgingly. 'Tell me what you hear,' Bishop said.

Bishop got in the driver's seat. He put the key in the ignition and turned it clockwise. The starter motor tried its best to cough into life again. With the driver's concentration elsewhere, Bishop kept his grip on the key and ducked down to look to the rear of the bus, checking under the rest of the seats. But there was nobody hiding back there either. The breakdown seemed legitimate enough, but Bishop knew there were endless ways to sabotage an engine without leaving a trace.

Because something was off here. He was sure of it.

He removed the key and stood up, still looking towards the rear. He could see a floor panel about three-quarters of the way down the centre aisle. Maybe that was worth a check.

Bishop heard movement behind him as the driver came on board. 'Hey, what's up?' he asked Bishop. 'You lose something?'

'No, I just—' Bishop began, and halted in his tracks. Through the rear windshield, he saw the figure of a mailman moving in their direction, pushing a standard USPS handcart. Bishop looked at his watch and saw it was only 07.16. The guy was a whole hour too early. And Delaney had said he didn't deviate.

Bishop was getting that cold feeling at the core of his gut. He put his hand in his pocket and clasped the .38. He heard the driver coming down the aisle behind him. When he figured the guy was less than a foot away, Bishop turned, pulled the gun out and stuck the two-inch barrel in the man's gut. He grabbed the guy's lapel and pulled him round so he could still track the mailman's progress.

'How many?' Bishop whispered into his face.

'What?' the driver said, his eyes wild. He glanced down at the gun, then back up. 'What are you—'

'I already made the fake mailman back there. Where are the rest? You got more hiding under the bus, or what? Talk.'

'Hey, man, I don't know who you think I—'

Bishop pulled back the hammer and the guy stopped. 'Gut shots are the worst, believe me. Keep it up and you'll find out why. Now answer me. Where are the rest?'

Instead of answering, the driver darted a look past Bishop's shoulder, then suddenly dropped to the floor with both hands over his head. Out the front windshield Bishop saw a white panel van at the intersection fifty yards away. It had an ADN COURIERS logo on the side and was turning into this street.

A courier delivery at a quarter past seven in the morning? That'd be a first. He heard the van's engine rise in pitch as the driver stepped hard on the gas.

No time to check the floor panel now. He needed to get back to the house, right this second.

As he turned, the guy on the floor suddenly grabbed at his right ankle and tried to pull him off-balance. Bishop pulled his free leg back and kicked him in the temple. Hard. The man's body immediately went limp. Bishop ran to the front of the bus and leaped out onto the sidewalk.

'*It's a hit!*' he shouted, and began sprinting towards the house.

Out the corner of his eye, he saw the mailman to his right pull a large automatic assault rifle from one of his satchels. Bishop aimed the .38 in his general direction and fired off two shots as he ran, knowing both had gone well wide.

Behind him, he also heard a sharp slamming noise coming from inside the bus, quickly followed by windows being smashed. That goddamn floor panel. He'd been right. How many men had been hiding in there? Two? Three?

There was the screeching of tyres to his left as the courier van mounted the kerb, then quickly overtook him down the driveway. The rear doors were swinging open and he saw at least three heavily armed men sitting inside, steadying themselves against the van's movements. The van was making for the wide passageway at the side of the house, towards Strickland's location at the rear. Making sure all sides were covered.

Ahead of Bishop, only ten feet away, the front door was already half-open. Delaney stood there, Glock raised in her right hand.

Then she began firing over Bishop's head as the sound of automatic gunfire suddenly erupted from behind him.

FIFTEEN

Bishop just kept running, trusting Delaney's aim. She continued giving him cover, edging back from the doorway as she emptied a magazine at whatever was behind him. He waited for the inevitable bullets in the back, but none came. As he got closer, a neat row of jagged holes suddenly appeared in the doorframe just above his head. More rounds punched into the wall next to the door.

Then he was diving through the gap and inside.

He landed on the tiled floor, twisting round until he was facing the doorway. Aiming the .38 at two vague human shapes in the bus a hundred feet away, he squeezed the trigger four times until the gun clicked empty. With no idea if he hit anything, he turned his body, kicked out with his foot and slammed the door shut. For all the good it would do.

But he wasn't injured. Yet. If he was going to help get the Stricklands out of this, staying in one piece was essential.

Delaney was crouched at the smashed window by the front door, still firing at the bus, and yelling, '*Reiseker, stay on the one on the left. Hammond, call for backup and keep shooting, dammit.*' She ejected an empty magazine and rammed home a new one. '*Lomax, stay with the principals. And where the hell are the others? TALK TO ME, DAMMIT.*'

Still lying on the floor, Bishop flipped open the Taurus's cylinder and ejected the six empty shells while he pulled one of the speed loaders from his jacket pocket. He could hear more semi-automatic gunfire coming from other parts of the house. From outside, fully automatic weapons hosed the property on all sides. The stench of gunpowder was everywhere, the noise relentless. It sounded like a wooden crate full of nuts and bolts being shaken side to side. The air was full of streaks of light as Delaney's team returned fire. Shattered glass tinkled on the tiles in front of him.

Bishop inserted the six new rounds into the six slots, twisted the loader's knurled knob and released them in a single motion.

He was snapping the cylinder closed when he saw Delaney go down.

She landed a few feet from him, her Glock skittering away along the floor. Blood was pumping from a neck wound and he could see she'd also been hit in the chest. He crawled over to her and she turned to him with glazed eyes. Her mouth opened and closed but nothing came out. He could see she'd taken a heavy hit to the jugular and was leaking blood at a rate of knots. She was dying, and she knew it.

'Get . . .' she managed to say. 'Get . . .' She coughed once and more blood erupted from her mouth. She tried again but no more words came.

'I will,' Bishop said. It was all he could think to say.

She stared at him blankly. She was going.

Bishop placed the palm of his free hand against her cheek and held it there for a moment, thinking of how soft her stomach had felt under his touch, two years ago. And he remembered that small compass tattoo just above her navel. So she'd always know where she was, she'd said. He remembered how the corners of her eyes crinkled when she'd laughed. And he thought of things left unsaid and how they'd now stay that way.

After a second or two Delaney closed her eyes.

We all die alone, she'd said. And she was absolutely right.

Knowing he couldn't do anything for her, Bishop silently bid her goodbye and rolled onto his stomach and began crawling down the aisle towards the bedrooms. Staying as low as possible, since people generally aimed high, even in combat situations. The shelves on either side gave him some protection, but not much. They looked ready to collapse at any second. The noise was relentless. It was like being in a busy lumberyard. Wood splinters flew in the air around him like angry insects. Bullets punched through the outer walls and ricocheted off the interior walls and fixtures. More glass shattered. There was gun smoke everywhere. The whole place was being torn apart.

Bishop made it to the end of the shelves and looked to his left. The pool table had lost two of its legs at one end and was lying at a tilt. A marshal lay on his back next to the table, with one leg was folded under him and his entire upper body drenched in blood. Looked like Hammond. Bishop looked to his right and saw the Stricklands' door was shut. With any luck they were both in there right now. And getting them out alive was all that mattered.

Slumped right next to their door was another marshal. Lomax. Hard to see where he'd been hit, but his whole right arm was covered in blood, although he was still gripping his Glock. In his left hand, he was holding a cell phone and trying to press numbers on the keypad. He looked barely conscious.

Using his elbows and knees, Bishop quickly crawled over to him. Bullets pinged all around him. The noise was just as deafening as before. He needed to get the Stricklands out, fast. Because the enemy would sure as hell be coming in. They'd want to make sure nobody was left breathing. And they'd do it soon, once they felt they'd lessened the odds enough. Bishop figured about thirty seconds had passed since he jumped out of the bus. No way of knowing how long he had left. But already an idea was forming in his mind.

He reached Lomax. '*The principals,*' he yelled over the noise of gunfire. '*They still inside?*'

Lomax turned and blinked at him. Bishop saw part of his left ear was missing, and blood ran freely down his neck. Bishop couldn't see where else he'd been hit, but he looked in bad shape. 'You bastard,' he said in a slurred voice. 'You bast . . .' He slowly started to lift the hand holding the gun.

Bishop took the Glock from his weak grip. 'Don't be stupid,' he said. 'Focus. The Stricklands. Are they inside? Who's with them? *Talk.*'

Lomax ignored him and kept pressing buttons on his phone. 'Gotta get through somehow. Gotta tell them . . .'

'*Shit.*' Bishop checked the Glock's magazine. It was empty. He dropped it at Lomax's feet and raised himself to a crouch. He tried the door handle, but it wouldn't turn. Locked from the inside. He pounded on the door with his fists. '*Strickland. It's Bishop. Open this door.*'

He kept pounding on it as he looked to his left. Stray rounds hit the frame by his head and he ducked as slivers of wood flew in front his face.

Somebody yanked the door open. Bishop immediately dived inside and slammed it shut behind him.

'*Jesus Christ.*' Strickland was on his hands and knees, staring wildly at Bishop. '*What do we do?*'

Bishop saw they were under siege in here, too. Barney was on the floor by his overturned bed, frantically pulling on his jeans. The shooters in the backyard were really pouring it on. A continuous stream of bullets rat-a-tatted against the exterior of the house like a never-ending drum roll. Sounded like at least three automatic weapons. Probably more. In the enclosed space, the barrage was almost deafening. Stray rounds flew over their heads, but the four-foot-high shield was holding. For now.

'*What do we do now?*' Strickland yelled again.

'I'm getting you both out of here,' Bishop said.

'And how the hell you gonna do that?'

Bishop saw the spare fibreglass corner plate lying on the floor next to the TV. Right now, it was the best plan he could come up with. He pocketed his .38 and scrabbled over on his hands and knees, grabbed the plate and dragged it back to Strickland.

'I need you to take another corner piece from the wall and link it with his one,' he said. 'Quickly, while I'm doing the same.'

Without waiting for an answer, Bishop went over to the north-west corner of the room and wrenched at the two corner pieces until the fibreglass plates came apart at the dowel joints. He took one of these corner pieces and disconnected it from its brother on the other side. Then he separated two more plates. He dragged all three back to Strickland, who'd already gotten his second piece and connected the two plates together so they were now standing at right angles to each other. Bishop quickly fitted the other corner piece to one of them, so he was left with a three-sided U-shaped box. Strickland understood immediately. He connected a further plate to one side while Bishop did the same to the other, thus extending the length of the U.

Bishop saw Barney was now dressed in jeans, hooded sweatshirt and sneakers. He looked scared out of his mind, but he wasn't crying.

'*Barney*,' Bishop shouted. '*Over here.*'

Barney quickly crawled over. His father placed his arm around him and held him close. Bishop estimated the assault had already lasted less than a minute. He didn't know how many marshals were still alive. Maybe none. They were running out of time. The enemy would be coming in soon. If the three of them were going to move, it was now or never.

Bishop quickly explained what he wanted from them, adding, 'I'll lead with the open section in front of me. Strickland, you take the rear, with Barney between us. You and I will carry the box as we move. Keep it about two inches off the floor. Barney, you just keep low and stay with us all the way. Okay? Everything clear?'

They both nodded agreement. Keeping low, Bishop trotted over to the door, pulled it open and quickly ducked back out of the way. If anything, the concentration of firepower worsened. It was incessant, and coming from all directions. The air was full of lead and noise. He'd been in *actual* warzones that had used up less ammunition. And he hadn't seen a single marshal anywhere. At least, not standing. He glanced over to the right, but all he could see of Lomax was his feet. If the guy wasn't already dead, he would be soon.

He re-joined Strickland and Barney. They'd already taken their positions within the U and were waiting for him. Bishop backed into it, crouched down and lifted the front two plates off the ground. He felt Strickland doing the same at the back.

'Okay, we're moving out now,' he said. 'Keep your heads down. Ready? Go.'

Bishop took one step forward. Then another. And another. Keeping his steps regular. Strickland managed to stay with him, step for step. Barney had a hold of his waist and was sticking close. Bishop aimed for the centre of the doorway and carefully guided them through. This was the worst part, when he was wide open to the gunfire coming from the front of the house. Bullets flew all around them. He held his breath. When he judged he'd cleared the doorway, he carefully turned right ninety degrees and breathed out again.

He carried on walking at the same stoop. They'd covered another ten feet when about a dozen rounds suddenly riddled the left side of the shield. The plates held, but Bishop was immediately pulled hard to the right until the wall stopped him. He fought to keep his legs under him. Strickland shouted something and dropped the back end. Barney cried out, too. They all came to a stop.

'Anybody hit?' Bishop shouted.

'No,' Barney said into his back.

'I'm okay,' Strickland said.

'We keep going, then,' Bishop said, picking up his part of the barrier again while Strickland did the same at the back. 'Don't stop. We're almost there.'

Bishop figured another twenty-five feet to the utility room. That was all that mattered. Getting to that room. They covered a few more feet. The shooting didn't let up for a second. How much longer could it last? And how much time had passed since it had started? Eighty seconds? Ninety? Bishop had lost track. The cops had to be already on their way. But by the time they arrived it would be too late.

More rounds hit the side of the shield. Nobody cried out. Nobody lost his balance. Bishop kept going. He saw the open doorway of the utility room was only ten feet away. Eight. Six. Four. His stepped up the pace a little and then they were right next to the doorway.

'*Turning left now*,' he yelled, then carefully turned them ninety degrees until he was facing the room. He moved forward, manoeuvring them between the bullet-ridden washing machines and the destroyed cleaning equipment stacked next to the walls. Thin snakes of electric wiring hissed and sparked. He made it to the end and used one hand to turn the door handle. He kicked the door open and continued on into the garage.

Hundreds of bullet holes already riddled the three garage doors directly ahead. Daylight poured through each hole, turning the garage into a nightclub from hell. Bishop could see the Ford was totally destroyed. All four tyres were flat. There was nothing left of the windows except jagged shards of glass. He aimed for the empty middle bay, turning them all ninety degrees so the open end faced the rear doors of the SUV. The Toyota was still intact, as it should be. The body was also covered with bullet holes, but none seemed to have penetrated more than a few millimetres. He was glad to see plenty of spent rounds on the floor next to the vehicle. There were also impact marks along the side windows, but the polycarbonate glass had held, too. So far.

'We're at the SUV,' he said and lowered his part of the box until it touched the floor. A few stray rounds thumped against the box. 'Stay where you are and keep your heads down until I tell you. When I say move, you both jump in the back, got it?'

Bishop dashed forward, grabbed the driver's door handle and yanked it open for cover. He realized the sound of firing was gradually lessening in intensity, which meant the marshals were all down by now. Or dead. The hit team would be preparing to storm the house and make sure Strickland was part of the body count. They were out of time.

He edged along the vehicle's side and opened the rear door. Holding it ajar, he said, 'Both of you get in now. *Move.*'

Barney jumped out of the box like a starter's gun had gone off. He quickly dived into the back seat and stayed down like he'd been told. Strickland followed him a second later. Bishop slammed the door shut after them and jumped into the driver's seat. As he pulled his door shut he lowered his hand to the right of the wheel, expecting to feel the key sticking out of the ignition.

But the key wasn't there.

The slot was empty.

SIXTEEN

Bishop felt around behind the steering wheel. Nothing. The key had to be here somewhere. *Had* to be. Because the alternative was to run back inside and search Delaney's pockets for the spare, then somehow get back here in one piece with only a .38 and twelve rounds against an unknown number of automatic weapons. The very definition of suicide.

'What's the hold-up?' Strickland said.

'Key's missing,' Bishop said, leaning forward in his seat and quickly moving his hands over the carpet at his feet. There was nothing there. He worked his fingers under the seat bar and moved his fingers along.

'Oh, man, I don't *believe* this,' Strickland said.

Bishop ignored him and kept looking. There was nothing under the driver's seat. He leaned over to the passenger seat and felt along the floor on that side. The floor mat had shifted position so part of it was in contact with the centre console, and now he noticed something lodged in the space in between. Something that glinted. He pulled the mat away and saw a thick black transponder key on the floor.

'Got it,' he said, sitting back up. 'Put your seatbelts on.'

As they both strapped themselves in, Bishop pulled his own seatbelt across and inserted the key in the ignition. He turned it clockwise. The engine caught instantly. The police scanner also lit up. He could see the numbers *159.21000* displayed on the screen. Based on what Delaney had told him, this was likely the North-east Dispatch frequency.

Bishop pressed down hard on the accelerator and the engine steadily rose in pitch. Once the needle was firmly in the red, he pressed his other foot on the brake pedal, released the handbrake and shifted the gearstick into Drive. 'Whatever happens next,' he said over the engine noise, 'make sure you both stay down.'

He waited for a few more seconds, still revving. Watching the garage door directly in front of them. Waiting for one of the shooters to get curious about the noise. He estimated a fifteen-foot gap between the front bumper and the garage door. Hopefully enough space to get some decent speed up before he made contact.

When he saw a shadow fall across some of the holes in the garage door, Bishop gripped the wheel and took his left foot off the brake.

The tyres screeched against the floor as the SUV shot forward like a rocket, covering the space in half a second. The vehicle slammed into the garage door and immediately burst through it in an explosion of timber and noise. Bishop was jolted forward by the impact, but kept his foot firmly on the pedal. He felt the vehicle wobble as the wheels went over an obstruction. With luck, one of the shooters.

Bishop kept the vehicle pointing towards the gap in the boundary wall directly ahead, forty feet away. The bus was on the street just to the left of it. In a flash, he identified three men in the immediate vicinity. All with automatic weapons. Two on his left were turning as they approached the front door of the house. The third, the mailman, was right in front of them. He was standing inside the wall, just to the left of the gap.

He raised his automatic weapon and fired at the SUV. In the back, Strickland shouted something. Bishop winced as a stream of impact marks riddled the lower part of the windshield. He kept the wheel steady. The man kept firing. But now he was shooting low, aiming at the wheels and the undercarriage. The noise of the bullets making contact reverberated throughout the vehicle's interior. More gunfire rained down on them from the left as the other two joined in. Bishop suddenly heard a harsh grinding noise under his feet he hadn't heard before and just kept ploughing through.

Then he was through the driveway entrance and on the street. They were out. Bishop pumped the brakes, wrenched the wheel hard to the left until they were pointed east and stepped on the gas again. The rear end started to fishtail to the right until he compensated and got it under control again. He passed the school bus and just kept going down Gulliver Street.

'You all right back there?' he said as he took it up to forty. Forty-five. Fifty.

'Jesus,' Strickland said. 'Yeah, we're okay. Where to now?'

'The nearest police station.'

Bishop had made a thorough recon of the area yesterday evening, so the various routes were still fresh in his mind. He knew every street around here. Every intersection. Three-quarters of a mile to the east was North 5th Street, which would take them to the downtown area of North Vegas. He knew the nearest police headquarters was on East Lake Mead Boulevard, about five miles south of their current location. But he didn't want to take such a direct route if he could help it. No telling who might be coming after them.

He visualized an alternative route. The next turn-off along Gulliver was for Longacres Street, a hundred yards up ahead on the right. The one he wanted for North Gramarcy Street was another hundred yards beyond that. He looked in the rear-view and saw a dark sedan suddenly screech into Gulliver from the intersection back at the house. It kept coming in their direction. A backup in case the hit team let them get away, had to be. It was moving too fast to be anything else, which meant they weren't out of it yet.

'There's another car,' Barney said breathlessly, looking out the rear windshield. 'It's coming after us.'

'I think you're right,' Bishop said.

The turn-off for Longacres was almost on them. Bishop made an immediate decision and tapped the brakes and yanked the wheel right. He swung the SUV into Longacres at forty miles an hour, straightened out and began to increase speed again.

'*Watch out*,' Strickland yelled from behind his shoulder.

Bishop had already seen it. Up ahead on the right, barely twenty feet away, a car was backing out of its driveway onto the street. Bishop pressed down on his horn twice and veered around the vehicle without braking, barely missing the rear bumper by inches.

'*Asshole*,' Strickland shouted. An angry car horn answered him.

Bishop kept going, checking the rear-view every other second.

Waiting for that sedan. It was sure to have seen him take the turn. That grinding noise under the engine was also getting progressively louder. Bishop didn't like that sound at all.

Up ahead about fifty feet away was the three-way intersection he wanted. He needed to reach it before the sedan turned into this street and saw which direction they took. He stamped down hard on the gas, giving it everything he had.

Seconds later, he reached the intersection and swung a hard left into Blackmore Avenue. The sedan still hadn't made the previous turn. Bishop straightened out again and aimed for the intersection for North Gramarcy two hundred feet up ahead. They reached it four seconds later, still with no sign of the sedan. Bishop braked and looked left and right. Saw nothing. He turned right into North Gramarcy and took them back up to thirty-five. Single-storey houses passed by on either side. Their car was the only one on the street. But it wouldn't be for long.

Bishop decided it might be better to stick to these smaller roads. It would take longer, but there'd be far less chance of their being tracked by the enemy. Especially as they stood out in this vehicle. The bullet holes were kind of hard to ignore.

Voices were coming from the police scanner and he reached down and turned the volume up.

'. . . *confirmed, Seven-Adam,*' a clipped female voice was saying. It sounded like the dispatcher. '*Address is 234 Gulliver Street. Same witness also reports three or four of the perps have just escaped the scene in a black Toyota Highlander. No registration available at this time. Be advised they are reportedly armed with fully automatic weapons and are to be considered extremely dangerous. Handle with caution, and don't take any chances. Helicopter surveillance is also on its way. ETA, six minutes.*'

What the hell? Bishop found himself slowing as he listened closely.

Another voice, this one male, said, '*Ten-four, Dispatch. En route now. Currently at the plaza on East Centennial Parkway, about to turn into North Gramarcy. Twelve-Adam's behind me. And don't worry, we definitely won't be taking any chances with these guys.*'

'*Shit,*' Bishop said and hit the brakes, bringing the Toyota to a sudden stop. 'East Centennial's just over half a mile ahead of us. We're on a collision course.'

'Hey, what are they talking about?' Strickland said. 'We're the *victims* here, not the perps. What the hell do we do now? Turn ourselves in? What?'

'I don't think so,' Bishop said, thinking fast. 'That cop sounds a little too gung-ho for my liking. The kind who shoots first and asks questions later.'

'But what can they do to us?' Barney said. 'We're in an armoured car.'

'Maybe so, but that's not the only reason to avoid them.'

Bishop studied the houses on either side of the street. The one just behind them on the left had a narrow driveway that ended in a carport at the side of the house. Driveway and carport were both empty. He could only hope the occupants had already left for work. It would only be for a few minutes anyway. He reversed a few yards until they were adjacent to the open gate, turned the wheel left and calmly steered the Toyota down the driveway until they were under the shade of the carport roof.

Bishop set the handbrake, but left the engine idling. He watched the rear-view. The cops would be racing past in a matter of seconds. He *hoped* they'd race past. He could already hear sirens approaching.

Strickland leaned forward. 'What the hell are they talking about, armed and dangerous? We're the victims here, like I said.'

'That witness the dispatcher mentioned,' Bishop said without turning. 'If he's one of the shooters, and I think he is, we're being set up. That's why I don't want to let the cops take us just yet. Even if there's no shooting, they'll arrest us and call in with their current location, and you can bet your ass the perps will be listening in on their own police scanners. There's that black sedan, don't forget. Maybe that courier van, too. Who knows how many more vehicles they've got on the streets searching for us? Once the cops call in that they've caught us, they'll simply converge on their position and take us *and* the cops out in one go. They've just wasted a bunch of US marshals to get to you. What's a few more cops?'

'The siren's getting louder,' Barney said.

'Get down,' Bishop said, lowering himself enough that he could still see using the side mirror.

Seconds later he saw a black and white whip by, the light bar flashing red and white as it went. Then a second one hurtled past immediately after it. The sirens gradually grew muted as they sped away. Bishop stayed where he was for a few more moments, watching and thinking. Mostly thinking.

Because getting them to police headquarters wasn't going to work anymore. Five miles was too far to travel without being spotted by either side. Especially in a bullet-ridden SUV. And to make matters worse there'd also be aerial surveillance within the next five minutes. They still had the police scanner, but he didn't dare use it to call for help, not with the perps listening in. And Bishop had left his cell phone back at the house, which meant they were completely on their own for now.

But one thing was for sure. They couldn't stay here. A nosy neighbour might be reporting their presence to the police right this second. They needed to move, fast. And they really needed to get out of the city altogether if possible. Go to some other town and make contact with the feds from there. Vegas was far too hot right now. But where?

Bishop mentally ticked off the available options using the road map in his head until he was left with the one they'd least expect.

He quickly reversed out of the carport and yanked the wheel left until they were pointing in the direction from which they'd just come. In the rear-view mirror he noticed a middle-aged guy in a red tracksuit about twenty feet behind them, just jogging on the spot as he stared at the SUV. No doubt curious about all the bullet holes. Bishop was about to hit the accelerator when he remembered the GPS tracker that Delaney had mentioned. Hidden in the armrest, she'd said. Probably a good idea to get rid of it now rather than later. With the engine idling, Bishop looked down at the leather armrest set into the door panel at his side and tried dislodging the thing with his bare hands, but it wouldn't budge a millimetre.

He said, 'Barney, you still got your multi-tool with you?'

'Uh, yeah. Why?'

'Let me have it for a moment. There's a GPS tracker in here we need to get rid of.'

Barney pulled out his multi-tool and handed it over. Bishop extracted the small one-inch knife and inserted the blade in the thin space between the armrest and the hard plastic of the door. After about fifteen seconds of jiggling, he felt the armrest start to loosen, so he removed the blade and used his fingers to pull it out the rest of the way. And lying in the space underneath there was a sleek-looking device that resembled a small, wireless, external hard drive. A pinhole-sized green LED light at the top showed it was currently active.

He pulled the device from its hiding place and pressed the switch to lower the window.

From the back, Strickland said, 'I been thinking, Bishop. Why don't you just let the two of us out of here, huh? I'll call the feds from one of these houses and—'

'Forget it,' Bishop interrupted, and tossed the tracker out the window where it landed on the sidewalk. 'There's no way I'm letting either of you out of my—'

He suddenly stopped when he saw the jogger had moved closer to the SUV, so that there was now only five or six feet between them. The guy had his arm outstretched and was aiming a cell phone in their direction, obviously taking a photo.

'Shit,' Bishop said, and quickly raised the window again, hoping the guy hadn't caught his face, but there wasn't a whole lot he could do about it. They were out of time and needed to move right now. He released the handbrake and stamped hard on the accelerator. They sped away.

Strickland said, 'So what now?'

'Now we go off-road,' Bishop said.

SEVENTEEN

Bishop slowed as they got to within fifty feet of the Beltway up ahead. They were currently driving across the rough terrain of the Mojave Desert, having left the smooth asphalt roads of North Las Vegas five minutes before. Nobody was following them. Yet.

'That noise is getting worse,' Strickland said. His voice came out shaky as he was rocked back and forth from the rough ride.

Bishop said nothing, but Strickland was right. Each time he turned the wheel that grinding noise recurred, a little louder than before. Whatever it was, it had started back at the house. Amazingly, three of the pneumatic tyres were still intact. The fourth had been shot out, though the polymer ring backup was working just fine so far. But something was damaged down there. Bishop had a feeling the undercarriage hadn't been as well protected as Delaney had thought. And if it was the front axle shaft that was damaged, as he suspected, then it could likely snap at any time, especially on rough terrain like this.

On the plus side, there was very little traffic using this section of the Beltway up ahead. A coupe and a sedan were approaching from the right. Once they sped past, Bishop couldn't see anything else approaching for at least half a mile in either direction.

The time was now.

He stamped on the accelerator and raced towards the highway up ahead. They climbed the slight incline and then they were driving across the almost empty four-lane highway. In less than a second they reached the other side and were back on rough desert again. Bishop kept them going in a northerly direction. Just over a mile north of the Beltway, he knew there were some old mining roads that ran parallel to the highway for another four miles. They weren't much more than dirt tracks, but smoother than the terrain they were currently on. And four miles was four miles.

Bishop kept driving towards the mountains in the distance, avoiding sagebrush where he could, until he spotted the old mining road he was looking for. He veered right, joined the track and kept going east. Almost instantly the ride became a lot smoother. They weren't being jostled about anymore. Bishop hoped there'd be less strain on the front axle too.

'That's *much* better,' Strickland said. 'So what happens now, Bishop?'

'We keep heading north-east, staying parallel to US 93 as much as possible. We'll travel alongside the old Union Pacific line for a few miles since it goes in the same direction and the terrain won't be as rough. Then we'll get on US 91 before joining up with the I-15. After that we make for the nearest decent-sized town and hole up for a couple of hours until the heat's died down. Then we call the feds and get them to come pick us up.'

'Sounds like a plan,' Strickland said. 'Hey, back at the house, what happened with Delaney? I didn't see her. Did you?'

'I saw her.' Bishop said, unconsciously recalling those final few moments as her life seeped out of her. Despite their limited time in each other's company she'd played a pretty significant role in his life, and he had a feeling he'd be reliving that scene for quite some time yet. 'She didn't make it. None of them made it.'

'Shit. I liked Delaney. She was all right.'

'Yes, she was.'

Less than half an hour later, they were heading along US 91 at a steady fifty. Bishop had stuck to the mining road for as long as possible. When that came to an end, it was more rough terrain until he saw the old railroad line and then he stayed close to that for another four miles. Then when that crossed paths with US 91, he'd transferred over to the old highway. It wasn't used much anymore, just a few trucks or pick-ups every now and then, occasionally a sedan, which made it perfect. For a while anyway. They'd soon have to join up with I-15 if they wanted to keep in this direction, but that wasn't for a few more miles.

Nobody was saying anything. Bishop watched the uneven landscape all around them as he drove. One minute it was rising hills to the left and sharp banks to the right. The next it was flat land, closely followed by deeply sloping ditches on both sides. Changeable was a good word for it. And always the ever-present telephone lines running alongside the road.

They were travelling along one of the flatter stretches when Barney said, 'Hey, Dad? I don't . . . I don't feel too good.' His voice sounded very faint.

'Barn? Hey, what's wrong?'

In the mirror, Bishop saw Strickland press a palm against his son's forehead. Barney did look a lot paler.

'Feel hot and dizzy,' the boy said. 'And sick. And . . . and I keep seeing black spots everywhere. I think . . . I think . . .'

Barney's eyes closed and he simply fell back against the rear seat like a rag doll. Strickland held him up and gently patted the boy's cheeks. 'Barn? Hey, come on now, wake up. Don't scare me like this, buddy. Barney?'

'He's fainted,' Bishop said.

Strickland turned to him. 'Huh? Fainted? From what?'

'A combination of stress, fear and mild dehydration probably. He's a tough kid, but he's only twelve years old and he's just survived a major assault by a team of heavily armed killers. That's enough to wipe out most adults. I'm surprised he's lasted this—'

At that moment the grating noise suddenly doubled in volume until it was almost deafening. At the same time a harsh vibration reverberated through Bishop's feet and up into his legs. He tried jiggled the steering wheel but got hardly any response.

'Uh-oh.'

'What was *that*?' Strickland yelled over the noise.

'The front axle going,' Bishop shouted back. He revved the engine a couple of times. He could hear the axle still spinning, but nothing was happening except the vehicle was slowing down. Already fifty miles per hour, and decreasing steadily.

'All we're doing now is grinding metal,' he said. 'I need to get this thing off the road while I can.'

Bishop stuck the gear into Neutral, switched off the engine and wrenched the wheel to the right as far as it would go. Gradually, the vehicle began to go in the direction he wanted, but it was a hard struggle. They left the road and entered the desert again. The vehicle was rapidly losing speed now. Forty miles an hour. Thirty. Twenty. Then they descended a mild incline before the landscape evened out again. After another forty feet the vehicle finally came to a complete stop. There was no cover at all, but with any luck the slight incline would mask it from casual road traffic.

'That's that, then,' Strickland said. 'Looks like we're walking.'

Bishop unstrapped his belt and opened his door. 'Without water, in the desert? I don't think so. We have to try and hitch a ride if we can. And don't try and wake Barney up anymore. We've got more chance of getting a lift if they see we've got a sick kid with us. Come on, let's go.'

Bishop got out of the Toyota and checked his watch. 08.04. Still early, but it was already heating up. And no shade, either. For the boy's sake, he hoped they wouldn't have to wait around too long. He helped Strickland pull Barney out of the car, then waited as Strickland placed one hand under the boy's back, another under his knees, and hefted him up. They headed back towards the road.

Bishop reached the roadside first and looked both ways and saw nothing. Not a thing in either direction. Just flat desert all around them, except for the mountains far off to the north. Strickland caught up after a few more seconds and found a spot a few feet away and gently sat the unconscious Barney down on the ground. He sat down too, and placed his arm round his son's shoulders, positioning the boy's head so it was resting against his chest.

'Does he suffer from low blood pressure at all?' Bishop asked.

'Not that I know about. Why? Does that cause fainting?'

'It can. Could be just something that runs in the family. You ever faint as a kid?'

Strickland frowned. 'No, but I remember Carrie . . .' He paused, then continued, 'My wife once told me she sometimes had fainting spells when she was going through puberty.'

'That's probably it, then. That and everything else he's gone through today has caused him to shut down. Right now his body's busy transferring blood to the brain to raise the pressure back to its normal level again. He should be fine in another half-hour or so.'

'Christ, I hope so. It tears me up seeing him like this.'

Bishop turned away and looked up at the clear azure sky. He was thinking through possible explanations for whoever might stop for them. He couldn't risk the whole truth, but he needed something that would explain what the three of them were doing in the middle of nowhere. He decided to stick as close to reality as possible. That they'd been heading for Mesquite, twenty miles away to the east, when the axle on the vehicle suddenly went, forcing Bishop to park it over the rise back there. That they'd already been waiting an hour and the boy had simply fainted from dehydration.

'I hear something,' Strickland said.

So did Bishop. He turned to his left and saw nothing, then turned right and spotted a truck in the distance, heading in the direction from which they'd come. Towards Vegas. Which meant it was no good to them.

'We'll let this one go,' he said.

It looked like a dump truck of some kind. It took about thirty seconds to reach them and it wasn't slowing down, either. As it got closer Bishop saw a silhouette in the cabin look their way and then it was past them. As it sped off Bishop saw a vast heap of gravel in the rear open bed. Bishop kept watching as the vehicle slowly receded into the distance.

'Here comes another one,' Strickland said.

Bishop turned back again and peered off into the distance. Straight away he could see this one wasn't a truck. It was a car. Dark in colour. And there was something else too.

Even though it was half a mile away, he could make out the light bar on the roof.

EIGHTEEN

'Hey, is that a cop car?' Strickland asked, squinting at the vehicle in the distance.

'Looks like Nevada Highway Patrol colours to me,' Bishop said.

They were about to be arrested. There was no way to avoid it. Not if the troopers had been listening to their radio. And Bishop still had the .38 still in his pocket, as well as the extra speed loader, and the very last thing he needed was for the law to find him packing an unlicensed piece. He pulled both items from his pocket and threw the extra rounds into the desert far behind him. After wiping his prints off the .38 he lobbed it sixty or seventy feet towards the other side of the highway. He didn't see where it landed. Somewhere amongst the sagebrush. But that was everything of his except for the Seiko watch.

They both watched as the cruiser gradually closed the distance. So far they were just three hitchhikers. Well, two. But once the cops pulled up and saw the bullet-ridden Toyota back there, things would turn serious, fast. The cruiser was still a hundred feet away from them when the LED lights on the roof started flashing red and blue simultaneously. So they'd spotted it already.

'Don't make any sudden moves,' Bishop said. 'These guys are expecting the worst so they'll be on edge. Just do what they say, don't wise off, and be cool.'

'Way ahead of you,' Strickland said.

Bishop stayed perfectly still as the patrol car came to a halt twenty feet away and two troopers in dark blue uniforms jumped out, one Caucasian, one Latino, both brandishing their service pistols in the standard Weaver stance. The Caucasian driver shouted, 'All of you, face down on the ground. *Right now.*'

Bishop slowly lowered himself until he was lying on the ground with his left cheek pressing against the rough asphalt. He also saw Strickland gently lay Barney on his back before assuming the same position as Bishop. Meanwhile, the Latino cop was advancing towards them, still aiming his gun in their general direction.

'That's real good,' he said. He sounded a little calmer than his partner at least. 'Now place your hands behind your backs. Slowly.' He frowned at the unmoving figure of Barney. 'Hey, what's wrong with the kid? What you do to him?'

'Nothing,' Bishop said, placing both hands behind him, wrists crossed. 'He just fainted. That's his father over there next to him.'

'Yeah, sure. And you must be the kindly uncle.' He called out, 'Steve, keep me covered, okay?'

His partner by the car said, 'I got you, Mateo.'

A moment later Bishop felt Trooper Mateo attach flex cuffs to both his wrists. Not too tight, but tight enough. Then hands expertly searched him from head to toe. Finding nothing, Mateo then stepped over to Strickland and went through the same routine. Bishop glanced over to the patrol car and saw Trooper Steve speaking into a mic. Calling dispatch, no doubt. Reporting their position and telling them what they'd just found.

Trooper Mateo shouted over to him, 'They're both clean. Hey, you wanna come and carry the kid? He's out cold. They must have given him something.'

'We didn't give him anything,' Strickland said, his voice rising. 'This guy told you, he's my son. He just—'

'Wanna stay on my good side, pal?' Mateo cut in. 'Then just keep your mouth shut unless I ask you a direct question. That goes for both of you. Unless you wanna speed things up and tell me where you stashed your weapons.'

'We're the victims here,' Bishop said, knowing it was useless. 'You can see we're both unarmed. Or do you think we somehow shot up that SUV back there ourselves?'

'Don't get smart with me, pal. Believe me, that'd be the absolute worst thing you could do right now. Now get up, the both of you.'

Bishop didn't bother arguing. It was pointless. Instead, he rolled onto his side and pushed his right elbow against the ground to get himself into a sitting position. Then he leaned his body forward to balance himself and slowly got to his feet. When he looked up again, he saw Trooper Steve walking towards them. He'd already put the gun back in his side holster. Strickland was also standing a few feet away.

Trooper Steve said, 'Dispatch said to search the SUV for weapons before heading back.'

'Sure, right after we get these two tucked away.' Trooper Mateo moved behind Bishop and nudged him forward towards the cruiser. 'Let's go.'

He and Strickland both moved off towards the patrol car with the trooper behind them. Bishop saw it was a regulation Crown Vic, but a slightly older model than usual. The vehicle was all black with gold markings. Once they reached it Trooper Mateo opened the rear door on the driver's side and then moved back to cover them both. Bishop looked over the car roof and saw Trooper Steve crouching down to lift up Barney.

'Okay, get in,' Trooper Mateo said, motioning to Bishop with the gun.

Bishop lowered his head and got in the back of the unit. Mateo ordered Strickland to go to the other side and wait while he leaned in and buckled Bishop's seatbelt. Then he slammed the door shut and went round to Strickland, who was waiting by the other door. He pulled it open and Strickland made a move to get in when Mateo placed a hand against his chest. 'Not yet,' he said. 'The kid goes in next.'

Through the window, Bishop watched as Trooper Steve, carrying the still-unconscious Barney in both arms, made his way back to them. Bishop used the time to inspect his new surroundings. The windows looked to be the usual reinforced glass. There was a steel mesh partition separating prisoners from those up front, connected to the roof by bolts that could only be accessed from the front. And there were the usual blank metal plates where the door handles and window controls would usually be. Up front, in addition to the scanner and mic, there was an upright shotgun rack next to the centre console on the passenger side. In the rack was a black Remington 870 12-gauge pump.

The other cop finally arrived with Barney. 'I don't like it,' he said. 'The kid seems to be breathing okay, but I can't wake him up.'

'I told you,' Strickland said, 'he just fainted, that's all.'

Trooper Mateo ignored him and said to his partner, 'Just put him in the middle seat and I'll buckle him in. Once we've checked the Toyota we'll haul 'em all back to the station and take things from there.'

Bishop watched them place the unconscious Barney next to him, while Trooper Mateo made sure the boy's safety belt was securely fastened. Then it was Strickland's turn. Finally Trooper Steve shut the door, activated the remote locking mechanism and both cops walked off towards the abandoned SUV, sixty feet away.

Strickland shook his head. 'Assholes.'

'I just hope they don't waste too much time over there,' Bishop said.

Strickland turned to him. 'Why?'

'Because I suspect the perps were also listening in to their call to dispatch and are putting two and two together as we speak. The sooner we get moving, the happier I'll be.'

Strickland looked out the window in the direction of the cops. Thirty seconds later, he said, '*Now* what are they doing?'

Bishop looked past him. The two cops had clearly found nothing in the SUV and had started searching the ground near the vehicle. 'They figure we must have tossed the weapons. The thing is I actually did throw a speed-loader not too far from where they're looking.'

'Well, once they get us to the station house and call the feds it won't matter what they find.'

'I know, but it's still wasting time. We're too vulnerable out here. We need to get moving, now.'

No more was said for a while. With the sun shining down and all the windows shut, it was hot in the back. Bishop could feel sweat start to drip down the back of his shirt. Barney's breathing sounded steady and regular, though, which was good. With any luck, when he next woke up he'd be in the middle of a police station with cops all around him.

Three more minutes passed in silence as Troopers Steve and Mateo searched the ground in ever-widening circles. Bishop began to feel more uneasy.

He turned to Strickland and said, 'I need Barney's multi-tool again.'

'Why?'

'So I can free my hands, that's why.' Struggling against the tight seatbelt, Bishop shifted in the seat so he was turned towards the door, then edged back as much as he could until his bound hands came into contact with Barney. He moved his hands down the boy's shirt and stopped when he reached his jeans, patting the left front pocket and feeling what had to be the boy's hand-held games console. He then reached behind the boy and checked the left rear pocket and found the adapter, but nothing else.

'Not there,' he said. 'I can't reach his right-hand pockets. You'll have to do it.'

With a sigh, Strickland manoeuvred himself until his back was turned and began to pat the front pocket of the boy's jeans. Almost immediately he said, 'Yeah, it's there. Wait one.' He grunted and shifted his body again for a better angle, then gingerly inserted his left hand into the boy's pocket. 'You sure this is a good idea?' he said. 'What if those cops search you again?'

'So what? The worst they can do is confiscate the knife and recuff me. But I don't like how they're taking their time over there. It's making me paranoid.'

'Why? You think they're on Hartnell's payroll, too?'

'I doubt it. But I don't like being hog-tied like this. Right now you two are my responsibility and if something does go wrong I want my hands free, just in case. Come on, hurry up.'

'Hey, give me a break here. I'm going as fast – *wait*. There, *got it*.'

Bishop watched as Strickland slowly pulled the keychain from his son's pocket. Once it was clear, Bishop said, 'Okay, toss it towards me. Carefully.'

Strickland turned his head to check Bishop's position and then flicked his left hand back and let go. The key fob landed on Barney's left leg and slid off into the space between them. Bishop arched his back and reached his hands down until his fingers felt the keychain on the seat. He grabbed hold of it and faced forward again. By feel alone, he extracted the knife, then leaned his body forward as much as he was able and began working on his left wrist.

It was difficult working blind, but less than two minutes later he brought his freed hands to the front and rubbed at his sore wrists. After placing the keychain back in Barney's pocket, he glanced out the window again and saw Trooper Mateo talk into his radio and call out to his partner. They started back at last, neither man carrying anything either. Bishop put his hands behind his back again, willing them to move faster.

The two state cops finally reached the cruiser and after unlocking the doors took off their hats and got in. In the driver's seat, Trooper Steve started the engine, then grabbed the radio mic and reported in. Trooper Mateo turned to look from Bishop to Strickland, then back to Bishop again. He was frowning deeply. 'I don't know what to make of you two,' he said with a sigh. 'I surely don't.'

'Look, it's very simple,' Bishop said. 'The guy on my right is a secret witness under federal protection. The boy is his son. The people he was due to testify against attacked their safe house on Gulliver Street this morning and killed a bunch of US marshals in the process. I was the extra man on the scene and was trying to get these two well away from the danger zone when our vehicle died. Then you found us. That's it.'

'Well, that isn't what dispatch told us.' With another sigh, he faced front and said, 'I guess we'll find out what's what pretty soon, though. Okay, Steve, let's get moving.'

'Right.' Trooper Steve stepped on the gas and they pulled away.

'So what was the story dispatch gave you?' Strickland asked.

Both cops ignored him, which was about par for the course. Bishop sat back and said nothing else. Further talk was pointless until they got to the station.

They continued down the highway at a steady sixty. There was no air con. Or if there was, it wasn't working. Out of habit, and since there was nothing else to do, Bishop made a careful note of every vehicle that passed them. There weren't many. At one point, a tan pick-up containing a lone driver went past, closely followed by a black Infiniti, containing two upfront and two more in the back. Bishop noted the licence plates and watched as both vehicles receded into the distance. A minute later, a silver Honda Civic also whizzed by with two male figures in the front. Again, Bishop turned his head and watched the car until it disappeared into the horizon.

He faced forward. Up front the police scanner made various noises, but the volume was turned right down so Bishop couldn't make out the actual words. Trooper Steve lowered his window. He leaned his left elbow on the frame as he drove. After a while, the other one lowered his, too. A pleasant draught swept through the vehicle's interior.

At some point, Bishop looked out the rear windshield again. There was a silver car back there. Maybe a hundred feet behind them and closing. Bishop thought it looked like a silver Honda Civic. He was well aware the Civic was one of the most popular vehicle makes in the country and that silver was the most popular colour. Still, he couldn't shake the feeling that this was the same car that had passed them a couple of minutes before. He strained to see the numbers on the licence plate, but it was still too far away to make out.

It closed the distance between them to eighty feet. Bishop noticed they were now driving through one of the more changeable sections of the landscape, with shallow hills off to the left and gradual sloping ditches to the immediate right of the road. Sixty feet between them now. And Bishop was finally able to make out the licence plate.

It was the same plate as before. The same car, with the same two men in front.

He faced front and said, 'You might want to speed up a little, Officers. We're being followed.'

Strickland turned to look out the back and groaned.

'Gee, you're absolutely right,' Trooper Mateo said, watching his wing mirror. 'And on a public road, too. Can you believe the nerve of some people?' He turned to his partner and shook his head gravely. 'What's the world coming to?'

'He's gaining,' Strickland said, still looking out the back.

Bishop saw the Civic was accelerating fast. In no time at all it closed the distance between them to twenty feet and then it began veering into the left lane, preparing to overtake. The front passenger window was rolled down and Bishop could see the two men clearly. Two grim faces, the driver staring ahead, the other watching the black and white.

'Hey,' Mateo said, 'these idiots must be doing at least eighty. Are they blind or just stupid? Don't they see the light bar on the roof?'

'They see it,' Bishop said, 'they just don't care. Don't let them come alongside.'

Ignoring him, the trooper pressed a button on the console and the siren suddenly blared out from the roof speakers. With the windows down, the noise was almost deafening.

The driver of the Civic paid no notice. He kept gaining speed until he was level with the patrol car, then slowed a little until he was matching their speed exactly. There was less than three feet of space between the two vehicles.

Bishop brought his hands round to the front, checked Barney's seatbelt and positioned the boy's head against his father's shoulder. 'Whatever happens next,' he said, 'try and keep your muscles relaxed.'

'Huh? What the hell are you talking about?'

There was no time to explain. Trooper Mateo was already jabbing a finger at the road ahead and glaring at the passenger only a few feet away from him. *'Pull over,'* he yelled over the noise of the siren. *'Right now.'*

Bishop saw the passenger in the Civic smile. He kept smiling as he pulled a very large revolver from his lap, aimed it at the cops and pulled the trigger.

NINETEEN

The next few moments passed before Bishop with crystal clarity. He could see the gun was a .44 Magnum Colt Anaconda. It was stainless steel with a huge six-inch ventilated-rib barrel, so the guy could feel like Dirty Harry. When Bishop saw the flash and heard the *BOOM*, he knew immediately that the first shot had missed the driver.

It hit his passenger full in the face instead.

Trooper Mateo's lower face disintegrated into a mass of blood and bone as he slammed against the far door, his body convulsing uncontrollably. Bishop felt tiny droplets of blood spatter against his face. Strickland shouted something. Trooper Steve still hadn't fully comprehended what had happened. They were still more or less moving in a straight line.

Then the second shot took out the driver.

A whole chunk of Trooper Steve's head was blown away from the force of the blast. A geyser of blood spurted from the left temple area. His foot reflexively pressed down on the accelerator and his body jerked to the right as far as the seatbelt would allow, while his hands also wrenched the steering wheel hard to the right.

Strickland cried out, and Bishop ducked a microsecond before a third bullet shattered the window next to him. Then the horizon tilted to a thirty-degree angle as the vehicle left the road, still racing at over sixty miles an hour. He saw they were speeding along the uneven incline at the side of the road, descending on a slight gradient, still veering to the right.

They were also totally out of control.

The car rocked up and down as the wheels hit natural bumps in the terrain. Bishop held onto Barney and saw he was still unconscious – the best thing for him at the moment. He felt one of the front wheels collide with something big. There was a loud thump against the axle, then the car suddenly banked to the left and the world shifted on its axis again as the vehicle began to roll over onto its right side.

And kept on rolling.

Strickland cried out again and Bishop lost his grip on Barney and relaxed his body as much as he could. The car passed through a quarter-turn and kept rolling until they were all upside down. Bishop heard the light bar on the roof beneath his head being wrenched off. He saw the roof flatten and warp. The driver's airbag activated. And still they kept rolling as the vehicle continued speeding down the incline. A three-quarter turn and the front windshield imploded, shattering into a hundred pieces. Small shards of safety glass made their way through the cage grille and rained down on the back of Bishop's head.

Then the car was upright again, but it continued to turn, flipping over onto its side once more as they continued down the incline at an angle. Through the open windshield he thought he could see the bottom of the incline racing towards them. They were at the second quarter-turn when the window next to Strickland exploded outwards. The car fell back onto its roof again and kept on its course for the bottom of the gradient.

Now no longer rolling, the grinding noise of the roof scraping across the bumpy desert floor at thirty miles an hour reverberated through Bishop's body like a jackhammer. He opened his eyes and looked at the upside-down world ahead and saw the ground rising up towards them at speed.

Then, a second later, *impact*.

The noise was immense. The car smashed against the side of the ditch, rose a few feet into the air before coming back down on its roof in a thunderous sound of mangled metal.

Stillness. The only noise came from the faint rumble of the idling engine.

Bishop took a second to check himself. He didn't feel any pain anywhere. Not yet anyway. No broken bones. He probably had bruises, but that didn't matter. He was still upside down, the safety belt still holding him in place. He saw Barney and Strickland still held in their seats, their arms hanging over their heads. Barney's eyes were still closed, but Bishop couldn't see any blood or obvious injuries. And he was breathing normally. Strickland was still conscious, though. He was just staring ahead with his mouth open.

'Holy Jesus,' he said, then turned to his son. '*Barn*.'

'He looks okay,' Bishop said. 'I don't think anything's broken.'

He got himself into a decent angle, pressed the release on his seatbelt and slid to the roof. He plucked the multi-tool from Barney's pocket again and extracted the blade. Reaching past the boy, he cut through Strickland's cuffs and said, 'Free Barney, then take cover behind the car. They'll be coming any second now.'

'Right.' Strickland brought his hands round and got to work on his belt.

Bishop needed some weapons, fast. Fortunately he had immediate access to two. Maybe three. He dragged himself through the window frame on his side and saw they were at the bottom of the incline. It looked like they were in a dried-up riverbed or something, or maybe an unused drainage channel. The road was somewhere twenty or thirty feet above them. No sign of the shooters yet, but they'd be coming to finish the job at any moment.

He turned and leaned into the front driver's seat. The airbag had already deflated and there were chunks of safety glass and blood everywhere. It looked like an abattoir in there. The smell was rank. He also noticed both the scanner and radio were destroyed.

Bishop reached up and pulled Trooper Steve's duty weapon, a Glock 22, from his side holster. He stuck it in his waistband and also took the spare magazine attached to the holster.

Now for the shotgun. It was still secured safely inside the gun rack, and probably unlocked via the control pad on the console. Bishop swept his eyes across the inverted buttons. *There.* Top left corner. The printed words, GUN LOCK. Bishop pressed the button and hoped the electrics were still working. A second later he heard a loud metallic click above his head and the shotgun clattered to the roof.

Bishop heard a screeching of tyres nearby and turned to look behind him. Nothing up there yet. He had seconds before that changed.

He pulled the shotgun out and tested the weight. It felt fully loaded.

These things had a seven- or eight-round capacity, but he didn't have time to check. He erred on the side of caution. Call it seven rounds. And one semi-automatic with two full magazines. Hopefully they'd be enough.

He racked the shotgun as he ran round to the other side of the overturned vehicle, what was left of it. But it was the only cover around. Strickland was there too, crouching next to the trunk and patting Barney's cheeks as he tried to wake him. And it seemed Barney was responding too. The boy's eyes were closed as he moved his head from one side to the other, groaning softly.

'Stay down, both of you,' Bishop said and moved to the front of the car, using the wheel for cover as he raised part of his head. Seconds later he saw the Civic's bumper and hood appear at the top of the crest fifty feet away. Then the rest of it appeared as the vehicle left the road and slowly made its way down the incline towards them.

Bishop waited. It was all he could do. At some point they'd see the empty rear seats and assume the worst. But the closer they came, the better for him. Bishop checked the Glock's magazine and made sure there was one in the chamber.

He was ready.

When the Civic was twenty feet away, it made a slow hundred and eighty until it was pointed back towards the road. Then the front passenger door opened and the passenger slowly got out. Stocky. Wide in the shoulders. Close-cropped hair. Wearing a sports jacket and jeans. He stayed where he was and kept his gun aimed in Bishop's general direction as he studied the wreckage. Bishop aimed his own Glock at the man's chest area. He was just squeezing the trigger when the man must have spotted the glint of metal and dived to his left.

They both fired at the same time. Bishop's shot went nowhere. The gunman's shot hit the underside of the car to Bishop's immediate right.

Bishop corrected his aim and fired off five more shots at the man's mass. He saw blood appear on his upper thigh and knew he'd scored at a hit, maybe two. He was about to fire again when the other door burst open and the driver jumped out of the car, dived to the ground and rolled along the desert floor. He was gripping a micro sub-machine gun of some kind. Bishop stood up and followed him with his sights.

When he stopped rolling, Bishop had time to miss twice before the driver got to his knees and fired.

Bishop ducked down as a stream of rounds pitter-pattered against the side of the patrol car then stopped. He stuck the Glock in his waistband, picked up the shotgun and crawled to the front of the car and peered round.

He saw the passenger slowly getting to his feet. He looked in pain. Good. Bishop quickly raised the Remington to his shoulder, aimed and fired. The explosion echoed throughout the area. The man yelled and went down again. Looked like a leg shot. Bishop swore. The aim on these things wasn't worth shit.

He pumped the forestock and the spent shell flew out the ejection port as a new one entered the chamber. Then he ducked back as the driver sprayed the hood of the patrol car again with the machine pistol. As soon as Bishop heard a loud click, he got to his feet. The driver was back at the car. He was crouching behind the open door of the Civic as he inserted another magazine into his weapon. Bishop aimed the shotgun at the door window and pulled the trigger. The shotgun roared. Glass smashed. The driver fell back to the ground with a large red stain in his left shoulder. He quickly raised himself up, pointed the machine pistol and Bishop ducked again.

More rounds sprayed the patrol car, followed by the sounds of a semi-automatic being fired. Which meant the passenger was back in the game. Bishop stayed where he was and waited for them to shoot their loads. Seconds passed. The shooting stopped. He didn't hear a gun click empty though.

He looked over at his principals. Strickland had managed to bring Barney round. The boy was crouched against the side of the trunk, hand pressed to his forehead as he stared groggily at the ground. Strickland said something and then left him there, quickly crawling the six or seven feet to Bishop.

'Give me a weapon,' he said.

'Yeah, sure.'

'I'm not screwing around here, Bishop. Give me a piece or I'll—'

Bishop snapped his head upwards as something small and cylindrical arced down towards them from the sky. '*Incoming!*' he shouted.

The M84 flash-bang landed on their side of the car directly at Barney's feet.

Pushing Strickland out of the way, Bishop yelled, '*Barney, close your eyes,*' and dived towards the device, clamping his own eyes shut in preparation.

He figured he was still two feet away when the grenade detonated.

There was a deafening explosion accompanied by a flash of white. Bishop felt a blast of hot air hit him in the face and he rolled away. Through his impaired hearing, he could hear a muffled scream nearby. Bishop opened his eyes and saw Barney was already on his feet with both hands pressed to his face.

'*I'm blind,*' he was shouting. '*Oh God, I'm blind.*'

'*Get down,*' Bishop yelled.

But Barney couldn't hear or see him. His primary senses and motor functions were gone. Before Bishop could get up, Barney was already stumbling blindly away from them, still shouting. Worse, he was moving in the direction of the other car.

Bishop fought his disorientation and got to his knees. He pulled the Glock from his waistband, shook his head and stood up unsteadily. The passenger was limping towards Barney. He was only a few feet from the boy. Bishop raised the Glock. Aimed for the man's chest. His hand wavered slightly. His vision blurred.

Then he immediately ducked as the machine gun played a drum roll against the car's underside. Bishop hadn't seen him, but it had to be the driver giving his partner cover. Another brief drum roll followed as he sprayed the car again, followed by another.

Bishop stood up and raised the weapon again and saw the limping passenger backing away towards the car, using Barney as a shield.

Barney.

The killer had one arm around the boy's neck and was dragging him back with him. The driver was no longer visible. But the car was now reversing towards them with the front passenger door swinging wide open. The passenger saw Bishop and aimed the Magnum. Bishop ducked and heard the blast and the round hitting the car. When he raised his head again, the Civic was right beside the man and his hostage. The passenger threw Barney into the front of the car. He fired another shot in Bishop's direction and got in after the boy.

Bishop just gripped the Glock tightly. Unable to fire. Unable to do anything.

Impotent.

The vehicle took off in the direction of the highway. Bishop watched uselessly as it climbed the gradient. It came to a stop at the top and Bishop saw the front passenger door open again. The killer leaned out, left something on the ground and closed the door.

Then the car took off and disappeared from view.

TWENTY

'What do you mean they took Barney?' Strickland yelled, grabbing Bishop by his jacket lapels. 'How could you let those bastards take my boy?'

'I didn't have a whole lot of choice,' Bishop said in a calm voice. His own vision was all right now, but both ears were still ringing from the blast. 'The stun grenade blinded Barney and he panicked and ran right into their hands. There was nothing I could do.'

Strickland let go in disgust. 'They took off, and you just stood there and *let* them?'

They didn't have time for this. Bishop sighed and said, 'Look, I was still feeling the effects of the flash-bang myself and could barely see straight. If I shot at the car in that state, I risked hitting Barney. I made the only decision possible.' He finished wiping his prints off the shotgun and dropped it on the ground. It was too big to be of any use anymore.

'Come on,' he said. 'We need to get out of here before somebody spots this wreckage and calls the cops. If they haven't already.'

Strickland's anger had already dissipated. He slumped to the ground with his head in his hands. 'Oh, sweet Jesus, they'll kill him. They'll kill my boy and it's all my fault.'

'That's the very last thing they'll do, Strickland. Think about it. It's you Hartnell wants, not Barney. If those two hitters hadn't both been bleeding like stuck pigs they would have tried to make the trade there and then. My guess is they're both heading off to get themselves fixed up, knowing they're already ahead on points.'

Strickland looked up at Bishop. 'You're just guessing. You don't *know*.'

'Of course I do. What other option is there?'

Strickland frowned as he considered the logic. He was an intelligent man, but he was also still groggy from the grenade. It was taking time to get through, and they didn't have any time left. 'Come on, Strickland, we have to move. Let's go.'

'Why? What's the point?'

'The cops, remember? Right now our only strength lies in our freedom of movement. As long as we control our own destinies we can negotiate for Barney. If the feds get you into their custody again we lose that ability. That's if they don't shoot us first. I hate to think what they'll make of this mess, but I can take a wild guess and it doesn't look good.'

'Okay.' Strickland nodded and slowly got up. 'Okay, I guess that makes sense.'

'Good. Now let's move.'

Bishop grabbed hold of Strickland's arm and urged him along as they ran up the shallow hill to the road. When they reached the top, he could see nothing but empty highway in both directions. Which was both good and bad. Bishop looked around until he spotted the item they'd left by the side of the road, about thirty feet away. A cell phone, of course. He jogged over and picked it up.

It was a cheap brandless pay-as-you-go job you could pick up at just about any 7-Eleven. It looked new. It was also currently switched off. Strickland caught up with him and saw what he was holding. 'They leave that for us?'

Bishop nodded and pressed the button that switched the phone on. A tinny chiming sound erupted from the speaker and a logo he'd never seen before lit up the small display screen. After a few seconds, a basic menu appeared. Then a large banner flashed up on the screen: *1 MESSAGE RECEIVED.* The sender's number was listed as *Unknown.*

Bishop opened the message. It read, *NO LAW OR U NO WHAT.*

Strickland was looking over his shoulder. 'Well it looks like you were right, thank God. They're gonna deal. So what do we do now?'

Bishop looked up and saw a large vehicle in the distance, heading back towards Vegas. Which was about the last destination they wanted. But beggars couldn't be choosers.

'We try and look friendly,' he said.

TWENTY-ONE

'Can't tell you how much we appreciate this,' Bishop said. 'It was just our luck to get a busted axle in the middle of nowhere, and with no credit left on my cell phone, either. You guys really saved our hides.'

Roger Souza gazed at him in his rear-view and said, 'Well, we couldn't exactly leave two poor souls hanging in the middle of desert country, could we?'

'Not on your life,' said his sprightly grey-haired wife, Eleanor, sitting opposite Bishop at the dining table in the RV's main living area. 'Besides, after eight weeks on the road it's good to have some outside company for a change.'

It had been a real stroke of fortune when the recreational vehicle had pulled up and the sixty-something driver asked if they needed a ride. Fortunately, the couple hadn't spotted the wreckage of the patrol car at the bottom of the incline or they might not have been so welcoming, although they *had* spotted the SUV a few miles back. Roger and Eleanor had said they were headed for Pahrump, a medium-sized town about sixty miles west of Vegas, where they planned to spend a few hours with Roger's infirm mother, who was staying in a care home. After introducing himself as Scott Lawson, and Strickland as his brother, Carl, Bishop had said that was perfect since they were also headed there.

Bishop had actually been to Pahrump many years before with a client who'd wanted to check up on a flight school he owned out there. He figured the town was as good a place as any to take stock and figure out their next move.

'Sure you don't want us to drop you in Vegas?' Roger asked. 'I mean, you'll want to contact a breakdown service to bring your SUV back, right? You don't want to leave it out there too long.'

'It can wait until we get to Pahrump,' Bishop said, improvising quickly. 'I know a good mechanic there who'll haul it back at a fraction of the price those outfits in Vegas charge.'

'Fair enough. Pahrump it is, then.'

It also meant Roger could avoid Vegas altogether by taking the Beltway route and then joining up with State Route 159. That would eventually connect up with SR 160, which would then take them west to Pahrump, fifty miles away. He looked out the front at the road ahead. They were currently doing a steady seventy down I-15. He saw a sign telling drivers the Beltway turn-off was only a mile away.

Eleanor turned to Strickland, sitting on the couch on the other side, and said, 'You okay over there, Carl? You haven't said much.'

'Sorry.' Strickland gave her a wan smile. 'Got things on my mind.'

'Woman trouble,' Bishop said under his breath.

'Ah,' she said.

She looked about to add something else, so Bishop quickly changed the subject and said, 'This is a real nice RV you got here, Eleanor. Very stylish.'

Eleanor smiled at the compliment. 'Well, we simply figured that since we planned to spend a large portion of our twilight years travelling all over this great country, we might as well do it in comfort. After all, it's only money, right?'

'That's right.'

Even to Bishop's untrained eye, the RV was clearly one of the high-end luxury models. It certainly had all the mod cons. Oak panelling, a fully stocked kitchenette, a Sony sound system, a 40-inch Panasonic flatscreen TV, and more. From the surround speakers, a subdued Frank Sinatra was assuring everybody that the moon was yellow and the night was young.

But Bishop was mostly thinking about the overturned cruiser they'd just left. He was sure somebody must have spotted it by now and reported it in, which meant the cops would be erecting roadblocks pretty soon, if they hadn't already. For sure though, things were going to get very precarious very soon.

He was proven right twenty minutes later.

Eleanor had just finished recounting their recent tour of Utah's Monument Valley, when Bishop looked out the front and saw they were coming to the crossroads that joined them with SR 160. There was a large gas station directly in front of them, and no other building in either direction. Roger stopped at the intersection, then flicked his right indicator and turned onto SR 160. At which point Bishop spotted two Highway Patrol vehicles blocking part of the westbound lane up ahead. They were about a hundred yards away. Two troopers were standing by their vehicle, hands on their belt holsters, as a third questioned the driver of the car at the front of the line. It was a small line. The eastbound lane was being left alone. There wasn't a whole lot of traffic going in either direction.

'Oh, great,' Roger said. 'What now?'

Bishop looked over at Strickland and noticed an Air Force baseball cap lying next to one of the cushions at the other end of the couch. He made a vague head movement until Strickland saw where he was looking. Then he understood. He reached over, picked up the cap and placed it on his head. Eleanor was watching him with a faintly puzzled expression.

'We're going to need your help here, Eleanor,' Bishop said, taking off his suit jacket and placing it on the seat next to him. He pulled the Glock from the side pocket and rested it on the table, not pointing at anything in particular.

'What – ?' Eleanor said, her eyes wide as she stared at the gun. 'What *is* this?'

'I'm afraid I wasn't being entirely honest with you before, Eleanor,' Bishop said. 'Now we're in a real bind here and we need to get out of the area fast, which means you and Roger are going to have to help us get past this roadblock.'

'Oh, God,' she said. Her voice sounded unsteady, but Bishop was just grateful she wasn't screaming.

'Honey?' Roger was watching them in the rear-view. 'You all right back there? What's wrong?'

'We just need you to stay cool, Roger,' Bishop said, 'and get us past this roadblock without any fuss. Can you do that?'

'Please just do what he says, Rog,' Eleanor said. 'He's got a gun.'

'A gun?' Roger turned in his seat and glared at Bishop. 'Mister, if you hurt her—'

'Nobody's getting hurt, Roger,' Bishop said calmly. 'Not if you get us past these cops, like I asked. The car in front just moved up a spot.'

Roger stepped on the gas and closed the gap. The trooper was now questioning the driver of the car in front. They were next. In the background, Frank was now singing about having one more for the road.

'Okay,' Roger said. 'Okay, what do you want me to say?'

'Just be natural and say what you'd normally say in these circumstances. If they ask about us two tell them we're family, but only if they ask. Don't make a big deal out of it. And no secret signals, Roger. That would be a very bad move. I can't emphasize that enough.'

'I'm not stupid,' Roger said.

'I know you're not,' Bishop said.

Then the car in front moved off and the trooper was waving for them to come forward and stop. Roger obeyed and pulled up beside the trooper. He lowered his window and said, 'What's the trouble, Officer?'

The trooper leaned an arm on the window frame without answering. He wasn't smiling. He looked in the back of the RV and saw Bishop and Eleanor sitting at the table. Then he glanced at Strickland on the couch.

He turned back to Roger. 'Where you folks coming from?'

'Utah,' Roger said. 'We been touring the national parks, and let me tell you it's some beautiful country up there.' His voice sounded very natural to Bishop.

'Uh-huh,' the trooper said. 'You folks all travelling together?'

'That's right, Officer,' Eleanor called out. 'What happened, did somebody finally rob one of the big casinos on the Strip or something?'

The trooper's face softened just a little. 'No, ma'am, nothing like that.' He turned back to Roger. 'Where you all headed?'

'Pahrump,' Roger said. 'Then we plan on heading on over to Arizona and spending a few days exploring the Grand Canyon.'

'Grand Canyon, huh?' The trooper looked at the road behind them and said, 'Okay, well, you can move along now.'

'Right, Officer.' Roger carefully put the vehicle into Drive, stepped on the gas and drove on through the gap.

As they picked up speed, Bishop breathed out again.

'So what happens now?' Eleanor asked.

'Now you take us to Pahrump and drop us off in town, as agreed. Then you'll continue on your way and forget you ever saw us. Deal?'

Eleanor swallowed and attempted a smile. 'Deal,' she said.

TWENTY-TWO

Just over an hour later, Roger Souza pulled up next to the sidewalk in the main part of town. They'd already passed a number of small casinos along the way, but thankfully no more roadblocks. On the other side of the street was the Pahrump Shopping Center with an Albertson's store serving as the anchor.

'Here okay?' Roger said.

'Perfect,' Bishop said, standing by the side door with Strickland. During the drive Bishop had explained their current predicament in fairly vague terms without mentioning Barney at all, so things weren't anywhere near as tense as before, but he knew the Souzas wouldn't be sorry to see the back of them. 'Thanks for the ride, folks. And I'm real sorry about the gun, but you wouldn't have taken me seriously otherwise. Now my advice is to continue with your lives as before and just forget we ever existed.'

'Don't worry,' Eleanor said at the table, 'we won't say anything.'

Bishop nodded his thanks and opened the door and pushed the still-withdrawn Strickland through and followed him down the step onto the sidewalk. He raised one hand to Eleanor. She gave a brief wave back, then he closed the door and Roger pulled away and off they went to their own lives. Bishop almost envied them.

'It's been over an hour now,' Strickland said, 'and still nothing. What's taking them so long?'

'They're just making you sweat is all. They'll call. Don't worry.'

'*Don't worry.* Easy for you to say. Barney's not your son.'

Bishop looked both ways. Traffic was very light. As they crossed the road, he said, 'Believe it or not, I want Barney back just as badly as you.'

Strickland gave a snort. 'Yeah, right.'

'Okay, maybe not as badly as you, but if those two morons back at the car wreck had wanted to make a trade there and then I would have still handed you over in a heartbeat.'

Strickland turned to him. 'No shit?'

'No shit.'

'So what makes Barn so important to you all of a sudden?'

'Aside from the fact that I like him, I also gave my word I'd keep him safe. And you too, for that matter. But Barney's still a kid, which means he takes top priority.'

'At least we agree on something then,' Strickland said.

They reached the opposite sidewalk and Bishop began walking across the vast parking lot towards the Starbucks he'd seen on the right. They needed to camp somewhere while they waited for the phone call, and the coffee shop would do as well as anywhere else.

'So who'd you give your word to?' Strickland asked, keeping pace alongside.

'To Delaney. During her last few moments.'

'Oh,' Strickland said. 'Okay.'

They kept walking until they reached Starbucks. There were also a couple of empty wooden benches along the walkway in front of the store. Bishop was motioning for Strickland to take a seat on one when the cell phone in his pocket began chiming. He pulled it out. *Unknown Caller* was displayed on the screen.

This was it. The worst-case scenario in actuality. Now he was doubly glad they'd gone through that role-play exercise the night before.

'Is it them?' Strickland asked, his face a mass of worry lines.

'It has to be,' Bishop said, and sat on the nearest bench. He looked around. Other than a couple of female shoppers exiting the Albertsons store fifty feet away, he and Strickland were all alone.

'It's you they'll want to talk to,' Bishop said, passing the phone to Strickland. 'And don't forget to put it on speaker. Okay?'

Strickland sat down next to Bishop and stared at the cell phone for a moment as though it were an alien object, then he pressed the green button and the ringing stopped. He pressed another button and from the small speaker a tinny, amplified voice said, 'Who am I talking to? No names.'

'The father,' Strickland said. 'Let me talk to my boy.'

'Maybe later, now's not convenient. He's in transit. But you know he's with us, right? And you also know we're not amateurs at this, and that he'll stay unharmed. For now.'

Strickland let out a breath. 'I know.'

'And you know what we want in exchange, don't you?'

'I can take a guess. Your, uh . . . your voice sounds familiar.'

'Thought it might. So if you know the voice, that'll save us unnecessary time-wasting. And since we don't want to risk attracting the attention of certain third parties who are probably already monitoring the airwaves, no names to be used from now on. Now I think we should keep things as simple as possible, so what'll happen is I'll give you the address of one of our people out there. You'll hand yourself over to him and then we'll release—'

Bishop watched as Strickland extended his index finger and pressed the red button, instantly ending the call.

TWENTY-THREE

Bishop raised an eyebrow as Strickland carefully placed the cell phone on the bench between them. His hand was shaking. Which wasn't too surprising, considering.

Bishop just looked at him, waiting. Things were starting to fall into place now.

'This is the only way to prove I'm serious,' Strickland said finally. 'He'll call back.'

'I know he will. I just wasn't sure if *you* did.'

In fact Bishop was certain this guy would call back, but that didn't stop him from being impressed with Strickland's handling of the situation. With his boy's life at stake he wasn't letting his emotions get in the way. But then, he probably knew better than anybody the kind of people he was dealing with.

'You're not quite the honest man-off-the-street Delaney made you out to be, are you, Strickland?'

'Huh? What are you talking about?'

'Just how long did you work for Hartnell? Was it months? Years?'

'Look, Bishop, maybe now isn't the time to get into—'

'Now's the perfect time. How long?'

Strickland sighed. 'Just over ten years.'

'And what was your role in his organization?'

'Mostly I was a bagman. You know, collection and delivery, that kind of thing. Usually money. Hartnell liked to call people like me middle management. It was his idea of a joke.' He looked up at Bishop. 'You don't look surprised.'

'I'm not. When Delaney told me how you supposedly witnessed the murder, the details didn't really add up for me. It just seemed so unlikely that you'd luck into witnessing the world's most paranoid man personally executing an undercover cop. I had a feeling there was something missing and now I know what it was. Did she know who you really were?'

'Yeah, I filled her in when she took over from the previous guy. A few others know too, but not many.'

Bishop wondered if that's what Delaney had wanted to tell him the night before, outside Strickland's room. Something else he'd never know. Not that it mattered now.

'So who's the guy on the phone?' he asked.

'His name's Dominic Callaway, and he's been Hartnell's right hand since forever. I hate to think how many people he's wasted for his boss, but it's probably close to three figures. This is not good, Bishop. Not good at all.'

None of it was. And Bishop knew it wasn't likely to change for the better anytime soon, either. He glanced around as Strickland fidgeted, but they were still alone. Strickland rubbed his forehead with an unsteady hand. Then the phone rang again and Strickland immediately reached down for it and paused. He let it ring twice before answering.

'You know close you came there?' the same voice said. 'I make one call and—'

'Skip it,' Strickland said. 'We both know what's in store for me, so don't waste time with pointless threats. Now we either do this my way or I go straight to the men in suits right this minute and nail our friend to the wall two days from now. What's it to be?'

There was a pause. Then, 'I'm listening.'

'Okay. You're aware I'm not alone?'

'Yeah, I know. The wild card who came to the party late, right? You listening in, pal?'

Bishop saw nothing to gain by speaking, so he stayed silent. It was usually best.

'He's here,' Strickland said. 'And what'll happen is this. We arrange a simple exchange. You get me, he gets my boy, then both sides go their separate ways.'

'That's reasonable.'

'Good. So we just need to agree a time and place. Now I think—'

'Thursday morning,' Callaway cut in. 'Six o'clock. Here in Ohio.'

'Why do I get the feeling,' Bishop said, 'that you had this in mind all along?'

'Is that you, friend? 'Cause I'm sure I don't know what you're talking about.'

'I'm not your friend. Why there?'

'Well for a start, my employer's currently unable to set foot out of this state and I know he'd like to keep a close eye on things. And there's the home advantage factor too. Plus a few other reasons that don't concern you. But it does mean you'll need to get your skates on if you want make it in time. Oh, and you'll need to steer clear of anybody in uniform, but you already know that.'

'Even if we were to run into them,' Bishop said, 'it wouldn't necessarily mean anything. Your man here can still refuse to say anything on Thursday.'

'Yeah, and you'll take my word that we'll release our bargaining chip the second the thing's dismissed? Come on, man. I'll respect your intelligence if you do the same for me. You get grabbed and we'll assume the worst, and you know what that means.'

'You're too smart to cancel him out just like that. You'd at least wait until Thursday and see what happened.'

'You're partly right, friend. I *am* smart, but I also work for a man who likes things to happen a certain way. If they don't he gets angry, almost vengeful. You know, Old Testament-style. And this is how he wants it. I'd like to guarantee the package would be released safe and sound if your pal there decided not to go ahead, but I know my boss. He'd want reimbursement for having to sweat out the past few weeks not knowing what was coming. And with the package so close to hand . . .? Well, what can I say?'

Strickland didn't look quite as composed as before. He said, 'Ohio's over two thousand miles away.'

'Gee, is it? So drive. Fly. Take a train. I don't care which. Just make sure you're here at dawn on Thursday.'

'Where, exactly?' Bishop said.

'We'll discuss the exact location later, but it'll be somewhere west of Columbus. Maybe Greenville, maybe Sidney. Maybe somewhere else. I haven't decided yet. I'll call back later so you can speak to the boy, but for now I suggest you get your asses into gear and start making tracks.'

The line went dead. Bishop took the phone and put it back in his pocket. He looked at his watch. It was 10.04. Which left them with just under forty-four hours to get to the meet.

'How long to drive to Ohio?' Strickland asked.

Bishop shrugged. 'Using the main highways? Day and a half, maybe. But we have to figure on more roadblocks between here and there, which means using the back roads for long stretches. So add another half a day at least. That's if we drive.'

'But why would the law assume we're going to Ohio?'

'The feds won't assume anything yet, but they'll figure it out in time. They're not dummies. I've had experiences with them before. Right now they'll be digging into my background and trying to gauge what my role is in all this. Was I really working for Delaney off the books, or was I in Hartnell's pocket all along? In which case, was I the one who led the assault team to the house or not? And if I *am* in league with Hartnell, what then? Have I got orders to deliver you to him in person or am I taking you to a pre-planned drop-point? And then there's Barney. They might figure I brought him along simply as a means to keep you in line. Or maybe I'm working for somebody else altogether. A competitor of Hartnell's who's decided you're worth your weight in gold. See what I mean? Lots of possibilities and they'll consider them all, then act on the most likely ones. Hell, maybe all of them.'

'Or maybe they'll assume you're exactly who you're supposed to be.'

One side of Bishop's mouth turned up. 'Anything's possible. But if I'm on the side of the angels, why did I run from the scene of that highway shooting? And why haven't I turned you and Barney over to the law by now? That's a big question mark right there.'

'But that highway shootout can only work *for* us,' Strickland said. 'Right? I mean, we were locked in the cage, so you couldn't possibly have shot the cops. The feds will have to figure Hartnell's people were behind it and you fought them off with the cops' weapons. Either that or they pulled us all out from the wreckage and took us with them to wherever.'

'On what evidence? A few bloodstains and some chunks of glass that could have come from anywhere? Because there's no other indication of a second car being involved, and no witnesses. And those rear windows aren't impossible to break out of. I've done it before. With enough leverage, I could have kicked it out, reached around for the driver's gun and killed them both.'

'Sounds pretty unlikely.'

'But it's not impossible, and that's what counts. Still, whatever they think they'll have to assume we're still out on the loose. I know *I* would.'

'Okay,' Strickland said. 'So do we go steal a car, or what? Because I don't like the idea of getting on a train. If somebody spots us there's no way off. And flying's out. They'll grab us the moment we set foot in an airport.'

Bishop had been thinking along the same lines. 'Maybe there's another way,' he said.

TWENTY-FOUR

Since Pahrump had no public transportation they had to walk the four miles to the Calveda Meadows Airfield, situated in the north-east section of town. Bishop still remembered how to get there from his previous visit. It wasn't hard. You just kept on the main Pahrump Valley Road until you got to Belle Vista Avenue on the right, which then led you directly to the private airfield and the private hangars surrounding it. The sky was a clear azure with not a cloud in sight, and Bishop estimated the temperature as somewhere in the early sixties. Which was pretty impressive for early November, even in Nevada.

They were walking along Belle Vista Avenue when Bishop said, 'Did you have much face-to-face contact with Hartnell?'

'You kidding?' Strickland snorted. 'Nobody gets too close to the Man, except for Callaway, maybe. Hartnell always keeps at least three layers of insulation between himself and everybody who works for him. That's one of the reasons he's never seen the inside of a court-room. I was just one of his many flunkies, that's all. A well-paid flunky, but nothing more than that. Sometimes I'd have to go and talk to him in person, one on one, but only when a real important matter came up, which wasn't often.'

'So what made you decide to testify against him in the first place?'

Strickland paused, then said, 'My wife, Carrie. It was mostly her who pressured me into it. You never knew her, Bishop, but you'd have liked her. She was always the best part of me, that's for damn sure. Once I finally admitted to her what I did for a living, instead of leaving me like any normal person she just patiently kept working on me, trying to get me out of the life. She never gave up on me. Never. And there's Barn too, of course. He also played a big part in turning my head around.' He sighed. 'And now my wife's in the ground and my boy's in the hands of a couple of major-league psychos. Jesus.'

'We'll get him back.'

'Correction: *you'll* get him back. In exchange for me. See, that's why I been so quiet till now, Bishop. It's a hell of a thing facing up to your own death, and if I know Hartnell like I think I do it'll be a drawn-out painful one.'

'You don't know that,' Bishop said.

'Oh yeah, I do. I worked for the man for over ten years and I know how he operates. Callaway wasn't lying on the phone. Hartnell takes things personally and he likes to inflict pain. Callaway even told me about one time a few years back, when he was ordered to grab a certain street dealer and bring him to this out-of-the-way place where Hartnell was waiting. See, this guy had been mouthing off to everybody about how he'd dated Hartnell's wife a few times before Hartnell and she had ever met, and what a real freak she was in bed. You know, playing the big man who's managed to get one over on his boss. So Hartnell decided he was going to personally teach this guy a lesson and just went to work on him. Callaway says he really took his time on the guy, using every kind of blade imaginable. He'd start at nine in the morning, finish at five, then go home to a nice hot dinner and have sex with his wife. Meanwhile, two doctors somehow kept the poor bastard breathing through the night and made sure the flies stayed off him, then Hartnell would come back and do the same thing the next day, while Callaway watched. Callaway said the poor, blind bastard lasted three days before his heart gave out. *Three whole days*. Can you imagine that? God only knows how long I'll last.'

Bishop said nothing in response. But he already knew a little something of Hartnell's character, and suspected this story wasn't an exaggeration. Hartnell was one of those people who were pretty much capable of anything. And now he had Barney in his hands.

Worst-case scenario, all right. The *very* worst.

They carried on walking in silence and it wasn't long before Bishop saw the first hangar about a hundred feet away on their left. It was completely closed up. Beyond it, running off into the distance, were twenty or thirty more hangars of different shapes and sizes, some old, some new, all either locked up or vacant. Further along on the right Bishop saw several administrative buildings and a couple more, larger, hangars. The last time he'd been out here those last two hangars and one of the administrative buildings had belonged to the flying school. And he knew that just beyond them lay the five-thousand-foot-long runway, running from north to south.

It was very quiet. They were the only things moving, it seemed. There were no planes preparing to take off, no vehicles on the road. Just the two of them, walking.

Five minutes later they came level with the admin buildings. Bishop was pleased to see the building nearest the two hangars had a sign affixed to the side with the words SAGUARA FLIGHT TRAINING in large letters. That wasn't the same name as before so it looked like his old client had since sold it on. Just outside the hangars there were a number of single- and twin-engine aircraft on the ground. Bishop counted five in total, mostly single-prop from the looks of things. Some looked in better shape than others. All could have done with a lick or two of paint. One of the large hangar doors was wide open, but Bishop couldn't see a single person, inside or out.

Strickland said, 'Sure looks dead around here.'

'There's bound to be somebody still working,' Bishop said. He turned to the other man. 'I don't suppose you got any money on you?'

Strickland made a face. 'Is that a joke?'

'Thought I'd ask. Guess we'll just have to improvise instead. Okay, let's go.'

They both walked across the uneven field towards the two hangars and the planes. There was no fence or anything to denote boundaries. As they got closer Bishop finally saw a burly male figure exit one of the admin buildings and march towards one of the single-engine planes. The man was wearing a dark polo shirt, tan chinos and sunglasses, and carried a clipboard or folder under his arm.

'There's our pigeon,' Bishop said, and aimed for him.

The pilot reached his plane, glanced briefly at the two men walking his way, then opened the door on the port side and bent down to look at something. It took Bishop and Strickland another minute before they reached him. Up close, Bishop saw the guy was probably in his mid- to late forties. He had a heavily lined face, and short brown hair that was thin at the back and greying at the temples. The aircraft he was working on was a single-prop Cessna. Possibly a Skyhawk. Bishop saw two front seats and two more in the back.

Perfect.

The guy was sitting half in, half out, and inspecting the floor and seat hinges as he made notations in the folder. Finally he turned from his work and stared at the visitors through his mirrored aviator sunglasses. 'Help you, fellas?'

'Possibly,' Bishop said. 'You free to take us up today?'

The pilot removed his sunglasses as he looked at each of them. Bishop noticed his eyes were of the palest blue, even more so than Bishop's own. 'You mean you want a lesson?'

'Sure.'

The pilot frowned as he studied them. 'You both just walked here from town?'

Bishop shook his head. 'A friend gave us a lift to the intersection back there. We walked the rest.'

'Oh, okay. So either of you ever been behind the controls of one of these babies before?'

'Not knowingly,' Bishop said.

The pilot smiled. 'First-timers, huh? Well, nothing wrong with that. And as you can see, we ain't exactly rushed off our feet at the moment so I guess we can go up anytime you want.' The pilot held out his hand. 'Charlie Hooper, by the way.'

They all shook hands and Bishop said, 'You the owner, Charlie?'

'Nah, just a lowly pilot. Owner's back in Oklahoma, I think. We rarely see much of him these days.' He stood up and said, 'So you guys wanna follow me back to the office? We'll fix the paperwork and take your credit card details, then get you started.'

Bishop sighed. He really hated doing this. He pulled the Glock from the back of his waistband and showed it to Charlie.

'Maybe we can just skip the paperwork part altogether,' he said.

TWENTY-FIVE

While Charlie was finishing his pre-flight checks, he looked over at Bishop sitting in the co-pilot's seat and said, 'Look, you sure you want to do this? I don't—'

'Save your breath,' Bishop said. 'All you need to know is that we both need to get out of this area as fast as possible. That's your job for today. Nothing else, just that.'

'Hey, you're not gonna hurt me, are you? I got a wife and kids back home.'

'Nothing'll happen if you do what I tell you. Now I noticed there's no control tower around here, so I assume you use standard CTAF procedures for getting clearance?'

Charlie blew air from his cheeks. 'Yeah, there's a UNICOM base station at Vegas Airport, and we use their frequency to co-ordinate all our landings and departures. They don't give us clearance or anything, we do that ourselves. They just warn us if there's a lot of traffic in the area, or if there's bad weather ahead, things like that.' He frowned. 'So you *have* flown before?'

'A little.' He wasn't about to tell Charlie his time in the air had mostly been in helicopters. A guy Bishop knew in Jersey named Mandrake had given him a few lessons, but work seemed to keep getting in the way for both of them recently. 'Better get them on the line then. And no hidden code words, Charlie. I'm not stupid. Just take us where we want to go with the minimum of hassle so we can all carry on with our lives. That sound good to you?'

'That sounds real good. You don't have to worry about me, fella. I'm no hero.'

'That's what I like to hear.'

'So where we heading?'

'East.'

'Anywhere in particular?'

'Just east for now.'

In the back seat, Strickland tapped his feet on the floor and said, 'Come on, come on, let's go.'

'Relax, will you?' Bishop said. 'Charlie, who's on office duty today?'

'Just Rosie, our receptionist. Guy, our other pilot, is probably napping in one of the old offices. Why?'

'I'm thinking maybe you better call this Rosie and let her know you'll be out the rest of the day. Just tell her you've got a couple of cash-paying customers who want to spend the rest of the day learning the ropes and that she shouldn't wait up for you.'

The pilot nodded, pulled a cell phone from a pocket and pressed a button. Bishop quickly took the phone from him and held it to his ear. Once he heard a female voice say, 'Saguara Flight School,' he handed it back and let Charlie say his lines.

Bishop had already read the Cessna's specs and knew what the plane was capable of. He leaned forward and checked the fuel gauge. The needle showed both tanks were almost full. He made a few quick mental calculations while he listened to Charlie. Fifty-plus gallons at an average cruise speed of a hundred knots or more meant they could probably cover five hundred miles in four to five hours, which would take them as far as Colorado. A quarter of the way. Possibly. If the wind was with them. Refuelling might be a problem, though, especially with no money. He'd have to think his options through carefully once they were up in the air and make a decision then. He checked his watch and saw it was 10.48. Amazing. It was hard to believe it was even the same day, let alone the same morning.

Charlie finished his call and hung up the phone.

'That was real good,' Bishop said, taking the cell and placing it on the floor at his feet. 'Now it's UNICOM's turn.'

He watched Charlie switch on the radio and adjust the frequency to 122.700 MHz. When he donned his headset, Bishop also put his on. He listened as Charlie spoke with an operator named Ben, giving his general heading and asking if there was any reason he couldn't take off this minute. There wasn't. It wasn't a long conversation.

'Before we take off,' Bishop said. 'You got anything to eat or drink in here?'

'There's some emergency rations I keep in the aft baggage hold,' Charlie said. 'You get to it through that small door on the portside.'

Bishop got out and stepped over to the small cargo door at the back. He opened the latch and saw an old knapsack lodged further in, alongside some tools and some rope. He pulled the bag out and undid the zip. Inside was an assortment of candy bars and energy bars, a single large carton of concentrated orange juice, two bottles of water, three packs of biscuits, three packs of beef jerky, one pack of dried mango and one of dried apricot. Charlie was clearly a man who planned ahead. Good for him.

Back in his seat, Bishop passed the knapsack to Strickland and then buckled his safety belt.

'Okay, here we go,' Charlie said, and made a few final checks before pushing the red fuel control button all the way in. Then he pressed the red master switch, jiggled the primer and pulled it out until it was locked into position. He turned the ignition key to the right. The engine turned over but failed to catch. He tried again, moving the throttle back and forth at the same time. This time the engine caught. The nose propeller kicked in and within seconds it was just a circular blur in front of them.

Bishop sat back as Charlie slowly taxied them towards the start of the landing strip. Once they were on the centreline and pointing north, he increased the throttle to two thousand rpms. They started moving down the runway, gathering speed as the engine rose in pitch.

The runway was a lot smoother than Bishop had expected. He kept his eye on the air speed indicator. At fifty-five knots Charlie pulled slowly back on the control yoke, the plane continued to gain speed and then the wheels left the ground and they were airborne. As they rose into the air Charlie dipped the right wing a little and kept them on a north-easterly heading for another mile before levelling out. Then he slowly turned the yoke to the right until the compass needle was pointing east.

'Excellent, Charlie,' Bishop said. 'No muss, no fuss. Just how I like it.' He turned to Strickland in the rear. 'Reach into that bag and pass me the orange juice, will you?'

TWENTY-SIX

Bishop looked out the portside window and tried to make out the Rocky Mountains he knew were down there, twelve thousand feet below, but there was too much cloud cover to see anything clearly. They'd already been in the air for just over four hours, with the sky gradually becoming more overcast the further east they went. Despite the heating in the plane, he was also feeling the sizeable drop in temperature.

Pulling up the collar of his suit jacket, he turned in his seat and saw Strickland in the back, also looking out the window and still looking as jittery as when they'd taken off. No doubt he was thinking of Barney, imagining what the boy must be going through right now. But Barney was a pretty tough kid for his age. Bishop had an idea the boy was probably handling the situation a lot better than Strickland gave him credit for. He hoped so, but he also knew it was pointless worrying about things beyond his power.

Instead his mind drifted to Angela Delaney again, and that brief conversation they'd had over coffee this morning. She'd clearly wanted to ask him to share her vacation time with her, and probably would have asked outright once the assignment was over. He would have accepted, too. He still liked her a lot. Or maybe she was thinking of something more than just another brief holiday romance this time, maybe she wanted something a little more concrete in her life. Or then again, maybe he was overthinking it. He'd never find out now.

All he knew for sure was Delaney was dead and that somebody on her side of the fence had leaked their whereabouts to Hartnell and set this morning's events in motion. In the end it always came down to one person, and Bishop knew he wouldn't be able to rest until he knew the identity of that person.

But that could all wait until the proper time. The boy was their number one priority now.

He looked at Charlie in the next seat, currently staring straight ahead, all his concentration on the sky before them. Bishop checked his watch and saw it was a minute to three, Vegas time, making it almost four o'clock here in Northern Colorado. Twenty minutes earlier Charlie had contacted the base station at the municipal airport where they were due to land and asked if it was possible to refuel while they were there. It was a small airport he said he'd used before, situated midway between the towns of Fort Morgan and Wiggins. The guy at the other end had remembered Charlie from before and said he'd get back to him.

If all went to plan, and with two or three more stops along the way, they could be in Ohio by tomorrow morning, a whole twenty-four hours ahead of schedule. This would give Bishop enough time to plan for the exchange to come. Although his first priority was getting Barney back, he wasn't planning on handing Strickland over if he could possibly avoid it. Bishop wanted Barney safe, but for a whole bunch of reasons he also wanted Hartnell's ass in a sling, and Strickland was the key to achieving that.

But of the few options available, all required some kind of outside help, which was where the problems lay. Because Bishop knew better than most how the Marshals Service worked. He'd had first-hand experience of their methods not too long ago, so he knew the first rule of evasion was to steer clear of all known associates. He had no idea of the scale of the search being undertaken, but he had to assume that pretty much everyone he'd ever known in his adult-life would now be under scrutiny by the various law enforcement agencies. Same went for Strickland. Which meant they were totally cut off.

But an answer would come. He was sure if it. Think long enough on a problem and a solution always presented itself.

A sudden jarring shift in the plane's altitude shook Bishop out of his thoughts. But it was just a little turbulence, and he watched Charlie calmly pull back slightly on the control yoke as he returned them to their original position.

A minute later, Charlie raised a hand to his mic. Bishop quickly put his own headset on and heard the same voice as before say, '. . . Echo One, this is Wiggins Ground, do you read, over?'

'Wiggins Ground,' Charlie replied, 'this is Cessna Calveda Golf Echo One, I read you, over.'

'Sorry for the delay, Cessna, but that's an affirmative on the refuelling. We should have enough on-site for you.'

'That's great, Wiggins. The only problem is I forgot my wallet. Can you charge it to the school?'

'No problem, Cessna. So, uh, tell me, how's things up there? Everything okay?'

Bishop's antennae suddenly shot up. He didn't like the sound of this.

'Sure, we're fine,' Charlie said. 'No problems this trip.'

That was it. Bishop glared at Charlie and made a rapid chopping motion with his hand. *Wrap it up, right now.*

'Gotta go, Wiggins,' Charlie said, eyes wide. 'See you on the ground. Over and out.'

'Over and out,' came the reply. 'Take care of yourself.'

Bishop switched off the radio and took off his headset. Charlie did the same.

'And you were doing so well up till then,' Bishop said. 'I thought you said you were no hero.'

'I'm not. I wasn't lying.'

'No? Then what was that I just heard? "*No problems this trip.*" That *is* what you said, isn't it?'

Charlie just looked at him.

'What's happening?' Strickland said from the back.

'Our pilot here just gave our friends down below a heads-up. I told you I'm not an idiot, Charlie. When I first started taking chopper lessons I read up on call signals, and using the word "trip" in a sentence is a trigger to alert the ground that you've been hijacked. Somehow it wouldn't surprise me to find a whole cadre of cops waiting for us once we landed. Or are you going to tell me I'm just imagining things?'

'Look,' Charlie said, 'it just came out before I could think it through. I didn't—'

'Don't make things worse,' Bishop said, and Charlie got the message and shut up.

'How did they even suspect something was up?' Strickland asked.

Bishop shrugged. 'Back during his first communication with the base station, he could have given them a signal I didn't catch. Something that got them worried. I thought it was taking too long for them to get back to us. How about it, Charlie? That what happened?'

Charlie didn't look at all well. 'Oh God,' he said, 'you're gonna kill me.'

'Relax, Charlie, I'm not a psychopath. Granted, you've complicated things for us, but you can still get yourself out of this by taking this thing down and landing at the first available opportunity. Then after I've tied you up, we'll go our own way and call it evens.'

When the pilot made no effort to move the control yoke, Bishop motioned with the Glock and said, 'That was me being reasonable, Charlie. Don't tip me the other way. Take us down, *now.*'

Charlie swallowed, then pushed the control stick forward and began their descent.

TWENTY-SEVEN

As soon as Charlie killed the Skyhawk's engine, Bishop reached past him and pulled the keys from the slot, just in case he got any ideas. At least the landing had been a fairly smooth one, despite the less-than-perfect terrain. He had to admit the guy was a pretty good pilot.

Charlie had managed to land them in the middle of a vast dry cornfield, with similar-sized fields surrounding them in every direction. No snow flurries yet, thankfully, but with less than a fortnight before ski season started it was surely only a matter of days. Far off in the distance, to the north and west, Bishop could see low mountains covered with evergreens. There was a long treeline about a mile to the south, with nothing but flatlands to the west. And no visible sign of habitation anywhere. No farmhouses, no barns, nothing. Just long-dormant farmland everywhere you looked.

And no means of transport other than their own feet.

So much for being ahead of the game, he thought.

'Great,' Strickland said from behind him. 'Stuck in the middle of nowhere again.'

'Look on the bright side,' Bishop said, 'we just covered five hundred miles in four hours. That's not so bad.'

'Shit, there's no bright side to *any* of this. Come on, let's get going.'

Bishop opened the door on his side and got out of the plane and stretched, rolling his shoulders one way then the other, getting rid of the stiffness. Under his feet, the earth felt dry and hard and as solid as rock. It also wasn't quite as cold as he'd expected. Maybe somewhere in the mid-forties, so at least they wouldn't have to worry about freezing to death. The sky was still overcast, though, and he figured they still had a couple of hours' daylight left. Maybe less. As Strickland pushed the passenger seat forward to give himself enough room to get out, Bishop went over to the baggage hold and from it grabbed the long coil of rope he'd seen before. Then he approached the pilot's door and pulled it open. Charlie just sat there and stared back at him with a worried expression. His skin had turned a lot paler in the last few minutes too. The poor guy really thought Bishop might waste him. He really hated scaring the hell out of innocent civilians like this, but he didn't have any other choice right now.

'Okay, come on out,' he said.

'Why don't I just stay here?'

'Just do as I tell you, Charlie.'

Charlie slowly manoeuvred himself out and then just stood next to the door. Bishop reached down behind him to slide the pilot's seat forward a few inches. 'All right,' he said, 'turn round and face the plane, hands behind your back.'

'You ain't gonna shoot me?'

Bishop sighed. 'No, Charlie, I'm going to tie you up, like I told you. That's what the rope's for. You'll stay here. We'll go away. Sometimes life *can* be that simple, you know.'

'We don't have time for this,' Strickland said. 'Just do what he says, Charlie.'

The pilot exhaled and turned round, then Bishop pulled both his arms back and went to work with the rope. A few minutes later, he had the pilot's arms, hands and feet bound to his satisfaction. He then carefully placed Charlie in the back seat and fastened the safety belt too, so he couldn't move around too much. He didn't bother gagging the guy. Nobody was likely to hear him out here anyway.

'I'll stick the keys behind those tools in the hold,' Bishop said.

'Hey, you really just gonna leave me tied up like this? I could die out here.'

'I doubt it. I made sure those knots aren't impossible to get through. Might take you a few hours, but with a little patience and effort you'll be able to free yourself easily enough. Then you can fly to that same little airport you were taking us to, refuel and head on home.' He paused. 'And now I've got a favour to ask, Charlie.'

The pilot's mouth hung open. He looked at Bishop as though he'd just produced a set of encyclopaedias from his nose. 'A favour? From *me?*'

'That's right. When the cops question you I'd like you to tell them that the two men who hijacked you wore baseball caps, dark glasses and false beards and moustaches, and you couldn't really tell what they looked like under all that crap. Can you do that?'

Despite being tied up Charlie actually looked a little more confident now, or at least less worried about his ultimate fate. It had obviously gotten through to him that he was going to live through this. 'I guess so,' he said, 'but why would I?'

Bishop rolled up his jacket sleeve, undid his watchband and removed his timepiece. 'This is a Seiko Prospex scuba watch that was given to me recently by somebody I did a favour for. I've been told it's worth about one-and-a-half grand new. This one's a couple of months old, but you should be able to get seven or eight hundred for it on eBay. That's enough to take care of the fuel costs both ways, as well as your time. And to earn it all you have to do is say you couldn't see us clearly. Not much to ask, is it?'

Charlie studied him for a few moments, then said, 'Eight hundred bucks, huh?'

'Maybe more.'

'I guess I could do that. Okay, gimme the watch and we got a deal.'

'Good man,' Bishop said, and laid the watch on the floor at Charlie's feet. When he backed out, he saw Strickland standing there holding the knapsack, watching them both.

'And you'll just trust him to keep his word?' he said.

Bishop shrugged. 'He will or he won't. Trust has to start somewhere, and Charlie strikes me as an honest man.'

He reached into the bag and pulled out one of the remaining bottles of water. It was half-full. Or half-empty, depending on your outlook. He left the bottle on the front seat and said to the pilot, 'For when you get yourself free. The rest of the rations go with us. We'll need them more than you.'

Charlie just looked at each of them, then said, 'I got one question.'

'What's that?'

'Just what the hell did you *do*?'

Bishop shook his head. 'I've been asking myself the same question these last few hours. Just remember our deal, Charlie.'

He shut the door. Strickland hefted the knapsack over his shoulder and both men started walking south, towards the treeline in the distance.

'So where the hell are we?' Strickland asked.

'As near as I can tell we're about halfway across Colorado, so probably in Grand County somewhere. From the air I saw that treeline marks the beginning of some woodland that keeps going for another mile or so. I also spotted a reservoir, or a lake, along the way with a river leading off from it on a north-easterly direction. The bad news is it's right in our path. I just hope there's a bridge somewhere so we can get across.'

'And some wheels.'

'Yeah, some wheels, too.'

They trudged on in silence for a while. The field wasn't too bad for walking in. The land was flat, more or less. It could have been worse.

'Pretty funny, huh?' Strickland said after a while.

Bishop turned to him. 'What is?'

'Me rushing to my death like this. Hard to believe that thirty-six hours from now I'll be a goner.'

'Nothing's set in stone. Anything can still happen.'

'I never knew you were an optimist, Bishop.'

'You could fill a book with what you don't know about me.'

'So where'd this positive outlook of yours come from?'

'What difference does it make?'

'Not much. But we got a long walk ahead of us. Why not just tell me?'

Bishop shrugged. 'There's nothing complicated about it. It just makes more sense to be positive than not. Go into anything with a negative attitude, you're already planning to fail before you've even started. What's the point of that? In fact, what's the point of anything? You might as well just curl up and die. A guy call Sun Tzu once said, "*He who's prepared and waits for the unprepared will be victorious*". I find that's a pretty good mantra to live life by.'

'Kind of like hope for the best, but prepare for the worst, right?'

'Pretty much.'

'But that second part isn't exactly positive, is it? Preparing for the worst? Sounds to me like you're already setting yourself up for a fall there.'

'No, it's saying you shouldn't keep your head in the clouds, either. Nothing's plain sailing. There are always obstacles. All you can do is prepare for them as best you can, then deal with them when they come.'

'And you really believe this can end on an up note for me?'

'It's a little too early to tell, but I'm still open-minded. Ask me again tomorrow, once I've given it some more thought.'

'Assuming I'm still breathing by then. Look, Bishop, you'll make sure Barn's okay, right? Because whatever happens to me, Barney needs to be alive at the end of this. With Carrie . . .' He paused and gave a small sigh. 'With Carrie out of the picture and me at the end of a very short rope, his life's all that matters to me now.'

'I'll make sure Barney's all right, don't worry about that.'

'Good. That's all I wanted to hear.' Strickland faced front again and they continued walking.

TWENTY-EIGHT

Bishop slowed to a stop when he saw the building about a mile away in the distance. It looked like a farmhouse, two storeys, with an old-style brick grain silo rising up on the left, and a large barn set a little ways back. There were a lot more trees in that direction too, many of them surrounding the property. Bishop figured whoever lived there probably owned the land they'd been walking on for the last three miles.

'What do you think?' Strickland asked.

'I think since we're out in the middle of nowhere, it's a good bet there'll be at least one useful vehicle on site. Other than a tractor, I mean.'

'Think they'll be good enough to let us borrow it?'

'I wasn't planning on asking for permission.'

They continued on. They'd already been walking for about half an hour and the sky hadn't gotten any darker. Since Bishop no longer had a watch he had to guess, but he figured it was probably around four thirty, so maybe another hour and a half until nightfall.

Ten minutes later Bishop reached the first of the trees, a mixture of oaks and birches that surrounded the property perimeter. Standing under cover of one of the larger oaks, he took a moment to study the white clapboard farmhouse a hundred feet away from them.

They'd approached from the side, and at the front he could see a long wide porch with wooden columns, with a swinging seat hanging from chains at one end. The house itself didn't look particularly new, but it looked well cared for. Somebody had given the place a new coat of white paint recently, maybe even in the last couple of months. There were no lights on inside, though, and Bishop couldn't hear any animal noises at all, which was odd. Not even a dog. There was also a large empty courtyard out front, but no vehicles in sight.

Directly opposite, with the doors facing them, was the large barn. It was the same white as the farmhouse, and probably housed the tractor, baler, and whatever other pieces of farm machinery were needed to keep the place going. And hopefully also a vehicle they could actually use. The double doors were the kind that slid apart, like those on aircraft hangars except much smaller. Just above the doors were two small hayloft windows.

About twenty feet away from their position there was a chest-high cyclone fence that circled the property. Bishop didn't see any insulator poles, though, which meant it wasn't electrified. When he reached the fence he climbed over and waited for Strickland to join him. There were some more trees on this side of the fence and Bishop led the way to one and said to Strickland, 'You stay under cover here while I circle round front and check the barn.'

Without another word, Bishop left him and followed the fence until he came to a long, wooden entrance gate. This had to be the front of the property. Beyond the gate, he could see the dirt driveway carried on down a gentle slope before disappearing between some more trees. Presumably it led towards a back road, or more likely a dirt track. But a road was a road. Bishop took a moment to check the gate wasn't locked, and then kept walking along the perimeter until he came to the side of the barn facing away from the house.

He was still waiting for the sound of a barking dog to break the silence. Or something. But he heard nothing, and saw nothing, which only put him on guard even more.

Bishop edged along the side of the barn and, when he reached the corner, peered round for a better look. He saw there were sliders at the top of the double doors and a metal rail at the bottom for the wheels. In the centre he saw two steel handles affixed to the doors, but no padlock. Knowing he'd be in full view of anybody looking out of the house, Bishop trotted over to the centre, grabbed the handle of the right-hand door and pushed it to the right. The door began to slide open. Fortunately, the caster wheels weren't too noisy. When he'd made a space big enough, Bishop slipped inside the barn.

He waited a few moments for his eyes to adjust, but the small windows in the hayloft above helped shed light on the situation. Looking around, he saw two large tractors at rest next to each other. Both looked old and well used. Further back, he also saw three old trailers, a large cultivator, a planter, and something that looked like a grain cart. There was also a selection of old machine parts and used tyres piled up at the rear of the barn.

But the machine that really caught his attention was the pick-up, an old square-bodied Chevy Cheyenne, standing on its own. A real relic from the seventies, it looked in even worse shape than the tractors. The cab was one of those with space enough for a driver and a single passenger. There was plenty of rust on the body, and at some point a large galvanized plate had been riveted onto the side of the bed.

Bishop went over and opened the driver's door and looked inside. It had a manual transmission, which was fine, but the ignition slot was empty. Well, there were other ways to start these old vehicles. Unfortunately, they were also noisy.

He was about to close the door when he frowned at the sun visor. He used a finger to flip it open and something metallic fell out and jangled as it hit the floor. Bishop smiled and picked up the keys. There were two of them, attached to a basic key ring. He inserted the ignition key and turned it a quarter-rotation, then flipped the switch for the headlights. The full beams suddenly flashed against the barn doors, lighting up the whole room. Excellent.

Turning the lights off, he exited the barn and made his way back to Strickland using the same route as before. 'There's an old pick-up in there,' he said, 'along with the keys. The headlights work, so it looks like it's been used recently.'

'Sounds like a second vehicle, then,' Strickland said. 'They're probably out somewhere right now in the good one.'

'Possibly. But I still don't want to risk starting the engine so close to the house.'

'So how do we play this?'

'I let out the handbrake and we push it out of the barn. Once we're through the gate, the driveway slopes down a little so I just need a start. Then you come back, slide the barn door shut as quietly as possible and follow me and jump in.'

Strickland nodded and said, 'Lead the way.'

Bishop took the same route as before with Strickland following close behind. They stopped when they reached the entrance gate and pushed it open all the way. Once inside the barn, Strickland dropped the knapsack into the cab while Bishop slid the barn door a little further along until there was a five-foot gap. Then he reached in the driver's door and let out the handbrake.

'Okay, let's do it,' he said. With one hand on the steering wheel, Bishop braced himself against the doorframe and pushed while Strickland did the same at the back. As the car began to move forward Bishop moved the steering wheel until the vehicle was pointed at the gap. Once they were through, he turned the wheel left and aimed for the open gate twenty feet away. After a few more seconds of effort they had a little momentum going and he got in the driver's seat and gently closed the door. The vehicle was moving at about three or four miles an hour when Strickland let go of the rear. In the rear-view, Bishop saw him run back to the barn. No sign of anybody else back at the house.

Bishop passed through the gate and reached the gradient and got the vehicle up to six or seven. The driveway was long and bumpy, but fairly straight and tree-lined on both sides. When he thought he'd covered enough distance, Bishop turned the key and stepped on the gas. The engine coughed once, twice, then it caught and he shoved the gearstick into second. The diesel engine was louder than he'd expected, but it couldn't be helped. He kept going for another twenty yards, then the landscape levelled out and he pressed down on the brakes. They felt a lot looser than he liked, but the vehicle eventually came to a stop. He left the engine running. Thirty or forty feet ahead he could see the driveway connected with another dirt track that turned off at a right angle. He looked at the dial and saw the tank was about three-quarters full. Not perfect, but better than nothing.

Strickland appeared a few seconds later and jumped in.

'Let's get the hell out of here,' he said. He sounded out of breath already.

'You see somebody?'

'No, but somebody might have seen me. I was shutting the barn door when I thought I saw one of the drapes moving back at the main house.'

'Wonderful.' Bishop said. He put the gear into first again and stepped on the gas.

TWENTY-NINE

The truck's suspension was almost non-existent. Every rut they drove over felt like a crater and Bishop's lower back starting aching almost immediately. The excuse for a road went on for about another mile before it connected up to another dirt track, although this one was a lot smoother, with fewer potholes. Clearly it was used a little more regularly. They passed a couple more isolated farmhouses along the way, and then the road turned into a bridge that took them across the river Bishop had spotted earlier. Once they were across that, it was another half-mile before they reached an intersection that connected to a two-lane highway.

'Finally,' Strickland said. 'Never thought I'd be glad to see asphalt again.'

Bishop paused at the junction and saw a single car approaching from the left, heading north. Once it sped by Bishop pulled out and headed off in the opposite direction. As he stepped on the gas he pushed the gearstick into third for the first time and the engine voiced its displeasure with a loud rattling sound. Fourth was a little quieter, but it was clear the Chevy's best days were far in the past. At fifty miles per hour the engine sounded like it was straining badly, and Bishop knew he'd be lucky to get sixty out of the thing.

At the next intersection he turned left. Soon, they passed a sign that said they were now on Highway 40 and about to enter the town of Granby, population 1,800. Bishop just hoped nobody would recognize this truck, what with that damn steel plate on the side. Still, there wasn't much he could do about it now.

They drove on. Traffic was very light for a major highway. This part of Colorado wasn't exactly densely populated, which had its pluses and minuses as far as Bishop was concerned. Over the next mile or so they passed another gas station, some residences, a scattering of business premises and warehouses, and a small row of storefronts. Bishop noticed a black and white parked in a bay in front of a tools and supplies store. There didn't seem to be anybody inside it. Then they passed a hotel, and after that it was nothing but more farmland on both sides.

The next few miles proved uneventful. Beautiful mountain country all around, but Bishop wasn't in the mood to appreciate it. He was too busy trying to recall the layout of this part of the country from his close protection days. He'd spent a period of time in Colorado on a job and, like always, had made sure he had a general understanding of the main routes between the cities. Most of it was still stored away in the back of his brain somewhere. He had a general feeling the highway they were on would take them through the mountains before eventually joining up with the I-70, and from there to the main cities like Denver and Broomfield to the east, which he wanted to avoid, and smaller municipalities like Boulder, Colorado Springs or Castle Rock. Along with a host of others whose names escaped him.

After another fifteen miles or so, Bishop began to see signs for a town called Cramer located just up ahead, along with a couple of vacation lodges and something called the Cramer Hill Shopping Center. They were passing through a small unnamed township when Bishop looked in the rear-view and almost wished he hadn't. About two hundred feet back, a black and white cruiser was joining the highway from a side road. And heading in the same direction as them. Bishop could see two silhouettes inside the cruiser.

'Check your wing mirror,' he said.

Strickland bent his head and saw it immediately. 'Oh, shit. Has he seen us?'

'Not sure. I don't see any flashing lights.'

'Yet.'

Bishop said nothing. It all depended on whether the owner really did see Strickland back at the house. If he did, it was a cinch he or she called the cops, which meant the moment this one spotted the steel plate on the side they could be in real trouble.

He kept going. It was all he could do. There were no more turn-offs ahead, just straight highway. He looked down at the dial and saw they were still doing just over fifty-five. The engine was making a hell of a noise, but holding fairly steady. If he needed to, he felt he could possibly get another five miles an hour out of it. For all the good it would do. Even a go-cart would be more than a match for them at this point.

'Doesn't look like he's in any hurry,' Strickland said, still watching his mirror.

Bishop checked the rear-view again and saw he was right. The black and white was falling back. Other cars were moving into the left-hand lane to overtake. The cop was at least three hundred feet behind them now. And fading.

Soon they lost sight of the cop, but Bishop wasn't about to start counting his chickens yet. Another mile went by. He was watching the rear-view as much as the road ahead.

Then behind them, in the distance, he saw flashing red and blue lights.

THIRTY

Strickland glanced in the wing mirror and said, 'I knew things were going too smoothly. You think it's us he wants?'

'I'm not waiting around to find out,' Bishop said, and stepped on the gas.

Whatever the cop was responding to could be entirely unrelated to them, but he had to assume the worst. Somehow Bishop got the vehicle up to sixty, but the steering wheel started vibrating badly and he had to fight to keep the vehicle in a straight line. Coming up on the right was a small turn-off, but he ignored it and kept going. He was thinking of that sign they'd passed and hoped the shopping centre wasn't too far away. The land round here was pretty flat, though, and he could clearly see a small town up ahead. It had to be Cramer. Industrial buildings started flashing by on their right and road signs warned drivers to start reducing their speed.

Bishop kept them at sixty. He kept his foot pressed to the floor, hoping to get more out of it, but the needle was stuck. And now it wasn't just the steering wheel that was shaking, but the whole damn truck. The thing felt like it could fall apart at any moment.

There was a Ford something in front of them, doing forty. Bishop steered round it and kept on going, the Chevy's engine screaming like a banshee. He caught a quick flash of the police cruiser gaining in the rear-view, but all his attention was focused on the road ahead of them. They were passing through the main part of town now, if you could call it that. Some kind of eatery over there on the right. To the left was a ski lodge. Traffic was still fairly light, which was bad. He would have preferred more vehicles to slow the cop's progress. He steered them round another car. The driver angrily beeped his horn as he passed.

Then they were past the lodge and Bishop saw a large parking lot coming up on the left. And further back was the shopping centre. It wasn't much. A large ALCO anchor store in the middle with a long line of much smaller stores on either side, maybe a dozen in all. And coming up directly ahead was a large four-way intersection. A few cars were waiting for the lights to turn green.

'They're gaining,' Strickland said, looking out the back.

Bishop ignored the red lights at the intersection and tapped the brakes, changing down to third as he veered round a couple of waiting vehicles. The engine was still screaming. He hung a left into the winding access road to the shopping centre and kept going. He could see the parking lot to his right was barely a quarter full. Maybe seventy or eighty vehicles. And it was coming up to five thirty. He didn't know what the opening times were like around here, but they'd have to be closing up pretty soon. That might work for them.

Strickland faced front. 'What the hell are you doing? This is a dead end.'

'We can't outrun them in this thing,' Bishop said. They were almost at the parking lot. 'They don't know what we look like yet so we make that work for us. Soon as we park this thing we'll split up and lose ourselves amongst all the other customers.'

'And then what?'

'I'm still working on it. Hold on.'

Bishop yanked the wheel to the right and sped into the lot entrance, narrowly avoiding an exiting vehicle coming the other way. He kept going, passing some of the smaller stores on their left. A few shoppers walking with bags or trolleys watched them as they sped past.

'Where are they now?' Bishop asked.

Strickland looked behind. 'They just took the turn.'

Bishop was watching the aisles, looking for spaces near the front. The cruiser should be far enough away that they wouldn't be able see where he parked, not straight away. But he still needed a space. And fast. There. There was one at the head of an aisle just past the ALCO store. He slowed down to twenty, turned into the aisle and then carefully slotted the pick-up into the space and turned off the engine. The muffler began ticking as it cooled.

'Head for the ALCO store,' Bishop said. 'Try and act casual, like you're just off to do some weekend grocery shopping. I'll take one of the smaller stores. Once I've come up with something I'll call you on the cell. Try not to look like a fugitive.'

Strickland stared back at him.

'Get *going*,' Bishop said, and got out. He heard Strickland doing the same. He studied the reflections in the store windows to the left. The cruiser was taking the same route as them, but moving a lot slower. Evidently they hadn't spotted them yet.

Bishop closed the door and ducked down, moving between the vehicles in front until he emerged in the next aisle along. He stood up and saw Strickland had joined a family of four also making for ALCO. He was walking confidently alongside them, as though he belonged. Good. It also meant the anchor store opened late. But what about the other stores?

As Bishop crossed the road he stared at the approaching cruiser fifty feet away, just like everybody else was doing. This was exciting stuff for a small town. He could see the driver slowing at each aisle while his partner checked the parked vehicles. They'd spot it any moment now. Bishop turned away and looked in the store windows as he walked. The first one, a travel shop, was closed. The next one, a Taco Bell, was open for business, but looked empty. He moved on to a Radio Shack, also open. Then a cell phone store with a few customers inside. He moved to the next shop along and stopped.

The store was smaller and narrower than the others. The sign above, written in a tasteful freehand script, said *Clea Arts & Crafts*. The items in the window were a mixture of artist's materials, ornaments for the home and general knick-knacks. Most of the items looked handmade. The sign behind the door read OPEN.

Without making it obvious, Bishop turned his head to the left a little. He could see the cruiser had stopped at the aisle where he'd parked. The driver was speaking into his mic, probably calling for backup. The other one was standing and peering at all the pedestrians walking around. Bishop opened the door and stepped into the shop.

He smelled the incense first. Just a faint odour, but noticeable. He was the only customer.

Looking around, he saw the place was packed with product similar to the things in the window. Two large display shelves ran the length of the narrow store and finished up at the counter at the rear. More items were arranged against the walls on both sides. Bishop saw picture frames, hand-woven baskets, string beads, rainbow bracelets, artist's easels, paints, scrapbooks and more. It all looked like good quality stuff. None of it looked tacky.

Bishop could hear somebody talking at the back of the shop. The voice sounded female, but he couldn't see anybody. He went back to the front door and looked out. One of the cops was walking towards the ALCO store. The other one stood by the cruiser, speaking into his radio.

He and Strickland needed to get out of here as fast as possible. That much was clear. Because more cops would be coming and once they did, the situation would quickly become untenable for both of them.

Bishop walked down the aisle until he reached the unmanned counter at the rear of the shop. Behind it was a door, partly ajar. Through the gap he could hear the woman's voice more clearly.

'Look, Howard,' she was saying in a calm, patient tone, 'this is getting us nowhere. We're just going over the same arguments as before, and I already allow Lucy to stay with you two full weeks out of every eight, which is far more time than the two weekends a month the judge awarded you. It's not like I haven't bent over backwards to accom . . .' Silence for a few seconds, and then, 'Well, you better make a decision now, then. You either choose this Tracy woman or you choose our daughter, because if I have to come and take Lucy away tonight, we're going to be reverting to the original legal agreement and sticking to that from now on.' Another gap. 'Fine. Well, it looks like there's hope for you yet. I'll talk to you tomorrow, or the day after. Right.'

There came the sound of a phone being dropped into its cradle or base unit. Bishop waited a few seconds before clearing his throat.

A small, slim, bespectacled woman emerged from the back room, dressed in black jeans, white T-shirt and black waistcoat. Auburn shoulder-length hair framed a pleasant oval face. She looked about

Bishop's age, possibly mid- to late thirties, and gave him a sheepish smile. Her pale grey eyes seemed to look everywhere but at him.

'How much of that did you hear?' she asked. Her face had coloured a little.

'Not much.' Bishop said. 'Are you the owner here?'

She nodded. 'That's my name on the sign out front.'

'Clea? Nice name. Short for anything?'

'Yes, it's short for Cleanthe. How can I help you?'

'Well, I actually came here to ask a favour.'

She looked at him for the first time and her brows immediately came together in a frown. Bishop watched her eyes and thought he saw something that looked like recognition in there. Which was bad news. Very bad news.

'Um, a favour?' she asked.

He reached behind him and gripped the Glock in his waistband. 'I'm afraid I need to use your phone, Clea.'

'My phone?' The frown deepened. 'Look, I don't really think I can—'

She stopped as Bishop pulled the gun out and laid it gently on the counter. 'Sorry, but I really have to insist,' he said.

THIRTY-ONE

Bishop lifted the hinged end of the counter and came round and joined Clea. Her eyes were huge circles and she was actually shivering with fear, which hadn't been his intention at all. Concerned she might lose control completely, he put the Glock back in his waistband. It had served its purpose. She knew he had it now and that was enough.

'Look, I'm not here to hurt you, Clea,' he said. 'What's your last name?'

'What?' She swallowed. 'My . . . my last name? It's Buchanan.'

'And are you here on your own? Please don't lie.'

'Yes, I . . . I can't afford help.'

'Okay. Good. But you recognized my face, didn't you? From where? The news?'

She nodded and wrapped her arms around herself. 'I've got a portable TV in the back office and . . . and there was a piece about you a couple of hours ago.'

'Great. And what did they say?'

'Well, they said you were involved in a shootout at a house in Las Vegas this morning that left seven marshals dead, and that . . . and that you escaped in an SUV with two other people. They showed a photo of you in the vehicle, and said anybody who sees you should call the police straight away.'

Bishop wondered where they could have possibly gotten a photo of him. Then he remembered that damn jogger with the cell phone and silently cursed to himself. He said, 'And were any names mentioned?'

Clea shook her head. 'I don't think so.'

'But it was definitely seven marshals who were killed, right?'

'That's what they said.'

So that was all of them. 'And did they say where I'm supposed to be heading?'

Clea shook her head. 'I only caught the first part. I had to turn the TV off when a customer came into the store.'

Bishop studied the woman as he rubbed his hand over his scalp. She no longer looked as though she might collapse from fear at any moment, but she still looked far from calm.

'Please don't hurt me,' she said. 'I've done nothing to you.'

'I know you haven't, Clea. Let's move into your office. I still need to use your phone.'

Clea backed up, pushed open the door and stepped through with Bishop right behind. The light was still on. The room was very small and very narrow, with another door at the other end. There were no windows. There was a work desk with a PC, some paperwork, and a cordless phone. Halfway down an old couch took up part of the wall. Next to it was a mini-fridge. At this end was a small table holding a small portable TV. It was currently turned off.

'What's behind that door back there?' Bishop asked.

She wrapped her arms around herself again. 'A small hallway and a restroom, and then the rear exit fire door.'

'Which opens onto what?'

'The rear loading area and staff parking lot.'

'Good.' He motioned for Clea to sit at her desk and said, 'What's the number for this phone?'

She recited the number, and he picked up the cordless and dialled the number of the cell phone. Strickland picked up after four rings. 'Yeah?' he whispered.

'It's me. I'm calling from a store a few doors down from you. What's the situation?'

'Right now I'm just walking around the men's clothes section, but I can see one of the cops standing outside the main entrance, watching people come and go.'

'Well, I've just been informed that my face is now public property, and possibly yours too, so don't leave that way. There's bound to be an employees' exit somewhere at the rear, though, so try and use that. See any baseball caps where you are?'

'Yeah, I got a whole bunch of them right in front of me.'

'Good. Rip the price off one, stamp on it a few times and put it on. Then leave by the rear entrance and turn right.' He turned to Clea. 'Is there a sign so he can identify this place?'

The woman nodded.

'Look for the sign that says *Clea Arts and Crafts*,' Bishop said. He gave Strickland the number in case of problems, and then hung up.

'What kind of car do you drive?' he asked Clea.

She stared at him. 'Sorry, what?'

'Your car. What make is it?'

'Oh, it's a Ford Explorer. Why?'

'New?'

'No, it's about twenty years old.'

'And it's parked out back?'

She nodded. 'I can give you the keys. My bag's right there in the desk drawer.'

'Later. So what happens when you close for the day, Clea? You got roll-down security shutters on this place, anything like that? What about alarms?'

'There's an alarm for the front door, but I don't use shutters or anything like that. Cramer's only a small town. We don't really get many thefts around here.'

'Lucky you. And you live here in town?'

'No, I . . . I live just outside Wellerby, the next town along.'

'And what time do you generally close?'

'Um, seven, usually. Eight o'clock on Fridays and Saturdays.'

'And your neighbours along here all close around the same time?'

'Mostly. Radio Shack closes about now. ALCO stays open till ten, I think.'

'And what time is it now?'

She checked her watch. 'Um, almost five thirty.'

'Okay. I think it's best if you finished early today, Clea. Let's see that bag of yours.'

Bishop waited as she went over and pulled out an ornate, multi-coloured shoulder bag from one of the desk drawers and placed it on the desk. It looked handmade, like the rest of the stuff outside.

He said, 'If I were to go through that bag, would I find a gun?'

The look of genuine innocence on Clea's face was better than any verbal denial she could have come up with.

'Never mind,' he said. 'All right, let's lock up. Bring your keys.'

She pulled out a large key ring from the bag and Bishop led her through the shop until they reached the front door. Bishop waited as she flipped the light switches, leaving them in darkness except for the light in the back room. He held onto Clea's arm as she locked the door and reversed the OPEN sign to CLOSED. After checking the door was actually locked, he peered out the window and saw a second cruiser had arrived at some point. It was parked outside the ALCO entrance. No flashing lights, though. They clearly didn't want to scare the shoppers over what looked to be a simple case of car theft.

Bishop stayed there for a while longer, just watching. After a couple more minutes, he saw one of the cops started to stroll down this way, looking in doorways as he passed.

'Let's go back,' Bishop said. He followed Clea into the back room and gently clicked the door shut. They waited in silence. Another minute passed before Bishop heard the sound of somebody knocking on glass out front.

'You're not here,' he said. 'Soon he'll move onto the next door.'

Clea closed her eyes and just nodded.

Bishop waited. There came another knock on the front door. Bishop waited another minute and finally relaxed when no more sounds came.

The sound of a ringing phone suddenly interrupted the silence and Clea gave a shriek of surprise. Bishop grabbed the cordless and handed it to her. 'You better answer it. Once you're calm again.'

Clea took a deep breath, then pressed a button on the keypad and brought the phone to her ear. 'Yes?' A pause, then, 'Yes, he's here.'

Bishop took the phone from her and said, 'Where are you?'

'Outside the rear door,' Strickland said. 'Let me in, huh? I'm feeling self-conscious out here.'

'Wait one,' Bishop said and hung up. To Clea, he said, 'Bring your bag.'

Clea slung her bag over her shoulder as Bishop opened the door. Beyond was a narrow corridor that ran back for about twenty feet and ended in a steel fire door. In the ceiling, a single fluorescent tube supplied light for the small space. Along the right-hand wall was another door that presumably led to the restroom.

Bishop turned off the light for the office, then shut the door behind him.

Clea went first. At the end of the hallway she pressed down on the crash bar and pushed the fire door open. Strickland was standing right outside, wearing a black baseball cap with a bat logo on the front.

He looked at Clea for a beat, and then turned to Bishop. 'You made a friend.'

'Kind of. You recognize this man, Clea?'

'No,' she said, frowning. 'Should I?'

'Well, that's something, I guess,' Bishop said.

He saw the whole rear area was just a wide open space, with various parked vehicles dotted around in haphazard fashion. A dark brown Explorer was parked just a few feet away from her door. About a hundred feet to the left, Bishop could see a Radio Shack delivery truck had backed up to the store's rear entrance. A guy in dark overalls was loading boxes onto a handcart. Another one wearing similar overalls was puffing on a cigar as he talked into his cell phone. Neither of them was looking this way.

But more importantly, Bishop couldn't see any cops. Yet. And it was getting noticeably darker too, which could only be to their advantage. He turned to Clea and said, 'All right, let's go.'

The woman's eyes grew wide behind her glasses. 'Go? But I thought you just wanted my vehicle.'

'I wish it were that simple,' Bishop said, 'but at last count there were four cops out front, and at least one of them will be checking every car that leaves this area. Which means we'll need you to help us get past them.'

THIRTY-TWO

'Oh, God,' Clea groaned, 'this is turning into a nightmare.'

'There's nothing to it,' Bishop said. 'You say you simply felt a bad migraine coming on, so you decided to close up earlier than usual and go home and get some rest. It'll be a cakewalk, believe me. Come on.'

Clea fumbled with her keys and finally deactivated the Explorer's power lock. The poor woman looked totally dispirited. Bishop couldn't really blame her. He hated doing it, but it seemed today was his day for threatening innocent civilians with firearms.

He looked the SUV over. It seemed in pretty good condition for its age, and clean inside and out. He checked the rear and saw a vinyl shade cover protected the cargo area. Patting the lift gate, he said, 'Unlock this for me, will you?'

Clea did so and Bishop grabbed the handle and raised the lift gate. He estimated the gap between the floor of the cargo area and the shade cover to be about a foot and a half. Currently the space was filled with various different coloured blankets, arranged in two neat stacks.

Bishop turned to Strickland. 'You'll go in here.'

'Why me?'

'Why not you? Transfer these blankets to the back seats first, though.'

Strickland grumbled as he began pulling the blankets out, while Bishop said to Clea, 'I'll be lying on the floor just behind you with one of those blankets covering me, so I won't be able to watch what you're doing. And that means I have to rely on your intelligence here, Clea. I hope you can understand that an animal's at its most dangerous when it's cornered.'

Clea winced. 'I understand. The last thing I want is any shooting.'

144

'That's the last thing any of us wants. Now I assume you've got a cell phone in that bag of yours, so I think you better hand it over to me for safekeeping.'

Clea pulled out an older Samsung model and passed it over. Bishop switched the thing off and stuck it in his pocket. 'You'll get it back,' he said.

'I'm ready here,' Strickland said.

Bishop led Clea to the back of the vehicle. He looked over at the delivery truck, saw nobody was watching, and nodded to Strickland, who ducked into the back and arranged himself into a foetal position.

'Don't take too long, okay?' Strickland said. 'I got a real problem with small spaces.'

Bishop had to sympathize. He felt the same way. 'We'll try,' he said.

He lowered the lift gate, made sure the shade cover lay flat, and clicked the door shut. Then he led Clea back to the driver's side. As she got behind the wheel, he searched the dash and said, 'No GPS?'

Clea shook her head. 'I've never needed one. I know this area back to front already.'

'Good point.' Bishop shut the door and quickly got in the back. He reached past Clea and locked her door as well as all the others. 'Right, let's get moving before more cops arrive. If they stop you, just smile and give them the migraine story like we agreed. Okay?'

'No, I'm not okay.'

'But you'll do it.'

'Of course I'll do it. What other choice do I have?'

Bishop said nothing. Just watched her take a few deep breaths before starting the engine. As she slowly pulled off, Bishop grabbed one of the darker blankets, inserted himself in the space between the seats and draped the blanket over his lower half. He stayed in a sitting position and watched as Clea drove past all the other stores before turning left at the end. Bishop could see they were now on the access road that led back to the highway. A little way ahead was the left turn he'd previously taken to get to the parking lot. Just past that intersection stood a uniformed cop doing vehicle checks. He was talking to the driver of an SUV, while two more vehicles waited their turn behind him.

Clea came to a stop behind the last car. Bishop saw the cop wave the SUV along and both cars in front inched forward a few feet. Clea followed suit.

'I think I know that policeman,' she said. 'He's been in my shop a few times with his wife.'

'Recently?'

'Uh, I think the last time was a couple of weeks ago.'

'You know his name?'

'If I do, I can't remember it. I'm too scared.'

'That's okay. Just relax and try and act natural, Clea. Remember, you're the only person in this car. Just ask what the problem is like anybody else would, and if he gets chatty say you don't feel too good and you're going home. That's all there is to it. Okay?'

She took a deep breath, let it out. 'I'll try.'

'Attagirl. You'll be fine.'

Bishop looked out the window to his left and saw the two police cruisers were still parked in the same positions. He couldn't see the other uniforms anywhere, though. They were probably searching the stores. Clea moved the car forward a few more feet and Bishop turned to look out the windshield. He saw the young cop stop the vehicle in front and lean in to talk with the driver. Bishop carefully lay down on the floor and pulled the blanket over himself until he was completely covered.

This was the worst part. It was all down to Clea now. If she freaked his only chance would be to use her as a hostage in order to get the cop's gun. But he was in an extremely vulnerable position and couldn't really see how that would work. All he could do was wait and see. If he heard something he didn't like he'd just have to improvise somehow, without putting Clea in harm's way.

The Explorer moved forward again and then came to a stop. Bishop heard the hum of an electric window being lowered, followed by Clea's voice saying, 'Is there a problem?'

'Hey,' a youthful sounding male voice said. 'It's Clea, right? From the craft shop?'

'Oh, hello there. Did your wife like that basket you got for her?'

'Yeah, she loved it. So, uh, you're leaving a little early today, aren't you?'

'I, uh, started to feel a migraine coming on, so I thought I'd go home and rest my eyes for a while.'

'Ah, sorry to hear that. Cousin of mine suffered from migraines a few years back so I know how painful they can get. What's that you got in the back there?'

Bishop held his breath and remained perfectly still. Not moving a muscle.

'Oh, uh, just some old blankets I picked up. I'm planning to convert them into ponchos and sell them in the shop. What's going on anyway?'

'Nothing you need to worry about. You head on home and take some Advil if you got 'em. They helped my cousin some. About the only things that did.'

'I will,' Clea said. 'Thanks.'

Then the car was moving. Bishop heard the window being raised and waited a few more beats before he removed the blanket and raised his head to peer out the back. He saw the cop back there was now talking to the driver of a station wagon.

Strickland's muffled voice said, 'Are we good?'

'Yeah, we got through,' Bishop said and faced front again. They were approaching the intersection. The lights were red. 'That was real fine, Clea. You're a natural.'

'I was just terrified of what might happen if I screwed up. So I did what you wanted. Now what happens?'

'Now take us back to your place.'

Clea let out another groan. 'God, I was afraid you were going to say that.'

THIRTY-THREE

Wellerby was situated about five or six miles south of Cramer and barely qualified as a town. There was a post office and a diner and a bar on the main road, and Bishop also spotted road signs for a local school and library nearby, but every other building off the main strip seemed to be residential. Once Clea turned off into a side street the gaps between the few visible houses and ranches gradually became larger, and the streetlights became fewer. There were also no road markings and no sidewalks.

Gentle suburbia in the high country.

It was ten past six and already getting a lot darker and a lot colder. Night fell fast around these parts, probably due to the high altitude. Once the streetlights thinned out to nothing they had to rely on the Explorer's headlights to see where they were going. Clea finally turned into a narrow tree-lined street and they passed three more houses on the left side, all set well back from the road, before stopping outside a garage next to a single-storey stucco house at the end. The house looked fairly new and had a neat front porch. In the large front yard, a thick copse of evergreens obscured the view of her nearest neighbour a hundred feet away. There were no houses opposite.

'Pretty isolated around here,' Bishop said.

Clea killed the engine. 'That was one of the main reasons we originally bought this place. I'm already regretting it.'

'Don't. We'll be out of your life soon and you'll be no worse for wear.'

'I really wish I could believe you.'

'Hey, get me out of here,' Strickland said from the rear. 'I feel like I'm suffocating.'

'Christ, my back's killing me,' Strickland said, stretching, after Bishop had helped him out. 'Next time *you* get to go in the back.'

'Sure. Next time.'

Bishop motioned for Clea to go first and both men followed her over to the front porch. He still felt bad about this whole situation, but with the cops closing in he'd been out of other options. Hopefully, they could soon retreat from this poor woman's life with the same ease with which they'd entered it.

As she inserted the key into the lock, he said, 'You keep any guns on the property?'

She paused. 'There's an old shotgun in the basement, but it's not loaded. It's probably rusted by now.'

'Just that? Nothing else?'

Clea opened the door. 'Nothing else. I don't like guns.'

'Good for you,' Bishop said, and followed her into the house.

She turned on the lights and led them down a long hallway with doors on either side, along with some framed photos on the walls. Some were prints, but there were also a couple of shots of Clea posing with a little girl, who had to be her daughter, Lucy. She looked a little younger than Barney, but Bishop had no idea when the photos had been taken. The click-clack of their shoes on the hardwood floor echoed throughout the house until they finally entered a large kitchen and dining area at the end. Bishop noticed the room was as neat and tidy as the vehicle they'd just left.

Bishop spotted the large refrigerator against one wall and said, 'How are you stocked for food? We haven't eaten anything solid in a while.'

'I've got some T-bone steaks in the freezer,' Clea said. 'And some eggs, I think. And there are some canned vegetables in the cupboard. So should I now consider myself your prisoner?'

Bishop took a seat at the table and brushed his hand over his head. 'If you want. But we're not here to hurt you so put that out of your mind. All we need is a place to lay low while I think through our next step.'

Strickland said, 'We've sure had a day of it, all right. And it isn't going to get better anytime soon.'

'And how long are you planning on staying here?' Clea asked.

'An hour or so,' Bishop said, 'no longer. We really need to keep moving.'

'In my Explorer.'

'Afraid so. Unless you got another vehicle stashed away in the garage.'

'I don't.'

'Got any atlases or maps in the house?'

'Yes, I have a few in the garage.'

'Good, I'll need those. And do you have a satellite dish?'

She frowned. 'Yes. Why?'

'Because I want to check the news.'

THIRTY-FOUR

The three of them watched the TV in the large living room at the front of the house. As expected, the massacre in Vegas was the hot story on all the major news channels. Bishop finally decided to stick with CNN, but it didn't make any difference. They were all showing pretty much the same thing anyway.

For example, film of the destroyed house on Gulliver was almost always used as a backdrop while the studio anchors attempted to give their own spin on what had happened. The footage was obviously taken not long after the incident, with police barriers already set up and plain-clothes detectives, uniforms, and crime scene technicians moving around the devastation, taking photos and marking evidence.

As for the story itself, there was plenty of conjecture and not much in the way of real facts, but one thing everybody seemed to agree on was that it had been a witness safe house, since the dead were all federal marshals. Clearly, nobody from the USMS was going to confirm any of that yet, but they didn't need to. Three residents – one male, two female – living directly across the street each gave interviews saying that they'd overheard one of the first uniforms on the scene comment to his partner that all the dead bodies inside had federal marshal identification. The media simply worked out the rest for themselves.

And the body count was six, not seven. The same male eyewitness from before said he'd seen just one victim being loaded onto the first ambulance with an oxygen mask over his face, and that he'd been missing part of his left ear. Another reporter had found out where he'd been taken and somehow confirmed that the unnamed victim had lost a lot of blood and was still unconscious, but that there was a half-decent chance he'd pull through.

The ear part was enough for Bishop, though. The survivor was Frank Lomax. It had to be him.

After that, they moved onto the subject of the SUV speeding away from the scene, which had everybody buzzing with all kinds of theories. This was accompanied by the damning photo Clea had mentioned and, of course, it was the one taken by that jogger on his cell, which he'd immediately posted on his Twitter account for the whole world to see.

It showed both doors on the driver's side, each one riddled with bullets, along with a three-quarter view of Bishop's face as he was turning away from the camera. It was far from a perfect likeness, but anybody who knew Bishop would know straight away it was him. Strickland could also be seen clearly in the back as he said something to Bishop, but it was a profile shot so it wasn't quite as obvious. And behind Strickland was the silhouette of a boy who could have been anyone. That was something to be grateful for, at least.

It got worse, though. Much worse.

The jogger, whose name was Amos Martin, was actually interviewed on camera, still wearing the same red tracksuit, and he said, 'Just before I took the shot, the driver lowered his window and I could hear the guy in the back saying, "*Just let us out of here,*" or something like that and the driver tossed this GPS tracker out of the window and said, "*Forget it, there's no way I'm letting you go,*" then he saw me and just sped off like a bat out of hell. But it was obvious to me that he was holding the guy and the kid against their will, man. I mean, you can see clear as day that those two in the back have been cuffed. It was only later on I found out about the shootout a few blocks away and put two and two together.'

It wasn't quite clear as day, but Bishop could see how anybody might get the wrong idea. In the photo Strickland was leaning forward with his arms down at his side and his hands out of shot, and Barney was in a similar position. And the dialogue Martin had spouted wasn't a million miles away from what had been said, but taken out of context it could easily be conceived as meaning something entirely different, which was clearly the case here.

The channel also broadcast footage of the bullet-ridden SUV on

Route 91, along with the overturned patrol car, both vehicles surrounded by numerous law enforcement officials. Naturally, one of the local crime reporters had been listening in on the police scanner at the time and said he heard one of the murdered state troopers saying they'd just apprehended two men and a boy and were bringing them into headquarters. That was the last anybody had heard of them until they discovered the two dead bodies.

An assistant sheriff from the Las Vegas Police Department also gave a statement saying it seemed likely, thanks to Martin's account, that the driver of the SUV was connected to the team that hit the house and he confirmed a nationwide manhunt was currently in progress, with every law enforcement agency in the country now on the lookout for the two men in the photo, along with the unidentified child. Citizens were also advised to stay alert and to call in straight away if they saw either of the men in the photo.

From bad to worse, Bishop thought.

On the plus side, it seemed unlikely that the feds would ever give out Strickland's or Barney's identities, not to the cops and definitely not to the media. But Bishop knew it was just a matter of time before somebody put a name to the face of the driver, and things were certain to go downhill from there.

CNN also showed a brief clip of Deputy Director Lawrence Whitaker of the US Marshals Service. Whitaker, a distinguished-looking fifty-something with hollow cheeks, thinning grey hair and piercing blue eyes, was carrying a briefcase and trying to make his way down the steps of a federal building in DC to his car, but his progress was being hampered by a small army of reporters and cameramen blocking his way.

One reporter called out, 'Sir, *sir*, can you confirm that the murder house in Las Vegas *was* being used to shelter a high-profile witness?'

'No comment,' Whitaker said, trying to get through.

'But surely you can confirm that the six murder victims at the house *were* federal marshals, as has since been verified by independent witnesses?'

'Again, no comment.'

Another reporter said, 'Isn't it true that the same man who took off with the alleged witness and an unidentified boy is also the same man wanted for the murders of those two state troopers on Route 91 this morning?'

Whitaker said, 'I have no comment to make on that.'

'From the information we've uncovered so far,' the same reporter said, 'it seems possible that a third party may also have been involved in the state troopers' murders. And if that's the case, it's possible that the SUV driver was working hand in hand with them, isn't it? That they killed the troopers in order to rescue him?'

'I still have no comment to make,' Whitaker said. 'And you should really be talking to the Las Vegas Metropolitan Police about this anyway.'

A female reporter said, 'Sir, isn't it feasible that this driver is merely trying to protect this alleged witness, and that he has no connection to the assailants at all?'

Whitaker finally reached his car at kerbside, opened the rear door and said, 'How many times do I have to say it? No comment. Now I'm late for an urgent appointment, people, so if you'll excuse me . . .' He got in the back, slammed the door shut and the driver of the car pulled away from the kerb.

Bishop could see the station was getting pretty desperate now. He pressed a button on the remote and the TV screen went black. He'd heard and seen enough anyway.

'Great,' Strickland said, staring up at the ceiling. 'That's just great. So now we got the whole world out looking for us.'

Bishop remained silent.

Clea was watching the two men from her chair, no doubt trying to digest everything she'd seen so far. Finally, she said, 'So *did* you have anything to do with the deaths of those two state troopers?'

'Well, we were there when it happened if that's what you mean,' Strickland said. 'Two goons came up alongside us and – *BOOM BOOM* – took 'em both out like it was nothing. Almost took us out too.'

'So why haven't you turned yourselves in? Has it got something to do with that boy in the photo not being with you?'

'It's got everything to do with that, lady,' Strickland said. 'See, that boy is my son, Barney, and during the firefight those two men managed to grab him and take off. One hour later we got a call saying he's on his way to Columbus, Ohio, and the only way we can get him back alive is to be there before dawn on Thursday and make a trade. Me for him. And if the cops grab us at any point, the deal's off and Barn's dead.'

Bishop let the talk wash over him. He was thinking over what he'd heard on the TV and what he hadn't. Although little mention had been made of the sole survivor other than his current condition, Bishop had to assume that once Lomax awoke he'd give his superiors his version of what happened. And if he *was* the leak behind the massacre, then it was a good bet he'd add a few extra details in order to lay the blame entirely at Bishop's door.

At least there had been no mention at all of Roger and Eleanor Souza, though, which suggested they'd kept their word, at least. That meant the cops would still be on the lookout for two men and a boy, instead of just two men.

And no mention of Charlie Hooper yet, which meant they still had a little breathing space. Not much, but some.

Time enough to grab some food and maybe to make some minor adjustments to their appearance before getting back on the road again.

THIRTY-FIVE

Bishop was first to finish his food. He was no expert in the kitchen, but it was almost impossible to screw up steak and scrambled eggs. Strickland was still making his way through his, though. He'd argued that he wasn't hungry, but Bishop had told him he had to eat something if he wanted to keep going and he'd grudgingly agreed to try.

Clea was also sitting at the table, silently staring into her mug of coffee as though there might be a way out of this at the bottom.

As Bishop took a sip from his glass of water, he looked out the rear windows and saw it was already completely black outside. They'd need to get going soon. Once a few more details were taken care of.

'There's more bad news to come, isn't there?' Clea said, still staring at her cup.

Bishop turned back to her. 'What do you mean?'

She raised her eyes to him. 'I mean that I've been sitting here thinking it all over and it's obvious to me that you can't afford to just take off and leave me here. Am I right?'

Bishop sighed. 'I'm afraid you are.'

'What are you talking about?' Strickland said, wiping his mouth with a piece of kitchen towel.

'Clea here will have to come with us. At least part of the way.'

'I knew it,' she said. 'I just knew this day was going to get worse.'

Strickland frowned. 'What's wrong with tying her up like we did with the pilot? We can take her down to the basement, tie her up and make her comfortable, then make an anonymous call to the cops tomorrow.'

Bishop shook his head. 'What we did with Charlie won't work here. For one thing, he'll have gotten himself free in a few hours and once he does he'll get straight on his radio, then meet up with whoever

156

was waiting for us at that airfield. Possibly local cops, possibly feds, but whoever it is, it won't take them long to figure out who else was on that plane.'

'You figure Charlie will talk, then?'

'Not straight away, but they'll get the whole story out of him sooner or later and then there'll be roadblocks set up from here to the East Coast.'

'Why? They don't know where we're going. Nor does Charlie.'

'He knew we were heading east, and that'll be enough. The feds will take one look at a map and figure we're headed for Ohio. They won't know the reason why, although they'll probably assume I'm taking you to my supposed employer, Hartnell.'

'Hartnell?' Clea said.

'The guy I'm supposed to be testifying against,' Strickland said. 'But they can't set up roadblocks on every single road. It's impossible. So all we have to do is stick to the back roads and we should be okay.'

'We can avoid most of them that way, sure, but if we *do* come up against a roadblock I'd prefer having the car's legitimate owner there with us, with the correct documents and everything.'

'Yeah, okay,' Strickland said slowly. 'I see what you mean.'

'Sorry, Clea,' Bishop said, 'but it's the only way.'

'But I can't go with you,' she said. 'Can't you see that? Just leave me here. I swear I won't tell anyone about you. Look, I'm a mother myself, with a daughter who expects—'

'How old is she?' Bishop cut in.

She gaped at him. 'What?'

'I said, how is old is your daughter? I saw photos of you with a pretty little girl in the hallway, but they could have been taken anytime. How old is Lucy now?'

'How do you know her name's Lucy?'

'From that phone conversation with your ex-husband back at the shop.'

Her face relaxed a little. 'Oh, yes, right. Well, she's eleven if you must know. Almost twelve.'

'Almost the same age as Barney,' Bishop said. 'And you must love her very much, right?'

'Of course I love her. She's the world to me. What kind of question's that?'

'I'm just trying to get across that my associate here is just as attached to Barney as you are to Lucy. The only difference being that your little girl's currently safe with her father, while his son's currently in the hands of some people who'll go to any lengths to get what they want. And I do mean *any* lengths. Ordinarily, I wouldn't dream of taking you with us, Clea, but with Barney's life at stake I really don't have a choice.'

'And that justifies you forcing me to come along, does it?'

'I'm not trying to justify anything. I'm merely explaining.'

Clea said nothing, just placed both hands on either side of her head and stared at the table.

There was no point in arguing the point any further, so Bishop let the matter rest. It was a shame, though. Clea seemed a decent person who'd ordinarily be willing to aid somebody in trouble, especially a kid, but being forced to help rather than being asked understandably played a major factor in a person's attitude. However it couldn't be helped. She had to come along, it was that simple.

After a few moments, he said, 'Does this Howard also wear spectacles?'

Her brow furrowed as she looked up at him. 'Only for reading. Why? Is this relevant?'

'I'm just wondering if you've still got any of his stuff here. Because an old pair of reading glasses would really come in handy right now.'

'There might be a pair of his old frames up in the attic, along with the rest of his junk. Why?'

'Well a little basic camouflage wouldn't go amiss, and a pair of glasses can often do wonders for a face. My face, in particular.' He studied her. 'Do you dye your hair?'

Clea made a face. 'And what's *that* got to do with anything?'

'Is that a no, then?'

'Yes, that's a no. Auburn's my natural colour. Why does that matter?'

Bishop ran a palm over his buzz cut. 'I was hoping you'd be able to turn me into a redhead or something, but never mind. The glasses will have to do. But if you've got some scissors or clippers lying around, maybe you could do something about my associate's hair.'

She turned to Strickland and studied his thick shoulder-length locks. 'No clippers,' she said finally, 'but I do have some hair scissors in the bathroom cabinet.'

Strickland brushed a hand through his hair. 'I guess it kinda stands out, huh?'

'Right now you look a little too much like that guy in the back seat for my liking,' Bishop said. Strickland also had a heavy five o'clock shadow. He was probably one of those high-testosterone types who needed to shave twice a day just to keep things on an even keel, which could only work in their favour. 'How about it, Clea? Can you do anything?'

She sighed as she got up from her seat, and said, 'If you think you can trust me with sharp objects, I guess I can give it a try.'

THIRTY-SIX

Bishop drove them through the mountains as they headed south on Route 40. It was almost nine and the sky was still overcast, so no moon, and no stars. And for long stretches no streetlights either, with the only illumination coming from the Explorer's headlights and those of the occasional vehicle coming the other way. The rest of the world was just various shades of black. Bishop had to keep almost all his concentration on the few feet of visible road directly in front of them.

Clea sat in the front passenger seat while Strickland stretched out in the back, occasionally rubbing a hand through his new haircut. She'd gone at it with the scissors and managed to pare it down to half an inch all round. It looked uneven in places, but that seemed to be the current style anyway. He'd told Strickland to take a wet shave but to leave the upper lip alone. The remaining hair still had a little way to go before it could realistically be labelled a moustache, but Strickland had assured him it would grow quickly.

The drive had been quiet so far. Clea hadn't spoken at all since leaving the house. She was sitting with her head at an angle against the seat rest as though she was looking out the side window, although Bishop wasn't even sure her eyes were open.

'I been keeping tabs,' Strickland said from the back, 'and I think we maybe passed five side roads in total since leaving Winter Park back there. What if the local law decide to surprise us with a road-block on this one? How do we get off it?'

'That's why I'm keeping us at a steady seventy,' Bishop said. 'The sooner we're off this, the better. Once this road bears east it's about another fifteen miles before Idaho Springs, and after that things start opening up again the closer we get to Denver. Meaning plenty of back roads.'

'We're not going through Denver?'

'No, I plan on avoiding major cities for a while.'

'Good.'

Clea turned to Bishop and said, 'And how long are you planning to keep *me* here?'

'Well, we have to be in Ohio by dawn on Thursday,' he said, 'so well before then I hope. I thought you were asleep, Clea.'

She turned back to the window. 'Sleep? How can I sleep when my life's been turned upside down like this? No offence, but I hate being in this car with you. I just hate it.'

'You think I like it?'

'Maybe not *like*, but I think you're the kind of man who'll do whatever it takes to get what he wants, and right now I'm just an asset to help you get from A to B. And if I get damaged along the way you'll cast me aside and find another asset to help you reach the next hurdle. That's what *I* think.'

'You're wrong,' Bishop said, although she wasn't. Not completely.

The thing was, whenever he was faced with a seemingly insoluble problem he knew it was only a matter of time before the uncompromising – some would say almost obsessive – side of his character came to the forefront: that all-devouring single-mindedness that had been with him since childhood, where the problem at hand began to override all other considerations, such as other people's needs and requirements, Clea's current involvement being a good case in point. But that was just the way he was, the way he had always been. He wasn't about to change now, even if he wanted to. And if he was honest he actually considered it more a strength than a flaw. After all, it was a state of mind that produced results. Most of the time.

'Why don't you just kidnap another pilot?' Clea said, turning to him again. 'You're good at that. Then you could fly out of my life and be in Ohio in just a few hours.'

'I considered it,' Bishop said, ignoring the sarcasm, 'and then discounted it. For a number of reasons.'

The main one being that there weren't many private airports still operating this late. Certainly no flight schools. And by the time they opened up again in the morning, word would have gotten out and the feds would have every municipal airport and private landing strip under close surveillance. No, not a good idea at all.

She said, 'I still don't understand why you don't contact the US Marshals and explain the situation to them like you've explained it to me. Instead of wasting time chasing after you they can then focus all their efforts on getting this man's son back. They'll have to.'

Strickland leaned forward and said, 'Well, there's a small problem there, Clea. See, my ex-boss has got a hell of a lot of people on his payroll, and a small percentage of those people are cops. I don't know who. He never shared that information with anyone. But I do know the moment word got out I was in police custody, Hartnell would hear about it. He might snuff Barney's light out in a fit of anger and I just can't afford to take that risk. No, we'll stick to the deal we made and trade me for my boy. It's the only way.'

'And then what happens? To you, I mean.'

'Once Hartnell gets his dirty little mitts on me I'll disappear forever.'

'You mean he'll kill you.'

'That's right. And it won't be quick, either.'

'And that doesn't bother you?'

'Well, I'm not exactly happy about it, but Barney's safety is all that matters to me now.'

'And how do you feel about that?' she asked Bishop. 'Does that bother you at all? Does anything?'

Bishop saw a pair of headlights suddenly appear in the distance. There must be a turn up ahead. He waited as the headlights flashed over them, and when the vehicle had passed by he said, 'I'd prefer to keep both of them alive if I can.'

'Really?'

'Of course. The moment Hartnell gets this man in his hands he wins again, just like he always does. I don't like the thought of that.'

'So this is all about winning and losing to you, is that it?'

He shook his head. 'Far from it. And I can't be summed up in a sound bite, Clea, so don't even try.'

Bishop slowed as a sharp left turn came into view up ahead. He took the speed down to forty, followed it round and immediately picked up the pace again. From now on they'd be heading east – and not before time.

As the car lapsed into silence again, Bishop thought back to the fiction that Delaney had given him back at the house, and said to Strickland, 'I'm still interested in the murder that started all this. So you actually witnessed Felix Hartnell personally pull the trigger on this undercover DEA agent?'

Strickland was silent for a moment as he looked out the windshield. Then he said, quietly, 'Yeah, I saw it.'

'So tell me how it all went down.'

'Why?'

'I want to know.'

Strickland took a deep breath and said, 'Okay, well I guess it all started four months back when I got a call from one of Hartnell's local dealers, a Salvador Ferrera. He was just a low-level street guy who worked out of Columbus, or so I thought at the time. Shows what little I knew. I'd collected some cash from him a couple of times so he knew I was fairly high up on the food chain, and he got a hold of my number and called me. Said he had something important he wanted to talk about. I met with him and he told me he wanted to talk to Hartnell about a police informer he knew about, high up in the organization. He said because the guy was so senior he'd only talk to Hartnell directly, otherwise forget it. And he added he'd also bring proof to back up his claims.'

'So you arranged a meet.'

Strickland nodded. 'I had to. I knew the guy was probably just trying to fast-track his way up the ladder by getting in Hartnell's good books, but I also knew he had to have *some*thing or he'd never have even brought it up. But it still wasn't easy, let me tell you. I wanted to talk to Hartnell about something, I had to pass through three layers of security before I even got to the front door and then I had to tell him face to face. That way, if the shit ever comes down it's his word against yours. Nothing provable. Either that or I could tell Callaway and *he'd* tell Hartnell. But I never really trusted that guy, so I preferred to do it myself. So I made an appointment with one of Hartnell's flunkies, drove over to his estate the next day and relayed to Hartnell what Ferrera had told me.'

'And how did Hartnell take it?' Bishop asked.

'Not too well. That guy's got a real temper, and you don't want to be in the same room when he loses it. And nothing pisses him off more than the possibility of treachery in the ranks. Especially at the exec level. He started to calm down after a while and I finally suggested it couldn't hurt to meet the guy and see what he had to say. Hartnell could choose the time and place, after all.'

'And he agreed with you?'

'Yeah. He said he'd get word to me about the final details, and that it would be my responsibility to make sure Ferrera came alone on the night. The following Friday I get word from Callaway that the meeting's set for midnight at an old, vacant trading estate in a place called Lima, about eighty miles north-west of Columbus. I'd used the place before for another meet and knew the general layout. It's located right out in the middle of nowhere, with three or four run-down old buildings set around a main square. It's perfect. So I told Ferrera I'd pick him up at ten at his place in town and we'd go on from there.'

Bishop nodded. 'So what went wrong?'

'What makes you think something went wrong?'

'Call it instinct.'

'Well, you're right. I, uh . . . well, I got held up by something and by the time I got to Ferrera's, he was gone. Since I'd already given him the general location, he'd already left for the meet in his own car. I tried calling him but he didn't answer, which really got me sweating. I was worried about him taking some friends along with him, you know? For all I knew this was some kind of hit he'd been planning all along, and if it was and it went wrong, I'd get the blame.'

'But it wasn't,' Bishop said. 'Ferrera was actually a deep-cover DEA agent.'

'Right. But I obviously didn't know that then. All I knew was that I had to get to Lima before Ferrera did and make sure everything was kosher.'

'And did you?'

Strickland paused before nodding. 'Just about. But it was close. I got there at about eleven forty-five and, uh . . . well, I parked round the back of one of the vacant buildings and quickly found Ferrera's car behind one of the others. I found the guy waiting nearby on his own. Hartnell arrived just a few minutes later in his black limo and parked in the main square, if you could call it that.'

'On his own?' Bishop asked, watching as another vehicle's headlights appeared in the distance.

'Guys like him never go anywhere on their own. His favourite boy, Callaway, was there to watch his back, and doing double duty as the driver. And there was also a third guy there, too.'

'Who?'

'Some high-up business associate, I guess. I never saw him before.'

'What did he look like?'

Strickland paused, then shrugged. 'Hard to tell. He was wearing a raincoat and baseball cap, and I couldn't see his face. Anyway, I show myself and bring Ferrera out. I say everything's okay and bring the guy over to Callaway who searches him and then takes him back to Hartnell and the other guy. Hartnell tells me my part of the job's done and to get lost. So I walked all the way back to my car and got in, ready to drive back to the main road.

'Except I started to think to myself that maybe I was missing a golden opportunity here, you know? And they don't come around too often. Not all gift-wrapped like this one was. And Hartnell came in with only Callaway for protection, remember, so obviously he felt the fewer witnesses to the meeting the better. So I decided to stick around for a while and see what all the fuss was about. I got out of the car again and quietly made my way back to the same building where Ferrera had been waiting. I crept in the back and worked my way up to the second floor and watched everything from up there.'

Strickland paused as he combed his fingers through his new haircut.

'Go on,' Bishop said.

Strickland smiled. 'Got you on the edge of your seat, do I? Well, there isn't much more to tell. By the time I got into position, Hartnell and Ferrera were already arguing about something, but I couldn't make out what they were saying. Then this other guy, the one in the raincoat, he pointed at Ferrera and said something. Hartnell turned to him and said, "Are you sure?" clear as day, and the guy nodded back and said something I didn't catch.'

'He identified Ferrera as a cop.'

'He must have done, 'cause Hartnell then pulled an automatic from his coat pocket, pointed it at Ferrara's head and pulled the trigger and kept on firing into his body until the gun clicked empty.'

'Jesus,' Clea whispered.

'Yeah,' Strickland said, 'that's pretty much what I was thinking. I knew Hartnell had a short fuse, but I never thought I'd see him actually pull the trigger himself. I do remember it was the first time I'd ever seen Callaway looking less than sure of—'

He stopped at the muffled sound of a ringing phone. They all heard it.

Strickland shifted in the seat and pulled the cell from his pocket. The shrill ringing tone echoed throughout the car interior. He looked at the display. 'Unknown caller.'

'It'll be Callaway,' Bishop said. 'Remember to put it on speaker.'

Strickland nodded. He closed his eyes for a second, then opened them and took the call.

THIRTY-SEVEN

Callaway's amplified voice said, 'Well, here we are again, as promised. Miss me?'

'Put my boy on,' Strickland said.

Callaway chuckled, the harsh sound reminding Bishop of paper being crinkled. 'Now that doesn't sound like the talkative fellow I used to know.'

'Look, do I get to I talk to him or not?'

'Keep your shirt on. He's right here. And remember, no names or I hang up.'

There was silence on the line for a few moments. As Bishop drove he strained to identify ambient noises in the background, but except for the steady hum of the Explorer's engine there was nothing.

Then a boy's voice said, 'You there, Dad?'

Bishop gave a long exhale. He hadn't realized he'd been holding his breath. It *was* Barney's voice, though. He sounded as though he'd just woken up, but he was okay.

'It's me,' Strickland said. 'I can't tell you how good it is to hear your voice again, Ba— my boy.'

'Me, too. I . . . I wish I could see you, Dad. I really do. Uh . . . so how are you?'

Good boy, Bishop thought. Barney hadn't forgotten what he'd been taught last night.

'How am *I*?' Strickland said, 'Forget about me. How are *you*? Are they treating you okay?'

'Well, I, uh, I got scared before, but then I did that breathing exercise you taught me and I'm okay now. And they're treating me all right, I guess. When I said I was hungry they brought me a few bags of chips and a big bottle of Coke.'

Bishop was watching Strickland and saw his eyes were already moist. He also kept rubbing his nose with his hand.

'That's good, son,' Strickland said, sniffling. 'That's real good. Sounds like they're taking care of you okay.'

'Yeah, I guess. Oh, and they let me keep my Dingoo too, so I can still play Tetris.'

'I'm real glad to hear it,' Strickland said. 'I know how you love that game.'

Bishop nodded to himself. He was a smart kid, all right. Ballsy, too. So far he'd learned that Barney was being kept in a room with no windows and only one exit, so probably a basement cell somewhere. And the mention of Tetris on his console meant there was just one guard watching him. But since he hadn't mentioned that the game was always on there, that meant the guard wasn't stationed in the room with him. Not that Bishop could really use any of that information right now, but it was enough to know that Barney was staying positive and keeping his cool.

The boy cleared his throat and said, 'Hey, Dad?'

'Yeah?'

'I'm sorry.'

Strickland suddenly wrapped a hand over his mouth and made a short choking sound. Clea was also watching Strickland with dewy eyes as he struggled to retain control of himself. Bishop's own eyes were dry as they always were. That didn't mean he wasn't affected, though. It was just the last time he'd wept had been on learning of the accident that had killed his parents. And, like him, Barney had not only lost his mother recently, but he had to know he was in danger of losing his father too, yet he was still holding it together somehow. Drawing on his inner strength to stay on top of things.

Remarkable.

Strickland finally took his hand away from his mouth, and in a tight voice said, 'You got nothing to be sorry about, son. Nothing at *all*. You understand me?'

'I just meant . . .'

'I know what you meant, and I want you to stop thinking that way. It won't do any good. If anybody's to blame it's me for wasting my life all those years, so don't be thinking like that, okay? You promise me?'

'Okay, Dad, I promise.'

'Good. Now I'm going to get you out of there. That's my promise to you. So I don't want you to worry, okay? You play your Tetris and do whatever it takes to get your mind off all this, because it's my problem, not yours. I need you to stay strong for me. Can you do that?'

'I'll try, Dad. Um, look, the man's making signals that he wants the phone back so I better go. I love you, Dad.'

'I love you too, son. Don't you ever forget it.'

'I won't. 'Bye.'

Bishop heard the speaker being smothered by something. There was silence for a few seconds.

'Son?' Strickland said in a tentative voice. 'You still there?'

''Fraid not,' Callaway's voice came back. 'Just thought I'd step outside for a moment. Some things a boy shouldn't have to hear, don't you agree?'

'Yeah,' Strickland said.

'All right, I let you have a good long chat with him so you can see I'm holding my end of the deal. And I know for a fact you've managed to steer clear of the boys in uniform so far, so it looks like you're doing the same. Where are you now?'

'On the road,' Bishop said. 'And closer to you than we were.'

Callaway did that crinkled paper sound again. 'So you're still with us too, friend?'

'All the way to the end. Don't you think it's time we discussed our final destination?'

'What's the rush? You just get yourselves over to our friendly state first, then we'll worry about the rest of it. You still remember our deadline, I hope.'

'We're not likely to forget.'

'Good. I'll call you at five a.m. on Thursday and then we'll talk about the location for the switch.'

'I'll want to talk to him again before then,' Strickland said.

'I figured you would, so expect another call tomorrow at around the same time.'

There was a click and the line went dead.

In the rear-view, Bishop watched Strickland sink into the back seat with his head lowered. Clea turned to look at him. She seemed about to say something, but Bishop shook his head at her. Sometimes silence was best. This was one of those times. Clea finally nodded back before facing front again.

Bishop just drove into the night and thought about Barney. And Strickland. And Hartnell and Callaway. And the deadline, of course. He couldn't avoid thinking about that. Not with the LED light of the dashboard clock flashing back at him.

20.23.

Less than thirty-four hours to go.

THIRTY-EIGHT

It was 05.25 the following morning when Bishop realized he'd have to stop pretty soon. He'd been driving most of the night and felt shattered. He'd had a couple of hours sleep earlier when Strickland took over the reins for a while, but that had come to an abrupt end when he'd woken Bishop up with news of some kind of roadblock ahead of them.

That had been around the Castle Rock area, south of Denver, and they'd been heading east on one of the less-used highways. Fortunately, the land was flat enough around that part of Colorado for the shimmering police lights to be visible from half a mile away. Bishop had instructed Strickland to turn off the headlights and pull over. After switching places, he'd then backtracked until he found a minor road that would take them south and then east again.

Somehow they'd travelled almost six hundred miles through the night, using Clea's dwindling cash reserves to twice fill the tank along the way, and now they were stuck on the back roads of Kansas, right in the heart of the Midwest.

As a result, he was tired. And when you were tired you made mistakes. And he couldn't afford to make a single one. He needed to rest, just for an hour or so. He also needed to eat something and to stretch his legs. But mostly he needed to get out of this vehicle for a while. They all did.

They were currently driving along a two-lane highway that ran parallel to Highway 160 five miles south of them. About thirty miles to the north-east was Wichita, which, being the largest city in Kansas, was to be avoided at all costs. The sky was brightening a little on the eastern horizon, although full sunrise was still about half an hour away. There was almost no traffic along the route they were on though, with just farmland and trees on both sides and the occasional farmhouse or ranch to break things up. They'd passed an old-style gas station a couple of miles back, but that was all. It had been closed.

'Some kind of sign up ahead,' Strickland said from the back seat.

'I see it,' Bishop said, although he hadn't. That was worrying. And yet another reason to stop.

Bishop slowed when he reached the road sign, which was illuminated by an old, dim spotlight hanging over the top. The sign itself was old and weatherworn and told them to call in at *Toby's Grill* one mile up ahead for *Local Grub at Local Prices*.

'I'd say we're overdue a pit stop,' Strickland said. 'I could do with some breakfast, or at least some coffee, and maybe a trip to the restroom.'

'I was thinking the same thing,' Bishop said. 'I just hope it's open.'

'Hey, this is farm country. Life starts early around here.'

Ninety seconds later, they had their answer. Bishop slowed the vehicle when he saw another weatherworn sign by the road, lit by another single bulb hanging over the top. There was a large red arrow pointing right and underneath were the words, *Welcome – We're OPEN!* Bishop turned into the entranceway a few yards up ahead and entered a small dirt lot. A dark pick-up and an old Chevy were parked in front of a small, single-level clapboard building. The lights were on and he could see several people sitting inside. To the left and set a little ways back was a wooden garage with a set of closed double doors.

'Guy must do a roaring trade around here,' Strickland said.

'Mostly local clientele, I expect,' Bishop said. 'He probably makes enough to get by.'

He swung the car in a U-turn and reversed until he was parked next to the pick-up. It was always a good idea to leave your vehicle facing outwards. Just in case.

As soon as he switched off the engine, Clea gave a yawn and hunched her shoulders as she reached into her jacket pocket and donned her spectacles. 'Where are we now?' she asked, looking around.

'Somewhere in West Kansas. I thought it might be an idea to grab some breakfast while we can. Are you hungry at all?'

She gave another yawn and shook her head. 'Not really.'

'Well, maybe some coffee then.' To Strickland he said, 'You and Clea better go in first while I wait here. You get any suspicious looks from anybody you come straight back out and we'll find somewhere else. If you're not out within sixty seconds I'll assume everything's okay and come join you.'

'Right,' Strickland said, and the pair got out and walked over to the main entrance. Bishop watched Strickland open the door, wait for Clea to go first, then follow her inside.

Bishop waited a few more seconds and then checked himself in the rear-view. The pale blue eyes that gazed back at him were red-rimmed and dull. He pulled out the old pair of frames that Clea had found in the basement and put them on, then inspected his face carefully in the mirror again. It seemed there was a slight softening of his facial features with them on, or maybe he was just imagining things. Either way, the glasses couldn't hurt.

Once ninety seconds had passed without any sign of Strickland or Clea, Bishop exited the car. It was a cold frosty morning, but the crisp air gave him the immediate boost he needed. He stretched his arms and ironed out the kinks in his neck before locking up and making for the main entrance. After making sure the Glock was in the back of his waistband where it should be, he entered the small, no-frills establishment with half a dozen tables arranged in the centre, and three booths set against the left wall. Clea and Strickland were sitting in the middle booth.

A grey-haired couple were eating breakfast at one of the central tables. They each gave Bishop a mildly curious look as he came in, but didn't stop eating.

At the rear was a small counter where two brawny farmer-types in baseball caps, thick coats and jeans were sat drinking coffee with the bearded guy on the other side. This man wore a cook's apron and looked to be in his fifties, with receding grey hair and a nose that was a darker shade of pink than the rest of his face. Either he was a boozer, or one who'd just given up. To the left of the counter was a hallway leading back to the kitchen. Bishop could hear the sounds of country and western music coming from back there.

The three men were all idly watching the new arrivals. Bishop didn't sense any recognition in their faces. The two customers drank their coffees and the guy in the apron said, 'Mornin'.'

'How you doing,' Bishop said.

Bishop went over to the middle booth and sat down next to Clea, so he was facing the front window. 'You ordered yet?' he asked.

'Not yet,' Strickland said. 'The guy said he'd be over in a minute.'

Bishop studied Clea's profile and said, 'So you managed to get some sleep?'

'Some.' She looked at him. 'How much longer do you think you'll last without any?'

'I got a couple of hours in earlier. I'll be fine.'

On the table, amongst the condiments, was a tube of wooden toothpicks. Strickland plucked one from the opening and stuck it between his lips. 'Maybe I should drive for a while,' he said.

'Yeah, maybe you should,' Bishop said. 'But still wake me if anything comes up.'

'Okay, but I can probably—'

Strickland stopped when he saw the guy in the apron coming over. He handed the two men a handwritten card menu each, ignoring Clea. Up close Bishop could see the man's nose was a mass of broken capillaries. He also noticed a folded *Racing Form* sticking out of the guy's back pocket.

Bishop gave the menu a cursory look and saw there were only three choices anyway. He passed it to Clea and said, 'I'll have the ham, scrambled eggs, and hash browns. And a large pot of coffee. Emphasis on large.'

Strickland ordered the same, while Clea quietly ordered the cheese and tomato omelette and a Coke.

'Be about ten, fifteen minutes,' the man said, 'since it's just me doin' all the cooking. That okay with you?'

'That's fine,' Bishop said and yawned.

The guy frowned at Bishop. 'Can't say we get too many strangers in here. You just passin' through?'

'Yeah,' Bishop said, 'we're on our way to Wichita. Old buddy of mine over there said he's got a business proposition for me and my brother here.'

'Yeah? What kinda business you in?'

'We buy and sell antique coins.'

The guy nodded. 'Antique coins, huh? What, by mail order?'

'Mostly over the internet these days. Listen, you're Toby, right?'

'Sure am.'

'Well, Toby, no offence but if I don't get some of your coffee in me pretty soon I think I might just pass out on your floor, and then you'll never wake me up.'

'Gotcha.' Toby's grin showed discoloured teeth. 'One pot of coffee coming right up,' he said, and left them.

Less than a minute later he came back with a tray bearing a large pot of coffee, two cups, two saucers, one glass tumbler and one can of Coke. After setting them all down on the table he returned to the kitchen. The two men at the counter had already lost interest by this point and gone back to their own conversation.

Strickland poured coffee into the two cups. Bishop slid one over, took a sip and deemed it satisfactory. Not as good or as strong as the stuff Delaney had made, but it was palatable. And hot.

Clea poured Coke into her glass. 'Don't tell me. I'm paying for all this too, right?'

'Sorry,' Bishop said. 'I'll pay you back once we get through this.'

Her mouth twisted. '*If* you get through this.'

'Let's try and stay positive, shall we?'

She studied him for a moment, then shook her head and looked away.

Bishop leaned his head back against the seat rest, took another sip of the coffee, and found his thoughts returning to Delaney again. He knew it was pointless, but he couldn't help it. He could still see that moment when she'd landed on the floor inches away from him, bleeding heavily from neck and chest wounds, and with a puzzled expression on her face, as though she was thinking, *It wasn't supposed to happen like this. I had plans.*

But she was only one reason why he wanted the person responsible for leaking the safe house location in the first place. The other was if he could discover that person's identity maybe he could use that information to his advantage when the time came to hand Strickland over. Or maybe not. But in any case, the more information he had the better.

As for the who, his thoughts naturally turned to the only other survivor, Lomax. Bishop felt sure the assault team in Vegas would have been under orders to finish off any remaining survivors, yet Lomax had been left alive. Why?

Well, what if Lomax's role had simply been to set them all up and then afterwards shift all the blame onto the newcomer, Bishop, thus taking the focus away from the real source? It was a possibility. A slim one, maybe, but you had to consider every alternative. Also, during that firefight Bishop had found the wounded Lomax trying to call somebody on his cell. At the time he'd assumed the guy was calling for more backup, but what if he had been trying to contact his real employer instead? Maybe to tell him that all the other marshals were either dead or dying, so get your men to stop the shooting and enter the house already.

But for what possible motive? Money? Bishop didn't think so in this case. Sure, marshals were human and susceptible to the same tempt-ations as everyone else, but Lomax would surely have known that he was setting up his colleagues for certain death, and no amount of cash would have been able to wipe that kind of betrayal away. Some people could do it. Bishop had worked alongside one or two who easily fit the profile, but Lomax really hadn't seemed the sociopathic type. Not with that look in his eyes when he'd been thinking about his dog back home.

But it didn't have to be money. What if his wife, Karen, was the motive?

What if Hartnell ordered some of his men to grab the wife in order to put pressure on the husband? He knew from recent personal experi-ence that a man would do almost anything to protect those he loves, maybe even sell out his whole team.

On top of which, there was that tense phone call Bishop had woken up to. Delaney had given him a very reasonable explanation at the time, but what if there was more to the call than basic marital suspi-cion and mistrust? Since Hartnell already knew their location at that point, maybe Lomax was being given some last-minute instructions.

That would certainly help explain the hidden keys in the SUV. Because Delaney was a pro, and a pro would have gone through the house and checked and rechecked everything on a continual basis. And she would have definitely noticed if the keys to the SUV weren't in the ignition where they were supposed to be. So maybe Lomax had been instructed to get rid of the keys as a final insurance to prevent anybody getting out. And since Lomax knew Delaney's habits, maybe he'd played it safe and had the keys simply 'fall' and get lodged under the floor mat instead.

Maybe, maybe, maybe.

It was a pretty good theory, but that's all it was right now. And Bishop couldn't exactly do anything about it anyway, at least not yet. He already had enough to worry about, such as getting them all through the rest of the day.

THIRTY-NINE

Bishop finished his breakfast and moved his empty plate to the side. He'd been a lot hungrier than he'd originally thought, and Toby hadn't skimped on the portions either. He poured himself more coffee and watched Clea pick at her omelette unenthusiastically. Strickland was almost done with his. As for the other customers, the elderly couple had settled their bill and left already, with the two guys at the counter following them shortly after. Nobody else had come in since they'd arrived.

Maybe business would pick up later on, although Bishop kind of doubted it. It was starting to get light outside, and Bishop noticed a faint ground fog rolling in from the surrounding fields, making it hard to see anything beyond the empty road out front.

Strickland finally put down his fork and said, 'There's still one thing I can't get my head around.'

'Only one thing?' Bishop said.

Strickland gave a thin smile. 'Just this one for now. And that's what the hell made you join up with us in the first place. I don't get it. What was in it for you?'

'If you must know, Delaney said she'd owe me a favour once it was over.'

Strickland shook his head. 'That's not it. Delaney told me she made you that offer when she came to see you before and you turned her down then. Yet a few days later you shoot me with that damned paint pellet and decide you want to join up, after all. So what made you change your mind?'

Bishop thought for a moment. He briefly considered fobbing Strickland off with another line, but instead he said, 'Paul Mechner.'

'Come again?'

'Take a moment. Does that name mean anything to you?'

Strickland's brow became furrowed as he thought it over. 'Paul Mechner . . . Paul Mechner.' Then recognition dawned and he patted the table with a palm. 'The accountant. Hartnell's accountant. Or one of them, at least.'

'Correct.'

'But that's, what, almost ten years ago. Just a few months after I started with Hartnell, in fact.' He studied Bishop. 'And this Mechner was something to you?'

'He was one of my very first protection assignments.'

'Whoa.' Strickland pulled his head back. 'Seriously?'

Bishop still remembered it all like it was yesterday. He wasn't much for backward thinking, but whenever he did go into recall mode the past invariably came back to life in dazzling detail, with barely any blurring around the edges at all.

He'd been working in RoyseCorp's close protection division for just under eleven months when he got promoted to team leader, which was a company record, apparently. And his very first assignment in the new role had been to head a team to safeguard an overweight accountant and his wife. Except this wasn't just any old accountant.

For over five years Paul Mechner had been a trusted employee of Felix Hartnell, one of the most successful and wealthiest cocaine distributors in the country. Mechner hadn't known that when he'd first taken the job, but he figured it out pretty soon after, once he saw the vast sums of money that kept pouring in week after week. That kind of money only ever came from one source, and it was Mechner's particular speciality to find new ways to launder it. It seemed he was very good at it, too, despite hating every second. Until that point he'd always been a law-abiding man, but he knew that when you worked for Felix Hartnell you couldn't just up and quit when you felt like it.

So Mechner gritted his teeth and put up with it for five long years, all the while keeping the truth from his wife, Emily. At some point he decided he deserved some recompense for the years of sleepless nights, so near the end he'd simply made a few minor adjustments in the books and siphoned off a few bucks for himself as a kind of unofficial safety net in case things ever went south. Unfortunately, not long after, a colleague tipped him off that Hartnell suspected something was up and that Mechner was under suspicion.

The accountant didn't waste any time. He knew all the stories about Hartnell by this point, had even gone to his house a few times to make occasional reports, and the man scared him to death. After finally explaining the full situation to Emily, he'd argued the only way they could escape Hartnell's influence and what he felt was certain death was by getting them new identities and making new lives for themselves overseas. Money wouldn't be a problem. After some long and heated arguments, Emily finally agreed to stand with her man.

They hid out in Oklahoma City, somewhere neither of them had ever even visited before, although Emily's parents *had* originally come from Duncan, a town situated about a hundred miles south-west of the city. Once there, Mechner used his few contacts to arrange new identities for himself and Emily, along with new passports and all the rest. But since it was all under the counter and had to be done just right, it would also take time. And Hartnell was sure to start looking for him soon, if he wasn't already. So Mechner decided to hire some professionals to keep them safe while they waited for their documents, and that's where RoyseCorp came in. The price was high, but their rep was second to none. And Bishop, along with his handpicked four-man team, was given the assignment.

He'd seconded them in one of the company's safe houses in Fayetteville, Arkansas, and life was pretty quiet for two weeks. Bishop always accompanied Mechner or his wife whenever they needed to go out for whatever reason. But mostly they stayed in, patiently waiting for the preparations for their new lives to be finalized.

Mechner was okay in Bishop's book. Sure, he was an embezzler, but since the victim was a sleazebag Bishop didn't hold that against him. In fact Bishop actually liked the guy, which was a rare treat as most of his principals thus far hadn't exactly been citizens of the year. And that's why he'd tried to convince the accountant to forget about all that new identity stuff, to take what he knew to the feds and go into the Witness Protection Program instead.

He still remembered the conversation in the kitchen, word for word . . .

'*Hartnell would find me eventually if I stayed in this country,*' Mechner had said in response, '*no matter what name the feds gave me, he'd find me. Believe me, that guy's got people in every state and in every town and in every alley. No, I've thought it all through and this is the best way. Once he knows I'm not talking to anyone, hopefully he'll just call off the dogs and forget about us.*'

'*You really believe that?*' Bishop had said. '*Knowing what you do about the man?*'

'*Depends on the time of day.*' Mechner smiled then. He sipped at his ever-present can of Dr Pepper and said, '*Funny thing is, I've already got something on him and he doesn't even know it. I locked it away in a safe place before I called you people, but I know that if it ever got out it would cause serious problems for Hartnell. And I mean serious.*'

'*All the more reason to take it to the feds and turn state's evidence.*'

'*It wouldn't work that way. It's not the kind of thing that would stand up in any court of law.*'

'*So what is it then?*'

'*It's an audio cassette recording in which Hartnell talks about how he manipulated his business partner over a personal matter. It's there as my last resort, only to be used if I've run out of all other options. I do have some paperwork I took out with me, mostly to do with the laundering side of things, but it's not nearly enough to convict him. He's too careful for that, and never puts his name to anything.*'

'*You won't know until you talk to the feds. I say it's worth a try. New name or not, I don't think Hartnell's the kind of man who gives up once he starts something. He'll keep looking until he finds you, and we can't protect you forever. Maybe the feds can.*'

'*No. I want to do this my way,*' Mechner said. '*Believe me, I've planned it all out to the smallest detail. I'm sure we'll be all right . . .*'

Bishop hadn't been quite so sure, but you couldn't argue with somebody whose mind was already made up. Knowing what came later, maybe he should have tried a little harder.

He gave Strickland a brief summary of the situation, only omitting the details of that kitchen conversation.

Strickland said, 'But Hartnell still tracked him down, though, right?'

'That's right,' Bishop said. 'How much do you know about it?'

Strickland glanced at Clea, who was silently watching them both, then he shrugged. 'Not a whole lot, and most of it's just rumours. But I'm sure Callaway was behind it. He never came right out and admitted it to me, but he laid enough hints. Besides, Hartnell wouldn't have trusted anybody else for the job. So what happened? Did he hit you guys at the safe house?'

'He tried.'

'It wasn't another massacre like Vegas, was it?'

Bishop shook his head. 'No, that wouldn't have worked where we were. We were in a much more heavily populated suburban neighbourhood, which was part of the reason I picked it. Or maybe Hartnell simply wasn't as desperate back then. No, they used the Trojan Horse method instead.'

'What? You mean like a parcel bomb or something?'

'Not quite. What it was, there was a neighbourhood kid of about Barney's age who lived a couple of houses down. His name was Andrew Truman and he came to the front door shortly after we moved in and asked if he could mow our front- and backyards for a few bucks. I'd already seen him mowing everybody else's, but our lawn wasn't too bad at that point and I told him we didn't need any work done right then. So we chatted some and he said he'd try again in a week or two and went home.'

What Bishop didn't mention was that he'd chatted to the boy on the doorstep for a good ten minutes or so before he went home. Primarily he'd done it as a way to fit in a little more and deflect any possible suspicion as to their presence in the area, but it turned out he and Andrew actually had a shared passion – soccer. Bishop was an avid follower of the New York Red Bulls, but he still kept up with the doings of some of the more notable European teams like Barcelona, Real Madrid, Inter Milan, and a few others. And Andrew was a major Juventus fan. So much so that his father had even subscribed to an expensive overseas satellite channel in order that his son could watch some of their games.

So they found they had plenty to talk about, discussing the pros and cons of goal-line technology, or the effectiveness of certain managers in elevating their teams to the top level, or how reliable the transfer rumours were concerning certain players. But Bishop had had to call an end to it at some point, and eventually Andrew returned home and that was that.

'Three weeks later,' Bishop said, 'Andrew came back and rang the doorbell and asked me again if he could mow the lawns, and this time I said okay. Only he seemed kind of nervous and distant for some reason, and he wasn't particularly interested in talking, either, which was very unlike him. But I just put it down to trouble at home and took him to the garage where there was an old mower at the back. So I let him get on with it while I patrolled the house again. It was a big two-storey ranch-type thing with six bedrooms and plenty of space, and it usually took me awhile to check everything to my satisfaction. At the time, Emily Mechner was in the kitchen while her husband was in the bedroom, working on his laptop. I still checked on Andrew's progress, though, and once he'd done the front I went out and led him through to the backyard. One of the other members of my team, Kwinell, was sitting out there in a deckchair, so I knew he'd be able to keep an eye on the boy from that point on.'

Bishop poured himself some more lukewarm coffee and took another sip. It left a bitter aftertaste. Although maybe that wasn't entirely down to the coffee.

Strickland said, 'And *did* this Kwinell keep an eye on him?'

Bishop sighed. 'Yeah, but he also made a mistake. Two, in fact. And they were big ones. I was on the phone to my supervisor at the time, giving him my daily report, when I realized I hadn't heard the mower in a while. I went round the back and saw the machine standing there on its own, with the lawn still only half done and Kwinell still sitting in his chair. When I asked where the boy had gone, he said he went inside a few minutes before to take a leak. And without searching him, either. Remembering Andrew's nervousness from before, I knew something was wrong then. I ducked inside and ran to the staircase at the other end of the house and heard faint movements on the landing above. I climbed the stairs silently, and when I reached the top I saw

Andrew crouching in front of Mechner's bedroom door, placing what looked like a tube of Lifesavers on the floor.'

'They weren't Lifesavers,' Strickland said.

Bishop shook his head. 'Semtex, as it turned out. In his other hand he held a miniature remote. That kid wasn't just nervous, he was terrified out of his mind. He kept rubbing his free hand up and down his jeans, trying to wipe off the sweat, and he was also shaking like a leaf. The last thing I wanted to do was startle him, though, so I holstered my gun and very quietly called his name. But at the sound of my voice he jumped and when he saw me standing there, he screamed and panicked. He clenched both his hands into fists and he must have activated the detonator and . . . well, you can guess what happened next.'

'Shit,' Strickland said.

'My God, that's awful,' Clea whispered.

'Yeah.' Bishop remembered the world turning white for a second, the noise of the explosion filling the house as the force of the blast propelled him into a wall, then down the stairs until he finally landed in a heap at the bottom.

Clea said, 'Was this Andrew . . .? I mean, did he—'

'He was gone.' Bishop snapped his fingers. 'Like that.'

'And Mechner?' Strickland asked.

'The explosion completely destroyed the bedroom door and part of the wall, so he took some of the blast, but his work desk protected him from the worst of it. He was basically uninjured. At least, physically. Once I confirmed he was safe, I ran out the front and sprinted over to the boy's house. I broke in, but Callaway and his people must have split the moment they heard the explosion. All I found were the bodies of Andrew's parents in the dining room. Callaway probably had them killed the moment the boy left for our house. No survivors, no witnesses.'

'Animals,' Clea said, shaking her head. Bishop had to agree.

Strickland had also turned a little pale at that last part. 'But Mechner couldn't have survived,' he said. 'Callaway wasted him. He practically admitted it to me.'

'Well, he got to Mechner eventually, but it wasn't on our watch.

After that breach, Mechner finally saw the light and decided to follow my advice. His wife had pretty strong opinions on the matter too. So I escorted them both to a meeting with the section chief of the Criminal Investigative Division at FBI headquarters in DC, and it turned out they were *very* interested in what Mechner had. They felt he had enough to initiate a tax evasion case that could put Hartnell behind bars for fifteen years. So they stuck them both in the Witness Protection Program, and that was that. Or so I thought.'

'What happened?' Clea asked.

'Three months later, my supervisor gave me the news that he'd been taken out with poison. Although there was never any proof of Hartnell's involvement, of course. Apparently his people found out where one of the marshals did the weekly food shopping and that was it. They must have known about Mechner's particular craving for Dr Pepper, so they injected strychnine into some cans of their own and swapped them over somehow. Probably created a diversion at the checkout till or something. That's what I would have done. My supervisor at the time said it was a very painful death.'

Strickland frowned. 'So that's why you joined up with us? To get back at the man who killed your old client?'

'No, to get back at the man who killed a young boy named Andrew Truman. I liked him. He was a good kid. And while that initial explosion may well have been set off accidentally, it was still murder whichever way you look at it. Especially as the investigators found out later that there were two explosions, not one.'

'What do you mean?' Strickland asked.

'I mean they found additional tiny traces of Semtex in what was left of Andrew's belt, as well as bits of an intricate blasting cap hidden behind the steel buckle. They theorized that both bombs were tuned to the same electronic signal, so even if Andrew had gotten out of the area before pressing the detonator, he still would have blown himself up. His parents were already dead at that point, and he was the last loose end. Callaway, and by proxy Hartnell, was simply making sure all bases were covered to ensure no comebacks.'

Strickland nodded. 'That sounds like them, all right. They never did like taking unnecessary chances.'

'They should have killed me too, then. Because I've got a very long memory, and the moment I realized it was Hartnell you were testifying against I suddenly developed a very great interest in your continued well-being.'

'I don't feel hungry anymore,' Clea said, and began edging out of the seat. 'I'm going to the restroom, if that's all right with you?'

'Don't mind if I check first, do you?' Bishop said.

'I think I can manage, thanks.'

'Better safe than sorry,' he said, sliding out after her.

FORTY

Bishop followed Clea down the narrow hallway, past the basic kitchen area on the right, and a little further down on the left was an unmarked door. Clea rolled her eyes as Bishop opened the door and stepped inside.

It was a small, not very clean, unisex restroom. There was a private cubicle on the left, a single urinal affixed to the right-hand wall, and a small sink on the adjacent wall. There was a long thin transom window above the urinal, too high up for Clea to reach. In the cubicle there was a small, double-hung sash window of frosted glass in the wall behind the john. Bishop tried the latch, opened the lower half and peered out and saw the garage doors to his immediate right. To the left was the driveway that led to the front parking area. He latched the window shut again. It was small, but just about big enough for Clea to get through if she wanted. All he could do was keep a watch on the front and check back after a few minutes, in case she tried to make a run for it through the fields.

He stepped back outside and said, 'Go right ahead. I'll check back in a while to make sure you're all right.'

'Do you really think I'm going to try and make a run for it?' she said. 'Out here? In the middle of nowhere?'

'People have surprised me before.'

She stared at him, sighed, then went inside, closing the door behind her. Bishop carried on down the rest of the hallway. He passed two more doors on the right, the first of which was partly ajar, and inside he could see a small, but well-stacked kitchen. He kept going down the hallway until he reached the rear exit door at the end. It was just a normal windowless wooden door. Obviously fire regulations weren't taken too seriously in these parts. He tried the handle. It was locked.

Satisfied, he walked back to the booth where Toby was busy piling their empty plates onto a tray.

'Any chance of some more coffee?' Bishop said.

'Be right back with another pot,' Toby said, and carried his load back to the kitchen. Clea's unfinished omelette he left on the table.

Bishop sat back down. He glanced out the front and saw the Explorer was still the only vehicle in the lot. The fog had thinned out a little, but there wasn't a whole lot to see. Just dormant farmland in the distance and a road that was still completely empty of traffic.

Strickland turned to look. 'You checked she didn't bring a spare key with her, right?'

'Back at the house.'

'Okay.' Strickland looked down at the table. 'I have to tell you, Bishop, I didn't like hearing that part about the kid at the end. I didn't like that part at all.'

'Be glad you didn't have to witness it first-hand. It's not an image I'll ever forget.'

'That isn't what—' Strickland paused as Toby came back and placed the same urn in the centre of the table.

'Anything else you need?' Toby asked.

'We're good, thanks,' Bishop said. The owner stared at them both for a beat, then gave a single nod and went away.

Bishop poured himself some more as Strickland continued, 'That isn't exactly what I meant, Bishop. All you did was highlight the fact that we're dealing with a couple of assholes who make a habit of tying up all loose ends, no matter what. And they haven't got too many scruples about wasting kids, either. When I heard you talking about that Andrew, all I could see was Barn's scared face as he hit that detonator. We both know what kind of animals we're dealing with here, so what makes you think they'll *ever* let Barney go free?'

'What happened before won't happen this time, Strickland. I'll be there to make sure Barney comes out of this in one piece.'

'But you can't *guarantee* that.'

'Nobody can guarantee anything. But you'll just have to trust me on this, that's all. I keep my promises, and if I'm not able to this time it'll be because I'm dead.'

Bishop needed to end this line of thought, fast. Further worrying about Barney's situation couldn't serve any useful purpose, not when they needed all their concentration for getting through the coming day in one piece. Recalling Paul Mechner's comment about Hartnell's business partner, he said, 'Where does he get his coke from?'

Strickland looked up from the table, mouth open. 'Huh? What?'

'Hartnell's been one of the US's leading distributors for the last couple of decades, right? And I assume it all comes from somewhere south of the border, but where? Colombia? Bolivia? Peru?'

'What difference does it make now?'

'How do I know until you tell me? At this point, all information is useful information. So who's Hartnell's supplier? You must know.'

Strickland jerked his shoulders. 'He's got a long-term partner over in Mexico keeps him supplied with shit. One of the major cartel bosses down there, name of Rafael Guzman. Ever hear of him?'

Bishop frowned. 'The name sounds familiar. Can't quite place it, though.'

'Well, he's a major-league badass, believe me. He's also been in the game for as long as Hartnell, and you know how long the average life expectancy is for guys like that, which means he must be doing something right.'

'But they don't manufacture coke in Mexico, so where does Guzman get it from?'

'Peru, I think. I don't know for sure. Hartnell and his higher-ups always kept everything nice and compartmentalized when I was working for him. You knew your part, and you soon learned everything else was none of your business.'

Bishop picked up his mug. Drank some coffee. He thought for a few moments, then said, 'And whose responsibility is it to get the coke into the States? Hartnell's?'

'Like I said, I don't know too much about that side, but I think they share the risk. No idea how they do it, but each time they've gotten the stuff through without any problems so I imagine we're talking some major payoffs somewhere along the line.'

Bishop nodded. 'How long is "long-term"?'

'What do you mean?'

'You said Hartnell and Guzman were long-term partners. How long is that?'

'Fifteen years, maybe twenty. Something like that.'

Bishop gave a low whistle. 'That's an unbelievable amount of time for a business relationship, especially for the drug trade. But surely if this Guzman survived as a cartel boss for this long, then it's a given that he's burned a lot of enemies and competitors along the way. And probably in very nasty ways. They like to make big statements down there.'

'I guess. What's your point?'

'So what the hell are Guzman and Hartnell still doing together? A man like that would surely have tried to take over Hartnell's part of the operation for himself by now. Too much is never enough for these kinds of people. Sooner or later, they always want to get their hands on everything, and Guzman doesn't strike me as the shrinking violet type.'

Strickland sat back in his seat. 'Well, there *were* some rumours back in the day that Guzman might try something like that, but it never came to anything. The way I heard it – and this is all third-hand, remember, so it's probably equal parts exaggeration and bullshit – was that one of the rival cartels decided to go after Guzman one time. The story is the hit team somehow got into his compound but he wasn't there, so they grabbed his sister instead. His elder sister, his only living relative, apparently. So they took her away and soon got in touch and told Guzman he had three days to hand himself over to them or they'd send her back to him in pieces.'

'Sounds familiar.'

'Yeah, right. This Guzman went crazy, of course. And he was probably half-crazy to start with. He had his men search that whole section of the country trying to find her, but they kept coming up blank, so Hartnell heard about this and sent about a hundred of his best guys over to Mexico to help find her. And a day before the deadline Hartnell's people helped locate the kidnappers' hideout, only to discover she'd been dead for a while already. The kidnappers had raped her repeatedly, then just slit her throat and let her bleed out. Or maybe she'd slit her own throat out of shame. Nobody knows. Of course, Guzman was ready to declare war on everybody at that point, but Hartnell's guys somehow managed to grab the head of the rival cartel and *his* family, and basically delivered them right to Guzman's doorstep. You can pretty much guess what happened to them next. But the end result was Guzman never forgot what Hartnell did for him.'

Bishop made a face. 'And that's why they're still together after all this time? Doesn't sound too likely, does it?'

'Hey, it's just what I heard. There's probably a lot more to it than that, but there has to be *some* reason why they're still pals.'

Bishop couldn't argue with that part. There was always a reason. Always.

He thought about this new wrinkle as he watched Toby stroll over to the front door. The owner just stood there, looking out as he straightened the OPEN/CLOSED sign. When he headed back towards the kitchen area, Bishop realized Clea had been gone for some time now. He no longer had a watch, but he guessed it was about five or six minutes – far too long for a bathroom break. But the Explorer was still out front, and he hadn't seen any other movement outside.

He was about to get up and check when he looked over at the front door again.

Something was different. The OPEN part of the sign was now visible, when it hadn't been before. It meant Toby had just turned the sign round, yet it was still only six in the morning, or thereabouts. It couldn't possibly be closing time yet.

'Uh, Bishop?' Strickland said, carefully putting down his cup on the table. He was staring intently at something past Bishop's left shoulder.

Bishop slowly turned his head and saw Toby standing behind the counter where the two previous customers had been sitting.

He was also holding a shotgun. And it was pointed right in their direction.

FORTY-ONE

'Hey, be cool, Toby,' Bishop said, adding a fake quiver to his voice. 'We weren't planning to stiff you on the check or anything. There's no need for guns.'

'Shut up,' Toby said, 'and don't neither of you move an inch.'

He raised the weapon for emphasis and Bishop saw it was a Mossberg 500 pump. He'd used the same model back in the Corps. It had a five-round tube magazine with one in the chamber, and could stop a rhino at fifty yards. So they said. He'd never thought to test it out. Toby's left hand was supporting the walnut forestock, while his right was tight around the grip, the index finger resting against the trigger. The black steel barrel remained very still.

'I never argue with a man with a gun,' Bishop said, staying just as motionless. His own Glock was still in his rear waistband, with no possible way to get to it. 'Mind telling me what's going on?'

'Sure, I don't mind,' Toby said. 'Remember those two guys I was talking to when you came in? Well, they're brothers who also happen to be good acquaintances of mine. And one of them called me a short while ago and told me something real interesting. He said they were listening to the radio in their pick-up and the news was going on about that massacre in Vegas yesterday when Zack all of a sudden remembered where he'd seen your face before. He said he was sure you were the driver of that SUV who took that witness guy and his kid, and that maybe it would be a good idea if I held you all here until they get back.'

Strickland said, 'Look, mister, I think you got us confused with—'

'Shut your hole,' Toby said and came over to their booth, stopping a few feet away from Strickland. 'You think I'm stupid? As soon as I hung up I checked the internet and pulled up that photo that guy took of you. And this one here's the driver and you're the other one,

192

the witness, just with a new haircut. Say you ain't and I'll wrap this barrel round your face. Pretty you up. You want that?'

Strickland shook his head. 'No.'

'Smart move. So who's the skirt? Some little piece you picked up along the way?'

'Just some storekeeper we ran into,' Bishop said, knowing there was no point in lying. 'We needed her vehicle, and brought her along in case we got stopped at a roadblock.'

'That's better,' Toby said. 'I'll go get her in a tick, but right now I want both of you to put your hands on the table, palms down, like you were at a séance or something.'

Both men did as they were told.

Toby pointed the barrel at Bishop. 'You, take off those glasses. One hand.'

Bishop raised his right hand and took the glasses off and set them down on the seat next to him. He put his hand back on the tabletop.

Toby studied him and slowly nodded his head. 'Yeah, you're him, all right. They also mentioned a kid on the TV. Where's he?'

'He was grabbed by the people who are after me,' Strickland said. 'We're on our way to get him back.'

'Bullshit.' Toby turned his attention to Bishop again. 'Now they said on TV that you were armed, so what I want you to do next is put your hardware on the table. What you packing?'

'A Glock.'

'Where is it?'

'In the back of my waistband.'

'Okay, let's see it, but slow.'

Bishop had been keeping his attention on Toby, but he'd also just seen something interesting out the corner of his eye. Some kind of movement along the bottom of one of the front windows. He was sure of it. It had looked like the top of somebody's head as they slunk past, towards the Explorer, which could only mean Clea had decided to make a run for it. That was good news. Maybe she'd make some kind of sound that would divert Toby's attention for a couple of seconds, just long enough for Bishop to overpower him and get everything back on track again. That was all he needed.

He was trying to remember if he'd locked the doors when Toby said, 'Don't make me tell you again.'

Bishop couldn't delay any longer. He raised his left hand from the table and slowly brought it back to his waistband. He was watching the shotgun barrel. It didn't waver at all. He gripped the pistol and just as slowly pulled it out. Bringing the gun round without making any sudden movements, Bishop gently placed it in the centre of the table.

'Okay,' Toby said, 'now slide it across to me.'

Bishop gave the gun a push with the edge of his hand. It slid across the table surface, fell over the side and clattered onto the floor. He heard Toby slide it away with his foot, but he was paying more attention to the window to the left of the front door: the one with the view of the Explorer. He watched as the driver's side door opened a few inches and then closed, all without a sound. But he now remembered he *had* locked the vehicle before coming inside. Clea must have hidden a spare key somewhere on the Explorer's undercarriage. He'd made a check of the vehicle back at the house, but it had already been dark at that point and he could easily have missed it. Now he was glad he had.

'Now open out your pants pockets,' Toby said. 'Slowly, and one at a time.'

Bishop pulled out his empty left pants pocket with his left hand. He placed that hand on the table and then used his right to pull open the other pants pocket, also empty. Then he put that hand back on the table. He was waiting for Clea to start the Explorer's engine. The moment Toby's attention was diverted he'd move. Not easy when he was stuck in a booth like this, but he had to try.

'Now your jacket,' Toby said. 'Take it off and throw it over.'

'There's just a cell phone in the inside pocket,' Bishop said. 'That's all.'

'Yeah? Well, my pop once said a man who don't check the important stuff himself deserves everything he gets, so just do what I tell you and take it off.'

Bishop began slipping his arms out of the jacket. He was precisely half in and half out when the Explorer's diesel engine suddenly roared into life out front, the whine quickly rising in pitch as Clea pressed down on the gas pedal.

'What the hell?' Toby said, stepping two paces back.

Clea's timing couldn't have been worse. Bishop was still trapped half in and half out of his suit jacket. He began to slip the jacket back on when Toby quickly said, 'Keep those arms where they are, boy. One wrong move and it'll be the last move you ever make. That goes for both of you.'

Bishop believed him. His chance had gone. He didn't move. Just glanced out the window again as the Explorer's rear wheels skidded against the dirt, then the vehicle took off like a rocket. Racing across the parking lot, Clea didn't even pause at the entrance opening. She just steered the vehicle left and took the turn, and disappeared from sight.

FORTY-TWO

'Well, how about that?' Toby said, a faint smile on his lips. 'Guess she just didn't like the food. But it does kinda put me in a pickle. And you, too.'

'I don't follow you,' Bishop said as he slowly put his jacket back on.

'Well, I figure she's probably on her way to the cops,' Toby said, grabbing the Glock from the floor and sticking it in his own rear waistband, 'and I wouldn't like that. Nor would my partners.'

Bishop frowned. 'You're not planning on handing us over to the law then?'

Toby gave a snort of derision. 'Shit, what good would that do us?'

'So what is it you want?'

'Money, of course. Dough. Payola. What the hell do you think?'

'I see. And where's this imaginary money coming from?'

'It's coming from you, pal. You, or the people you work for.'

Bishop shrugged with genuine puzzlement. 'You've completely lost me now. What are you talking about?'

'Don't try that innocent act on me, pal. I told you we ain't stupid. Now on the news this morning they all been figuring that this guy here has to be the main witness in that big murder trial tomorrow morning in Ohio. The one with that Hartnell fella. Am I right?'

So the media finally narrowed things down and made the connection to the Hartnell trial, Bishop thought. *Sure took them long enough.* 'So what?' he said.

'So, they also figured you must be working for this Hartnell guy and are getting paid to deliver this witness to him before the trial starts. And we happen to agree with them.'

'Well, they're wrong. I was hired by one of the marshals as an extra man on site, in case there was—'

'No more bullshit,' Toby interrupted. ''cause it ain't gonna wash with me. Now we all reckon if this witness here is worth so much to this Hartnell, then he surely won't mind paying a teensy little bit extra in order for us to let you go on your way as soon as possible. Especially as we ain't greedy types. We figure fifty grand per man, which is chicken feed to someone like him, but for us it's enough to pay off our bookies at the track and still have a few bucks left over.'

Bishop glanced at Strickland, unable to believe what he was hearing. These idiots had to be living in another world. There was no other explanation for it. Even if half of what they believed was true, did they honestly think a truly ruthless bastard like Hartnell would ever submit to a shakedown by a trio of amateurs such as themselves? He'd have them executed without a second thought. That's after he'd roasted them over an open fire first.

But what could he say? This Toby was clearly convinced Bishop was part of Hartnell's organization and that was that. And Bishop wasn't about to change his mind now it was made up. The guy could already smell the money he knew was coming his way. But it gave Bishop an idea too.

'We are so screwed,' Strickland groaned, his head in his hands. 'It's a choice of the Three Stooges here or the cops. Either way, we're done.'

'Watch your goddamn mouth,' Toby said.

'The cops aren't about to show,' Bishop said.

'No?' Toby raised an eyebrow. 'How come?'

'Yeah,' Strickland said. 'What's stopping Clea from heading to the nearest station right now?'

'Her own conscience,' Bishop said. 'Last night in the car she was clearly affected by the conversation between you and Barney, and she knows if the cops get a hold of you he'll suffer for it. She's got a daughter the same age, remember. No, right now she's heading back to her normal life and her little shop in Colorado. She won't be calling the cops. In fact, she's probably hoping we make it.'

'I don't know what the hell you're talking about,' Toby said, 'but it don't matter. I see a cruiser out front I'll stick you both in the basement and tell 'em you took off after the woman. So now why don't you two both be good boys and just relax till my pals get here?'

'And how long will that be?' Bishop asked.

'Ten minutes, probably less. I reckon ol' Tyler's gonna keep his foot pressed to the floor all the way.'

'What about your regular customers? Won't they be kind of curious as to why you've closed up so early?'

Toby shook his head. 'The few regulars I got all know I sometimes close up and go into town and top up supplies. Don't worry, we ain't gonna be disturbed.'

'So what's the plan? How do you expect me to deliver this money to you so fast?'

Strickland sat up straighter. 'Hey, what are you doing encouraging him?'

'Be quiet,' Bishop said, and turned back to Toby. 'Well?'

Toby briefly turned to the table behind him to take hold of a chair. The moment he looked away, Bishop quickly grabbed the steak knife next to Clea's plate and tucked it under his left shirtsleeve with the blade pointing outwards. Strickland watched him, his face expressionless. Toby then turned back, set the chair down and sat facing them. He placed the shotgun on his lap, still pointing in their direction.

'Well now,' he said, 'the way Zach figures it, you must be in regular contact with the guy who gives you your orders, right? So all you do is call him up and tell him you got a slight problem and you need some business expenses straight away. Then he wires the hundred and fifty to this special bank account Zach set up years ago with a false name and ID, over in Wichita. See, we were gonna use it for stashing our horse winnings without the taxman finding out, but things didn't work out and we never got around to using it much. But now we got the perfect reason.'

'Sounds like you've really thought this through,' Bishop said, even though they clearly hadn't. Even if Bishop *was* working for Hartnell they would never live long enough to spend a single cent, but what did it matter? It was all fantasy anyway.

Toby smiled, showing discoloured teeth. 'Damn right we thought it through. Once my pals arrive, we'll go over the details. Until then, we wait.'

Bishop nodded, as though it all made perfect sense. But he was already busy thinking through possible scenarios and making plans. He knew he'd only have one chance at getting them out of this, and he had to make it count. And the best time to act would be when the two brothers, Zach and Tyler, arrived. When Toby was distracted, even just momentarily. All Bishop had was a small steak knife, but it would have to be enough. He'd often had to work with less. Then there was the psychological aspect too. Bishop was already formulating a couple of ideas on that score.

The three men waited in silence. Strickland shook his head in despair every now and then while Toby sat silently watching them both, not moving at all. The occasional vehicle passed by outside, but none pulled in.

Bishop estimated about nineteen additional minutes had passed when he heard the sound of tyres on dirt and gravel outside. He looked up and saw the dark pick-up from before pull into the entrance and approach the front of the diner.

Toby stood up and smiled. 'Well, better late than never,' he said.

FORTY-THREE

Bishop watched the pick-up slowly come to a stop in almost exactly the same spot where the Explorer had been. A few seconds later the two brothers, Zach and Tyler, got out. They were dressed the same as before. Thick coats, jeans, matching baseball caps. The driver arched his back while the other one arranged something at the back of his pants and looked around. The driver then patted the right-hand pocket of his jacket and said something to his brother. The other one said something back.

Bishop almost smiled. Time to plant the seeds of doubt in Toby's mind. 'Your so-called partners have come armed,' he said.

Toby turned to him. 'So what?'

'So why would they do that?'

'To help keep you two covered, of course. Why else?'

'One of them, maybe. But both of them? I don't think so. No, I think it's far more likely they're planning to stiff you. In both senses of the word.'

'You better shut your damn mouth, else I shut it for you. I known these boys a long time. We're practically family.' But even as Toby said it, he was frowning at the two brothers. They were still out there talking.

'But you're not family, Toby,' Bishop said, and shook his left arm until the knife blade emerged at his inner wrist. One more good shake and it would fall right into his palm. 'Not *real* family, I mean. Not like those two are to each other. And it worries me that it took so long for them to get here. You said ten minutes. They took twenty-five. The way I see it, that's more than long enough for two smart men to formulate a whole new game plan altogether. One that doesn't involve you at all.'

'What?' Toby turned back to him. 'What the hell are you talking about, asshole?'

'I'm saying that if I was them, I'd make the most of my presence here and cut you all the way out. Especially as they can pull the trigger on you easily and then blame it on me, since I won't be around to argue. I'll be long gone. And let's face it, seventy-five grand sounds a hell of a lot more appealing than just fifty, don't you think?' He faced front again. 'I wonder what they're discussing out there. Must be something real important if they don't want you to hear it.'

Toby said nothing. Just watched them out there, talking between themselves. For all Bishop knew the two brothers *were* planning to freeze Toby out, but it didn't make any difference. The suspicion that they might be was all he needed. The brothers had now finished their discussion and were strolling casually towards the front entrance.

'You're just trying to screw with my head,' Toby said. 'I known them both a long time. We're partners in this.'

'With a hundred and fifty grand at stake? Accessible via a dodgy bank account that only Zach has access to?' Bishop chuckled. 'You're a lot more trusting than I would be in your position, Toby. All I'm saying is it wouldn't hurt to keep an eye on them, that's all.'

The men appeared at the door. The driver tried the handle a couple of times, but the door was locked. Probably by Toby when he turned the sign round.

'Use your spare key, Zach,' Toby called out. 'I'm watching these two.'

As the driver, Zach, reached into his pants pocket Bishop shook his arm and the steak-knife blade slid into his palm. He quickly rotated it a hundred and eighty degrees until he had the knife in a reverse grip, with the blade running parallel along his elbow. Toby was maybe four or five feet away. And Bishop was in a sitting position with a table obstructing his movement. It wasn't good, but then life was never perfect. He began slowly, carefully, inching himself along the seat, towards the aisle. And towards Toby.

There was the jangling of a key in a lock, and then Zach pushed the door open and they each stepped inside. The other one, Tyler, closed the door and latched it shut, then stood just to the side of it.

Zach came forward a little and smiled at Bishop. 'Yeah, it's him all right. Didn't I tell you, Ty?'

'Sure did,' his brother said.

'Look,' Toby said, his gun wavering between the two groups, not pointing at anybody in particular, 'you guys . . . uh, you guys just stay there a minute, okay? I need to think.'

Zach stopped and frowned at the shotgun. 'Better watch yourself there, Tobe. Seems to me that thing's almost pointing our way, don't it, Ty?'

'Seems like,' the other one said, and started slowly moving his right hand to the back of his waistband.

Bishop had almost progressed to the edge of his seat now and figured there was about three feet between himself and Toby. He glanced over at Strickland and mouthed the words *Stay down*. Strickland nodded understanding and made himself small in the seat. Under the table, Bishop began lifting the balls of his feet and lowering them again. He also raised each leg and rotated the ankle one way, and then the other. He'd been sitting a long time and wanted to make sure all the muscles down there were limber and ready.

'Well, well, well,' Zach said, and took a few steps towards them. He was still about fifteen feet away, though, and his right hand was now in his coat pocket, the same pocket he'd been patting before. 'What's this guy been saying to you, Tobe? Don't tell me, he's been trying to play you against us, am I right?'

'Yeah, Zach, that's what he's been doing, all right.' Toby said, his shotgun still pointing at nothing in particular. But his hands no longer seemed as steady as before. To Bishop, he looked nervous. Unsure of himself.

Bishop knew he wouldn't get a better chance than right now.

Zach said, 'But you know better than to listen to him, right, Tobe? I mean, he's liable to say just about any –'

At that point, Bishop leaped off his seat and ducked out of the booth towards Toby. Staying low, he swung the steak knife towards Toby's midsection, narrowly avoiding the hands holding the shotgun. But Toby instinctively swivelled his body at the last moment and the knife blade missed his abdomen and sunk into his side instead.

Toby gave a hoarse scream as he stumbled back and as he fell to the floor, the shotgun went off with a thunderous boom.

Bishop immediately heard gunshots coming from somewhere up front. He dived to the floor and grabbed the Mossberg's barrel and yanked it from the man's weak grip. The metal was still hot from the blast. Bishop ducked under the nearest table as more gunshots came from the front.

Scrambling under the table on his hands and knees, Bishop heard the sounds of rounds hitting walls and quickly emerged on the other side. He knew the Mossberg had five more shots at most. Maybe less. And he had to assume the brothers had spare magazines for their weapons. Which meant his only chance was to end this fast.

The room went quiet for a heartbeat.

Then one of them shouted, 'Over *there*,' and there was a barrage of gunshots and Bishop heard a grunt of pain behind him and turned. Toby had been hit. Which meant the brothers were still focused on his previous position. Good. Bishop immediately got to his knees, faced front and brought the shotgun up. He could make out a human-shaped silhouette standing in front of the left window, both arms raised in a shooting position.

Bishop aimed the shotgun and fired. There was a tumultuous explosion followed by a single shout. The man went down.

The other brother yelled, '*Zaaach*,' then more gunfire boomed from Bishop's right.

He ducked down again, swept a chair out of the way and crawled under the next table, moving closer to the front of the diner. He racked the pump and the empty shell flew out the ejector port. As he crawled he quickly scanned the floor of the diner, looking for a pair of feet that wasn't Strickland's.

There. About five feet to the right of the front door. A pair of shoes with the toes pointing in his direction. He was a good fifteen feet away from Bishop's own position. Bishop brought the Mossberg round and was about to fire when the shoes' owner let loose a half-dozen shots of his own.

Bishop felt the table above him shake as the bullets hit and he saw a couple of rounds ricochet off the floor just inches in front of his nose.

He aimed the shotgun at the feet and fired. He racked the pump and fired again. At the same place. Then once more. The smoke from the gun blasts immediately obscured his view and he waved it away. A second later he saw a human shape lying in a heap on the floor. Bishop quickly backed out from under the table and jumped to his feet, keeping the shotgun pointed at the fallen man.

Tyler lay on his back with his eyes open. Blood covered most of his legs and midsection. He raised a bloody arm off the floor and then it slowly fell back onto his chest. Bishop racked the pump again and the spent shell flew out the side port. He aimed the gun at the man, but he was no longer moving. He wasn't even breathing.

Bishop turned to his left and saw the other one, Zach, about ten feet away. He was lying on his stomach and also not moving. Bishop manoeuvred himself between the tables and went over and crouched down next to him. As he felt the man's carotid artery, he shouted, 'Strickland, you hurt?'

'Bishop?' Strickland called out.

'It's me.' He couldn't find a pulse in Zach's neck. 'Are you hit?'

'No, I don't think so. Jesus *Christ*.'

Bishop stood up and went over to the other one again. Tyler was still in the same position, both eyes still staring sightlessly up at the ceiling. Bishop looked around, saw a Colt Automatic lying on the floor a few feet away. He was about to pick it up when he paused and decided it would be better to just leave it where it was. Then he went back to the booth and retrieved his glasses while Strickland emerged from under the table.

'You get 'em both?' he asked.

'Yeah.' Bishop turned and looked at Toby lying on the floor. Strickland got to his feet and joined him.

The owner had managed to pull the knife from his side, but it had made little difference in the end. His partners had managed to get a couple of good ones in. One bullet had taken him in the centre of the chest, while another one had got him in the right shoulder. The man's off-white apron and most of the shirt underneath was almost entirely crimson. There was also a large puddle of blood on the floor around him. Yet the man was still breathing somehow. It came in short rasps, but he wasn't dead, at least not yet.

Toby groaned, then whispered, 'Am . . . Ambulance.'

Bishop slowly shook his head. 'Can't help you there, Toby. Wouldn't make any difference, anyway. Not with that chest wound.'

'You made your own bed,' Strickland said. 'You should have just left us alone.'

There was the sound of a vehicle whizzing by outside. It didn't even slow as it passed.

Toby closed his eyes. Opened them again. 'Wa . . . water,' he whispered.

The man's breaths were getting shorter. Bishop knew he had minutes left, if that. Bishop didn't particularly feel sorry for the guy, but he didn't hate him, either. He was just one more greedy loser whose mistakes had finally caught up with him, and his last wish on this earth was for a simple drink of water before he died.

'Go get him some from the kitchen,' Bishop said.

'Screw him,' Strickland said. 'He was ready to sell us out quick enough. Besides, we got our own problems. Let's just get the hell out of here.'

'Just get him some water, will you? It's easy enough.'

'Okay, okay,' Strickland said, and marched off to the kitchen.

Bishop stayed where he was and watched the man slowly bleed out. It wasn't pleasant, but he'd seen worse. Caused worse, too. Thirty seconds later Strickland was walking back from the kitchen with a glass of clear liquid in his hand when Toby coughed a couple of times and gave a long slow exhale. And he didn't breathe in again. Nothing dramatic about it, but there rarely was.

'Never mind,' Bishop said. 'He's gone.' He crouched down, felt for a pulse and found none. He then shifted the body and pulled the Glock from the man's rear waistband and stood up.

Strickland had already drunk the glass of water. 'So now we go?'

'Not just yet,' Bishop said.

FORTY-FOUR

After making sure the front door was latched, Bishop searched for the light switches and then turned them all off, plunging the diner into semi-darkness. He could still see his way around well enough, but nobody would be able to see in.

After wiping his prints off the Mossberg, he went back to Toby and placed the dead man's hands around the grip before dropping the gun on the floor a couple of feet away. He was pretty sure neither shotgun nor rifles left gunshot residue on the shooter's hands, but if he was wrong Toby would already have them on his, since he'd shot first. He left Zach's and Tyler's guns where their owners had dropped them.

Watching him work, Strickland said, 'I can't even imagine what the cops'll make of all this.'

'I don't care what they make of it,' Bishop said, still kneeling. 'All that matters is that we were never here.'

'No argument there. You want me to grab the keys to the pick-up?'

'Probably not a good idea,' Bishop said and looked at him.

Strickland paused, then nodded. 'We take their car, then how did they get here in the first place, right?'

'Exactly. Go check what's in the garage while I finish wiping our prints from this place. And make sure you use a rag before you touch anything.' Bishop checked Toby's pants pockets, and when he felt a large set of keys he pulled them out and tossed them to Strickland. 'Go via the back door, just in case anybody passes by outside.'

'Right.' Strickland said, and disappeared down the hallway towards the rear.

Bishop had pretty much finished wiping every surface or item they might have touched when Strickland came back to the dining room and said, 'We're out of luck. Again.'

Bishop blinked at him. 'You're kidding. There's no vehicle in the garage?'

'Oh, yeah, there's an old station wagon in there, all right, but for some reason it's missing its battery. I had a good look around but couldn't see it anywhere.'

'Wonderful.'

'I used another word, but it didn't help much.'

'So we're walking then. At least until we can find another vehicle we can borrow.'

'Maybe some good Samaritan'll give us a ride.'

'We can hope. Let me have the keys.' Strickland handed them over and Bishop put them back in Toby's pocket. He checked Toby's watch and saw it was now 06.35. They really needed to get moving. 'Okay, let's go.'

Bishop got to his feet and they both went over to the front entrance. The road was still empty. He unlatched the door using his shirt cuff, set it to self-lock, and they both stepped outside. Bishop decided it was a little warmer than before, but not much.

Their shoes made faint crunching noises on the hard gravel as they crossed the small parking lot. Strickland glanced at the pick-up and said, 'Damn thing looks almost new too. The answer to our problems just sitting there, and we can't use it.'

'It'll cause more problems than it'll solve,' Bishop said. 'We've already got enough on our plate without the cops connecting us to another shootout.'

'Yeah, I guess.'

When they reached the road, Bishop looked both ways and saw nothing in either direction. They turned right and started walking along the grassy verge by the side of the road. Neither man said anything. There was no point.

After about five minutes of walking, Bishop thought he heard the faint, distinctive sound of a vehicle approaching from behind them and turned to look. So did Strickland.

About half a mile in the distance, Bishop could make out what looked like another SUV coming their way.

Strickland said, 'I hope this guy isn't planning on an early breakfast or we're in real trouble.'

'Just look friendly and hope for the best.'

Strickland put out his thumb while Bishop concentrated on the car. When it reached the turn-off for the diner it didn't even slow, but just kept on coming, which was good. He could see it was moving at a fair clip.

'Hey, maybe we'll finally get lucky for once,' Strickland said.

Bishop said nothing. He was watching the SUV as it quickly closed the distance between them. He frowned. It actually looked like an Explorer. Not only that, but it was a dark colour, possibly brown.

It couldn't be. Could it?

When it was only thirty yards away from them, the vehicle began to slow and Bishop was finally able to make out the Colorado plate. Unable to help himself, he smiled.

'Hey,' Strickland said from behind him, 'wait a second, is that . . .?'

The vehicle skidded to a complete halt right next to them, the engine still idling. Bishop opened the front passenger door and saw Clea looking back at him from the driver's seat.

'I have to say you're about the last person I expected to see on this road,' Bishop said. 'I thought you'd be halfway back to Colorado by now.'

Clea shrugged and said, 'I changed my mind. Now do you want a ride or not?'

FORTY-FIVE

Strickland got in the back again while Bishop took the front passenger seat. Without another word, Clea got them moving and gradually took their speed up to sixty. Their car was still the only vehicle on the road, and Bishop watched as the flat Kansas farmland passed by them on both sides.

'I'm real glad you came back, Clea,' Bishop said. 'We both are.'

'That's right,' Strickland said. 'Can't tell you how much we appreciate this, especially after what we had to go through back at that diner.'

'Why?' Clea was frowning. 'What happened back there?'

Before Strickland said something they'd all regret, Bishop cut in with, 'Toby threatened to call the cops when we couldn't pay the check and I had to do some fast talking before he calmed down, that's all. I ended up giving him my watch as payment instead.'

'Yeah, that's right,' Strickland said. 'That's all I meant.'

'You mind if I ask you a question?' Bishop asked, hoping to change the subject.

'I came back because of Barney,' Clea said.

'I thought that might be it.'

She shrugged. 'The thing is, I'd been so focused on just escaping from you two and getting back to my own life that I completely forgot all about the possible consequences. For a while there I was just driving along and congratulating myself on how resourceful and daring I'd been in getting out of that restroom, then finding the spare key hidden under the rear wheel arch, when it started to hit me. Every time I visualized my little Lucy's smiling face, I'd think about your friend's son and what might happen to him if you two don't make it to Ohio before your deadline. And I kept thinking of that story you told in the diner about that other boy, Andrew, and how . . . and what they did to him. I knew that if I let that happen again I'd never be able to look myself in the mirror without feeling guilty, so I came back.'

'Thanks, Clea,' Strickland said. 'That means a lot to me. It really does.'

'I'm just glad I can stop pointing a gun at you,' Bishop said. 'Believe me, it's not my favourite thing.'

'Think how *I* felt,' she said. 'Although this does kind of make me an accessory if we do get stopped by the police.'

Bishop shook his head. 'We won't. And if the worst does happen we'll tell them we forced you to come along at gunpoint.'

After a minute or so of silence, Clea said, 'So where am I going?'

'Just continue on this road for now,' Bishop said. 'If my memory serves me well, according to the map we've got the city of Wellington about twenty or thirty miles up ahead. How are we for gas, by the way?'

She looked at the odometer. 'Less than a quarter-tank left.'

'Okay. We'll skirt around the edges of Wellington and see if we can gas up somewhere. Look, I hate to bring it up, Clea . . .'

'If you're going to ask me how much cash I've got left,' she said, 'the answer is twenty dollars and some change. I can probably get some more from an ATM, but—'

'No ATMs,' Bishop said, 'and no credit cards, either. We don't know how much the feds know by now, but we have to assume the worst. Which means no paper trail.'

'So where does that leave us?' Strickland asked. 'We can't drive on fumes. Unless you're planning on stealing us another ride.'

'That's out too,' Bishop said. 'Stealing vehicles is simply another pattern we have to avoid. No, we'll just have to think of something else.'

Bishop stared out the windshield and rubbed his palm back and forth over his scalp as he tried to think of an alternative. He knew there had to be one. There always was. Like everything, the conundrum was simple enough when reduced down to its essential basics. To continue their journey they'd soon need gas, and for that they needed far more than the twenty dollars Clea had left. Which meant taking the required money from somebody else. And the best people to steal from were those who'd gotten it through illicit means themselves. Like street dealers, for example. But that meant heading into a large city, which would be counterproductive at best. And at worst? Well, how long was a piece of rope?

Strickland cut into his thoughts by saying, 'How far are we from Tulsa, Oklahoma?'

Bishop thought for a moment. 'It's about a hundred miles southeast of us, I think. As the crow flies. Why?'

'Because if it's cash we need, I've got some stashed there.'

FORTY-SIX

Bishop turned to look at Strickland. He didn't need to ask if the guy was being serious. They were long past all that.

'How much are we talking about?' Bishop asked.

'Just over fifty grand in small, unmarked bills. It was supposed to be my emergency fund and I meant to keep adding more to it, but I just never got around to it. But I'd say this sure qualifies as an emergency.'

Frowning, Bishop faced front again and checked the dashboard clock: 06.48. Less than twenty-four hours to go, with over eight hundred miles still to cover. But it was definitely doable, even if they took into account another small detour along the way. Besides, they didn't have any other choice. He pulled out the Kansas map again from the glove compartment.

Unfolding it, he saw it also covered only the top part of Oklahoma, to the south of them. But he was able to see that the I-35 was the main route south, with US 81 running almost parallel until it morphed into US 177 at South Haven. Since they wanted to avoid the interstate at all costs, and since US 81 was closest to their current position, that was clearly the way to go. At least to start with, until they got onto the back roads.

'What do you want me to do?' Clea asked.

Bishop looked out front and saw a turn-off for Caldwell Road coming up. Then he looked down at the map again until he found it. 'Okay,' he said, 'In about two miles we'll take a right turn and keep on that for about a mile. At the end we'll turn left and stay on that until it joins up with US 81. I'll give you further directions once we're on that, okay?'

She nodded. 'As long as I know ahead of time.'

He turned back to Strickland. 'So where are we going, exactly?'

'To an apartment complex in West Tulsa, north of the Arkansas River, just a few miles south of the Sand Springs Expressway.'

'And whose apartment is it?'

Strickland shifted in his seat and looked uncomfortable. 'It, uh . . . belongs to an old friend of mine from high school, name of Nicky.'

'You kept in touch with an old school pal over all these years?'

'Yeah, it's no big deal. He's an okay guy, Bishop. Plus he was always willing to listen to me pour out my troubles whenever I was feeling down, back before I met Carrie. And also I'd sometimes come and, you know, help him out whenever he got in trouble.'

'What, money trouble?'

'No, the physical kind, usually. He's, uh . . . well, he's gay.'

Bishop shrugged. 'So?'

'So nothing, I guess.' Strickland gave a nervous laugh. 'It's just I never talked about him to anybody before, not even Carrie. I guess I've always been a little embarrassed about him, especially as he's one of those real blatantly gay guys, know what I mean? Sure doesn't help that he tends to go for the rough trade either. But at school I always felt protective about him for some reason, and it seemed like I was always helping him out of one scrape or another. And then after school we just stayed in touch, that's all.' He shrugged. 'Like I said, no big deal.'

Bishop looked at him. 'You're just full of surprises, aren't you? So this Nicky is just holding all this money for you?'

'Oh, no way, he doesn't even know it's there. If he did, believe me, that money'd be gone in seconds. No, he's a flight steward with Delta, see, or he was last time I talked to him, and one time when he was out of the country I used my spare key and hollowed out a space under the floor of one of the bedroom cupboards and hid some cash down there in a knapsack. Just in case I ever needed to make a quick getaway, you know? I actually planned on adding to it over time, but then I met Carrie and all my priorities changed and I just left it there. And then after I got married Nicky and me just kind of naturally drifted apart, like people do.'

Bishop nodded. 'Who else knows about your connection to him since high school?'

'Nobody. Like I said, I never talked about him to anybody. Not even Carrie.'

'And when was the last time you and he spoke?'

'I dunno. Maybe five or six years ago. I'm not sure.'

'You realize he could have moved since then.'

'Anything's possible, I guess, but he once told me he really felt at home in that place of his, so I think he's probably still there.'

'What are the chances he'll be at home today?'

'Well, he's usually away for long periods so the odds are good that the apartment'll be empty, but I'll phone beforehand to make sure. And getting in won't be a problem. I kept a spare key hidden nearby in case I ever needed to lay low for a while.'

Bishop thought it over. He wasn't entirely sure about this. This Nicky didn't exactly sound like the introverted type, so there was no telling how many people he'd told about their friendship. But on the other hand Bishop couldn't ignore the fact that this was the only sure way out of the bind they were in. They needed cash. And they needed it soon.

'Well, since it's the only option we've got right now,' Bishop said, 'let's head on over and check it out.'

FORTY-SEVEN

'See that intersection up ahead?' Strickland was pointing as he leaned forward between the front seats. 'Take a left and then you'll see the Lakewood Apartment complex on the left-hand side. You can't miss it. It's the only thing there.'

The dashboard clock said it was 08.12. They'd kept to the back roads mostly, keeping to a steady seventy-five for much of the journey, and had made good time. And they hadn't seen a single roadblock either, which was even better. But that was probably because they were heading *away* from Ohio, rather than towards it.

Clea slowed at the intersection in question, waited for a car to pass by, then took the left turn into a heavily tree-lined street. It was actually a cul-de-sac that came to a natural stop fifty feet ahead. There were no houses, but Bishop could make out some kind of large building behind the trees on the left, with an entranceway further down. Clea slowed, turned into it and Bishop saw a large tasteful sign on the right telling them they'd reached the Lakewood Apartments.

Directly ahead of them was a parking lot with spaces for about a hundred vehicles. It was currently less than a quarter full. The building itself was a long, intricate-looking, two-storey adobe building, with a terrace outside every second-floor window, although some terraces were larger than others. There was plenty of tree cover all around. To Bishop, it all looked very upscale and expensive. It was probably even nicer at the back. In the centre of the building was an open area that looked to be the main front entrance.

'Residents just park where they want?' he asked.

'Uh-uh,' Strickland said. 'They get given numbered spaces. We'll want to take a look at forty-three. It's to the left of the entrance over there, Clea.'

With a nod, she steered them in that direction, then turned into the aisle closest to the main building and drove down it slowly.

Bishop looked out his side and saw each space contained a number spray-painted in the centre. They passed a vacant bay thirty-nine and Bishop saw a shiny black Infiniti was parked in bay forty. A grey panel van bearing the logo of a landscaping business took up bay forty-four. The three spaces in between were all vacant. Clea stopped the vehicle just before forty-three, but left the engine running.

'Well, it looks like he's out,' Strickland said.

'Let's make sure,' Bishop said, 'Call his landline.'

Strickland pulled out his cell phone and keyed in four numbers. Then he thought for a moment before keying in five more. He raised the phone to his ear.

While he waited, Bishop remembered the cell phone he'd taken from Clea yesterday. Deciding there was no reason to hold onto it any longer, he pulled the phone from his pants pocket and handed it back to her.

'I'd forgotten all about this,' she said. 'Sure you can trust me with it?'

'Let's say I'm willing to give you the benefit of the doubt.'

'Thanks. I think.'

They waited another minute until Strickland hung up and said, 'Nobody home. You can park up.'

Clea steered the Explorer into forty-three's space and killed the engine. 'Do you need me to come in with you?'

Bishop shook his head. 'It's not necessary. You can wait here if you want.'

She thought for a moment, then said, 'No, I'll come in with you. I could really do with a drink of water. I'm parched.'

At the main entrance they were greeted by a set of tinted glass doors. Strickland went over and keyed in a six-digit code on the security keypad affixed to the wall. There was an electronic click and then he pulled one of the doors open and they all went inside.

The lobby was a long, narrow, tiled area with a row of mailboxes on one side and a large noticeboard and a few community posters on the wall opposite. It looked spotless. The whole place smelled pleasantly of floor polish and carpet cleaner. There was an open stairwell on the right, and Bishop could make out a fire exit at the end. Halfway down, there were hallways leading off from the left and right.

'Where do you keep this spare key?' Bishop asked.

'In the laundry room.' Strickland said. 'It's this way.'

He led them to the left-hand corridor and entered the first opening on the right. Bishop paused to study the hallway beyond. It was well lit and stretched off into the distance with numerous apartments on each side. Bishop turned the other way and saw the hallway opposite was identical. There was nobody else around. He followed Strickland into the laundry room, a long, narrow, tiled room with a long concrete bench running down the centre. It was also empty of people. There were two rows of heavy-duty washing machines running along the left-hand wall. Running along the opposite wall were a dozen dryers.

Strickland pulled out Barney's multi-tool and extracted the flat-edge screwdriver. Then he walked over to the fifth dryer down, reached down to the back of the machine and began working on something there. A minute later he came back holding a key.

'As advertised,' he said. 'The apartment we want is this way.'

Strickland led the way out of the laundry room and turned right. The three of them carried on down the hallway, passing a number of heavy oak doors, each one identified by a silver embossed number. Up ahead an overweight, grey-haired businessman with a briefcase exited an apartment on the left and began walking quickly towards them, as though late for a meeting. He nodded amiably as he rushed past and Bishop absently nodded back, watching him until he disappeared round the corner. Finally, Strickland stopped outside number twenty-two on the right-hand side. He inserted the key into the lock and paused for a moment.

'Something wrong?' Bishop asked.

Strickland shook his head, opened the door and stepped inside.

Bishop and Clea followed, entering a short hallway with two closed doors on the left, two on the right, and one more at the end. The one at the end was partly ajar, and Bishop could see part of what seemed to be the living room beyond. It was hard to tell because the drapes were drawn. Bishop gently closed the front door behind them and frowned when he sniffed the air. 'I smell stale food,' he said.

'I was just about to say that,' Clea said. 'It smells like old pizza.'

Strickland paused just before the last door on the right and nodded. 'Maybe Nicky had to leave in a rush and left the dishes for later.'

Bishop didn't think that was it. Something didn't feel right here. As Strickland opened the last door, Bishop moved his left hand towards the Glock in his rear waistband.

'Oh, shit,' Strickland said, and halted in his tracks as he stared at something in the room beyond.

Bishop's fingers were actually brushing the Glock's handle when the door to his left was suddenly yanked open. Clea gave a short shriek of alarm as a stocky Latino man with small hard eyes appeared in the doorway, aiming a large revolver directly at Bishop's head. At the same time, the door to his immediate right was pulled open and Bishop saw another Latino, burly, shaven-headed, standing there holding a .45 automatic. He raised the barrel until it was pointing midway between Clea and Bishop.

'*Alto,*' this one said.

Bishop's limited Spanish was rusty, but that one was obvious. 'Nobody make any sudden moves,' he said, raising his own hands.

Clea turned to him with wide eyes, and then raised hers as well. Strickland already had his hands up and was being urged back into the hallway by a third armed man.

A fourth man emerged from the main living area and stood at the end of the hallway, watching them all. He was clearly the man in charge here. He had slicked-back hair and stubble covered the lower part of his face. He was also holding what looked to be a very large Desert Eagle 9mm at his side.

'See, Ramon?' he said to the man watching Strickland. 'Didn't I tell you today was our lucky day?'

FORTY-EIGHT

Nice to know it's somebody's, Bishop thought as the Glock was plucked from his waistband.

'Anybody else got weapons on them?' the man with the stubble said, with barely any trace of an accent. 'If you lie, we'll know.'

'Just me,' Bishop said.

'Okay, bring them all in here,' Stubble said, and went back into the living room, turning on the lights as he went. Strickland and his guardian followed him. Bishop felt something hard prod him in the spine and he started walking with Clea, their two shadows following close behind. But not too close. They weren't stupid.

'What do we do?' Clea asked, her voice almost breaking.

'Whatever they tell us to do,' Bishop said. 'We don't have any other choice.'

'I'm scared.'

'I know.'

They entered a large, sparsely decorated living room that contained two small couches, an easy chair, a large wooden coffee table, and a flatscreen TV affixed to one wall. It was currently turned off. Bishop saw old pizza boxes strewn all over the floor, some containing partly eaten food. The coffee table also held a sizable amount of empty beer bottles and cans. There wasn't too much mess, though, suggesting they hadn't been there long. He also detected a vague scent of marijuana in the air, faint like an old memory, but there were no ashtrays in sight. They'd probably smoked out on the balcony so as not to completely stink the place out.

'Everybody face the wall,' Stubble said. 'And keep those hands up.'

Bishop did as he was told and placed his palms against the wall.

219

They all did. He felt himself being expertly patted down by his watcher, who eventually said, 'Clean, Geraldo.'

The one checking Strickland said, '*Mismo.*'

'Hey, *watch* it,' Clea said.

The fourth man chuckled and said, '*Nada*, Geraldo.'

Strickland turned his face from the wall and said, 'Look, who the hell *are* you people? You're not cops, I know that. But I don't—'

'Shut your mouth, *pendejo*,' Geraldo said, 'or I'll do it for you. Now all of you turn round and face me.'

Bishop turned and looked at the man with the stubble, Geraldo. He already had a pretty good idea who they were. So would Strickland once he'd thought it through. He just couldn't figure out the why yet.

'Now sit on the floor,' Geraldo said.

Bishop lowered himself to the floor and sat with his legs crossed. The other two did the same.

'Watch them,' Geraldo said, and walked out into the hallway. Bishop looked around and saw the first man – the stocky one with small hard eyes – was standing next to the draped windows, while another stood against the opposite wall. The third was somewhere behind them. Bishop sighed. They were clearly professionals, automatically spacing themselves out at three of the compass points for maximum cover.

'My fault,' Strickland said quietly, shaking his head. 'I should have known.'

Bishop turned to him, remembering his pause just before turning the key in the lock. 'You heard something at the front door.'

'No, but I thought I saw some scratches around the lock. I should have known.'

'Water under the bridge now.'

The guard behind prodded Strickland with his boot and said, '¡*Cierra la boca!*'

The man by the window chuckled. 'That's Felipe telling you nicely to shut your mouths. I do what he says if I was you. He got a bad temper.'

A few seconds later, Geraldo returned holding a black holdall. He placed the bag on the coffee table and used one hand to casually sweep the empty beer bottles and cans onto the carpet. Then he pulled out a metallic grey laptop from the bag and set it down on the table, along with a smartphone and a small webcam. He moved the easy chair closer to the table and sat down and opened the laptop. He was partly side-on to Bishop, so Bishop was able to see a condensed, distorted view of the screen.

'What's happening now?' Clea whispered at Bishop's side.

Geraldo was moving his index finger across the trackpad as he activated a program.

'Probably calling his boss,' Bishop whispered back.

'You mean Hartnell?'

'No, not Hartnell. Worse.'

'What could *be* worse?'

There's always something worse, he thought, but said nothing. It wouldn't help matters.

Another display screen opened up and Geraldo keyed in a password. Probably Skype, or a more secure variation of the same. There was a sharp ringing tone, which lasted for about thirty seconds, then it stopped and Bishop saw a face appear on the screen as the person he was calling answered. Geraldo repositioned the webcam until he was satisfied and started speaking rapid Spanish, ending almost every other sentence with a *jefe*. The man at the other end said nothing for the most part, just listened.

Finally he said a few words in a low, guttural voice. Geraldo said, '*Momento, jefe*,' and turned the webcam round until it was facing the three captives. He also repositioned the laptop so they could all see the man onscreen clearly. Bishop saw a fairly handsome, dark-skinned man in his mid- to late fifties. He had heavy jowls and his thick black hair was greying at the temples, just like it was supposed to. He was wearing a white shirt open at the neck. He looked like a benevolent uncle, except Bishop knew better.

'Oh, shit,' Strickland whispered.

Bishop had to agree. Although he'd never seen that face in his life before, he knew without a doubt that he was now looking at Hartnell's partner, Rafael Guzman.

FORTY-NINE

On the screen, only the man's eyes moved as he took in the three captives. Then he gave a single nod of his head and said, '*Bueno*. It is him. Good work, Geraldo.'

'*Gracias, jefe.*'

'English for our guest, I think.'

'Whatever you say, boss.'

'And how are you, Señor Strickland?' the man on the screen asked. 'You look healthy enough.'

Strickland kept his gaze on the floor and shook his head slowly from side to side, muttering, 'Oh, this is bad, this is *so* bad.'

'Yes, I suppose it is.' The man's eyes shifted and he said, 'As for these other two, I recognize the man from the news, but who is this woman?'

Geraldo turned to Clea. 'Tell the boss who you are.'

She swallowed and said, 'My name . . . My name's Clea Buchanan. I . . . I own a craft shop in north Colorado. These two men . . . they came into my shop yesterday and took my car and forced me to go with them. I don't have anything to do with this. I didn't even know this man's name was Strickland until just now.'

'Yes, yes, very interesting.' Guzman's eyes became hooded. 'Geraldo, I do not understand why these two are still breathing. Señor Strickland is the only one I want.'

'I know, *jefe*, but you didn't give me specific orders about what to do if he had people with him. And I didn't want to do something I might regret later.'

The older man's lips slowly transformed into a smile. 'Good, Geraldo. I approve of this kind of thinking. And now you mention it, I *do* have some questions I want to ask them.'

'I've got a few I'd like to ask you, too,' Bishop said.

Without warning, something hard suddenly connected with the back of Bishop's neck. He toppled over, putting a hand out to stop his head hitting the floor while he pressed his other hand to his neck. It was already throbbing in pain.

'Talk when the boss asks you something,' Geraldo said. 'Not before.'

'Why, what's he afraid of?'

Bishop expected more pain for that one, but the man on the screen said, 'Wait, let him speak. Señor, you are either very brave or very stupid. Which is it?'

'Since I've got four guns aimed at my head, probably the second one.' Bishop sat up again. 'You are *the* Rafael Guzman, I take it?'

'You have heard of me?'

'Word gets around, Señor Guzman, even in my circles. I have to say I'm curious as to how you even knew about this place.'

Guzman smiled. 'Curiosity. Now that is a quality I value. It is because I am *also* a curious man that I have remained in my current position for so long, while the more ignorant have fallen by the wayside, bleeding, often begging for their lives. Do you understand?'

'Sure. Information is power, especially in your business.'

'Exactly. And over the years I have collected a great deal of information on associates and competitors, as well as people close to them. I believe you can never know too much about anybody. As for Señor Strickland here, a few years back I simply had one of my people compile a complete dossier on him, just as I have done with many others in Hartnell's employ. Such a simple little strategy, yet you would be amazed at the kind of results it can produce. I am surprised those in my position don't do it more.'

'Maybe they don't have your kind of unlimited manpower.'

Guzman tilted his head as though this thought had never occurred to him, although Bishop was sure it had. 'Perhaps. In any event, I soon learned of this long-term friendship with his little friend from high school and filed the information away for possible future use. Once I learned of Strickland's escape with you yesterday I decided to post some of my men at that apartment in case he decided to drop by. It seems my instincts were correct. And now you will answer some questions for me.'

'Seems only fair,' Bishop said.

'Firstly, am I correct in assuming your name is James Bishop?'

Bishop frowned. 'How'd you know that?'

'My sources are everywhere. Now why *did* you come to this apartment, Señor Bishop?'

'We're running low on gas, Strickland and I don't have any money, and Clea here's down to her last twenty. And we can't use her credit cards for obvious reasons. So Strickland told me about this old pal of his and said he might be able to supply us with enough to send us on our way. Instead, we ran into your boys here.'

Guzman was silent for a few moments, thinking. Then he said. 'Next question. From the photo I saw on the news, it appeared as though Strickland's son also escaped with you, yes?'

'That's right.'

'So where is he?'

'He's currently in the hands of your business partner, Felix Hartnell.'

Guzman sighed. 'Geraldo. *Barriga.*'

'Yes, boss.' Geraldo got up, took a few steps towards Bishop and kicked him in the belly with everything he had.

It felt like somebody had just pitched a four-seam fastball straight at him. Bishop let out a whoosh of air and doubled over at the sudden flaring agony, clamping both arms around what was left of his stomach. He wheezed and hacked as he tried to take in more oxygen, and it took him about thirty seconds before the pain lessened enough that he was able to breathe more like a human being.

Clea was looking at him with wide eyes. He shook his head at her, hoping she wouldn't ask if he was all right. She was supposed to be their unwilling hostage. He looked up and saw Geraldo had already sat back down and was watching the laptop screen, where Guzman was watching the scene with mild interest.

'Listen to me very carefully, Señor Bishop,' he said. 'I do not have, and never have had, a business partner of any kind. I have only associates with whom I do business, that is all. Do you understand the difference?'

'I do now,' Bishop said, wincing. 'You make your point very convincingly.'

'I find it saves time. Now you were saying, about the boy . . .'

Bishop took a few more deep breaths, and when he felt he was more in control of himself he said, 'Two of Hartnell's men ambushed the three of us yesterday morning outside Vegas. There was gunfire, Strickland's son panicked in the confusion and they grabbed him and took off. Later on, Hartnell's man – Callaway – called and said the boy dies unless we get to Ohio by tomorrow before dawn and hand Strickland over instead.'

Guzman raised a single eyebrow. 'Ah, things begin to fall into place now. And if you go to the police . . .?'

'Hartnell will find out, and he'll kill the boy. He'll probably wait until the trial's dismissed, but he'll still do it. There's no reason for him not to.'

Guzman nodded. 'Yes, of course he will. But I still do not understand. You are clearly not a member of the law enforcement community, so why does any of this concern you?'

'I made a promise that I'd keep the boy safe.'

'I see. And do you always keep your promises?'

'If I can. It's what separates us from the animals, after all.'

Guzman nodded in approval. 'We have something in common then.'

'In that case, you mind if I ask you another question? Or do I risk getting another kick in the stomach?'

Guzman's smile returned. He seemed to be enjoying himself. 'Everything in life is a risk, as you know. Ask your question.'

'Well, it's pretty obvious why Hartnell wants Strickland, but I don't get *your* interest in him. Mind enlightening me?'

Guzman tilted his head a little. 'It is very simple. Hartnell is an important business associate of mine. If he is convicted my organization will be forced to seek other outlets for its product. That takes much time and effort. Also, buyers for my product are often unreliable when it comes to payment. In my business, I stick to what works and make changes only if I have no other choice. And the system Hartnell and I have developed over the years works. Also, with Strickland now in my possession, my negotiating power with Hartnell instantly increases by the power of ten. So as you can see, by keeping Hartnell out of jail I am simply looking out for my best interests. And all with the very minimum of effort.

'Unfortunately for you,' he continued, 'my interest is *only* in Strickland here. I have enjoyed this chat, but I'm afraid you and the woman are now surplus to requirements.'

Geraldo slowly got to his feet and said, 'Orders, boss?'

'Yes,' Guzman said. 'Finish them both.'

FIFTY

Clea began to cry. Strickland kept his gaze on the floor and said nothing. Bishop thought furiously as he watched Geraldo take the huge Desert Eagle from under his jacket and pull back the slide. The noise echoed loudly throughout the room. Bishop knew they only had seconds left, but he also knew there had to be a way out of this. *Had* to be.

He quickly went over the main parts of the conversation in the diner this morning, when Strickland had been talking about Guzman, and decided there *was* a possibility there. Just a very tiny spark of something, but would it be enough?

'Please,' Clea said, wrapping her arms round herself. 'I've done nothing to you people. God, I just work in a *shop*.'

'It was just your bad luck to get involved, lady,' Geraldo said. 'But I'll make it quick.' He slowly raised the gun and aimed it at her head.

'Don't we get a last request?' Bishop said.

'Wait, Geraldo,' Guzman said, holding up a hand. Geraldo lowered the gun. 'And what do you want, Señor Bishop? A cigarette, maybe? A shot of whiskey? What?'

'Just some answers to a few questions.'

Guzman frowned. 'And what difference will the answers make to you, knowing what will happen afterwards?'

'Maybe no difference at all, but I think I can offer you some food for thought. Why not indulge me? Other than a few minutes of your time, what have you got to lose?'

After a short pause, Guzman said, 'Very well. Talk.'

'Okay, you said you're doing all this to protect your business interests, to keep the whole operation running smoothly, as well as to increase your bargaining power with Hartnell. But that's not the *only* reason, is it?'

Guzman raised an eyebrow. 'Is that a question?'

'Just a rhetorical one. The thing is, I know the media paint all you cartel boys as bloodthirsty psychos and maybe a good percentage of you are, but I've also met enough of your countrymen to know personal debts carry a lot of weight in your part of the world. You people are big believers in honour and paying off obligations, all that stuff. Which is something I can relate to.'

'So?'

'So, it's my opinion that there's also a personal element to your involvement here, over and above the business reasons. To be more specific, I think you're doing all this as a way to pay off an old obligation to Hartnell.'

Silence from Guzman, whose face remained impassive. Geraldo was looking at Bishop open-mouthed, as though he couldn't quite believe what he was hearing. The other three guards just stood still, mutely watching everything, waiting for the word.

Finally, Guzman said, 'Go on.'

Bishop continued, choosing his words with great care. 'Okay. Now Strickland told me about how a rival cartel grabbed your sister a decade ago, and what they did to her. He also told me how Hartnell helped you track her down. And when that ended badly, how he then brought those responsible right to your door so you could deal with them in your own way. Have I got the general gist of things or am I totally off the mark?'

Guzman's eyes were now two dark marbles. 'I'm still listening.'

'Now the way I figure it, an act like that from a business associate would surely leave a large impression on an honourable man. And it's just possible that if the opportunity ever presented itself, this man would then want to try and pay that associate back in kind. If he could.'

'Such as handing him the source of all his current troubles, for example?'

'It's possible, don't you think?'

'I think you are seriously mistaken if you believe there is room for *any* kind of sentiment in my business. And even if you *were* right, what is your point?'

'My point is, if that is the case then I think you're doing it for the wrong reasons, because I don't think you actually owe Hartnell any favours at all. In fact, I think Hartnell knew a hell of a lot more about your sister's initial kidnapping than he claimed.'

There was silence in the room. Everybody waited to see how Guzman would react, Bishop most of all.

After a few moments, Guzman said, 'You will now explain yourself, Señor Bishop. And if I suspect that you are wasting time in order to delay the inevitable for a few extra seconds, then I will make sure your death is very slow and very, very painful.'

Bishop tried not to think about that part. He went on, 'Okay, do you remember an accountant of Hartnell's called Paul Mechner? He left under a cloud about ten years ago.'

Guzman frowned. 'Mechner. Yes, I remember this name. According to my informants he stole some money from Hartnell and then tried to disappear.'

'That's him. And the way he tried to disappear was by arranging new identities for himself and his wife. So, conscious of the fact that Hartnell would undoubtedly be scouring the earth for him, Mechner decided to approach the country's number one private security company, RoyseCorp, to keep them safe while they waited for the finished documents. And if you know as much about me as I think you do, then you'll know I worked for RoyseCorp around that time.'

Guzman nodded. 'Yes, I know this. And you were part of his protection team?'

'I was in charge of it. And over the following weeks I got to know Mechner pretty well, and one time he let slip that he had something on his old employer that if it ever got out would cause serious trouble for the man. And not legal trouble, either.'

'What, then?' Guzman said.

'He told me it was an audio cassette tape,' Bishop said, 'and that on this tape, Hartnell was boasting about how he manipulated his business partner over a personal matter. He also said this tape was safely locked away and he'd use it only as a last resort. Now after Hartnell found us and made a failed attempt on Mechner's life I managed to convince him to forget about running and go to the feds instead, which he did. Yet Hartnell still got to him somehow, and so it appeared that Mechner's secret tape ultimately died with him.'

Guzman shrugged. 'All very interesting, but what is this to me?'

Bishop swallowed. This was it. The moment of truth. Except this part was all a bluff, based on a throwaway comment by a dead man ten years ago. Still, Mechner wouldn't have mentioned it if it hadn't existed. He had an accountant's logical mind, and wasn't prone to flights of the imagination. But none of it changed the fact that Bishop was grasping at straws here. If he blew it now they'd all be dead, without question.

'I don't think Mechner's secret *did* die with him,' he said. 'I think whatever he had on Hartnell is still out there, and moreover I think it relates directly to you and your sister.'

Guzman pursed his lips. 'You are implying Hartnell had something to do with Luiza being taken from my compound?'

'That's what I'm implying. I mean, I don't know too many of the details, but when Strickland told me about it, it did strike me as odd that Hartnell could send a bunch of his own people down to Mexico and then *some*how they manage to find Luiza's location. Whereas you know the country back to front and yet you couldn't find one clue as to her whereabouts. I mean, what are the chances?'

Guzman gave a patient smile, as though Bishop were a child. 'Do you not think that this thought occurred to me also? I am a suspicious man, Señor Bishop, and I had the same doubts concerning Hartnell's motives, but I conducted my own long investigation into the matter and finally came away satisfied. And I am not an easily satisfied man. As you say, you do not know all of the details, but I can tell you that Hartnell's men were only *partially* responsible for locating Luiza. Besides, they were all working under my direct supervision anyway.'

'Are you absolutely sure about that? I mean, you couldn't be everywhere at once, could you? What if one of Hartnell's men already knew without a doubt where Luiza was, and simply laid down a few hints to direct the search into that area? Maybe all it took was one whispered remark to one of your men. We both know it doesn't take much for an idea or a rumour to steadily work its way up the ladder until nobody's sure where it originated from.'

Guzman sighed. 'All I am hearing so far are fanciful theories, Señor Bishop, and my patience is nearing its end. Besides, even if I took you seriously, which I do not, what would Hartnell's motive be for taking Luiza?'

'Well, Strickland also told me about some rumours going round that you might have been planning to take over Hartnell's side of the operation before all this. Is there any truth to that?'

Guzman shrugged and said nothing.

'I'll take that as a maybe,' Bishop said. 'In which case, I think Hartnell decided to get proactive in order to get you on his good side and demonstrate what a worthy friend he could be in a scrape. I'd say helping you find your missing sister and then delivering her supposed murderers right to your door would certainly have helped his case rather than hindered it. Wouldn't you?'

Guzman's eyes gave nothing away. 'Your point?'

'Okay. I think this cassette of Mechner's is actual proof of Hartnell's direct involvement in the kidnapping and murder of your sister.'

'And?'

'And I propose that I go out and get it for you,' Bishop said. 'Right now.'

FIFTY-ONE

Guzman's smile slowly returned. Bishop wasn't sure if that was a good thing or not. Probably not. The cartel boss said, 'And this so-called proof. You know where it is located.'

'Not exactly,' Bishop said, 'but I believe it's close at hand. I've got some ideas.'

Bishop knew if it wasn't close by then it was all pointless anyway. They were all dead. But he didn't voice that thought. He was already walking a tightrope as it was, and the slightest gust of wind could send him plummeting.

'You have some ideas,' Guzman said without inflection. 'And if you *do* find this mysterious cassette and bring it to me, and it *is* as you say, what then?'

'Then you free us and let us go on our way, unharmed.'

'All three of you.'

'In this case it has to be all or nothing.'

'And if I agree to this you will trust me to keep my end of the bargain? Strickland is a very valuable commodity, after all.'

Bishop shrugged. 'I think you're a man who once he gives his word, keeps it. I hope you are. Besides, what other choice do I have?'

'None.'

'Exactly. Simplifies things from my end, doesn't it? So what do you think? Do we have a deal?'

After a few moments, Guzman said, 'And if this evidence is not close by? I can be a patient man, but my patience has its limits.'

'If it's not close by then I'm screwed. I know that. But one way or another I have to get Strickland to Ohio by tomorrow morning to have any chance of getting his son back alive, and right now this is my only chance to do that.'

Guzman was silent as he considered. Their lives were completely in his hands now. Bishop turned and saw Clea next to him, eyes closed and biting her lip as she rocked back and forth. Further along, Strickland was watching the laptop screen intently.

Bishop refused to think about Guzman turning him down. That line of thought was pointless. Instead, he contemplated his next step in tracking down Mechner's evidence – assuming it had anything to do with Guzman at all, of course. But he couldn't worry about that now. He'd have to make a phone call first. There was a man he'd used before who might be able to help. Bishop concentrated until he was gradually able to recall the guy's phone number, then he quickly turned his thoughts to the Mechners. And Emily Mechner in particular. He thought back to every conversation he'd had with her, recalling every detail she'd given him about herself.

Guzman's voice suddenly pulled him back to the present. 'Geraldo, what is the time there?'

'Eight twenty-five, *jefe*.'

'Very well,' Guzman said. 'My curiosity has been aroused by your story, Bishop. I have decided to grant you a reprieve. You will locate this tape for me.'

Bishop let out a long breath. Clea finally stopped rocking back and forth.

'But you have until one o'clock to produce results.' Guzman continued. 'That is less than five hours from now. And if they are not forthcoming by that time, then I will have no further need for you or the woman. Do you understand?'

'Perfectly.'

'Also, one of my men will also accompany you at all times.' Geraldo sat up straighter at this, but Guzman said, 'No, Geraldo, you are to stay there and watch over Strickland and the woman. Who else amongst your team speaks English?'

'Dario's English is as good as mine,' Geraldo said.

'And which one is he?'

'The man by the window.'

Bishop turned to the stocky man with the small, hard eyes who'd first greeted them on their arrival. Dario, knowing that he was under the scrutiny of the most powerful man in his world, was practically standing at attention.

'Dario, you will go with him,' Guzman said. 'You will not let him out of your sight. You will also call Geraldo at thirty-minute intervals and give him progress reports. Do you understand?'

'*Si, jefe*,' Dario said, 'I understand.'

'You are wasting time, Bishop,' said Guzman. 'I suggest you get started.'

Bishop said, 'I have to make a call first.'

'Then make it.'

Bishop turned to Clea. 'I'll need your cell phone again.'

Clea quickly nodded and reached into her jeans pocket for the cell he'd handed her in the parking lot. Bishop took it and keyed in a Brooklyn number. He brought the phone to his ear and listened to it ring. And ring. And ring.

Finally, the ringing stopped and a familiar voice said, 'Muro Investigations.'

'No names,' Bishop said. 'Do you remember a short while back when I hired you to watch over my sister for a few days? She was on life support at the time.'

There was a short pause. Then Scott Muro said, 'I remember. And I'd say you're in one hell of a spot right now.'

'You don't know the half of it. Look, I'm currently in a situation where I need somebody found fast, and your name immediately came to mind. Can you help?'

'What, I'm a charity now?'

'I'll pay you for your time. You know I'm good for it.'

'That kind of depends if you're still around or not, if you know what I mean.'

'So take a chance.'

'How fast would you want it?'

'Put it this way, I'll be waiting here on the line while you do your thing.'

There was a sigh at the other end. 'Okay, tell me what you need.'

'I need contact information for a lady whose married name was Emily Mechner. Her husband, Paul, died almost ten years ago so

234

there's a good chance she's either remarried since then or reverted to her maiden name, which was Landry. By my calculation she'd be forty-eight years old now. I was never given her exact date of birth.'

'Okay. What else you got?'

'Not much. I know her folks originally came from a place called Duncan, Oklahoma, so there's a chance she did too. That's about it. A phone number for her would be great. Anything on top of that is gravy.'

'Well, I've worked with less, but then I was usually given more time to play with.'

'In this case seconds count. And keep me on the line while you work, okay?'

'Sure, but I'll have to mute the phone. I got sources I need to protect.'

'Understood,' Bishop said. 'So don't waste any more time talking to me.'

There was a short bark of laughter, then the line went silent. Bishop took the phone from his ear, pressed the loudspeaker button and placed it on the floor. On the laptop screen, Rafael Guzman was currently distracted by something. Bishop saw part of one of those iPad tablet things come into shot for a second, then disappear. The guy was probably working out how many millions he'd made since he started this conversation. Nobody else spoke.

Bishop counted the seconds and tried not to think about the possibility of Muro not coming up with anything. For all he knew, Emily Mechner could have emigrated to Australia or moved to the South Pacific after her husband's murder. Unlikely, but not beyond the realms of possibility. She might even have died of natural causes. In fact, almost anything could have happened to her during the past ten years, thus making further conjecture pointless. And since there was even less point in formulating a plan without more information than he already had, Bishop just kept counting the seconds.

Five hundred and twenty-six of them had passed when from the cell phone a tinny voice said, 'You still there?'

Bishop grabbed the phone, deactivated the speaker and raised it to his ear. 'I'm here. Find anything?'

'I found out our Emily's no longer a Mechner or a Landry, but a Rylander.'

Bishop smiled. 'Tell me more.'

'Okay. She got married seven years ago in OK City to a commercial artist named Christopher Rylander, who's a widower himself with a son and daughter who'll both be teenagers now. Anyway, I got not only a number for you, but an address too. So on a scale on one to ten, just how good am I?'

'You're off the scale. So where are they now? Still in Oklahoma City?'

'No, they moved away about five years ago, but they're still in the same state. Some place called Okmulgee. You ever heard of it?'

'No, but that doesn't mean anything. You say you have an address for me?'

'Yeah, they're living at 924 South Walker Avenue.' He also reeled off a phone number and said, 'Now that's just a landline, okay? But I learned that this Christopher is now a freelancer who works from home, so you should be all right. I could probably get you their cell phone numbers too, but that takes more time.'

'Which I don't have.'

'Which is what I thought.'

'Thanks,' Bishop said. 'You really came through for me. I won't forget it.'

'I won't let you,' Muro said, and ended the call.

Bishop keyed in the number he'd been given and brought the phone to his ear again. After about thirty seconds, the phone was answered and a gruff male voice said, 'Hello?'

'Hello, is that Mr Christopher Rylander?'

'It is. Who am I speaking to?'

'Somebody who was a friend of your wife's first husband, Paul. Would it be possible to speak to Mrs Rylander, please?'

'Well, Emily's not here right now.'

'Any idea when she'll be back? It's very important that I speak with her.'

'So important that you can't give me your name?'

'I'm afraid so. For a number of reasons, I really can't say too much

236

on an open line, Mr Rylander. Let me ask you a question instead – has your wife told you anything about the conditions under which her first husband died?'

Silence.

'Mr Rylander?' Bishop prompted.

'Emily told me,' Rylander said. 'What part did you play in that?'

'I was one of the men who helped keep them both safe until the feds took over and . . . well, the rest happened.'

'What, like a private bodyguard, you mean?'

'That's right. But right now I need to talk to Mrs Rylander about something Paul left behind, and it's very important. Does she have a cell phone number I can call?'

'She does, but it won't do you any good.'

'Why not?'

'Because I'm looking at her phone right now. Seems she forgot it again.'

Bishop sighed. As if things weren't already difficult enough. 'Will she be back soon?'

'Well, she's gone to the store. She should be back by nine, but I can't guarantee it.'

'Okay,' Bishop said, 'now I see from the phone book that you live in Okmulgee. So would it be all right to come over and speak with Mrs Rylander in person?'

More silence on the line. Then, 'Well, I don't know. Where are you now?'

Bishop wasn't about to give his real location over an open line, but he had to give the guy something. And somewhere fairly close. 'Oklahoma City,' he said.

'That's about a hundred miles west of us. You sure you want to make that kind of trip?'

'It's worth it to me.'

Another pause. 'Well, if you think it's necessary, I guess you better come on out.'

Bishop breathed out. 'I'm much obliged, Mr Rylander. I'm starting off now, so I'll see you both soon.' He ended the call before the guy could change his mind, and handed the phone back to Clea. 'Geraldo, check on Google Maps for me and see where Okmulgee is in relation to us.'

Geraldo stiffened in the chair. 'I don't take orders from you, *pendejo.*'

'But you take them from me,' Guzman said calmly. 'Do as he asks.'

'*Si, jefe.*' Geraldo immediately pulled a smartphone from his jacket pocket and swiped a finger over the screen. 'Spell this place for me.'

Bishop spelled out the name of the town and Geraldo continued to move his fingers over the phone for another thirty seconds. Finally he said, 'Okay. It's about fifty miles south of here, on Route 75.'

Meaning it was less than an hour's drive away. Finally, a break. Bishop turned to Dario standing by the drapes and said, 'So which one of us is driving?'

FIFTY-TWO

Bishop drove.

They were using the gang's own vehicle, the grey panel van parked in bay forty-four. The landscaping logo on the side was also great cover. Dario sat in the passenger seat with his .38 resting on his lap, chewing gum while watching Bishop's every move. Neither man had much to say to the other. Other than a brief call to update Geraldo, the journey was spent mostly in silence, which was fine with Bishop.

The highway was essentially a straight line from north to south, with little in the way of variation, or traffic, for that matter. But there were no roadblocks, either. In fact, no sign of any police presence at all.

They reached Okmulgee at 9.12. The town wasn't much to look at, at least not on the outskirts, with one-storey shacks scattered along the highway in seemingly random fashion. But things started to look a little more affluent once they entered the downtown area, and Dario, acting as navigator with the aid of his cell phone and Google Maps, gave Bishop directions until they found the street they wanted.

South Walker Avenue was a quiet, tree-lined, suburban road with large houses lining both sides, all set well back from the road. 924 had a distinct Spanish hacienda look, with barrel-tiled roofing and a covered front porch set behind four stone pillars. The front yard was large, with well-tended grass that looked as though it had been cut recently. Bishop also spotted two cars in the driveway: a blue Toyota Corolla and a black Chevy Malibu. He could only hope one of them belonged to Emily Rylander.

Steering the van into the driveway, he stopped a few feet behind the Toyota, killed the engine and turned to Dario. 'You better wait here while I talk to them.'

Dario stopped chewing his gum. 'You think I'm *stupido,* asshole? You heard the main man back there. Where you go, I go. So let's go.' He reached for the door handle.

'Put the gun away first,' Bishop said.

Dario paused and looked at him. 'You telling me what to do now?'

'Look around you, Dario. We're in a nice working-class suburban neighbourhood in the heart of the Midwest, full of housewives on constant lookout for anything that doesn't fit into their comfy little world. And I guarantee one of those housewives is watching this van right now, wondering why the Rylanders have decided to get some landscaping done all of a sudden. The moment they see you with a gun at your side they'll be dialling 911. Then you'll end up trying to explain to your boss why you screwed everything up while his men calmly pull your intestines out and feed them to the rats. That what you want?'

Dario didn't look quite so sure of himself anymore. He'd know better than anyone what Guzman was really capable of. Maybe he'd even taken part in similar interrogations himself. Finally, he holstered the gun and buttoned up his leather jacket. 'Screw with me and you're dead, *comprendes?*'

Bishop opened the door and got out. 'Just let me do all the talking. The last thing we want to do is scare these people.'

'You do your job, man,' Dario said, getting out his side. 'I do mine.'

They both mounted the steps to the porch and Bishop pressed the door buzzer. Dario scanned the neighbourhood behind them while Bishop just faced front and waited.

He soon heard approaching footsteps and when the door opened he found himself looking up at a very tall, somewhat familiar-looking man, dressed in a sweatshirt and tan chinos. For a brief moment Bishop thought it was his old principal, Paul Mechner, staring back at him, but the feeling of recognition faded almost as soon as it arrived. There were some facial similarities between the two, but they were very faint. Also, this man was at least six-four whereas Mechner had only been five-eleven. He wore rimless glasses and his receding grey hair was cropped close to his head. Bishop guessed his age at some-where in the mid-fifties. He was frowning at the two men on his porch, and Bishop hoped it wasn't because he recognized one of them from the news.

'Morning, Mr Rylander,' Bishop said. 'I'm the one who called you earlier. This is my . . . associate. Is your wife back yet?'

'She's back.' The man's voice was somewhat deeper in real life. He opened the door wider and said, 'Well, I guess you better come in.'

'Thanks.'

Bishop entered a wide hallway with doors leading off both sides. Further down on the left was a staircase, and at the end of the hallway he could see a door leading to a large kitchen area. Rylander led them both to the kitchen, which was modern and spacious and overlooked a large backyard. Emily Rylander, a slim, handsome woman wearing faded jeans and a dark pullover, was currently at the large industrial-sized refrigerator, placing a covered dish onto one of the shelves.

'Em,' Rylander called out, and his wife shut the refrigerator and turned to them.

Her eyes widened. 'Bishop,' she said. 'So it *was* you. I wasn't sure.'

'Good to see you again, Emily,' he said. 'You look well.' In fact, she appeared to be the same age as when he'd last seen her. A few extra lines around the eyes, maybe, but still a great advertisement for healthy living.

'And you do realize you're all over the news, don't you? You shouldn't have come here, Bishop. You really shouldn't.'

'Wait a minute,' Rylander said. 'This is *that* guy? The one from the photo that everybody's chasing after? *Jesus*, Em.'

'Relax, Chris,' she said. 'I told you I didn't believe what they were saying about him, and I still think that.' She went over and sat at the small kitchen table. 'But he isn't exaggerating either, Bishop. You're in a world of trouble right now.'

'Oh, it's even worse than you can imagine.'

She looked from Bishop to Dario, then back again. 'What do you mean?'

Without mentioning names, Bishop quickly summarized recent events, including Barney's kidnapping, and explained his mission to get Strickland to Ohio before dawn for the swap. 'Except there's now a new complication. The guy standing next to me represents a third party who wants the witness for his own reasons, and who's currently holding him at an apartment not too far away. But the only way I can get the witness back, and in so doing get his son back, is to exchange him for something this third party wants even more. Hence my presence here.'

'I don't understand,' Emily said. 'What on earth could I have that anybody would want?'

Bishop took a seat next to her and said, 'Okay, Paul told me one time that he'd hidden away an audio cassette tape that could cause Hartnell a lot of trouble if it ever got out. And I'm pretty sure Paul never got a chance to use it or we'd have heard about it long before now, so I figure it's still out there somewhere. Now did Paul ever mention anything about it to you?'

Emily was already shaking her head before he'd even finished. 'Never,' she said, tapping her fingernails against the tabletop for emphasis. 'Paul never once said anything about that to me. I'm absolutely sure of it. Maybe he was just kidding you around?'

'That wasn't really his style, was it?'

She smiled. 'You're right. Strike that last comment from the record?'

'Done. What about Paul's possessions? Did you keep anything of his after his death? Anything at all?'

'Well, as you know, we didn't really take much with us.' Emily thought for a moment. 'I think I *may* have put some of Paul's stuff in a box somewhere, but I can't really remember. A lot of that period after his death . . . well, a lot of it's just a blur, even now. But there were some things of his – or *ours*, I should say – that I would never have thrown away, so they'd have to be around somewhere.'

'Any idea where?'

She gave a shrug. 'Well, if it's still in the house there's only one place it can possibly be, and that's up in the attic.'

FIFTY-THREE

The attic entrance was a simple ceiling trapdoor located at the very end of the long L-shaped corridor on the second floor. Attached to the inner frame of the trapdoor was a set of aluminium folding stairs, now unfolded. The three men were all silently standing at the foot of the ladder while Emily rummaged around the attic up above. They'd been waiting for five minutes already.

Dario spent his time busily chewing his gum as loudly as possible, while Bishop stared up at the square hole in the ceiling and pondered his next step if Emily came up blank. There had to be an alternative, but he was currently having trouble thinking of one. And he was also acutely aware of the one o'clock deadline too, which further limited his options. If the worst came to the worst, all he could think to do was incapacitate Dario and grab his gun, and then head back to the apartment and somehow neutralize the other three gunmen without risking Strickland's and Clea's lives.

Sure. No problem. As easy as falling off a bridge.

Finally Emily called out, 'I think I found something.'

There was the sound of something being slid across a flat surface above them. The sound stopped and Emily appeared at the opening and climbed down the ladder. Once down, she said, 'I did find a box of our old stuff up there although I don't know how much good it'll be to you. There's not much of Paul in there. Chris, can you bring it down? I left it by the opening there.'

'Sure.' Rylander climbed a few steps and grabbed a medium-sized cardboard box and brought it down with him. Bishop saw a number of picture frames and LPs peeking out the open top, along with a pile of other stuff. Rylander handed it to him and said, 'You three go back to the kitchen while I close up here.'

Emily led the two men downstairs again. Back in the kitchen, Bishop placed the box on the table and pulled out the LPs first.

'Those albums are mostly mine, actually,' Emily said, taking a seat.

Bishop went through the record sleeves quickly and counted eighteen in all, mostly of the easy-listening variety. Tony Bennett, Dionne Warwick, Neil Diamond, that kind of thing, although there were also several John Coltrane and Charlie Mingus records in there too.

He pulled out the picture frames next. There were four of them, each containing a shot of husband and wife together. One was an old wedding photo. Two others looked as though they'd been taken on holiday. One was on a beach somewhere, while the other was on a boat harbour, possibly in Florida. In contrast, the last had been taken in a backyard on a grey overcast day when neither Paul nor Emily had been in much of a smiling mood.

So far, so useless.

Shaking his head, Bishop placed the pictures to the side and reached into the box again, hoping against all odds that there was something here that might give him a lead. *Any* lead. He pulled out half a dozen old John MacDonald paperbacks and a couple of hardcovers and placed them next to the LPs. Emily took one of the paperbacks and opened it to a random page while Bishop pulled out an old Kodak Retina Reflex camera and looked it over. A quick check revealed there was no film inside. There were also some souvenirs from various holidays: a miniature Eiffel Tower, fake French francs, a lighter from Tombstone, and plenty more knick-knacks besides.

But no old diaries, no notebooks, no paperwork of any kind.

He soon reached the bottom of the box where all that was left was a stack of postcards, held together by a rubber band. There were about a dozen of them, all showing scenery from a variety of foreign locations, and all blank on the address side.

Sighing, he quickly riffled through each paperback, hoping something might fall out, but all he got out of it was a single blank bookmark. And nothing inside the LP sleeves either.

'Not much help, is it?' Emily said.

'No, but it was always a long shot. Can I ask why you held onto these things in the first place? The choices seem fairly arbitrary.'

Passing a hand over the stack of records, she said, 'Memories, I guess. Isn't that why people usually hold onto stuff? I mean, I haven't looked inside this box for a while, but I can see each item is a reminder of a pleasant moment in my life. Paul and I both loved these old records of mine, for instance, although the jazz ones were Paul's particular favourites. And we both loved anything John MacDonald wrote too. We'd usually pass them along to each other once we were finished. The photos kind of speak for themselves, of course, and these holiday trinkets are just—'

'Wait a second,' Bishop interrupted. 'I can understand the wedding photo and the two shots of you on holiday, but what's this one all about?' He extracted the last framed photo, showing the unsmiling couple in somebody's backyard, and showed it to her.

'Oh, *that* one,' she said, shaking her head. 'Not exactly showing us at our best, is it?'

'So why keep it?'

'Because Paul told me to. I even threw it out once, frame and all, and Paul nearly had a meltdown over it. He said I shouldn't ever throw anything out of his unless I asked first. And he said this photo meant a lot to him. God only knows why. I mean, look at my *hair*.'

Bishop could already feel his pulse picking up speed. This picture was an anomaly, and right now that was enough. He looked up and saw Rylander entering the kitchen.

'So did you find anything useful?' he asked.

'Not sure yet,' Bishop said. He flipped the picture frame over and saw the backing board was attached to the frame by old masking tape. He carefully pulled the tape away to reveal four metal clips, one on each side of the frame, holding the board together. He reversed each clip and then pulled the board away to reveal the back of the photo underneath. Resting against it was a small yellow envelope, like the kind that usually came with Christmas presents. He picked the envelope up and opened the flap.

There was a plastic card inside. And a thin key.

FIFTY-FOUR

Bishop pulled the key out first. It was a flat little thing with a shaft full of intricately cut teeth. There was also a number engraved on the face: 119643.

'What's it open?' Dario asked.

'Excellent question,' Bishop said, and set the key down on the table. He pulled out the plastic card and saw it was an Arizona Driver's Licence. According to the dates the card had been issued some twelve years before, and still had another fifteen to go before it expired. The background was a shot of the Grand Canyon. The photo showed the same Paul Mechner that Bishop remembered: a serious bespectacled man with close-cropped salt-and-pepper hair. The address listed was 906 West Wilson Avenue in Coolidge. The printed name underneath was for a *Mark Tamill*. The signature sample on the lower left showed the same name written in a terse script.

'I don't understand,' Emily said, looking at the licence. 'Who's this Mark Tamill?'

'Paul, obviously,' Bishop said. 'Is the signature in his handwriting?'

Emily nodded. 'Yes, it is. Without a doubt.'

'And the Coolidge address? Does that mean anything to you?'

'Not a thing.'

Bishop studied the licence more closely as he thought it all through. The key and the licence clearly went hand in hand, or else Mechner wouldn't have hidden them together. So one was no good without the other. Which made it a good bet that Mechner had stashed his evidence somewhere with half-decent security measures. Like a bank, maybe. He frowned. No, not a bank. That wouldn't work for a number of reasons. So something else.

'How on earth did Paul get a licence under an assumed name?' Emily asked.

'It's a fake,' Bishop said, turning it under the light. 'The actual card itself, I mean. And a pretty good one with a hologram that works, although I guarantee if you swiped the barcode through a proper scanner you'd get some pretty random data popping up. And I doubt it's got a proper watermark either. But if all he needed it for was to pass a basic security check to get at his stuff, then that wouldn't matter.'

Emily frowned. 'Where would he have gotten it from?'

'It's easy enough over the internet. Outfits in China do them for a couple of hundred bucks a pop. High-school students use them all the time.'

'Why an Arizona licence?' Rylander asked.

Bishop said, 'In most states you have to renew your licence every few years, but an Arizona licence remains valid until your sixty-fifth birthday. Meaning Paul could just stash this one away without the worry of it expiring anytime soon. *If* it had been real, of course.'

'Yeah, yeah,' Dario said, 'but what does the key open? That's all I care about.'

Bishop couldn't actually fault him on that one. To Emily, he said, 'You and Paul hid out in Oklahoma City for a while before he eventually decided to hire RoyseCorp for protection, correct?'

'That's right. I suggested it as I knew Paul had never been there before, and I knew the area a little since my folks originally came from that part of the country.'

'Duncan, right?'

She tilted her head. 'How did you know that?'

'It doesn't matter now. And how long did you stay in the city altogether?'

Emily puffed her cheeks. 'About three weeks, I guess. Maybe a little less. We were both getting real nervous just waiting around in the open, so Paul called your company and soon after you showed up with your team and took us to that house in Arkansas.'

'Three weeks would be more than enough time to find himself a good hiding place. During your time there did Paul ever go to one of those self-storage places, or mention that he was going to visit one?'

She shook her head again. 'No, nothing like that. At least, not that I know of.'

Bishop nodded vaguely. He'd had to ask, but he'd never heard of a self-storage place requiring a customer to show ID in order to access their locker. And even if Mechner *had* rented one he would have added his own padlock, or disc lock, for extra security. And the key on the table wasn't big enough to open either.

'And if you're thinking about a safe-deposit box,' she said, 'Paul made it clear that he wasn't going *any*where near a bank. He wasn't stupid. He knew that was the best way for Hartnell to track us.'

'There's no way he could rent a box with fake ID anyway,' Bishop said. 'Banks tend to check little things like that.'

He rubbed a palm over his head as he thought it over. He was getting one of those feelings again. After all, who said it had to be a *bank* safety deposit box? He knew there were plenty of private companies around who supplied the same service, and they didn't have to adhere to the same federal and state regulations as banks did either. A place like that would have been perfect for Mechner's needs. As long as you paid enough upfront, your valuables could remain untouched for years. Decades, even. And they'd be far more secure there than in some self-storage locker.

Turning to Dario, he said, 'Let me have your phone for a second.'

'What for?'

'I want to see how many private vault companies there are in Oklahoma City.'

Dario pulled the phone from his pocket and swiped the screen. 'I'll do it. Private vault company, yeah?'

Bishop nodded and waited while Dario tapped his fingers against the display. After about thirty seconds, he started frowning as he used a finger to scroll down.

'Anything?' Bishop asked.

Dario scrolled back up and nodded. 'Only one place. Called the Greystone Vault and Safe Deposit Box Company, at 1640 South May Avenue.'

'Greystone,' Bishop said, turning back to Emily. 'That name ring any bells?'

Her brows came together as she repeated the name to herself. 'You know, it kind of does? But I know for a fact that I never visited . . .' She closed her eyes for a few moments, then opened them again. 'Wait, *I* know what it was. I was darting out of the motel bathroom one morning to grab my toothbrush from the desk and Paul was talking to somebody on the room phone and I heard him say *Greystone*, or *greyhound*, maybe. Something like that. At least, I *think* I did. It was so long ago, and I never heard the rest of the conversation. I could be totally wrong.'

'Well, it's all we've got to go on now,' Bishop said, and turned to Dario again. 'Let me have your phone. I want to give this place a call.'

Dario slapped the phone into Bishop's hand. Bishop then scrolled down the web page until he found the contact information. There were three phone numbers. He memorized them, quit out of the browser and keyed in the first number. He brought the phone to his ear and heard a brief ringing tone and almost straight away, a female voice said, 'Greystone. How may I help you?'

'Oh, hello,' Bishop said. 'My name's Mark Tamill. I currently rent a safety-deposit box from you. I opened the account about ten years ago and paid for a long-term rental upfront, but I can't remember the exact date, and I'd just like to know roughly when my next payment's due. I don't have those details to hand for some reason.'

'That's no problem, sir. If I could just have your name again, please?'

'Mark Tamill. That's two Ls.'

'Thank you.' There was the sound of fingers tapping a keyboard. And then more tapping. Bishop found he was holding his breath. The tapping stopped for a few seconds, then started up again. Finally, the woman said, 'And can I have your wife's middle name, sir?'

Bishop breathed out and smiled to himself. That single question meant Tamill *was* on their system. To Emily, he whispered, 'What's your middle name?'

'Victoria,' she whispered back.

Bishop repeated the name into the phone. The woman thanked him and kept on tapping. After a few more seconds, she said, 'I have your details here, sir, and you don't have to worry. Your account is fully paid up for six more years. Do you want me to give you the exact date for your next renewal?'

'No, that's not necessary. But thanks, that's a real weight off my mind. Oh, while I'm here, can you remind me of your opening hours again?'

'We're open nine till six, Monday through Saturday. Any time outside those hours would need to be by appointment only.'

'And I assume I still need to present you with photo ID as before?'

'That's correct, sir. A driver's licence will be fine. And your key, of course.'

'Of course. Well, thanks again for your help.'

'You're very welcome, sir,' she said. 'Have a nice day.'

Don't push it, lady, he thought and hung up. He handed the phone back to Dario and said, 'You all heard. It's there, all right.'

'So let's go get it,' Dario said. 'What we waiting for, man?'

Bishop was looking down at the fake licence in his hand. Nobody else had grasped the problem yet, even though it was staring them right in the face.

Holding up the card, he said, 'The thing is, before I can access Mark Tamill's safety deposit box I'm going to have to first present them with Mark Tamill's ID here. And unless the person checking has got cataracts he's going to notice that not only am I the wrong age but I don't look anything like the man in this photo.'

Then he turned to Emily's husband and said, 'But *you* do.'

FIFTY-FIVE

'Oh, no, no, no,' Rylander said, shaking his head from side to side. 'Not a chance, Bishop. You can put that little idea out of your mind right now.'

'Look, I need your help, Mr Rylander,' Bishop said. 'It's that simple. I can't do it without you.'

'But I don't look *any*thing like Paul.'

'I disagree,' Bishop said, and turned to Emily. 'How about you?'

Emily sighed. 'There's a resemblance, Chris. You know there is. That's part of the reason I said yes when you first asked me out, remember? We've joked about it before.'

'But that was just us kidding each other, Em. This is about me trying to pass myself off as another man entirely. Plus I'm almost a head taller than Paul was.'

'So stoop a little,' Bishop said. 'We're not talking about a major inspection here. Whoever's on security will take a quick look at the photo on the licence, then make a comparison with the face in front of him, and then he'll let you through. Easy.'

Rylander snorted. '*Easy*, he says. Well, maybe I don't want to risk it. What do you think of that?'

Dario started unbuttoning his jacket and Bishop gave a minute shake of his head. That was the very last thing they needed at this point. Fortunately Dario saw sense for once and slowly lowered his hands.

'I can't force you, Mr Rylander,' Bishop said, 'but I wasn't lying when I said lives were at stake here. Besides, whatever's in that box is actually Emily's property now, so it's not like you'd be doing anything wrong. At least, not in the moral sense.'

'And what about the legal sense, Bishop? What if they see straight away I'm not the same man, which they *will*, and call the police? What then?'

'You're worrying about nothing. Even if the worst comes to the worst, which it won't, about all they *can* hold you for is for impersonating some guy named Mark Tamill, who never actually existed in the first place. Believe me, cops have got better things to do with their time. Look, all I'm asking is for you to drive to Oklahoma City with us, get whatever's in the box and bring it out to us, and then we'll go our separate ways. That's all.'

Rylander was still shaking his head when Emily said, 'I think we should help, Chris.'

'You do?' He blinked at his wife. 'How come?'

'Because there *are* lives at stake here, and it's really not much to ask. Besides, Bishop saved Paul's life ten years ago, back at that house in Arkansas, and this is a chance for me – for *us* – to return the favour.'

Rylander stared at his wife for a few moments, then turned to Bishop with a sigh. 'Okay. So what do you want us to do?'

Bishop said, 'Emily, can you go grab him some flat-soled shoes? He's tall enough as it is. No sense making things worse.' She nodded and left the room, while Bishop handed the licence to Rylander. 'And I'd like you to get a pen and paper and spend a few minutes practising that Mark Tamill signature until you're happy with it.'

'What for?'

'You'll probably have to sign in, and maybe sign out, too. But you're a commercial artist so I can't see it being a problem for you. And it doesn't have to be perfect anyway. Just a close approximation will be fine.'

Rylander walked over to one of the drawers in the kitchen, from which he pulled out a spiral-bound notebook and a pencil, and came back and sat at the table. As he began writing, Bishop turned to Dario and said, 'What's the time?'

Dario glanced at his watch. 'Nine forty. Less than three and a half hours left, *amigo*.'

'Maybe you should call Geraldo, then. You can update him on our progress, let him know things look promising.'

'You don't give the orders here. I call him when I'm ready, understand?'

Bishop just smiled in response. Small men trying to talk big always amused him, regardless of the situation. Lapdogs, especially.

'We all going in the one vehicle?' Rylander asked, still writing.

'No,' Bishop said, 'Dario and I'll go in ours, while you and Emily follow us in yours. There's a time factor here, so once we've got the item in question we'll need to take off fast.'

And even then, Bishop couldn't see them making it back to Tulsa before 13.00. He figured at least a two-hour drive to this Greystone place, then maybe another half an hour for Rylander to get the stuff, which meant it would be around midday by the time they set off to Tulsa. Assuming everything else went okay, that is. Pointless worrying about it this stage, though. If the cassette was everything Bishop claimed it was, then he felt sure Guzman's basic curiosity would win out over his impatience and he'd extend the deadline a little.

Emily came back carrying a pair of tan suede slip-ons. 'This old pair of Chris's is the only ones I could find without heels.'

'Perfect,' Bishop said.

Rylander was sitting back and inspecting his efforts so far. Bishop looked over his shoulder and saw the notebook page was filled with Mark Tamill signatures. They started out fairly rough at the top, but improved very quickly. To Bishop's eye, the signatures near the bottom were almost identical to the one on the licence.

'That's close enough for government work,' Bishop said. 'All right, people, I think we're good to go.'

FIFTY-SIX

It took them just over an hour and three-quarters to reach South May Avenue in Oklahoma City. Most of it had been spent on US 62, where traffic was light and free-flowing for the most part. Once again Bishop drove while Dario sat chewing his gum, speaking only when he had to make his half-hourly report to Geraldo or give Bishop directions from his phone. Never more than three car-lengths behind them was the black Chevy Malibu, with Rylander at the wheel and Emily in the passenger seat.

It turned out 1640 South May Avenue was actually a fairly large shopping centre, with a CVS Pharmacy as the anchor and various smaller franchise stores trailing off either side. Bishop pulled into the entrance and drove slowly down the parking lot's central aisle, scanning both sides. Directly opposite CVS was a large branch of the Wells Fargo Bank. And to the left of that was a smaller single-storey stucco building with a portico entrance, above which was a sign bearing the words GREYHOUND VAULT AND SAFETY DEPOSIT BOX COMPANY in block letters. Bishop could make out the tinted glass of the entrance doors further back.

Bishop peeled off the main aisle and had no difficulty finding a pair of connecting spaces close to the Greystone building. He parked up and killed the engine, and a few seconds later the Chevy pulled in next to them.

The digital dashboard clock said it was 11.14. Bishop got out and stretched. He walked round the front of the van where Dario was already waiting. Rylander and Emily were both standing next to the Chevy and looking at the Greystone entrance. Back at the house, Rylander had replaced the sweatshirt for a dark sports jacket over a plain white shirt so as to look more presentable. He still didn't look very happy.

'How you feeling?' Bishop asked him.

'Nervous,' Rylander said. 'This really isn't my thing, Bishop.'

'Don't worry about it. It'll be a piece of cake, believe me.'

The bigger man snorted. 'I'm glad *you* think so.'

'You'll be fine,' Emily said. 'And we'll be right here, waiting for you.'

'That's right,' Bishop said. 'And don't forget to slouch. It probably won't make much difference, but it's a good idea to keep those big shoulders of yours pointing at the floor as much as possible.'

Rylander slumped his shoulders and immediately lost a couple of inches in height. Bishop nodded his approval. 'Much better.' Pulling the fake licence and the key from his jacket pocket, he said, 'Don't forget these.'

'How could I?' Rylander said. As he was slipping them into his own pants pocket, a man in a tan windbreaker walked passed them carrying a canvas sports bag. He approached the Greystone entrance, opened one of the doors and went inside.

'See?' Bishop said. 'Plenty of customers visit their safety deposit boxes like it's nothing it all. Okay, tell me your name.'

'Mark Tamill.'

Bishop smiled. 'Right, you're good to go.'

Rylander took a deep breath and said, 'Well, wish me luck.'

'You won't need it,' Bishop said.

'Go get 'em, tiger,' Emily said.

They all watched Rylander lope off towards the portico entrance as though he were being led to the electric chair. He opened the left-hand door and disappeared inside.

Now it was just a waiting game. Bishop hadn't been lying to the guy before. He felt certain they'd only give the ID a cursory check, but Rylander's nervousness could be a problem. Well, it was out of their hands now. All they could do was wait.

Dario, still chewing loudly, leaned against the side of the van and started playing with his cell phone. Emily turned to Bishop and said, 'How long will it take, do you think?'

'Ten, fifteen minutes, maybe.' Bishop gently steered Emily to the front of the van until they were just out of Dario's earshot. 'No way of telling really.'

She searched his face. 'Just how bad *are* things for you, Bishop?'

He shrugged. 'Well, they're not good. All I can do at the moment is take things one step at a time. To be honest, everything kind of depends on what your husband brings out with him. And if it's what I hope it is then at least I'll get some extra breathing space.'

'And if it's not?'

'That's a bridge I'll cross if and when I come to it.'

They both lapsed into silence after that. Bishop found his thoughts turning to the two hostages back at the apartment. Clea, in particular. Not only was she an innocent civilian in all this, but she was also a lone woman amongst a gang of thugs used to taking what they wanted, whenever they wanted. But the deal had been to let them all go *unharmed*, and Guzman had ordered Geraldo to stay put and watch over them for a reason. And Geraldo had struck Bishop as a pro, much more so than Dario and the other two.

But the rule was, never waste time worrying about things over which you have no control. And the situation at the apartment was very much out of his control right now.

Instead, he turned his thoughts to Deputy Marshal Frank Lomax again – the possible source of the leak that started all this – and that tense phone call Bishop had overheard yesterday morning with the guy's wife. They lived in Bloomington, he'd said. Bishop remembered seeing it on a map and knew it was somewhere south of Indianapolis, in which case they'd probably be passing the place on the way to Ohio. Maybe he could afford to make a short detour before continuing their journey. *If* they had time, of course. And assuming he and Strickland survived the next few hours, which was far from guaranteed at the moment. Still, he'd learned long ago that it was always better to be prepared than not.

He turned to Emily and said, 'Did you bring your cell phone with you?'

'I certainly did.' She frowned. 'At least, I think I did.' She began patting both sides of her coat and stopped when she felt the left-hand pocket. Smiling, she pulled out a basic Samsung and handed it to him.

Thanking her, Bishop keyed in the same number as before and brought the phone to his ear. It rang. He waited.

When the call connected, the same voice said, 'Muro Investigations.'

'It's me again,' Bishop said. 'We talked a short while ago.'

'Hello, man-with-no-name. And using a different number this time, I notice.'

'The phone belongs to the lady I asked you to find before, who's actually standing here right next to me.'

'That's good, isn't it? So what do you want from me now?'

'The home address for a man named Frank Lomax. He's a US marshal who lives in Bloomington, Indiana, with a wife named Karen. That's about as much as I know.'

'Well, that doesn't sound too hard. You want to wait on the line again?'

'I'll be here.'

The line went silent. He and Emily watched as a young stockbroker type in a smart three-piece suit exited Greystone and trotted off towards the pharmacy directly opposite.

Less than a minute later, Muro came back to him. 'Got it. He's not in the phone book, but that's not the only book I use around here. The address is 844 West Evergreen Drive, Bloomington. I'm checking it out on Google Streetview right now, and I can see it's a nice little one-storey house at the end of a cul-de-sac. Lots of trees.'

'And where's Bloomington in relation to Indianapolis?'

'Indianapolis? Uh, about fifty miles south of it, I guess. So is that all you want?'

'That's all, thanks.'

'Then consider this one a freebie. Watch your back, man. I mean it.' The line went dead and Bishop handed the phone back to Emily, who put it back in her pocket.

From behind him, Dario said, 'Who you calling?'

Bishop turned and saw Dario still leaning against the van, still playing with his own phone. 'The same guy I called before.'

'Yeah? Why?'

'I needed somebody else found.'

'Sure you weren't calling the cops, man?'

'How would calling them help me? Or my friends, for that matter?'

'Now you're getting the picture.' Dario casually scratched his crotch with his free hand and said, 'So how much longer we gotta stick around here?'

Bishop turned away without answering. It would take as long as it took. Assuming Rylander hadn't completely lost his nerve in there. That seemed unlikely, but you never knew.

They waited. After a couple more minutes, the Greystone doors opened and a fifty-something woman in a smart business suit, carrying a laptop bag, exited and went straight to her Audi parked a few spaces away. A short time after she drove off, a casually dressed man in his sixties walked past Bishop and Emily and turned into the entrance.

After five minutes of nothing else happening, Bishop was staring absently at the ground at his feet when Emily said, 'Chris is back.'

FIFTY-SEVEN

Bishop looked up and saw the glass doors swinging shut behind Rylander as he walked towards them carrying a very slim black brief-case. He looked fairly pleased with himself.

'Hail, the returning hero,' Emily said when he reached the van.

'Cut it out,' Rylander said with a smile. His cheeks had coloured a little.

'No problems then?' Bishop asked.

'None,' Rylander said as Dario came over and joined them. 'It all went just like you said. I signed in at reception, went downstairs to the vault where the guy took a quick look at the licence, checked it against my face and let me through to the anteroom. Then he checked my key against the computer and took me into the vault itself. I couldn't believe it.' He gave the case to Bishop and added, 'Paul rented one of those large flat safety-deposit boxes. That case was the only thing in there. Nothing else would have fitted anyway.'

Bishop quickly inspected the case. It looked new but the design was pure retro. It was made of black aluminium, measured about sixteen inches by twelve, and was less than two inches thick. Instead of key locks, it had the old-style numbered wheels next to the two latches. Both locks were set at *0000*. Bishop tried flipping the release tabs, and wasn't surprised when nothing happened. The case was also fairly hefty. Maybe twelve pounds all told, three of which probably accounted for the case itself.

He gently shook it from side to side, but nothing rattled round inside.

'I did exactly the same thing in the viewing room,' Rylander said. 'No idea what's inside. And I don't know the code either.'

'When you took it out of the safety-deposit box,' Bishop said, 'both combinations were set at zero like this?'

259

Jason Dean

'That's right.'

And Mechner had been an accountant too, which meant the right combo could be pretty much anything. And with a four-number lock, that meant a total of ten thousand possible combinations to choose from. Per lock. Bishop walked back to the van and slid open the side door. He took a seat and placed the case on his lap. The others came over and Emily sat down next to him.

'Any ideas?' he asked her.

'I couldn't begin to guess what the combination might be,' she said.

'When were you born? If you don't mind me asking.'

She smiled. 'I don't mind. I was born on the second of July, during the so-called Summer of Love, although my dad said it was anything but.'

Bishop moved his thumb over the left-hand rotary dials until he had *7267*. He moved the latch to the side. Nothing. He then tried it on the right-hand lock. Again, no result. He tried *0702* on one side and *1967* on the other. Nothing. When he asked her for Paul's birthday, she told him it was the twentieth of November, 1962. He tried *1120* on one lock and *1962* on the other. When that didn't work, he reversed them. Again, no success.

'Hey, let's go,' Dario said. 'We'll open it back at the apartment.'

'Be patient,' Bishop said. 'Let me think for a minute.'

He wasn't about to explain to Dario that they had to open it here and now. There was no other way. If he took the case back to the apartment unopened only to discover that its contents weren't what he'd said they were, then Bishop, Strickland and Clea would all be dead within seconds. That's if they were lucky.

No, Bishop needed to know what was in the case now. If Mechner's evidence was related to Guzman and his sister, all well and good. But if it wasn't he'd have to act accordingly. That meant disarming and incapacitating Dario to start with, then working out some kind of game plan to somehow get Strickland and Clea back alive.

But first he needed to get inside.

There *was* another way to do it, of course. Back when Bishop had been in prison his old cellmate, Jorge, had shown him a thing or two about picking locks, and that had included numbered combination locks on cases. But the whole process was time-consuming. It would be better all round if he could just figure out the actual combination somehow.

'Paul would have written it down somewhere,' Emily said. 'I'm sure of it. Unless it was something obvious, that is.'

Bishop turned to her, eyebrows raised. 'Really?'

'Really. Paul had a pretty awful memory for numbers and dates. Hard to believe, but it's true. He was always very precise in writing down everything, though, and he rarely made mistakes in his job. I mean, if he had, he wouldn't have lasted very long, would he?'

'No, I guess not.' With his eidetic memory Bishop was just the opposite. He rarely had a need to write anything down, but he knew he was an anomaly in that respect. Yet Mechner hadn't left any written code in the envelope to help jog his own memory, and the safety-deposit number engraved upon the key was unlikely to open the case. Not only was it too obvious, but it was made up of six numbers. So something else then.

Then he got it. It was the only answer left. He said to Rylander, 'Let me have that licence again.'

'Oh, sure.' Rylander pulled the card from his pants pocket and handed it over.

Bishop checked the address again: 904 West Wilson Avenue. And the zip code was AZ 85128. He joined the two numbers together and tried *9048* on the first lock, and got nothing. He tried it on the other lock. Same result. But on the upper right of the card, just above the issue and expiry dates, was the fake licence number itself: *024357695.* It was also eight digits long, if you discounted the zero.

Bishop thumbed the left-hand dial to read *2435.* He slid the release tab to the side. There was a click and the latch snapped open.

'All *right,*' Dario said.

'Hey, you cracked it,' Rylander said.

Bishop tried *7695* on the other rotary dial. He slid the release tab to the side. There was another click and that latch snapped open too.

He quickly glanced at the three anxious faces above him, then he opened the briefcase.

FIFTY-EIGHT

Lining the black, padded, faux-leather interior were stacks of used fifty-dollar bills, each one wrapped in a blank paper currency band. Bishop guessed there were maybe fifteen or sixteen stacks altogether. And assuming each stack contained a hundred notes, that meant there was somewhere between seventy and eighty grand in there. So it looked as though Strickland wasn't the only one who believed in keeping a little extra tucked away for emergencies. Not that it had done him much good in the long run.

Rylander's eyes were wide. 'Whoa.'

'Is that for real?' Emily asked.

'Wouldn't be much point in locking it all away if it wasn't,' Bishop said.

Money wasn't all the case contained, though. He'd already spotted a flash of something grey under one of the stacks. He moved the money out of the way and underneath was a Sony microcassette recorder. It was only a small thing, measuring about twelve inches by six. He opened the front lid and inside was a TDK MC-60 cassette, wound back to the beginning.

Bishop had never seen anything so beautiful.

He almost smiled until he remembered the tape could contain anything. There were no certainties yet. He pulled the cassette from the player, pressed the Play button and watched as the two sprocket wheels began rotating in tandem. So even after all this time, the batteries were still working. That was good. He replaced the cassette and snapped the lid shut.

He looked up at Dario. 'There. Didn't I tell you?'

But Dario's concentration was on the stacks of money in the case. The young hood lifted one of the bundles and flipped through it

262

slowly. He smiled just as slowly, his mouth making smacking sounds as he continued to chew his gum. He stuffed the money in the left-hand pocket of his leather jacket, and then pulled out three more wads. They went into the same pocket.

'That's not your money,' Bishop said.

'Sure it is,' Dario said, grinning. 'Look.'

He reached down and grabbed the rest of the money and stuffed the wads in his other jacket pockets. 'You got a problem with that, amigo?'

Bishop ignored him and turned to Emily. 'Look, I really want to thank you two for helping me out here, but you should probably head on back now. I think the less you're seen with me, the better.'

Rylander was frowning at Dario. 'Yeah, I think he's right, Em.'

'Okay,' Emily said. 'I really hope things work out for you, Bishop.'

'You and me both,' he said. 'Thanks again.'

She nodded once, then she and her husband went over and got in the Chevy. Bishop watched as Rylander started the engine and slowly backed out of the space until they were pointing the way they'd come. As they pulled away, Bishop slid the now-empty briefcase into the van's interior and stood up, still holding the microcassette recorder.

Dario slid the side door shut. 'I wanna hear this tape.'

'You're not the only one,' Bishop said. 'Let's get inside first.'

Because if it turned out the recording was no use to him, he'd be in a much better position to put Dario out of action if they were both sitting in the front seats. He'd already decided that a knife-hand strike to the throat would probably work best, although he hoped it wouldn't be necessary.

He opened the driver's door and got in. Dario got in the passenger side. Shutting his door, Bishop thumbed the cassette recorder's volume control to its maximum setting, set the machine down on the dashboard and pressed Play.

FIFTY-NINE

First, there were some muffled clattering noises as the recorder was turned off, then on again. This was followed by a high-pitched giggling, then a child's voice said, '*And thank you for that, studio. I'm gonna—*' Something covered the microphone for a few moments, and then the same voice said, '*Hey, no way. You're not allowed to touch it, Julia. Mom told you before, it's my present, and you gotta wait your turn. You ain't—*' This was followed by sounds of a scuffle, as though somebody was trying to grab hold of the cassette recorder.

The voice had sounded as though it belonged to a boy. Maybe five or six years old.

'Hey, what is this shit?' Dario said.

'Be quiet,' Bishop said.

The unidentified sounds suddenly stopped and another child's voice said, '*Okay, get on with it then.*' This once sounded female, so possibly the aforementioned Julia. And she sounded a little older than the boy. Seven or eight, maybe.

The boy said, '*Okay, then. Right. So, like I was saying, thank you, studio. And now . . . and now this is ace reporter Richy Hartnell at the scene, reporting for ABC . . .*'

Bishop and Dario glanced at each other at the mention of Hartnell. Sounded like these two were his own kids then. And from the sounds of it, it was either Christmas or this Richy's birthday.

The boy went on, '*. . . and yes, the fire is totally out of control now and I think they're gonna have to call in the army to put it out.*'

'*That's the fire brigade, stinko,*' the little girl said, her voice dripping with sarcasm. '*Army's for riots and wars and things. Don't you know anything?*'

'Shut up, *Julia. You're the stinko, not me. And you gotta wait until I ask you the questions. You can't just say stuff when you want.*'

'*Okay, okay. Ask your dumb questions before the tape runs out.*'

'*Right. Okay, then. So you saw what started this fire, right, Miss?*'

'*Yeah, I did. It was this big fat elephant with wings, and he kept aiming his trunk at the buildings and rays of fire shot out of his trunk, and one of them hit . . .*'

Both kids collapsed into uncontrollable giggles that went on for about ten seconds. This was soon followed by more clattering noises as the boy messed around with the Pause and Play controls.

Dario gave a loud sigh and turned his face to the window. On the tape, Bishop heard silence for a while, and then the sound of somebody knocking on a door. '*Can I come in, Daddy?*' the boy said.

There followed the sound of a door opening. Then a deep male voice said, '*Hey, if it isn't my little birthday boy. You enjoying all your presents?*'

'*I'm a reporter for ABC, Daddy,*' the boy said. '*I'm here to interview you.*'

'*A reporter, huh? Well, I don't know about that. What about?*'

'*You know. Stuff. And you too, Uncle Dom.*'

So it was Hartnell *and* Callaway, both in the same room.

'*Well, as long as it's short, Richy,*' Hartnell said. '*Daddy's working, you know? What do you want to ask us?*'

Bishop heard something that could have been somebody sitting on a leather seat, or a couch. Then the boy said, '*Okay, you first, Daddy. I've just got a report that all the animals in the zoo have been let out of the cages. Now when the rhino and the lion get into a fight with each other, who do you think's gonna win?*'

'*Well, I'd have to go with the lion on that one, what with him being a carnivore and all. And let's not forget those teeth.*'

'*Thank you, sir,*' the boy said. '*And what about you, mister?*'

'*I don't think you can rule out the rhino,*' a familiar voice said. Callaway. It was him all right. '*That horn of his could do a lot of damage, Richy.*'

The boy coughed. '*Yes, I see. Thank you, sir. Now I'd like to ask you about the dinosaurs. If a Tyrannosaurus—*'

A woman's voice suddenly interrupted them. '*Richy, what are you doing in here?*'

'*I'm interviewing people for ABC News, Mom.*'

'*You know you can't interrupt Daddy in his office like this. Come on, now. Let's go to the kitchen where Daisy's making lunch.*'

'*But, Mom—*'

'*No buts. Come on now. Let Daddy get back to work.*'

'*Better do what Mom says,*' Hartnell said. '*You can finish up some other time.*'

'*Oh, all right.*' There was a muffled scuffling and then a few seconds later, the sound of a door being closed.

Hartnell's voice said, '*So where were we?*'

Bishop smiled to himself, and watched Dario slowly turn from the window to listen. It was obvious to both what had happened. The boy must have not only left the cassette recorder in Hartnell's office, but left the tape still running as well.

'*I was only saying you had nothing to worry about, Felix,*' Callaway said. '*I kept things tight all down the line and I've cleaned up after myself. Of the five men I used for the job, only one's still walking around, and I'll be taking care of him tomorrow night.*'

'*Which one is it?*'

'*Ayers. It's all arranged. It'll look like a gangland dispute that got out of hand.*'

'*Why can't you do it today? Or tonight?*'

'*We set up this whole meet a week ago and if I change it now, he'll suspect something's up. Also, one of the men I'm using is finishing up another job right now.*'

There was a sigh. '*All right, but the sooner this is all sealed up, Dom, the better. I don't need to tell you that if our wetback friend ever discovered we were the ones behind his sister's death, there'd be war on the streets. You know how emotional they get down there. If Rafael ever got his hands on us . . .*' He left the sentence unfinished.

Bishop's heart was already beating a mile a minute. The tape was turning out to be everything he could have hoped for and more.

'*Yeah, I read you,*' Callaway said. '*But after tomorrow there won't be anyone left who can connect us to that whole mess. And now Rafael's got his bloodlust out of his system, everybody's happy again.*'

'*Well, let's wait until tomorrow before we start celebrating. Come see me once it's done, okay?*'

'*Naturally. I better shoot off now. I still got a few details I need to finalize. Want me to send Mechner through on my way out?*'

'*Yeah. Send him through.*'

Bishop reached over and pressed the Stop button. They'd heard the most important part, the rest they could hear back at the apartment. But it sounded to Bishop as though Mechner had been summoned by the boss for whatever reason and sat in the same spot Richy had been sitting. He must have seen the tape was still running, decided it was an opportunity he couldn't ignore, and taken it away with him to listen to later. Which had been a pretty risky move for him at the time. But one for which Bishop was now profoundly grateful.

As he rewound the tape back to the beginning, he checked the clock and saw it was already 11.52. Time to go. He handed the tape machine to Dario and said, 'You better call Geraldo and tell him the good news. And that we'll be about half an hour late.'

Smiling, Dario pocketed the player. 'Sure, I'll call him, amigo.'

Bishop started the engine, then backed up and got them out of there.

SIXTY

Since there hadn't been any police presence coming in, Bishop decided to shave a few minutes off the driving time by taking the I-44 all the way back to Tulsa. Dario seemed in a good mood for much of the return journey, chewing loudly and humming to himself as he surfed the net on his phone. But then eighty grand for a minute's work would make anybody happy. Oddly enough, Bishop hadn't heard Dario mention Hartnell by name when he'd updated Geraldo. Or maybe he simply didn't want to be the bearer of bad tidings, preferring his boss to find out for himself. Geraldo had just told them to get back as fast as they could.

It was 13.22 when they reached the Lakewood Apartments. Bishop parked the van in the same spot as before and saw Clea's Explorer was still in its rightful space. The moment he turned off the engine, a stack of cash landed on his lap.

He turned to a now-grinning Dario and said, 'What's this for?'

'Gift from me to you. You keep that, I keep the rest. Nobody else needs to know about it. Are we good?'

Bishop spent a moment thinking it over. Then he smiled and stuffed the money in his own jacket pocket. It would come in very useful later, assuming Guzman kept his word. 'We're good,' he said.

'I like you, Bishop,' Dario said as he opened the door. 'You're okay for a gringo.'

After locking the van, both men made their way through the building to apartment number twenty-two. Dario rapped his knuckles on the door. After a few seconds, the one called Ramon opened it and let them in.

Bishop went first, the other two following close behind. In the living room, he saw Strickland and Clea still sitting cross-legged on the floor, both seemingly in good health. Both looked up at Bishop when he entered. Clea even managed a smile, which was a positive sign. Geraldo was still sitting in the chair, while the other armed goon had taken Dario's place by the window.

'You two okay?' Bishop asked his charges.

'We are now,' Strickland said, and Clea nodded in agreement. Strickland added, 'So you weren't bullshitting then? There really was a tape?'

'Oh, there was a tape, all right.'

'Sit,' Geraldo said, and Bishop lowered himself to the floor next to Clea. Geraldo then spoke rapidly in Spanish, and Dario stepped forward and handed over the microcassette player. '*Bueno*,' Geraldo said. He darted another quick look at Bishop, then opened the laptop and started on the trackpad again. Meanwhile the guard who'd opened the door took his position behind the three of them. Dario stood a few feet to the right of Bishop.

Bishop turned to Clea and whispered, 'You okay? They didn't try anything, I hope.'

Clea got his meaning and shook her head. 'No, they left me alone, thank God. I think they're all too scared of Señor Guzman to try anything, which I can understand. He sure scares the hell out of me. They haven't given us any food or water, but I don't think I could eat anything anyway.' She looked at him. 'It's good to see you again, Bishop. It really is.'

He smiled and said, 'That goes both ways.' He faced front when he heard the computer emitting the same sharp ringing tone as before.

Geraldo repositioned the webcam and when the call was answered, a face appeared on the computer screen. Geraldo spoke some rapid Spanish and then turned the laptop so everybody could see the display.

As expected, it was Guzman again. Bishop saw he was now wearing a powder-blue shirt. He looked as cool as a cucumber, with not a lick of hair out of place. 'So, Señor Bishop. I hear from Geraldo that you have a tape for me. Will I be pleased when I hear it?'

'Well, "pleased" isn't the term I'd use, but I think you'll find it very interesting.'

He gave a single, stern nod and said, 'Proceed.'

Geraldo placed the cassette player on the table and pressed Play.

The tape started. Everybody listened intently to the young boy playing at being a TV personality with his sister. Bishop was watching Guzman. His expression never changed at all at the mention of the boy's name. Then came the knock on the office door, followed by Hartnell and Callaway patiently indulging the boy's cute interview questions. Other than the occasional blink, Guzman's face still remained a mask.

Then came the good stuff. With both men unaware of the tape still running in the machine, Callaway went on to reassure Hartnell that he was taking care of all the unspecified loose ends.

And then finally, Hartnell's voice again: '. . . *All right, but the sooner this is all sealed up, Dom, the better. I don't need to tell you that if our wetback friend ever discovered we were the ones behind his sister's death, there'd be war on the streets. You know how emotional they get down there . . .*'

Bishop watched Guzman slowly clench his jaw muscles as his face grew darker and his eyes grew smaller. The man was clearly trying to contain his rage, and not entirely succeeding. As the tape continued, Guzman gradually gained control over his emotions until his face took on the same mask-like qualities as before. But they'd all seen what was waiting underneath. It even brought a chill to Bishop's spine, and he wasn't exactly a pushover in these kinds of situations.

'*Apagar*,' Guzman hissed, and Geraldo leaned forward and pressed the Stop button. The room lapsed into complete silence as Guzman pondered on what he'd just heard. Nobody in the room moved. Nobody made a sound. Even Dario had stopped chewing his gum. They all waited for what was coming next.

After a minute, Guzman said, 'Dario.'

'*Si, jefe?*'

'Did Bishop spend time alone with this tape at any point? Did he have any opportunity to doctor the recording?'

Dario frowned. 'I don't understand, *jefe. Doctor?*'

Guzman gritted his teeth and said, 'I mean did Bishop have time to mess with the cassette? Is what I have heard genuine, Dario? Yes or no?'

Understanding immediately came to Dario's face and he nodded enthusiastically. '*Sí, jefe*. I witnessed Bishop unlocking the briefcase and I was with him all the time after that. The tape was never out of my sight for a second. It's genuine.'

'I see.' Guzman rubbed his cheek. Quietly, he said, 'This changes many things. *Many* things.'

The room went silent again. Bishop gave it another minute, then said, 'I held up my end, Señor Guzman.'

Guzman frowned as he peered into his own computer screen. 'And now you expect me to honour my part of the bargain?'

'To be honest, after hearing that tape I can't see how Strickland would be any use to you now anyway.'

Guzman paused, considering. Bishop waited.

The seconds grew longer until it seemed to Bishop time stood still. Finally Guzman said, 'Geraldo, you and your men return to California. I may have further instructions for you there.'

'And these three, *jefe*?'

Guzman gave a casual shrug. 'I do not need Strickland now, and there is no profit in killing them. Leave them.'

Next to him, Bishop heard Clea exhale loudly at the reprieve. He knew how she felt. '*Gracias*, Señor Guzman,' he said.

'A deal is a deal,' Guzman said, 'and I always keep my word.'

'That's what I thought. Just one more thing before you go, though.'

'Oh?' Guzman said. 'What is this?'

Bishop pulled the small stack of money from his inner jacket pocket and lobbed it towards Geraldo, who caught it one-handed.

'Besides the cassette recorder,' Bishop said, 'Mechner stashed about eighty grand in that briefcase. That's five grand of it right there. Dario gave it to me in the parking lot to keep me quiet. The rest he's keeping for himself. I just thought you should know.'

Dario turned to Bishop, his eyes burning with hatred. 'This is a *lie*. I never—'

'*Silencio*,' Guzman said calmly. 'Geraldo, find out if this is the truth or not.'

Geraldo stood up, turned to Dario and said, '*Manos arriba*.'

The guard standing behind Bishop stepped forward and prodded

Dario's back with the barrel of his gun. Dario slowly raised his hands. His arms were shaking. Geraldo checked the man's left-hand jacket pocket and pulled out the three stacks of bills it contained. Then he pulled the other dozen or so bundles from the remaining pockets. He turned to Guzman. 'Looks like about seventy-five thousand, *jefe.*'

'You disappoint me, Dario,' Guzman said with a sigh. 'You really do. Geraldo, make it quick.'

Dario started to speak and stopped when Geraldo made a rapid movement with his right hand. All of a sudden, Bishop saw him holding a small thin knife that hadn't been there before. In less than a second he flipped the blade until he had it in a reverse grip, then raised his hand and immediately plunged the knife into Dario's fore-head, all the way to the hilt.

Clea gave a loud gasp. Strickland said, '*Jesus.*'

Dario's head had snapped back from the force of the strike. Staring upwards and with his hands still raised, the dying man tottered back a few steps until he connected with the wall behind him. Then his legs gave way and he oozed down the wall like maple syrup. There was almost no blood at all, just a thin red line running from the wound to his chin. Bishop watched the drops land on his shirt. It took a few more seconds for Dario's eyes to close and shortly afterwards his chest stopped moving altogether.

The room was silent.

Naturally, it was left to Guzman to speak first. 'Why did you tell me this, Bishop?'

'I hoped I might bank a small favour from you in return.'

'You wish a favour.' Guzman stared at him, his dark eyes resembling black holes. 'From me.'

'It wouldn't be much, just some information. Once we get out of this mess we're in. But I know that with your unlimited resources, something that might take me months to find out would most likely take you only a few seconds.'

'Maybe I should just have Geraldo kill you now. That would be even easier, no?'

'Is that what an honourable man would do, Señor Guzman?'

Guzman paused, frowning to himself. 'You puzzle me, Señor Bishop, and I am not puzzled by many things anymore. And so I think maybe I will honour your request for that reason alone. Geraldo will give you a number where you can contact him, and he will contact me. Then once I have heard what you want, I will decide if I will help or not.'

'That's all I ask.'

The man who could order a death as easy as blinking nodded once and said, 'Geraldo, leave Señor Bishop his gun. And take that body with you and dispose of it properly. I want no traces.'

'Understood, *jefe*,' Geraldo said, at which point Guzman immediately brought the video conference to an end. His face disappeared from the screen and Geraldo spoke rapid Spanish to the other two. To Bishop, he said, 'Stay right where you are until we've gone. I'll leave your piece by the front door.'

Bishop nodded, then watched as one of the other men reached down and extracted the knife from Dario's forehead. After using Dario's jacket to wipe the blood off his face, he hefted him up in a fireman's carry and took him out to the hallway. Meanwhile, Geraldo began packing his laptop and peripherals into the black holdall.

Clea said, 'Is that it? They're just going to let us go?'

'That's it,' Bishop said, turning to her. She had a confused look on her face, as though she couldn't quite grasp what was happening around her. Bishop understood how she felt. For the past few hours she'd been mentally preparing herself for a bullet in the head, and now it seemed that none of it had been necessary. Her life had been handed back to her by a single nod thousands of miles away. That was a hard thing to grasp in one go.

Bishop looked past her at Strickland, who was staring blankly at the ceiling. He'd know that he'd been handed nothing more than a twenty-four-hour reprieve. But that reprieve meant they still had a chance of saving Barney, and that's what this was all about.

Finally Geraldo hefted the holdall strap over his shoulder and spoke to the remaining guard in Spanish. The guard went out into the hallway. Geraldo stopped before Bishop and handed him a scrap of paper with a handwritten number on it.

'Two weeks from now,' he said, 'this number will be useless. Maybe sooner.'

'Fair enough,' Bishop said, taking the piece of paper.

Geraldo walked off and joined the others in the hallway outside. Bishop heard some faint mutterings from out there and the sound of the front door being opened. Then shut.

Bishop got up and went over to the hallway. It was empty of people. He also spotted the Glock lying on the floor mat. 'It's okay,' he said. 'They've gone.'

After retrieving the gun, he went back and helped Clea to her feet. She still seemed shaky and unaware of her surroundings. Strickland was already standing, watching them both.

'So that's us out of the frying pan and back into the fire,' he said. 'What now?'

'Now you go get that money you promised us,' Bishop said.

SIXTY-ONE

The moment Strickland exited the living room, Clea removed her glasses and began sobbing quietly. She barely made a sound, but her shoulders shook with pent-up emotion. Bishop took her other hand and held it. He understood delayed shock. He'd seen it countless times before.

'It's all right,' he said in a soothing tone. 'You're okay, Clea.'

Between sniffles, she said, 'I know I am. It's just . . . it's just . . . ' She stopped, took a deep breath and wiped her eyes with the sleeve of her jumper. Then she put her glasses back on and looked at him. Sniffing, she said, 'Don't you get it, Bishop? All those hours we were sitting here while you were gone, I thought I was going to die. I thought we were both going to die. I really did.'

'And now you're alive and confused and you don't know what to think. I understand. It's common amongst survivors of traumas.'

She looked at his face, then she looked at her hand in his. She gently removed it and said, '*Do* you understand, Bishop? Because I don't think you do. A few minutes ago I sat and watched you sign that man's death warrant like it was nothing.'

'You mean Dario? He was a stone-cold killer, like the rest of them. Don't waste your tears on him.'

'And what does that make you, Bishop? You're no different to any of them. Even Guzman recognized a kindred spirit when he agreed to help you later. Riding with you in the car I almost forgot your true nature, but I've seen the other side of your face now and it's not something I'll ever be able to forget.'

'I never claimed to be a saint, Clea. I did what I had to do, that's all. And I'd do it again if I needed to.'

'Yes, I realize you are who you are. But by the same token, you can't expect me to carry on with you two after this. I can't do it anymore. I just can't.'

'I understand. I was actually going to suggest you head on back now anyway. You've already done enough for us, and you've got a daughter back home waiting for you.'

Frowning, she used a hand to wipe away the last remnants of tears. 'Seriously? You don't mind?'

'No, I don't mind. Although I'd like you to do something for us before you take off.'

'That depends. It's not something illegal, is it?'

'No, nothing illegal.'

Strickland came back into the room then, dragging a bulging rucksack in one hand. 'It's all here, exactly where I left it,' he said. 'Although Nicky won't be too happy when he sees the mess I made of his bedroom cupboard.'

'He'll get over it,' Bishop said. 'Take out three or four grand for us. That'll be more than enough.'

Strickland reached in and took out a stack of messy bills wrapped in a thick rubber band. 'That's about five grand, I think. What about the rest?'

Bishop looked at Clea. 'It's yours if you want it.'

'I don't.'

'Not even a couple of hundred for breakfast and gas?'

'I don't want *any* of that money.'

'Your choice.' He turned to Strickland. 'You might as well leave the rest here for your friend, then. All right, let's get out of here.'

'Where to?' Clea asked.

'The nearest used car dealer,' Bishop said.

SIXTY-TWO

Heartland Cheap Autos, located at the north-eastern tip of Tulsa, wasn't the nearest used car dealer but it was definitely the cheapest. Located out on its own with no neighbours in the near vicinity, the establishment was a simple lot behind a chain link fence, containing about thirty vehicles, with a long mobile home serving as an office, and a larger wooden building set further back behind it.

Strickland stayed in the Explorer while Bishop and Clea dealt with the proprietor, a bald, fiftyish guy named Sandy. Bishop chose a brown, ten-year-old Nissan Altima with over 170,000 miles on the odometer, and managed to haggle the price down from $2,995 to a single cash payment of $2,500.

Ten minutes later he and Clea exited the converted mobile home, two and half grand lighter, but carrying a bill of sale and a title deed made out in Clea's name.

Clea exited through the open gate and got into the Explorer parked by the side of the road. Strickland started the engine and took off. Bishop got in the Nissan, started her up and took off in the same direction. The engine was pretty noisy and the wheel was a little stiff, but that was okay. Right now he only cared that it ran and that it had a full tank of gas.

After a couple of hundred yards, Bishop saw the Explorer at the side of the road with Clea and Strickland standing at the rear, waiting for him. Bishop slowed and brought the Nissan to a stop a few feet away. He got out and joined them.

'This is where we part ways, Clea,' he said. 'We couldn't have gotten this far without you.'

'Amen to that,' Strickland said.

Clea gave a faint smile. 'I could say it was a pleasure, but we know it would be a lie. You two live in a world very different from mine. And I'm not sure I'll ever be able to forget what happened back at that apartment. Not ever.'

'You'd be surprised at how well the mind can cope with unwanted memories. But you're right. What happened today isn't for you.'

'But it *is* for you?'

Bishop shook his head. 'Not out of choice, believe me.'

'I'm not sure I do believe you. I think a part of you actually craves these kinds of situations.'

Bishop said nothing, although he saw an element of truth in there. Maybe he'd look into it further one of these days. Or maybe not.

Strickland offered Clea his hand. 'Thanks for coming back to the diner. You didn't have to do that.'

Clea shook the hand. 'Yes, I did. I really hope you make it back to Ohio okay. And I'll be thinking of Barney all the way back, and praying he comes out of this all right.'

'I'll makes sure he does,' Bishop said.

He gave her a final nod, then got back in the Nissan and waited as Strickland joined him on the other side. Bishop drove them away from there on the empty road. In the rear-view, he saw Clea get in the Explorer and close the door. A second later, the vehicle made a U-turn and took off in the opposite direction. Bishop kept watching until it had completely disappeared from view. Then he focused on the road ahead, making sure the needle stayed around the seventy mark.

The dashboard clock said it was now 14.13. They still had a little less than sixteen hours left and a little under seven hundred miles to cover. Which, barring further obstacles, should be easy enough, even with what Bishop had in mind.

'Weird,' Strickland said.

Bishop turned to him. 'What?'

'I was starting to get used to having Clea around. Feels funny with her gone. But look, are you sure it was a good idea letting her go? If the two of us get stopped now we're really screwed. At least with her here we had a chance.'

'If Guzman's men hadn't grabbed us I'm sure she would have stayed the course without a problem, but those few hours at the apartment took her close to breaking point. If she was here now and we got stopped, the slightest provocation would cause her to break down entirely. No, best we go our separate ways while we're still able.'

'If you say so.' Strickland paused, then said, 'Still, one good thing that came out of it is you sticking Hartnell in the meat grinder like that. Whatever happens to me now, at least I know that bastard's not long for this world.'

Bishop smiled. 'He did it to himself. I'm just glad I could speed things along.'

Strickland snorted. 'Yeah, you did that, all right. So what now?'

'Well, from here it's a straight north-easterly route to St Louis three hundred miles away, then on through Indianapolis, and then another couple of hundred miles till we hit Ohio, I think. We'll want to skirt the cities themselves, but I'll use the I-44 for the initial part of the journey, which should speed things up. We'll get off it just before St Louis, then find a Walmart or something where we can get ourselves a GPS unit for the rest.'

'And some coffee.'

'Yeah, coffee would help too.'

Bishop also knew that roadblocks would remain a risk whichever route they took, but he felt the odds would be with them in this case. Assuming Charlie had talked to the feds, then they'd be expecting Bishop to head for Ohio from the west, via Colorado and Kansas. But instead, thanks to Guzman's intervention, they were now approaching from Oklahoma, which should be the last thing they expected. The cops couldn't cover every single road in and out of this part of the country. It simply wasn't possible.

Bishop slowed when he saw a sign pointing right for the entrance to the turnpike for the interstate. He signalled, took the next turn and starting accelerating again. 'By the way, once we get to Indianapolis I'll be making a short detour.'

Strickland frowned at him. 'Detour? What detour? What are you talking about?'

'That marshal, Lomax, has got a house in Bloomington, Indiana, which is practically on the way. I want to check it out.'

'Why?'

'Why? Because the way things currently stand I'm the odds-on favourite for being the one that started all this, and I'd like to do something about it while I'm still able.'

Strickland slowly nodded his head. 'Okay. So?'

'So I think Lomax's wife was held as a bargaining chip to force him to give away our location and to make things easier for Hartnell's hit team when they showed up on Tuesday morning. Like hiding that ignition key under the mat, for example. And maybe a few other things too. I've been thinking about the busted axle on that SUV, for example, and the more I think about it the more I'm convinced the damage was done *before* the assault. I've had plenty of experience with armoured vehicles in the past, and I just can't see how automatic gunfire, no matter how intense, could have affected the axle like it did.'

'But you don't know.'

'Exactly. I don't know. But a search of Lomax's home might give me something I can use against him. Something I can show to the feds when they eventually stick the cuffs on me, which they undoubtedly will the moment I turn Barney over to them. I already served time for a crime I didn't commit, and I'm not about to let it happen again.'

'Sure you're not overreacting here, Bishop? I mean, all they got against you now is vague circumstantial evidence.'

'Circumstantial evidence was enough to put me behind bars before. If it happened once it can happen again.'

Strickland was silent for a moment. 'So how long will this detour take?'

'Not long. Bloomington is still on the way to our final destination. Kind of.'

Strickland faced front again. 'All right, I guess we can do that. As long as we're at the exchange before the six o'clock deadline.'

'We will be,' Bishop said.

SIXTY-THREE

The first part of the journey went as well as could be expected. The I-44 was pretty much plain sailing, although the traffic started getting heavier the closer they got to St Louis. But there were no roadblocks at all, which was the best news possible. Strickland stayed quiet most of the time, allowing Bishop to spend much of the drive alone with his thoughts. Thinking about Frank Lomax, about what he might or might not find at the house, but also thinking about the dawn exchange and what he could do to prepare for it.

The problem was all the odds were currently on Callaway's side. Not only did he have the manpower advantage, but more importantly he had the choice of final location for the switch, and he was sure to know the terrain like the back of his hand. In fact, he was probably there now setting everything up. Whereas Bishop had only himself, and wherever this location was it was sure to be completely alien to him.

But there were ways to counteract each of those problems. Possibly. One he could get on to fairly soon, but the other he couldn't do anything about until much nearer the time.

They left the interstate at the Valley Park exit at 18.55. It was already dark by that point, which immediately made Bishop feel less exposed. Once in town, he soon found a medium-sized shopping centre containing a Target and a Caribou Coffee store. While Strickland got them some caffeine and sandwiches, Bishop made a phone call and when he got the answer he wanted, he went into the Target store and used some of the money to purchase a TomTom GoLive GPS unit. He also picked up a Cobra Handheld CB radio, since that was still the best early-warning system around for avoiding roadblocks. Even better, this one had a Close Call RF Capture function, where the radio instantly tuned itself to signals coming from nearby transmissions.

Back in the car, Bishop placed the CB radio on the dash, switched on the Close Call function and made sure the volume was turned up. Almost immediately a ragged male voice began blaring from the speaker as he cursed in colourful language about the state of the road he was driving on. Bishop immediately reduced the volume until the tirade became little more than background noise. He expected to hear a lot more transmissions like that one, but you had to take the bad with the good.

Then Bishop quickly planned out the quickest route to Bloomington on the GPS, which seemed to involve getting them onto US 50 as soon as possible. After topping up the tank at a nearby gas station, Bishop decided it might be a good time to get a couple of hours' shuteye while he could. He switched seats with Strickland, and then watched the road for a few minutes until they both saw the signs for US 50.

It seemed to Bishop he'd only just shut his eyes when he felt a hand shaking his left shoulder. Instantly awake, he sat up, taking in everything at once. It was 21.33. The CB radio was transmitting white noise. On the GPS display he saw they were a couple of miles west of a place called Lawrenceville, not far from the Indiana state line. They were also slowing. But there were no police lights ahead of them, and no traffic coming towards them either. Just a set of tail-lights in the distance, and slowly getting further away. He could also see a small intersection ahead. He was about to ask what the problem was when Strickland handed him his cell phone. It was vibrating and the display was flashing *Unknown Caller*.

'Callaway,' Bishop said.

'Has to be,' Strickland said. 'You answer it while I get us off the road.'

Bishop pressed the green button, raised the phone to his ear, and said, 'Hello?'

'That you, friend?' It was Callaway's voice.

'It's me,' Bishop said, not wanting to get into semantics again.

'Where's the other guy?'

'He's driving. Just finding a place to stop so he can talk to his boy.'

While Bishop had been speaking, Strickland had taken the left turn at the intersection. It was just a dark dirt track, probably leading to a farm or a ranch further in. Strickland stopped the car after twenty feet and turned off the headlights. The only illumination now came solely from the dashboard light.

'So how goes the journey?' Callaway asked. 'Making good progress?'

'We're doing okay,' Bishop said. 'And we'll be on time.'

'Glad to hear it. And so is the boy . . . Yeah, he's here, nodding his head. So here we are again. I'm keeping my word, like I said I would. Aren't I good?'

'So put him on.' He saw Strickland looking at him, waiting for the phone. Bishop pressed the loudspeaker button and handed it to him.

'Son?' he said. 'Are you there?'

'I'm here, Dad,' Barney said. 'It's real good to hear your voice again.'

'It's great to hear yours too. So how you doing over there? You still okay?'

'Yeah, I'm all right, I guess. I tried playing Tetris but I lose track of the lines after an hour and I have to start again. I keep thinking about you, and about Mom. I been thinking about Mom a lot lately. I try not to but it's real hard. I . . . I really miss you.'

Strickland closed his eyes. 'I miss you too, son. More than you can imagine. I wish . . . I just wish there was some way . . .' He trailed off into silence.

'Me too, Dad, but it's done now. And at least I know I'll see you tomorrow. That's what I'm looking forward to now.'

'Good. I know it's hard, but try and remain positive. And stay strong. We're on our way.'

'I know you are, Dad.'

There was a second's silence. Then two.

'Excuse the interruption,' Bishop said, 'but have you ever heard of a guy named Lao Tzu?'

'No,' Barney said. 'Why, who is he?'

'An ancient Chinese philosopher. He founded Taoism. He also came out with a lot of wise proverbs, including one my sister told me when I was younger. He said, *Being deeply loved by someone gives you strength, while loving someone deeply gives you courage.* It's a bit hokey, I know, but I've always liked it. How about you?'

'Yeah, that's pretty good. Can you say it again?'

Bishop repeated it, and Barney said, 'Yeah, I really like that. I'll try and remember it from now on. Thanks.'

'Now isn't that touching?' Callaway broke in. 'I'm getting teary-eyed here.'

'*You bastard,*' Strickland shouted into the phone. '*Put him back on. Now.*'

'I don't think so,' Callaway said, unruffled. 'I already explained why we need to keep these conversations brief, so suck it up and get your asses back on the road. I'll call you again at around five so we can talk location.'

The line went dead.

'Son of a *bitch,*' Strickland said, smacking his palm against the wheel.

'You all right?' Bishop asked.

'What do *you* think?'

'In that case I better drive. Let's switch.'

Strickland gave a long sigh, then opened his door and got out. Bishop did the same. Once he was in the driver's seat again, he pressed the GPS display to zoom out and saw the turn-off for State Road 67 was only a few miles away. That would then take them most of the way to Bloomington, which was currently about eighty miles to the north-east. Bishop wanted to get there before 23.00, if possible. It was now 21.38.

He turned on the headlights, swung a U-turn and took them back to the intersection. There was a pair of headlights approaching from the east, about thirty yards away. He waited for them to pass.

'Hey, Bishop,' Strickland said quietly.

'Yeah?'

'Thanks.'

'What for?' The oncoming vehicle, a large pick-up, sped past and Bishop pulled out after it and stepped on the gas.

'For what you said to Barn just now, that quote from that Chinese guy. That was a good thing to say.'

'I just wanted to keep his spirits up, and that was the first thing that came to mind.'

'Well, I think it worked, and not just for him.' He paused, then cleared his throat. 'So, anyway, thanks.'

'No problem,' Bishop said, and increased their speed.

SIXTY-FOUR

They reached West Evergreen Drive without incident by 23.03. It was located just off State Road 37 on the north-west side of Bloomington, in a very quiet section of town. The street had no lights, no road markings, and not that many residences, but there was no shortage of evergreens in the vicinity. They were everywhere you looked, with large copses covering the grounds between the houses and lining almost every driveway. All in all it seemed a nice, peaceful, rural setting. Bishop could see why Frank Lomax had chosen it for his base.

Bishop cruised slowly down the street with his headlights off. He didn't want to announce his presence if he could help it. The quarter-moon peeking through the thin clouds provided them with just enough light to see by. They passed about two dozen single-storey houses. These varied in size, but most were dark, which suggested early nights were the norm around here. Bishop checked the numbers of each mailbox they passed. As they approached the end of the road the trees gradually became thicker and the houses fewer and farther between. Finally, just before the woods threatened to take over entirely, Bishop saw a mailbox on the right with 844 on it.

Just past the mailbox was a narrow driveway that angled through more trees. Bishop could just about make out part of a single-storey brick house beyond, maybe fifty feet away from them. He couldn't see much from the road, but the house looked dark.

'That it?' Strickland asked.

'That's it,' Bishop said. 'Let's go take a closer look.'

He swung a U, parked on the other side of the road and killed the engine. After deactivating the interior light, he got out. He carefully closed the driver's door without a sound, and was glad to see Strickland acting with the same caution. Then they crossed the road and walked down the dirt driveway towards the house.

As they got closer Bishop could see Lomax's place was a fairly large brick bungalow, with a couple of steps leading to a front porch with a wooden railing. There was a prefab double garage to the right of the house, also wooden, with a narrow pathway running between the two buildings. There were no lights on in the house, and no vehicles parked on the driveway. The only sounds were some faint traffic noises far off in the distance.

They stopped before the house and just stood there for a moment.

'So we breaking in, or what?' Strickland whispered.

'Only as a last resort,' Bishop whispered back. 'Lomax told me they've got a German shepherd and I don't want to get him worked up if I can avoid it. I'm hoping for an unlocked door or maybe an open window. I'll try the front. You check the back, but do it quietly. If you see anything come get me.'

Strickland nodded and disappeared down the pathway towards the rear while Bishop climbed the steps to the porch and moved carefully over the wooden decking towards the front door. There was an elaborate lion's-head steel knocker in the centre and an oval doorknob on the right. Bishop tried turning the doorknob, but there was no give at all. Locked.

He stepped off the porch and began walking towards the large window on the right-hand side of the house when he heard a *psst* from the direction of the pathway. He saw Strickland waving. Bishop went over to him and Strickland said, 'Both back doors are locked, but I found an unlatched window we can use to get in.'

'Good.'

Bishop followed him down the pathway, passing a couple of dark windows, and soon entered a vast backyard bracketed by even more trees. He turned to the house and saw a pair of sliding window doors in the centre, but with the drapes drawn. There was a frosted window to the right of it, which suggested a bathroom. At the far left of the house was a panel door with a sash window next to it. The window's lower panel had already been raised a couple of inches.

They walked over to the window and Bishop slowly raised the lower panel as far as it could go. Inside, he saw a small, narrow utility room containing a washer, a tumble dryer, a clothes hamper, and a few other appliances. Bishop could just about make out a partially open door at the other end of the room.

'Wait here,' Bishop said. 'I'll unlock the door for you.'

'Right.'

Bishop climbed up and swung his right leg over the sill, then brought his other leg round and gently lowered himself until his soles touched tile. He stood there for a moment, listening to the house. Listening for anything.

Other than his own pulse ringing in his ears, he heard nothing at all.

But he could smell something like dog food. Stale dog food. He looked around the room and saw three small dark round shapes on the floor a few feet away, arranged in a row. Edging past them, he went over to the door and felt along the wall until he found a single light switch. He pressed it and the room was immediately flooded with light. The three round objects were dog bowls. One held a smattering of doggie snacks in the shape of bones, one held water, the other contained the remnants of the dog food he smelled.

Old leftover food and a partially open door to the rest of the house. It didn't bode well for the dog. Or the wife. But there was no lingering smell of death or decay either. So maybe he was wrong. He hoped so.

'You planning on letting me in or what?' Strickland whispered from the window.

Bishop went and opened the door, and Strickland entered and gently closed it behind him. Bishop retraced his steps to the other door and pushed it open, the light spill from the utility room allowing him to see a large, open-spaced, sparsely furnished living room beyond, with a couple of archways leading off from it.

Strickland, just behind him, said, 'You sure turning on the lights is a good idea? What about that dog?'

'Look at the dishes on the floor behind us,' Bishop said in his normal voice. 'If the dog hasn't heard or smelled us by now, he isn't going to. That goes for the wife too.' He looked to the wall at his left and saw another panel, this one with three switches. He stepped inside, flicked all the switches and the living room instantly lit up.

There was a familiar canine odour in this part of the house, which immediately reminded Bishop of his old mongrel, Casper. His childhood bedroom had smelled exactly the same, no matter how many times he was forced to clean it.

The living-room furnishings consisted of a large L-shaped couch, two easy chairs and an oak coffee table arranged around a large TV. Against the left-hand wall were three chest-high bookshelves, filled with a combination of paperbacks and magazines. Directly ahead was a large archway that led to a hallway with more doorways on either side. At the other end, Bishop could see the front door of the house. To the right, another large archway led to what looked like a dining room. Next to the archway was another door, which was shut.

'You check through there,' Bishop said, pointing to the archway that led to the front of the house. 'I'll check the rest. Turn the lights on if you need to. Whistle if you find anything.'

Strickland moved off ahead and Bishop went to the right, passing the long drapes that covered the sliding glass doors. He went to the closed door first, and opened it. It was a bathroom. Set into the right-hand wall was the frosted window he'd seen outside.

Exiting, he stepped through the adjacent archway into a large windowless dining area with a large round table and four chairs in the centre. The table surface was completely clean. There were various framed photos on the wall. Many featured Lomax with his wife at home or on holiday. There were also a number of shots of a German shepherd pup playing in the grass. Bishop noticed the room smelled faintly of burnt toast, mixed in with stale tobacco.

Directly ahead of him was another open doorway leading to a darkened kitchen area. He stepped through and looked around, but there wasn't enough light. He found the wall switch and pressed it and two harsh, fluorescent tubes in the ceiling came on instantly.

Looking past the breakfast bar on the right, he saw only the usual kitchen appliances. Ahead was a window that looked out onto the garage. Underneath the window was the sink and various kitchen cabinets, to the left more cabinets and a wooden door. Probably the entrance to a basement.

By the door, Bishop pressed his ear against the wood but heard nothing on the other side. He grasped the handle and pressed it down.

Pulling the door open, he saw only darkness.

But only for a moment.

Bishop heard a low menacing growl and saw a brief flash of sharp fangs, then something resembling a demon from hell leaped out of the darkness and slammed right into his chest.

SIXTY-FIVE

Bishop swore and crashed to the kitchen floor with a hundred pounds of snarling dog on top of him. Completely winded, Bishop struggled for breath as the German shepherd's huge front paws scrabbled against his chest and he felt hot, sickly breath close to his face. The dog gave a single bark that almost deafened him, and Bishop instinctively rolled his body to the left, forcing the animal off him and onto the floor.

The dog didn't stop moving. His rear paws scrabbled against the tiles and he immediately swivelled his body so he was facing Bishop again. His eyes were wild, his fangs bared in a terrifying grin. Without pause, the muscles in his hind legs bunched and he suddenly launched himself again. Bishop barely had time to raise his left arm for protection when the dog crashed into him and forced him onto his back once more.

Bishop, expecting to feel sharp incisors ripping through his left jacket sleeve, was surprised when he felt something like sandpaper moving up and down his palm instead.

It was the dog's tongue. He was licking Bishop's hand. And he wasn't growling anymore, but whimpering.

Strickland appeared at Bishop's left. '*Christ*, that thing's *huge*. You okay, man?'

The dog turned to the new sound with his ears folded back. He snarled and bared his teeth. Bishop quickly reached out with his other hand and massaged the dog's head, spreading his fingers between the soft fur between his ears. The snarling stopped.

'Be quiet and stand still,' he told Strickland. To the dog, he said in a soothing tone, 'There's a good boy. We're all friends here. That's right. That's a good boy.'

The dog, clearly calmed by the petting and the soft voice, answered by whimpering and trying to lick Bishop's other hand again. The dog's tongue was completely dry, though, and Bishop noticed his eyes also seemed dull. Clearly weakened from thirst and hunger, jumping out of that basement must have used up his last vestiges of strength. Still massaging the dog's fur, Bishop noticed a circular metal tag on the dog's collar with the word BIFF engraved in large capitals.

'So where the hell did he come from?' Strickland said.

'The basement over there. You thirsty, Biff? You want some water, boy?'

The dog gave a weak wag of his tail at the sound of his name and his whimpers became more plaintive. 'Go get that water bowl from the utility room,' Bishop said.

Strickland trotted off, returning a few seconds later with the half-full bowl of water. He put it down next to the dog and Biff immediately sunk his muzzle into the bowl and began lapping up the contents, splashing most of it onto the floor. He finished it off in a matter of seconds and Bishop filled it up again from the cold tap in the sink. As soon as he placed the bowl on the floor, the dog dived in again.

'That's one thirsty animal,' Strickland said.

'Check the basement,' Bishop said, as he began searching the kitchen cabinets for dog food. 'See what else is down there.'

'Right.' Strickland went away and Bishop finally found a cabinet full of tinned goods, including about half a dozen cans of Lamb and Chicken Pedigree. Bishop opened two of the tins, grabbed a soup bowl from another cabinet, and emptied both tins into it. He placed the soup bowl next to the water and Biff immediately switched his attention to the food, lapping up the chunks with great enthusiasm.

Bishop turned to see Strickland emerging from the basement stairs.

'Some kind of office space down there,' he said. 'It's pretty pokey, but there's a desk with a PC and stuff. Not much else except a few boxes of old clothes and books they must have been saving for Goodwill or something. Some of the clothes are torn to shit, thanks to your new friend there. He had a few accidents down there too, so it doesn't smell too good.'

'What about the other rooms?'

'Well, there's two bedrooms at the front. The big one's got its own bathroom and a double bed that looks slept in on one side. The smaller one's been converted into some kind of office for the wife, with computer, printer, and all the usual stuff.'

'You sure it's her office area, and not his?'

'Pretty sure. The room's got pink drapes, and there's flowers on the desk.'

Bishop nodded and watched the dog eat, wondering how he'd got locked down in the basement in the first place, without food or water. On the surface, it suggested his suspicions had been correct, that some of Hartnell's boys had paid Karen Lomax a visit recently. And since they would have simply shot the animal rather than risk being ravaged, it seemed likely Karen was the one who locked Biff down there. Maybe she'd planned to put some food and water in there, too, but didn't have time before she was taken away. But taken to where?

'It's eleven twenty,' Strickland said, pocketing his cell phone.

Bishop blinked at him. 'Okay.'

'I mean, it's eleven twenty so let's get *moving*. We got a date, remember?'

'We've still got time. It'll take us less than three hours to reach the Ohio state line.'

'But then we still have to drive to whatever location Callaway gives us when he calls at five, and that could be anywhere.'

'He already said it'll be somewhere like Greenville or Sidney, which are both cities in the western part of the state, so it's likely to be somewhere around there. And besides, I've already got something in mind that might improve our odds on that score.'

'What do you mean?'

'Later. But for now, we're staying until I can get a handle on what happened here.'

'What's the point? If Hartnell's people grabbed Lomax's wife then she could be just about anywhere now. We don't have time for a search and rescue mission.'

'I already told you I'm not going down for something I didn't do,' Bishop said, ruffling Biff's fur. The dog ignored him and continued eating. 'That's why we're here, remember. To find something that tells me for sure it was Lomax behind the leak. Finding Mrs Lomax also falls under that category. Now just be quiet for a minute and let me think.'

Without waiting for a response, Bishop thought back to Delaney's comments regarding Lomax. About how he was convinced his wife was screwing around behind his back, despite there being no evidence to the contrary. But maybe there *was* evidence to the contrary. Or signs, at least. Maybe Lomax wasn't just creating imaginary problems out of nothing. Maybe he had reason to be suspicious, and maybe he'd done something about it. Because that PC in the basement puzzled Bishop. If the computer in the converted office was Karen's, then the one in the cellar had to be Lomax's. But why stick it in a tiny hovel?

Unless he was using it for purposes he didn't want his wife to know about. And not internet porn either. Maybe he had another reason to keep it from her. And Bishop had a faint idea what that reason might be.

Conscious of the seconds ticking away, Bishop pushed off from the kitchen counter and marched back to the living room, where he turned right and then entered the open doorway on the left. He turned on the light and saw it was a fairly large bedroom. As Strickland had said, only one side of the double bed had been slept in, which at least suggested that Lomax's suspicions about his wife were of his own making. But that didn't matter now. Bishop was just hoping Lomax had acted on his paranoia.

Sticking close to the walls, he walked slowly around the room, studying the ornamental moulding near the ceiling. Looking for any kind of anomaly at all. But after completing a full circuit he found nothing. He stood in the middle of the bed and stared up at the light fixture inches above his head. It was a recessed downlight, like the one in the living room, with four small Phillips screws in the circular metal trim to hold the housing above in place.

But everything looked as it should be. He couldn't see anything out of place.

Exiting the bedroom, he tried the converted office opposite, which was a much smaller room and clearly feminine in nature. If nothing else, the pale mauve wallpaper was a dead giveaway. Bishop paced the room, checked the cornice plastering and the light trim as before, but once again saw nothing of any interest.

The living room was next.

After a complete circuit of the main living area, he once again looked up at the light fixture. Keeping his eyes averted from the bulb itself, Bishop stared up at the trim and tilted his head, frowning deeply. All the screws had Phillips heads as before, but one of them didn't look quite right. It looked as though somebody had placed a tiny drop of black paint in the centre of the head.

Except Bishop knew it wasn't paint.

Strickland was standing a few feet away, watching him. 'What the hell are you looking at?' he asked.

'The man in the moon.'

'Yeah? Well, I don't think you'll find him up there.'

Bishop smiled. 'You'd be surprised.'

SIXTY-SIX

Bishop descended the stairs to the basement, where the smell of urine and faeces was so strong he had to breathe through his mouth.

Strickland was right. It was a tiny space. Maybe ten foot by twelve, with a low ceiling and brick walls, more a storage room than an actual basement. There was a naked bulb in the centre of the ceiling. Against one wall was a cheap wooden work desk containing three drawers, and a Samsung PC, tower hard drive, and keyboard on top. In front of the desk was a basic office chair on casters. Set against the opposite wall were three large boxes full of old clothes and books. There was a pile of excrement in one corner, and probably elsewhere too. The floor was also covered with torn clothes, some stained with urine.

'Didn't I warn you about the smell?' Strickland said from the doorway above.

Bishop turned towards the desk. Next to the tower hard drive was a modem, out of which three cables ran down the back of the desk. Bishop grabbed the edge of the desk, slid it away from the wall, and saw one of the modem cables was plugged into a double wall socket, while a second plug led back to the tower hard drive. But more interestingly, in amongst the wealth of cables back there he noticed a thin one running from the back of the hard drive into a hole at the rear of the middle desk drawer. He also traced the route of another one that ran from the back of the hard drive and up the wall, disappearing into a hole in the ceiling.

After sliding the desk back against the wall, Bishop opened the middle desk drawer. There was a mass of official-looking paperwork inside. Most of it was loose, although some batches were held together with large paper clips. He reached in, grabbed hold of all the paperwork and placed it on the desk. And there at the bottom of the drawer he saw the same cable connected up with a small black external hard drive.

'What did you find?' Strickland asked from behind him.

Bishop turned to him. 'How good are you with computers?'

Strickland shrugged. 'I can hold my own. Why? What do you need?'

'I think Lomax has a fibre-optic surveillance camera installed in the living-room light. Probably motion-activated.' He pointed at the wire that disappeared into the ceiling. 'I think that leads to the camera, and I think the footage is stored on this little hard drive here.'

'Why would he do that?' Strickland was frowning. 'This isn't exactly a high crime area, is it? Plus there's that huge dog upstairs, too.'

'I think he was less concerned with matters of security and more concerned with keeping an eye on his wife. Delaney said he had major trust issues. Anyway, it won't take long to check, will it?'

'I don't know,' Strickland said, switching on the monitor and hard drive as he sat down. 'Don't PCs usually need a password? Because if this one does, we're screwed.'

Bishop had been thinking the same thing. But they had nothing to lose by trying.

The hard drive made a few electronic clicking noises, while the monitor showed a Microsoft logo on a black screen with a message informing them that Windows was starting. Soon, the display changed to a blue background and a password prompt appeared in the centre.

'Like I said,' Strickland said gloomily. 'It wants a password.'

Bishop leaned in closer. The screen showed an icon of Scooby-Doo next to a user name, *FrankL*, with a space underneath for the password. Which could be anything. But on the other hand, people often came up with pretty lame passwords for their computers. He recalled his sister Amy, who was an otherwise highly intelligent woman, had simply joined up her son's and daughter's first names for hers. And it seemed fairly obvious that Lomax was a man who loved dogs. Even cartoon ones. Bishop looked over to the stairwell and saw the family German shepherd lying at the base of the doorway with his head resting on his outstretched paws, watching them both.

'Try *Biff*,' Bishop said, and the dog began wagging his tail at the sound of his name.

Strickland turned to him. 'Huh?'

'The dog's name is Biff. B-I-F-F. Try that.'

Strickland faced the screen and keyed in the four letters and hit Enter. Nothing happened. He then typed in the same four letters and added *1* at the end. He pressed Enter again.

This time the password prompt was immediately replaced by a green-tinted shot of the Pyramids of Giza, with two columns of icons running down the left-hand side.

'How about that,' Strickland said, pulling his head back. 'We're in.'

'People should take more care with their passwords.' Bishop checked the icons until he found the hard drive one on the second column. He pointed and said, 'Open that.'

Strickland moved the mouse and clicked on the icon and a folder opened up. Inside the folder were twenty-two .mkv video files. The title of the first one was *000243* and it was recorded three weeks before on October sixteenth. The next one, *000244,* was recorded a day later, and so it went down the line, which meant the footage was automatically saved in twenty-four-hour chunks. And since there was only file for each day, it also meant there was only the one camera. The files all varied greatly in size too, although that made sense if the camera was motion-activated.

The largest file was 756 MB while the lowest was yesterday's instalment, at only 4 KB. Obviously, with the dog in the basement and Karen Lomax absent, there'd been nothing for the camera to record. Today's recording was only 17.3 MB, and would contain a few minutes of Bishop and Strickland's entrance along with a few seconds of Bishop looking right into the camera lens. But he was more interested in the file from two days before, the day of the massacre.

The file size for that one was 34.7 MB. Bishop pointed at it and said, 'Let's take a look at this.'

Strickland double-clicked on the file, which automatically launched the VLC Media Player. A video screen with basic navigation controls appeared in the top left corner of the screen. In the lower right corner of the video screen was the date and a time counter. The time read *00.01.24.*

Strickland moved the cursor to the navigation controls and clicked the Play button.

SIXTY-SEVEN

The video screen showed a black-and-white, fish-eye aerial shot of the living room. The camera was at a very slight angle, so the view also included the lower part of the archway entrance leading to the front of the house. Bishop guessed it was the living-room light coming on that must have activated it. As the seconds ticked away on the time counter, all Bishop saw was a static view of the couch and the chairs and the coffee table.

'Isn't there any sound?' he asked.

Strickland edged closer. 'Should be. The volume's on max.' He pressed a button on the control panel and the video enlarged to completely fill the screen. The video quality wasn't too bad. Hardly high definition, but then you couldn't expect too much detail from a fibre-optic.

All of a sudden there was a series of loud barks, and a few seconds later Bishop saw a dark-haired female figure in a knee-length dressing gown backing into the living room from the direction of the front door. She had both arms around Biff's neck and was dragging him back with her. Then Bishop saw the reason why. Two men followed them into the room, each holding a gun. The man on the left – stocky, black, with close-cropped hair, wearing a leather bomber jacket and light pants – kept his gun on Karen Lomax, while his Caucasian partner – leaner, fair-haired, wearing army jacket and jeans – kept his piece aimed at the dog. Biff kept on barking at the two intruders, even with Karen talking into his ear.

'*Get away from the mutt, lady,*' Army Jacket shouted, still aiming the gun at the dog.

Biff's barking began to tail off. Karen, still holding onto him, said, 'Please don't shoot. I'll lock him away in the basement if you want, but please don't kill him.'

300

'I said move away, bitch,' the same one said. He was no longer shouting, but he sounded no less threatening.

'Be cool, Roy,' Leather Jacket said. 'Lady, you go ahead and lock him up if you want.'

Roy turned to him with his mouth open. 'You shittin' me, Curtis?'

Leather Jacket, or Curtis, shrugged. 'I got no problem popping a cap in somebody, but I ain't shootin' no dogs. All right, Mrs Lomax, where's this basement?'

'Through the kitchen over there,' she said. 'You know my name? But I thought—'

'Yeah, I know what you thought.' Curtis chuckled. 'But home invasions ain't exactly our style. Now let's get this dog of yours stashed away before my partner here starts getting impatient. Move it.'

Curtis followed Mrs Lomax and Biff out of shot, while the other one placed his gun in his waistband and pulled a pack of cigarettes and lighter from his jacket pocket. He extracted and lit a cigarette, then grabbed the gun again. This at least explained the faint tobacco smell Bishop had noticed before.

Less than a minute later, Curtis and a sniffling Karen Lomax came back into shot, without Biff. He said, 'All right, lady, we still got a short drive ahead of us so you better get some clothes on. It's cold out and you're gonna be with us for a while.'

'Clothes?' she said in a breaking voice. 'But . . . but I still don't understand what you want from me.'

'You just need to make some phone calls to your old man when we tell you. That's all. Easy as pie.'

'Phone calls? But why? And for how long? What about my dog? He's locked down there with no—'

Roy grabbed her harshly by the arm. 'No more questions, bitch. From now on you just do as you're told, understand?' He smiled at his partner and said, 'I'll make sure she gets dressed okay,' as he dragged the poor woman towards the bedroom.

Curtis sat on the coffee table and waited.

Less than a minute later, there was a muffled ringing sound and he pulled out a cell phone from his jacket pocket. He checked the display and then brought it to his ear and said, 'Hello? . . . Yeah,

yeah, we're there now. It all went like clockwork. We're just about to leave for the . . . Yeah, that's right . . . Well, don't blame me, *I* didn't pick it out. You know how Roy goes apeshit over anything to do with the movies. We were out scoping the area and he saw the old place and his eyes just lit up. Said it reminded him of his childhood.' He laughed at something, then said, 'Well, that's where he gets all his tough-guy dialogue from . . . Yeah, well, it's pretty cold in there, but we picked up portable heaters and lights from a camping store, and there ain't any neighbours so we should be all right for a few days.'

He paused, listening to the person on the other end for a few moments, then said, 'That so? So where's he planning to make the exchange? . . . Same place he used last time, huh? . . . Well, he's got a long history with the main man, so I guess he can play it however he wants . . . Yeah, I know . . . Okay, I'll call you again in a couple of hours . . . Right.'

He hung up the phone, then walked off towards the bedroom and disappeared off the screen. With nothing to see, Bishop strained to listen. He could make out very faint voices, mixed in with equally faint barking. Obviously Biff, voicing his displeasure at being locked away from his mistress. For all his talk about not wanting to shoot dogs, Curtis sure didn't seem too bothered about locking them underground and starving them to death.

Two more minutes passed with nothing happening. Then at 01.32.18 Bishop saw a pair of tan pants and black shoes and then the living-room light went off. A few seconds later he heard the slam of a door, after which there was nothing but darkness and the faint sound of barking. It seemed the three of them had just left the house.

At the bottom of the screen, the playhead was about an inch from the end of the timeline. 'Fast-forward the rest,' Bishop said.

Strickland slowly dragged the cursor across the playhead. The video screen stayed dark for another two minutes until the movie simply stopped. He sat back in the chair and looked at Bishop. 'So did I hear right? This Curtis character actually *knows* the final location for the switch?'

'We both heard it.' Bishop leaned against the wall facing the stairs, where the dog was still in the same position, still watching them. 'And if we can locate him quickly and I pry that same information out of him we've got a good chance of reaching the site before Callaway gets there, and who knows what might happen then?'

'Yeah,' Strickland said, nodding. 'That'd sure be something, wouldn't it? But at least you know Lomax *was* the leak now too.'

'No, he wasn't.'

'Huh? What are you talking about? You heard what that Curtis said to—'

'Think it over for a moment,' Bishop said. 'According to what we've heard, it seems Karen Lomax was told to call her husband yesterday morning at regular intervals and make sure he was doing what he was supposed to, such as sabotaging the getaway vehicle and hiding that key. But why didn't those two break into the house the night before, or *two* nights before? Why wait until the morning of the attack to grab her?'

Strickland looked at him. 'You lost me. What difference does that make?'

'It makes all the difference. It means that while her husband probably did sabotage the getaway car, he couldn't possibly be the cause of the leak that led them there in the first place.'

'Why not?'

'Because the whole thing would take too long to set up. The assault on the safe house started at a quarter past seven yesterday morning, yet those two goons didn't show up here until a quarter past one that very same morning. So even if Lomax gave them our location the moment he was contacted, that still only gives Callaway six hours at most to organize and prep everything. Which is impossible. It simply can't be done, not within that timescale. His hit team still have to fly to Vegas and familiarize themselves with the location and work out getaway routes. Then there's the fake courier van to arrange, and the fake mailman. And then there's that bus driver too, don't forget.'

'Hey, you lost me again.' Strickland patted the air. 'What bus driver?'

Bishop realized he was thinking out loud, and that Strickland couldn't possibly know what he was talking about since he'd been in the bedroom with Barney at the time.

'There was a school bus that faked a breakdown near the front of the house,' he said. 'That's how it all started. Sweeney said it was the same guy as the day before, and I know for a fact that the driver was one of Hartnell's people, which means they *had* to know the location at least a day before they hit us. Probably longer. There's no other way. It was all too well planned. Also, this Curtis told Karen Lomax she'd be staying with them for a while, so obviously they're holding her on ice for good reason. But I can't figure out what they could be waiting for. Unless it's for Lomax to regain consciousness . . .'

'Hey, look,' Strickland cut in, 'this is all real interesting, but how about we just focus on one thing at a time, huh? The clock's still ticking, in case you hadn't noticed.'

Bishop smiled at the mild rebuke. 'Okay, so depending on what Curtis classifies as a short drive, then it's reasonable to assume Karen Lomax is being kept not too far from here. Either somewhere in Bloomington or in a neighbouring town. And if they've got any intelligence at all, probably the latter.'

Strickland scratched at his chin stubble. 'What's wrong with this place, though? We're in a remote location with not many neighbours. Seems like a perfect spot already.'

'And if Lomax wakes up and decides not to play ball anymore, and says his wife's currently being held hostage? Where's the first place the cops are going to check?'

Strickland nodded. 'Okay, I get you. But this Curtis said they were heading out to some old place they'd found, where they needed to bring in their own heaters and lights. So somewhere abandoned, you think?'

'I think. And from the comments he made about his partner, Roy, I'm inclined to believe it's an old deserted movie theatre, or something along those lines. Is that modem switched on?'

Strickland reached forward and clicked something at the back of the box. Green lights started flashing. 'It is now. Hey, maybe he was talking about an abandoned drive-in site. You know, like an old ticket office or something. There's plenty of those in Indiana.'

'That's possible, I guess, although we could be here the rest of the night checking those. Bloomington's smack in the centre of Monroe County, though, so let's restrict the search to that area.'

Bishop watched as Strickland opened a browser. He keyed *abandoned drive-in monroe indiana* into Google's search panel and pressed Enter. He checked the results, then shook his head and went to the next page. As he scanned the third page of listings, he said, 'Turns out they got a few drive-ins still doing business in this area. They even got a big one in Harrodsburg, about twenty miles to the south of us.'

'If it's still in business, then it's no good as a hideout. What else?'

'There's an abandoned one in Huntsville to the north, which is *well* out of Monroe, and another one in Bedford, forty miles south of us.'

'That's too far away. For them, and for us.'

'Well, that's it for old drive-ins, then. At least as far as Google's concerned.' Next, he typed *abandoned movie theatre monroe indiana* into the search panel and pressed Enter. More results came up. Strickland leaned in close to the screen and when he reached the bottom of the first page, he said, 'Hey, I might have something here.'

Bishop looked as Strickland clicked on the mouse. A new page opened up with *The Breeden Gazette* in large red letters at the top. So clearly a local newspaper. Under the headline, *Business Consortium Puts Forward Offer for Downtown Properties*, were two short paragraphs accompanied by two photos. One showed a line of rundown, one-storey, retail premises with shutters over the fronts. The other photo depicted a dilapidated two-storey building out on its own, but in a similar area. There was a half-destroyed marquee out front, while thick wooden planks had been nailed over the front entrance. THE CARDINAL was written in large faded red script along the side of the building.

Bishop skimmed through the article. It didn't say much more than the headline. Just that a newly formed consortium of local business owners had put in an offer for two blocks of Breeden's downtown area along South Shelbourne Road, and were already talking to investors and contractors about constructing a shopping mall and multiplex on the site. They were also talking to city councilmen about zoning permissions.

'The Cardinal,' Strickland said. 'For a temporary hideout, I'd say that place pretty much fits the bill.'

Bishop had to agree. 'And no other prospects in the vicinity?'

Strickland clicked on the next page of search results, quickly perused the entries, then tried the third page. Finally he shook his head. 'Can't find anything.'

'Okay, so how far's Breeden from here?'

Strickland went to Google Maps and keyed *Breeden Indiana* into the search box. The resulting map showed a small township along Route 46. Strickland zoomed out until they were able to see it was only about fifteen miles north-west of their current location.

'Good,' Bishop said.

He checked the time in the top right corner of the screen: *00.04.* Only six hours left. Call it three and a half hours to get to the Ohio state line, then possibly another hour or so to reach the final site. Assuming things went as he wanted them to.

And how often does that happen?

No doubt about it: it would be tight. But if they could find out the final location ahead of time, it would be more than worth the risk. Added to which, there was also the matter of Karen Lomax. Bishop couldn't just stand by and leave her in the hands of those two, especially as there was no possible way they were going to leave her alive afterwards. And it had nothing to do with the fact that she could put in a good word for him, either. He'd feel the same way if she were a complete stranger. Besides, the footage they'd just seen would be enough to get the cops off his back once this was all over, so in effect he didn't actually need the woman at all anymore. But he still had to do something.

He watched as Strickland sat there, quietly thinking things through. Bishop also found it odd how his feelings for the guy kept fluctuating. For instance, after learning of his true connection to Hartnell, Bishop's opinion of the guy had immediately taken a downward swing, and it hadn't been all that high to begin with. Yet during their time together on the road Strickland had gradually grown on him again. His clear unambiguous love for the boy and his willingness to lay down his life for him was the main reason for that, of course. It was an attitude Bishop couldn't help but admire, and respect.

And Strickland also knew that if Hartnell had his way his final moments wouldn't be easy. That was a hard thing to grasp for most people. Bishop had long ago come to terms with his own demise, for example, and he knew when it came it would probably be violent. But it was different when it was in the abstract, whereas Strickland had a fairly good idea of *when* he was going to go. And that it would be painful.

But the man didn't falter. Like all single-minded people, he just kept on going until he reached his goal. Bishop liked that. And he was also coming to realize that Barney's inner strength might not have been inherited solely from his mother's side.

Strickland finally raised his head, and said, 'You waiting on me?'

'I'm ready to go whenever you are.'

Strickland stood up. 'Then let's get to it,' he said.

SIXTY-EIGHT

They reached the township of Breeden – *pop. 3,400* – at 00.23.

Before leaving the house Bishop had left some extra food and water to keep the big guy going for a while, and he'd also found a mini LED flashlight with working batteries in one of the kitchen drawers and taken it along, knowing it was bound to come in handy. Once back in the Nissan, Bishop had then taken them north-west on Route 46 until they reached their destination a quarter of an hour later.

There were very few places still open in the main part of town. Just a handful of bars, an all-night diner and an Esso gas station. Turning onto South Shelbourne Road at 00.26, Bishop reduced his speed to twenty and watched both sides, looking for something he recognized. There were no pedestrians at that time of night and their car was the only moving vehicle on the street, which seemed to be made up entirely of business premises and retail units. The further south they went the more impoverished things became, although there were still a few cars parked along both sides of the street.

'*There*,' Strickland said, pointing to something up ahead on the right.

Bishop followed his finger and saw, under the glow of a streetlight, a row of shuttered stores that looked similar to those on the website photo. As they cruised slowly past Bishop saw they were the very same units, and in the same state of disrepair. It didn't look as though the consortium had made a whole lot of progress so far.

To the left of the units was a large vacant lot. And past that, about five hundred feet further along, was the old movie theatre.

Bishop could just about make out the CARDINAL letters on the side of the building, while a ten-foot-high wooden fence partly screened it off from the vacant lot on its right. As they came closer he saw the ancient marquee hanging over the front and the thick wooden planks still nailed over the front entrance and windows. As they were passing it, Bishop saw a narrow passageway between the building and the fence, no doubt leading to a parking area at the rear. It was protected by a chain-link fence and steel gate halfway down.

Then they were past it. Two more shuttered-up businesses served as neighbours before they came to the end of the block. Bishop turned right at the intersection into McNeely Street and saw an old Chevy sedan parked by the kerb twenty feet away. He pulled in behind it and brought the vehicle to a stop. He switched off the engine.

It was 00.29.

'You stay in the car,' he said. 'I'll leave the keys in the ignition. If something happens, like cops showing up and showing an interest, anything, you drive away.'

'What? You mean leave you here?'

'Preferably not, but do what the situation demands. Circle the block and come back if you can, but only if you think it's safe.'

'What if you don't come back out? Hey, don't look at me like that. It *could* happen.'

'I won't let it. Remember what I said about a positive attitude? But if the worst *does* happen, then you've got no other choice but to go to the feds and tell them everything.'

Strickland looked incredulous. 'Yeah, right.'

'I mean it. At least with them Barney'll have a chance. Without them he's got none at all. But it won't come to that. One way or the other I'll be out of there within the next half an hour. Hand me the multi-tool, will you?'

Strickland pulled out the multi-tool and handed it over. Bishop then pulled the Glock from his waistband, checked to make sure there was a round in the chamber, and put it back. He got out.

'Don't be late, man,' Strickland said as he slid across into the driver's seat.

'I won't be,' Bishop said, then walked back towards the old theatre.

SIXTY-NINE

Bishop moved briskly past the two closed-up retail units on his left, slowing his pace a little when he reached the old movie house itself. The cold night air felt good against his face, and helped sharpen his senses until he felt they were close to their maximum setting. There were streetlights every fifty feet or so, more than enough to see by. He could also hear some faint traffic noises filtering through from adjacent streets, but he was still the only thing moving on South Shelbourne.

Passing the theatre's heavily boarded-up entrance, he turned left at the side passageway and kept on until he reached the chain-link fence and gate. The fence was about eight feet high and looked old and rusty. The gate itself was about seven feet wide, just big enough for a vehicle to pass through. Bishop smiled when he saw the padlock. It was on the other side of the gate. That alone told him he'd come to the right place.

Looking to his left and right, he noticed that the steel terminal posts at each end and the two line posts on either side of the gate were permanently set into the concrete. That was good. He stepped over the left-hand terminal post and tried shaking it. The thing barely moved. Old, but solid. Bishop grabbed hold of the fence ties and climbed up without making a sound. Upon reaching the top rail, he dragged himself over and dropped down on the other side.

Sticking close to the side of the building, Bishop carried on walking and when he reached the end, peered round the corner and saw a large open area that must have been a customer parking lot once. Without streetlights he had to rely on the faint moonlight filtering through the clouds, but he was able to see the wooden fence continued all the way round the lot. Laid alongside the fence thirty feet straight ahead were three abandoned wrecks – a sedan, a pick-up, and a station wagon of some kind. They were all missing windows and doors. None of them had wheels. It looked as though they'd been there for years. About fifty feet to his left, set close to the fence, were three very large dumpsters.

A dog howled somewhere far away. Then another one joined it.

Bishop turned the corner and kept going along the rear of the building. The few windows he passed on the first floor all had thick timber planks nailed across the openings. There were also a number of windows on the second floor, but they'd been left alone. Bishop finally stopped when he came to the rear exit, which was a rusty-looking steel fire door. Lying on the ground nearby were several two-by-fours, which indicated this was now the sole entrance and exit. The door itself looked pretty solid. And, of course, there was no handle.

So how the hell did those two punks get in initially?

Then he looked to his right and saw that not *all* the ground-floor windows were boarded up. There was a small awning window about ten feet to the right of the fire exit door, at about head height. Bishop went over and saw somebody had smashed one corner of the frosted safety glass, leaving a hole about the size of a fist. The window itself was about two feet across and a foot-and-a-half deep, and it opened inwards. He pressed an ear to the gap and listened. After a few seconds, he thought he could hear very faint music coming from somewhere inside. Maybe a radio, he wasn't sure. But definitely signs of life.

Pulling the mini flashlight from his pocket, Bishop switched it on and moved it around the gap. Beyond was a small men's room, containing a single booth and two urinals against the right-hand wall. The room looked old and dirty. Probably a staff restroom, since the general public would have required something much bigger. Set in the left wall was a doorway, but no door. Bishop was able to see part of a corridor beyond that presumably led to the fire exit at his left.

Bishop carefully reached his hand through the gap and felt around the frame until his fingers touched a metal catch at the bottom. He unlatched it and pushed the window up as far as it would go. The space was big enough. Just.

He let it close again, clicked off the flashlight, and went over to the dumpsters. He still hadn't seen their vehicle and felt certain they wouldn't have risked parking on the street outside. So it had to be back here somewhere. And sure enough, as he got closer, he could make out a large SUV sitting between the nearest dumpster and the fence.

He walked up to it. It was a Nissan Armada and looked about ten years old. He tried reaching under the hood, but there was barely any gap there at all. He couldn't get a purchase. Pity. He'd have liked to remove the fuses that controlled the ignition, but there were always other ways to disable a vehicle.

Removing the multi-tool, Bishop extracted the knife and circled the Nissan, making deep slashes in each tyre as he went. All four radials were flat within seconds. Satisfied his targets wouldn't be making any quick getaways, Bishop turned back to the building and looked up. Now he was far enough away, he could see a faint light coming from the second-floor window directly above the fire exit door.

So *that's* where they were. Good.

Bishop returned to the first-floor window and pushed it all the way open. Then he climbed up and slipped through the gap.

SEVENTY

Bishop gently lowered himself to the floor and sidled over to the doorway. It was as chilly inside as out, and the room also contained a strong musty smell. But no other odours, which suggested they were using another restroom upstairs. He peered round the doorway and saw a long, featureless corridor leading back into the building. There was also a faint light source coming from somewhere on the right, about thirty feet up ahead.

Bishop pocketed the flashlight and pulled the Glock from his waistband.

He stepped through the doorway and began walking slowly down the corridor towards the light source. He kept close to the left-hand wall, making sure not to step on the old food wrappers and ancient newspapers that littered the floor.

The sounds he'd heard before gradually became a little more noticeable. It was a radio station, and he could make out a late-night DJ yacking on about something or other. But it was still very faint. Finally he came to the light source itself, which originated from above a concrete switchback stairwell on his right.

The rest of the corridor was shrouded in darkness. Bishop guessed there was a door somewhere down there that led to the auditorium, as well as the lobby and box office.

Still keeping close to the wall, Bishop began climbing the staircase. At the half-landing, he turned and climbed the rest of the steps until he reached the top. He saw the upper landing opened out onto another corridor that continued left towards the rear of the building, matching the one downstairs.

From somewhere to his left the radio was now playing some old techno track, but the volume was very low, even up here, which proved these two weren't complete dummies. If Bishop made a wrong sound, they'd hear it.

Bishop poked part of his head out and saw the corridor went back another thirty feet or so, ending at the window he'd spotted outside. The main light was coming from a lantern on the floor, one of those battery-operated camping jobs with the handle at the top. A second light source was coming from an open doorway on the right, about ten or twelve feet away from Bishop. There was a second open doorway further down on the right, but that remained dark.

He stepped fully out into the corridor, Glock at the ready.

Now he was able to see there were also two more doorways on the left side. But these actually had doors, both of which were shut. He couldn't hear anything else over the faint sound of the radio. Bishop inched along the corridor towards the first open doorway, the Glock hanging at his side.

When he reached the doorjamb, he peered round into the room and saw the black guy from the footage: the one called Curtis.

He was sitting in profile to Bishop with his back to the wall, still wearing the same leather jacket, and moving his fingers over an iPad. It looked like he was playing a computer game. That seemed to be where the music was coming from too. There was an open bottle of beer lying on the floor, just by his right hip. Next to the bottle was a large-calibre revolver. The light came from another lantern in the far corner.

Bishop edged round the doorjamb and raised the Glock, aiming it at the man's chest while he took in the rest of the room. But other than the lantern and some empty pizza boxes stacked against one wall, the room was empty. No other furnishings and, more importantly, no Roy and no Karen Lomax.

The song faded out and a car commercial came on.

Curtis must have sensed movement. He looked up from the iPad and stared at Bishop. He began to open his mouth, but Bishop immediately raised an index finger to his lips and he clamped it shut. He still didn't look worried, just surprised. Dropping the iPad on his lap, he glanced down at the gun a few inches away from his right hand. He then looked up at Bishop, who slowly shook his head.

Bishop was just about to step into the room when he heard the sound of a door opening behind him.

'*Shoot him!*' Leather Jacket shouted, and rolled his body away from the wall.

Bishop, already half-turning towards the corridor, squeezed off two shots at the black man as he lunged for his own piece. There was a hoarse grunt from within the room, and Bishop had just enough time to hope he hadn't hit anything vital as he brought his gun round to the darkened doorway opposite. He saw a flash of a fully dressed Roy raising his arm and immediately dived to the right as a shot fizzed past his head. Then a second shot followed right after. Both gunshots were deafening in the enclosed corridor. Somewhere close by a woman screamed.

Bishop landed in the corridor on his right shoulder, turned his body and aimed the Glock at the doorway where he'd seen Roy. But Roy wasn't there. Bastard must have ducked back into the room.

Keeping his arm perfectly steady, Bishop raised himself to his knees, watching for movement of any kind. He could hear muffled female sobbing from somewhere behind him, which could only be Karen Lomax.

Bishop was painfully aware of the camping lantern on the floor directly behind him, outlining him and turning him into the perfect target. He briefly considered shooting it out, but then thought better of the idea. More darkness would only prolong things, and he needed this over with fast. Instead, he gave a long, drawn-out groan, as though he'd been hit.

At the same time he silently edged over to the wall at his left. He kept his gun on the right-hand doorway, but watched both sides. Waiting for the first hint of movement from either doorway.

It wasn't long in coming.

A semi-automatic and part of a man's hand emerged from the right-hand doorway, the barrel pointing at the floor where Bishop had been. The gun roared once, twice, three times. All three rounds pounded into the concrete floor two feet from Bishop and he felt tiny shards of plaster pitter-pattering against his right cheek. Then hand and gun disappeared.

Bishop didn't fire back. Didn't groan again. He just waited. As patient as the dead.

After five long seconds of silence, part of a face poked out from the doorway on the right. Bishop saw a hint of blond hair, aimed, squeezed off two rapid shots.

The face disappeared.

Shuffling forward at a crouch, Bishop kept his gun aimed at the dark doorway and halted when he saw a blond head and part of a shoulder on the floor near the entranceway, lying half in and half out of the shadows. The blond hair was completely soaked with blood, as though it had been washed in the stuff. There was no sign of movement at all.

But there was still Curtis to worry about. Bishop felt certain he'd scored a hit before, though. Hopefully nothing life-threatening, although the light was still on inside, which suggested the guy wasn't in any fit state to turn it off. Bishop wasn't about to take unnecessary chances, though. That was how fools died.

He got to his feet and stood with his back to the wall, next to the lighted doorway. The radio had stopped too. Possibly the iPad had been damaged during the shooting. Either that or Curtis had turned it off himself. Whatever the cause, the building was now completely silent.

'We don't have to do this,' Bishop called out. 'I've got no beef with you. I just want the woman and the location Callaway picked for the exchange later. Roy's dead, but you don't have to be. In fact, you give me what I want and I'll let you go. What do you say?'

No answer. No sounds from within the room. Nothing.

Fearing the worst, Bishop pulled the multi-tool from his pocket and extracted the small knife and raised the blade until it was level with his eyeline. It was old and dirty, but it held a reflection. Holding the knife in his right hand, Bishop moved the blade towards the doorway, angling it slightly until he could see the part of the room he wanted. He found the light first, then angled the blade downwards until he saw an unmoving humanoid shape on the floor. He held the blade steady for a few more seconds, but the shape still didn't move.

Pulling his hand back, Bishop pocketed the knife and lowered himself to a crouch position. Then he swung his body round the doorjamb, gun first.

But Curtis wasn't in any fit state to fire back at him. Nor was he about to provide him with the information he'd come for. He was lying on his back and staring blankly up at the ceiling. Bishop stood up and walked towards the body. As he got closer he saw a small pool of blood on the floor near his head, then he saw the gunshot wound above his left ear.

'Shit,' he said.

He must have got the guy with the first shot, resulting in instant brain death. Kneeling down, he checked for a pulse, but it was pointless. Curtis was now just another statistic. All this time and effort, and for nothing. Bishop picked up the lantern and took it with him to the room opposite. Roy was still where he'd left him, and still just as dead. His head was now a gory mess.

Then he heard a faint sound from behind the other closed door on Roy's side of the hallways. In his disappointment, he'd almost forgotten about Karen Lomax.

So it hadn't *all* been for nothing.

SEVENTY-ONE

Carrying the lantern, Bishop walked to the end of the hallway and opened the last door on the left and stepped inside. He moved the light around until he could make out a dirty mattress in one corner of the room. On it, Karen Lomax, wearing a short-sleeved sweater and jeans, lay in a foetal position with one arm wrapped over her head. The other arm was outstretched and cuffed to an old water pipe that protruded from the wall. Bishop saw the room's sole window was boarded up on the outside, which meant she had to have been living in perpetual darkness all this time.

Bishop raised the lantern for a better look at her and saw numerous bruises and cuts all over her arms. Her long hair was matted and wild.

'Mrs Lomax?' he said softly and the woman suddenly jumped at the sound of his voice. 'You're safe now. They can't hurt you anymore.'

Slowly the woman removed her arm from her head, and looked up at Bishop. He noticed the left eye was all puffed up and surrounded by dark bruising. The right side of her mouth was also heavily swollen and covered in dried blood. The poor woman looked as though she was sucking on a golf ball.

'Y-you mean . . . you mean they're dead?' The words came out muffled, as though she were talking from behind a towel.

'Both of them. You're okay now, Mrs Lomax.' He knelt down in front of her and cleared his throat. 'Uh, did they . . .?'

'No,' she said, looking over towards the doorway. She shivered involuntarily and gave a humourless chuckle. 'No, I was spared that, at least. But that blond one, he . . . he liked using his fists on me. That's what turned him on most, I think. I've lost two teeth at least. Is he . . . is he really dead?'

'He really is.'

'Good,' she said. 'I'm glad.'

'I'd be surprised if you weren't. Let me go find the keys to those cuffs, okay? I won't be a second.'

Leaving the lantern with her, he picked up the light in the hallway and took it back to Roy's body. He searched the corpse's pants pockets and then his jacket pockets, but he didn't find any keys on the guy. Then he went over to Curtis's body and quickly found a large set of keys in his pants pocket, and a cell phone in his jacket. He went through the keys and when he saw one that looked small enough for the cuffs, he returned to Mrs Lomax in the other room.

'Who . . . who are you?' she asked, as he used the key on her wrist.

'A friend.' The key turned and the cuff clicked open.

'Thank you,' she said, pulling her wrist free. She began rubbing it with her other hand. 'But I've never seen you before. How do you know my name? How did you even find me here?'

'It's a long story, Mrs Lomax, and it doesn't really matter right now.' He figured about fifteen minutes had passed since he'd left Strickland in the car, and he desperately wanted to get back on the road again, but he couldn't leave the poor woman just yet. He still had to call 911, plus he had a few questions of his own to ask.

But then Mrs Lomax suddenly slumped forwards and began sobbing quietly. Bishop wanted to comfort her somehow, but wasn't sure what her reaction would be from being touched, so he did nothing. 'It's all right,' he said.

'No, it's not all right,' she said. 'They killed my dog, the *bastards*. That blond one there kept laughing about it when he was beating me, and said he must have already died of hunger by now, alone in the darkness.' She closed her eyes. 'Oh, my poor baby.'

'He was lying,' Bishop said. 'It's only been two days and Biff's perfectly fine, although he misses you.'

Mrs Lomax's head jerked up and she gaped at him. 'You saw Biff? He's all right? *Really?*'

'Really. I let him out of that basement and fed him before coming out here. I also left him enough food and water to last a couple more days, just in case.'

'Oh, thank God.' She said and gave a long sigh. Then she frowned at him. 'Wait a minute, you said I've only been here *two* days?'

'That's right.'

Her shoulders slumped again. 'And I thought I'd been stuck in this room for a week. Only two days. Jesus.'

'Look, Mrs Lomax, I'm calling 911 and then I'll have to leave you before the ambulance and the cops get here. Will you be okay on your own?'

She looked up at him and nodded. 'Now I know my baby's all right, I'll be fine.'

Bishop studied her face. Despite the haggard features and the bruising and the dried blood, it was still a very beautiful face, and he now saw steel behind the woman's eyes that hadn't been there before. He believed her. Nodding, he picked up Curtis's cell phone and dialled 911. When a male dispatcher asked him which service, Bishop quickly gave him the South Sherbourne Street address and said there was an injured woman in need of medical attention on the second floor of the old theatre, as well as the bodies of the two men responsible. He hung up when the dispatcher tried to press him for details, then wiped his prints off the phone and placed it on the floor.

'Before I go,' he said, 'are you up to answering a question or two?'

'Questions? About what?'

'Well, those two were obviously keeping you here for a reason other than just beating up on you. What was the reason?'

Mrs Lomax wiped her good eye and said, 'I don't know. They didn't tell me much. When we first got here I had to call Frank – that's my husband, he's a US marshal – and convince him to do certain things at this safe house he was staying at, or they'd kill me.'

'I know about Frank. Was it hard to convince him?'

'No, not once he realized they were serious. But . . . you know about Frank? How?'

'It doesn't matter. What kinds of things did he have to do?'

'Well, he had to hide some car keys under a mat, I remember that. Then he had to remove the firing pins of certain guns in the house. Oh, and he had to loosen an axle nut on one of the vehicles. The black man told me later that there was some kind of shootout and that Frank was wounded and in hospital, and that the police were all waiting for him to regain consciousness and tell them what happened. Once he woke up, I was to call him and tell him what to do next, but I don't know what I was supposed to say.'

Bishop had a pretty good idea of what she was supposed to say, but he'd heard enough. He had more pressing matters at hand, like vacating the area before the cops arrived.

He got to his feet and said, 'Okay, thanks. I better go now.'

'But what shall I tell the police when they ask about you?'

'Tell them everything that happened. Don't worry about me. I can handle myself.'

'Yes, I can see that. Well . . . thank you. I don't know how I can ever repay you.'

'You already have,' he said, and left her.

SEVENTY-TWO

Bishop was just emerging from the passageway at the side of the building when he heard the sirens in the distance. He couldn't tell from which direction, and there were no tell-tale flashing lights either. But they were getting closer. It seemed they didn't waste any time responding to 911 calls around these parts.

He sprinted down to the end of the block, passing the two remaining buildings, and turned right at the intersection where the Nissan was still where he'd left it.

Strickland must have spotted him in the rear-view. He opened the driver's door, got out and smiled when he saw Bishop approaching. 'Man, I was getting worried for a moment there. Are those sirens for you?'

'Yeah. Get in the other side. I'll drive.'

Strickland jogged round to the passenger side and shut the door. Bishop got in the driver's seat and checked the dashboard clock. It was still only 00.52, which matched his own estimate. He started the engine, but didn't switch on the lights yet. He just sat there watching the front, while checking the rear-view every other second.

'So what are we waiting for?' Strickland said. 'Let's get going.'

'You saw how empty the streets were coming in,' Bishop said. 'A cop seeing us drive away from the scene might wonder what we're doing out so late and decide to check us out. No sense inviting trouble. Let's just wait.'

Bishop counted the seconds as the approaching sirens steadily became louder. Forty-three had already passed when he saw flashing blue and red lights suddenly appear up ahead, about a hundred feet from their position.

'Get down,' Bishop said, sliding down in his own seat until his head was just below the window frame. Strickland quickly did the same.

It took another nine seconds for the vehicle to speed past them, siren blaring and lights flashing. Bishop heard a screeching of brakes as it reached the intersection behind them, and he raised himself up and looked out the rear window. The driver made a sharp left turn and a second later the car was gone, though he could still see the red and blue lights reflecting against the buildings on the other side of the street.

Sitting up again, Bishop turned on the Nissan's headlights and pulled out onto the street. He kept the speed at a steady thirty and headed up McNeely until he reached the next intersection where he turned right. The sirens seemed to be getting fainter, which was a good sign. And while they saw a few more vehicles in the main part of town, none of them were police cars, which was even better.

Finally Bishop got them back on Route 46 and kept them on a south-westerly heading. Once they got close to Bloomington, he'd get onto State Road 37 and head north until they could join the eastbound 252. Then they could really start laying down the miles. As long as there were no more distractions.

'So you planning on telling me how it went back there,' Strickland said, 'or am I supposed to guess?'

Bishop sighed. 'It went badly. They're both dead, so we're no better off than we were before. Karen Lomax is still breathing, though, so it wasn't a total loss.'

'Shit, I knew it all sounded too good to be true.' He shook his head. 'So she's okay, at least?'

'Well, the blond one got his rocks off by repeatedly beating the crap out of her, but she'll heal. She's a born survivor. I even managed to ask her a few questions before I left, and she was able to confirm a few things for me.'

'Yeah? Like what?'

'Like how I was right about her husband. They forced her to call him the morning of the assault and got him to loosen one of the nuts on the SUV's axle, and he also removed firing pins from some of the guns, probably the reserve automatic weapons. And a few other things besides.'

They were approaching a four-way intersection with a red traffic light. There was no other traffic. Bishop drove straight on through without slowing.

'So why were they holding on to her?'

'They were waiting for her husband to regain consciousness, she said. She didn't know why, but if I had to guess, I'd say they were going to put pressure on him to confess that *he* was the inside man right from the start.'

'Why?'

'So Hartnell can protect the real source of the leak, I imagine. And since he wouldn't go to all this trouble just to protect another lowly marshal, it has to be somebody pretty high up on the food chain. Somebody who can still be useful to Hartnell somehow. And I also remember Delaney telling me she was reporting straight to Director Christiansen on this job, which kind of narrows things down.'

'You mean the director of the US Marshals Service? The man at the top?'

Bishop just shrugged.

'Jesus.' Strickland paused, then said, 'But that doesn't make sense. Say Lomax wakes up, does what they want and 'fesses up. What then? Those two bozos back there aren't about to let the wife go, are they? She knows too much.'

'No, they'd have wasted her. Without a doubt.'

'So how can that work then? As soon as Lomax finds out his wife's dead, he retracts his confession and it's back to square one.'

Bishop shook his head. 'Once you confess to a major felony, it's not so easy to go back on it. Especially when all the pieces fit together so nicely. And Lomax actually *did* sabotage the safe house, don't forget. And anyway, how would he ever know for sure that his wife's dead? Those two back there weren't likely to tell him, were they?'

'But the empty house . . .'

'. . . could mean anything,' Bishop finished. 'Everybody knew how suspicious Lomax was in regards to his wife. As far as the feds are concerned she could have simply gotten tired of her husband's attitude and decided to take off. Happens all the time.'

The headlights of an oncoming vehicle lit Strickland's face as he turned to Bishop. 'After leaving her pet dog to starve to death in the basement?'

'That's been known to happen too.'

'Well, you sure screwed up their plans on that score. Those two are dead, the wife's still alive, and her husband's in the clear once he wakes up. So now Hartnell's got something else to worry about. I like that.'

So did Bishop. Lomax had told him on Monday that he was like a loose screw rattling around, messing up the works. Turned out he was right, just not in the way he intended.

There were some overhead signs just up ahead. Bishop saw the next exit was for Route 37 and steered the vehicle into the far right-hand lane. It was 01.03. Four hours before the next phone call, and over two hundred miles still to cover.

Bishop increased their speed.

SEVENTY-THREE

At 02.32, Bishop was heading east on State Road 44 when he heard something interesting on the CB. For much of the journey he'd been listening to static and white noise, interspersed with the occasional snatch of random conversation from nearby operators. But then he caught the middle of a conversation with some guy complaining about a '. . . *shitload of advertising on the 44, east a Connersville. Just cost me half-a-goddamn-hour, and I was already behind. Assholes.*'

Checking there was nothing behind them, Bishop took his foot off the gas and the vehicle began to slow. He knew that, in CB terminology, 'advertising' meant a police car with its lights on. And the speaker, who sounded like a trucker carrying a heavy load, was saying there were a lot of them. Which could only mean a roadblock. And Connersville was the next town along this route, less than three miles away from their current position.

Close. Very, very close.

Pulling over to the side of the road, Bishop listened as another voice came back with, '*I hear you, hoss. They sure know how to screw up a workin' man's timetable.*'

'*You got that right, man,*' the first guy said. '*I tell you, it's gettin' harder and harder to earn an honest buck in this damn country. Assholes, every goddamn last one of 'em. Next time I'll . . .*' Then the signal began to fade out, gradually morphing into static again.

'Trouble?' Strickland asked.

'Roadblock just up ahead, by the sounds of it,' Bishop said. As far as he was concerned the CB radio had just paid for itself. He checked the GPS and quickly came up with an alternate route that would take them past the problem area. Checking his rear-view and seeing nothing behind them, Bishop made a U-turn and then took them west for a few hundred yards until he spotted the turn-off he wanted. It would add another ten or twelve miles to their journey, but they were making pretty good time, so it shouldn't be a problem.

Strickland soon lapsed into silence again. He'd been that way since Breeden, but then the man had plenty to think about. The most important of which was that in three more hours he'd see his son again, probably for the last time.

Bishop had told Strickland that he wanted both father and son alive at the end of this, but he knew how unlikely that was. He was under no illusions, and saw reality for what it was. And with the odds so stacked against them, Bishop knew that just getting Barney back safe and sound would put them well ahead of the game. Anything over and above that would be verging on the miraculous. And he'd never believed in miracles. Not even as a child.

Leaving Strickland alone with his private thoughts, Bishop kept his eyes on the twin beams of light spreading out before them and just drove.

At 04.22, they were still travelling east on the little-used State Road 122 when they crossed the state line into Ohio. At least that's what the GPS said, and Bishop had no reason to doubt it.

'We're in Ohio,' Bishop said, breaking the silence for the first time in an hour.

Strickland rubbed a hand over his face. 'Yeah?'

'Yeah. Didn't you live here when you were working for Hartnell?'

'Well, we lived in Lancaster,' Strickland said. 'That's about a hundred and fifty miles east of here. But that was only for the last couple of years. Before that, I operated out of Cincinnati, where we had a little place out in the suburbs. Why?'

'So you don't know this western section of the state all that well?'

'Not all that well.'

'Good.' Bishop nodded, satisfied. As ever, all information was useful, and that little fact could very well be made to work in their favour when the time came.

Which would be just over half an hour from now.

* * *

At 04.53, they were heading north on County Road 25A when Bishop spotted the lights of an all-night Marathon gas station about a half-mile up ahead. Since they were down to a quarter tank, he reduced his speed.

Strickland was still looking at the cell phone in his hand. He'd taken it from his jacket pocket ten minutes before and had been staring at it ever since, waiting for the call.

Bishop turned into the station entrance and saw it was a pretty basic set-up, with a steel canopy overlooking two pumps, and a small one-storey shop set further back. Inside the store, the night guy was sitting next to the cash till, staring at a portable TV. The only other vehicle was a sedan parked to the right of the building, which was probably his. There were no other customers.

Pulling up next to the first pump, Bishop killed the engine and got out. He went into the store, gave the guy a twenty, and walked back out again. The guy had barely glanced away from the TV the whole time.

As he was filling the tank with unleaded, Strickland got out of the car and came over. He was frowning at the cell phone in his hand. 'We just got some kind of text. I can't figure it out, though. And there's a phone number with it, so it can't be from Callaway.'

'Let's see. Take over for me.' They switched places. As Strickland continued filling the tank, Bishop took the phone and looked at the number first, and then the text message. The message read, *Good to go.*

Bishop pressed Reply and keyed in *Posit?* He pressed Send.

Strickland said, 'So you know who it's from?'

'I know.'

Strickland waited for more. When none came, he said, 'So? You want to fill in the blanks for me?'

'Not yet. It might all come to nothing anyway.'

The cell phone chirped as a reply came back. Bishop opened up another message. It was just as brief as the first one: *Penthouse. 360.*

Nodding to himself, Bishop keyed in his reply – *Gear?* – and sent it off. Less than twenty seconds later, a reply came back: *ATCO.*

'ATCO?' Strickland said, looking over Bishop's shoulder as he gripped the pump. 'What the hell does *that* mean?'

'It means *all taken care of*,' Bishop said.

'Huh? What's taken care of? What are you talking about? And while I'm at it, just where the hell *are* we anyway? I just checked the GPS and all of a sudden we're heading north when we should be—'

Strickland stopped mid-sentence at the shrill ring of the cell phone in Bishop's hand. Not another text message, but a call. *The* call. The one they'd been driving towards these past two days.

It was 04.59.

This time Bishop answered.

SEVENTY-FOUR

He brought the phone to his ear and Callaway's familiar smug voice said, 'So who am I talking to this time?'

'The other one,' Bishop said.

'Uh-huh. So where are you?'

'At an all-night gas station in west Ohio, somewhere on US 127, five or six miles north of Greenville.' Strickland was frowning deeply at the obvious lie. Bishop ignored him and said, 'Let me talk to the boy, make sure he's all right.'

'No can do. He's not with me at the moment.'

'Get him then. Even if it's only by phone. I need to hear his voice before we can go any further.'

'Relax, he's fine. You think I'd risk queering the deal this late in the game?'

'I'm not here to guess what you may or may not do. Just get hold of him, right now.'

Callaway sighed. 'Like playing hardball, don't you, pal? Okay, wait one. I'll see what I can do.'

The line went silent. Strickland removed the dripping nozzle from the gas tank and placed the hose back in the dispenser. Bishop got in the driver's seat, shut the door and put the phone on loudspeaker. Strickland got in the other side.

Less than half a minute later Callaway came back on and said, 'Okay, I got him on another line, so make it quick.'

'You there, son?' Bishop asked.

'Yeah, I'm here,' a tinny, high-pitched voice replied. Even one step removed, it still sounded like Barney, but Bishop needed to be sure.

'Answer a question for me. When we first met a few days ago, we

330

compared Tetris records and you told me you couldn't get past a certain amount of lines. What was that figure you gave me?'

A brief pause, then, 'It was five thousand.'

'That's the one. So how are you? Are you okay?'

'Yeah, I'm all right, I guess. You and Dad are still coming to get me, aren't you?'

'We sure are, son,' Strickland said. 'We're just sorting out the final details now.'

Callaway's clear voice came back on the line. 'Time's up. As you can see we're keeping up our end. So you satisfied?'

'I'm satisfied he's healthy,' Bishop said. 'Now let's get down to it.'

'Okay, now we got a nice little place set up for the exchange, and I figure you should be able to get to it within the hour without too much trouble. You can come up with your own route if you want, but from Greenville you head east on Route 36 for about fifty miles before you come to a town called Urbana. And at the northernmost tip of this town, there's a big industrial estate. There's still a couple of factories operating out there, but most of the places have gone out of business so there'll be nobody to bother us. Now the place you'll want is an old warehouse with a big faded sign on the side with the words, *Big Discounts on—*'

'Forget it,' Bishop interrupted.

There was a brief pause. 'Say what, friend?'

'I said forget it. Forget this warehouse, forget Urbana altogether. We need to decide on a new location or the deal's off.'

'Okay, pal, I've given you all the leeway I could up till now, but you're really starting to piss me off.'

'Come on, *pal*,' Bishop said. 'You must have suspected I'd say no to whatever location you came up with, so don't act all shocked. Not only have you got access to as much backup and hardware as you feel is necessary, but you've had two full days to prepare for our arrival. Now call me cynical, but somehow I can't see the two of us lasting too long once we show our faces at this warehouse, can you?'

Callaway's silence was answer enough. Then he said, 'So what do you want?'

'I simply want us to meet at an alternative location, some place where you haven't had time to arrange a welcome party for us.'

'And you just happen to have the perfect location in mind, right?'

'No, that part I'll have to leave up to you. You know this state. I don't. My only stipulation is that it has to be somewhere my associate here is also familiar with, since neither of us is prepared to go into this completely blind. And obviously it needs to be somewhere both parties can reach before the imposed deadline. Unless you're willing to extend it.'

'No extensions. My employer's very specific about that.'

'Okay, then. So the ball's now in your court.'

A pause. Then Callaway said, 'Let me think on it.'

The phone went silent.

Strickland opened his mouth to say something, but Bishop quickly shook his head and he clamped it shut again. It was all down to Callaway now. Bishop had set the parameters, but the actual location had to come from Callaway alone. Bishop already knew the guy would want a place as remote as the other one, and that was fine. He also knew that if he or Strickland dared to make a further suggestion, Callaway would instantly nix the idea out of hand. So best to say nothing.

The numbers on the dashboard clock changed to 05.07.

And Bishop couldn't rush him either. He just had to be patient and hope the man at the other end of the line would make the right choice.

If Strickland had been telling the truth, the *only* choice left.

The clock had already changed to 05.08 when Callaway spoke again. 'All right,' he said, 'I think I've got a site that satisfies everyone's needs.'

'We're listening,' Bishop said.

'Lima.'

'Lima?' Bishop said, aware that Strickland was now staring at him. 'I've heard of it. That's north-east of us, right?'

'That's right. And I'm thinking of a certain abandoned manufacturing and storage complex on the south side of the city, close to the gas refinery. A place your associate knows all too well. In fact, you could say that's where all this current trouble sprang from.'

'I know where you mean,' Strickland said.

'Sure you do. And it's nice and deserted, so we're not likely to be disturbed by anybody. What do you say, friend? That meet with your approval?'

'If he's okay with it,' Bishop said, 'then so am I.'

'Gee, I'm so glad. Now as your pal there will tell you, this place is basically a large vacant plot of land with three derelict buildings grouped together in the middle of it. That's where we'll meet. And since this Lima's about sixty miles away from your current position, I suggest you don't waste any more time talking to me.'

The line went dead.

Strickland was still staring at him. 'Son of a bitch,' he said.

Smiling, Bishop started the engine, then got back on the road and continued heading north, feeling as though a great load had been removed from his shoulders. Callaway had indeed made the right choice, as Bishop hoped he would.

'You sneaky son of a bitch,' Strickland said. 'That's why you were happy when I said I didn't know this part of Ohio too well. Except for Lima. That's why you kept driving north on this old road. You had it in mind all along that he'd pick that place to meet.'

Bishop nodded. 'After you described the site to Clea the other night I knew it would make a perfect alternative. But since I couldn't exactly suggest it myself, I simply pushed Callaway into thinking along the same lines, that's all. Although if he hadn't gone for it, we would have been well and truly screwed.'

'Nice.' Strickland glanced at the GPS unit. 'So how far away are we from Lima now?'

'Twenty miles or so.'

'And how far away is this Urbana from Lima?' Strickland asked.

'About sixty miles. If they really push it, they should get there within the hour.'

Strickland smiled for the first time in hours. 'Where we'll already be waiting for them.'

SEVENTY-FIVE

05.45. Fifteen minutes to zero hour.

Bishop and Strickland stood in the darkness of the largest of the three buildings at the designated site, waiting for the first sign of approaching headlights. So far, nothing. But it wouldn't be long now.

Although it wasn't quite dawn yet, the first signs of light were already beginning to peek over the eastern horizon, transforming that part of the night sky into a slightly lighter shade of black. In the distance, Bishop could make out the lights of the vast, sprawling, industrial complex that made up the gas refinery. In addition to the three huge cooling towers, he saw numerous oil storage tanks, refining factories, waste water treatment plants, loading stations, and more besides. Even from half a mile away, he could hear the constant hum of heavy refining machinery at work.

This old trading estate hadn't actually been listed on the GPS map, but Strickland still remembered the directions and got them to the site by 05.32. The place was located on a tract of wasteland, maybe ten or twelve acres in total, bordered by the refinery to the west and the old railroad lines to the north. But there were no fences protecting the southern or eastern boundaries, so you could still enter and exit the site pretty much wherever you wanted.

As Strickland had described it before, at the centre of the vast lot were three abandoned buildings – ruins, really – arranged in a basic U formation, and overlooking an empty square overgrown with grass.

The east building was a single-storey, windowless brick building that must have once been a storehouse or depot of some kind. The roof had caved in long ago. The west building was a two-storey office building with caved-in outer walls and a second floor that looked ready to collapse at any moment.

The north building was also a two-storey structure, but it looked a little more stable than the other one. Great chunks of the outer walls were still missing, though, leaving large areas of the ground floor open to the elements, both at the front and at the back. In almost every room, the ceiling had either collapsed or been pulled down to get at the fixtures and copper piping, allowing you to see straight into the area directly above. There was also a concrete stairwell in the centre of the building that provided access for anyone brave enough to go up there. There were large piles of rubble and bricks everywhere.

Bishop and Strickland were standing in one of the front rooms that looked directly out onto the square. It was the best spot. A large triangular chunk was missing from the front wall, giving them a clear view to the south and a partial view of the east. Bishop felt pretty sure the enemy would be coming from one of those two directions. He'd parked the Nissan at the rear of the building in a semi-covered area that had probably once been a loading bay. Strickland said it was the exact same spot he'd parked the night he'd witnessed his ex-boss murder an undercover DEA agent by the name of Salvatore Ferrera.

That was a night that changed everything for a lot of people. And it was all about to come to a head right here. Today.

Strickland wrapped his arms round himself and shivered, even though it wasn't a particular cold morning. But Bishop knew that wasn't the reason he was chilled.

'How you holding up?' he asked.

Strickland turned to him. 'Not too good.' Then he shrugged and said, 'Still, a little better now that I . . . well, you know.'

Bishop nodded. He understood all too well. Now that they'd reached the endgame, everything had become a lot clearer to each of them. They now knew exactly what needed to be done and, more importantly, when.

'And knowing I'll be seeing Barn helps a hell of a lot too,' Strickland continued. 'Have I told you how much I love that boy, Bishop?'

'You told me. And even if you hadn't, it's pretty obvious. He's a special kid.'

'You're not kidding. I tell you, that boy's everything I hoped he'd be and more besides. You just don't know, Bishop. You just can't . . .'

He shook his head and sighed. 'I just wish I could have been a better role model to him, that's all. I wish I could change a lot of things about my life, like never getting involved with Hartnell in the first place, but being a better father's the one I wish most.'

'You're making up for it now.'

'Maybe. I hope I am. You know I tried everything not to turn out like my old man, Bishop, and I think I succeeded on that one, at least. Man, that guy was such a loser, it's no surprise I turned out the way I did. Did I ever tell you about him?'

'No.'

'Well, we lived out in Chicago and he was a pharmacist. Just a normal nine-to-five guy, you know? Had his own shop and made pretty decent money as far as that went. But as a sideline he also ran numbers for the local mob, and he loved to impress his drinking buddies by bragging about all his so-called connections with street guys. Even as a kid I could see they all thought he was a joke.

'And he loved to drink, too, especially after Mom died. He'd usually come home steaming, and he'd start ranting about my bad grades and tell me how useless I was and how I'd never amount to anything in this life. Like *he* was anything special. Then he'd get the belt out and really give me something to remember. And this would be a twice-weekly thing too, sometimes more. Best day of my life was when I walked out of that house at sixteen. Never went back neither.'

Dawn was breaking now. The grey, overcast sky was steadily getting lighter, allowing Bishop to finally make out Strickland's haggard, drained features. He looked as though he'd aged ten years overnight. But then again, maybe he had.

'Is he still alive?' Bishop asked.

'No idea. Haven't spoken to the bastard in over twenty-five years, so he might as well be. But at least he did do one good thing for me, Bishop. He made me promise to myself that if I ever had kids of my own, I'd make sure they had a father who always supported them and let them make their own decisions instead of forcing them into the same mistakes I made. And I'd clap 'em on the back when they did good, but I wouldn't make them feel like the world's smallest piece of shit whenever they didn't come up to expectations either. And I kept my promise too. I wasn't always there for Barn, but whenever I was I'd make sure he knew he was one of the two most important things in my life. Him and Carrie both.'

'I'm sure Barney knows that.'

'Man, I hope he does.' Strickland wiped at his eyes, then cleared his throat. 'You're all right, Bishop. I know we had our differences before and everything, but when the chips are down you're a good guy to have around. Like me, you don't go for half measures and I respect that. Kind of makes me wonder what would have happened if the two of us had met, say, five or ten years ago.'

'We wouldn't have got along,' Bishop said, smiling. 'At all.'

Strickland snorted. 'Yeah, you're right there. I would have drawn on you, or you would have drawn on me. Either way, one of us would have ended up bleeding on the floor. Funny how things work out sometimes.' He paused, then reached inside his jacket and winced a little as he rubbed his stomach.

'You okay?' Bishop asked.

'I'll be fine. So you think Hartnell will be coming to the meet himself?'

'Hard to say. Delaney told me Hartnell's on an eighty-million-dollar bail bond, but he still has to wear an electronic tag that forbids him from leaving the state. So that could be why Callaway insisted the exchange take place in Ohio. I wouldn't bet the farm on him showing, though. Hartnell's nothing if not careful.'

'Yeah, you don't need to tell me.'

Bishop, staring off into the distance, finally spotted a small convoy of headlights approaching from the south, all moving up and down as the drivers negotiated the bumpy terrain. There were four pairs of lights. About a thousand yards away and closing.

'Here we go,' he said.

SEVENTY-SIX

Bishop checked the display on his cell phone and saw it was 05.53. Callaway and his people must have really been pushing it to get here so fast. Still not fast enough, though.

When the vehicles were about three hundred yards away the drivers turned off their headlights one by one, but still kept on coming. Bishop and Strickland slowly retreated deeper into the building. Bishop positioned himself behind a stone pillar next to a huge pile of old bricks that had once been part of a partition wall, of which only a fraction still existed. He made a hand motion to Strickland, who moved further back into the room until he was completely enveloped in darkness.

Bishop stood at his spot. Watching. Waiting.

The day was getting noticeably lighter now, so he was able to make out details without too much trouble.

The first vehicle finally reached the large open area between the two other buildings five hundred feet away and came to a slow stop. The next car parked a few feet from it. The doors opened on both vehicles and Bishop counted six men as they got out. They were of various sizes, ages and ethnicities, and all wearing casual clothes and thick coats. Meanwhile, the other two vehicles, a sedan and a large black SUV with tinted windows, kept on coming until they reached the main square. They both came to a stop about two hundred feet away.

The six men from the first two cars all began walking towards the main square. One man carried a large holdall. Probably spare ammo. Three others had rifles slung over their shoulders and were studying the three buildings as they walked: obviously the snipers.

Bishop had to smile. Callaway probably couldn't believe his luck when Bishop agreed to this place. It was perfect for an ambush. You couldn't ask for better. Two or three carefully placed snipers on the second floor of this building and the one to his left would easily be able to cover the kill zone in the square below. Actually, just one sniper would be enough. It would still be like shooting ducks in a barrel.

But only if Bishop allowed things to get that far.

Three more men had already exited the sedan, making nine so far. Then the SUV's driver and a passenger in the front exited, making eleven. Finally the SUV's rear passenger side door was pushed open and a stocky, heavyset man stepped out. Number twelve. The man was dressed the same as Bishop – dark suit, pale shirt, no tie. About five-nine or five-ten. He had a hard, serious-looking face with a thin straight line for a mouth. His dark hair was cut short and was heavily receding.

'That's Callaway,' Strickland said from behind him.

Bishop said nothing. He'd already guessed as much.

The other men all gathered round Callaway as he gave them their instructions. Bishop saw the man point quickly towards both two-storey buildings as he spoke, no doubt ordering his snipers find themselves decent spots on the upper floors. Always take the high ground when you could. Everybody knew that.

'Stay here,' Bishop told Strickland. 'Don't make a sound, and don't move until I tell you.'

Moving away from the pillar, Bishop walked over to the remains of the front wall, stepped through the gap and just stood there in the open, waiting for one of the men to notice him. When none did, Bishop joined the tips of his thumb and index finger together, clamped both between his lips and gave a shrill, ear-splitting whistle.

Everybody immediately turned in his direction. Then they moved. Half the men dropped to the ground with their weapons out. Most had handguns, but he saw one guy with what looked like a Skorpion vz 61 sub-machine gun, which meant there'd be more. One of the snipers crouched next to the sedan's front fender, aiming his rifle at Bishop, while the rest of the men took cover behind the two vehicles.

All except Callaway. He just stood there watching Bishop, right out in the open, as calm as anything. He shouted, '*Nobody fires a shot unless I say so.*'

Without waiting for a response, Callaway gestured for Bishop to come forward.

Bishop stayed where he was for a moment, watching those shooters still out in the open. Looking for a jittery one. Only needed one wild card to think he knew better than the boss and that'd be it for Bishop. And for Barney. Be a hell of a thing to have it all fall apart so close to the finish line. But they all seemed calm enough. For the moment anyway.

Callaway waved him forward again, and this time Bishop began walking, arms out at his sides. He walked slowly, watching everyone and taking in everything, ready to dive to the ground at the first sign of trouble. As he advanced most of the men on the ground slowly raised themselves up to sitting or standing positions, still holding him in their sights. Callaway watched him approach with his hands on his hips, wearing a faint smile.

When Bishop had closed the distance between them to just fifteen feet, he stopped.

'Bishop,' Callaway said. 'So we meet at last.'

'So you're Callaway,' Bishop said. 'Funny, I expected someone taller.'

Callaway's smile didn't even falter. 'If that's an attempt to get under my skin you're wasting your time. Mind telling me how you got here so fast?'

'What difference does it make? All that matters is we arrived before you.'

'I'd still like to know.'

'Maybe I wasn't entirely truthful in regards to our location when you called earlier. As it turned out we were a little closer to this place than you were, that's all. Lucky for us.'

Callaway's brow became furrowed. 'Or maybe it was more than just dumb luck.'

Hoping to forestall that line of thought before it could even begin, Bishop said quickly, 'I've been counting and so far I make it twelve against two. Don't you think you're overdoing things a little?'

'A man takes every edge he can get,' Callaway said, shrugging. 'And it's thirteen actually. I got another man in the SUV, guarding the boy.'

'Don't suppose that would be Hartnell himself?'

'Afraid not. He's far too busy getting ready for his court appearance three hours from now, although I'll be keeping him fully updated on the situation here.'

'How? By carrier pigeon?'

Callaway smiled. 'You shouldn't believe every rumour you hear. My boss never talks over the phone, but that doesn't mean he's not a good listener. He's one of the best, actually, since he never interrupts. So where's Strickland?'

'Around. I told him to drop me off here, then take off in the car. He's currently parked somewhere in the general area, awaiting my call. And if I don't give him the correct password when I do call, he'll know that everything's gone to hell and head straight to the cops and turn himself in.'

Callaway studied Bishop for a beat, then slowly shook his head. 'I don't like it.'

'That's the whole idea.'

'No, I mean there's something wrong about this whole set-up. I can't put my finger on it, but there's something not right here, I can feel it. Or maybe it's just you that's not right, Bishop. Maybe this is all a bluff on your part and Strickland's still here somewhere, possibly watching us right this very second.'

Bishop kept his face expressionless. 'You willing to bet everything on that?'

Callaway's brows came together as he considered. This was a very dangerous moment. If he followed his own line of thought and began to suspect Bishop had manipulated him into picking this location, he'd have to assume Bishop had stretched the truth in other ways too. Which would automatically open up to all kinds of possibilities in his mind, none of them good.

Finally, Callaway said, 'Ramirez, Stack, get over here.'

The white guy with the Skorpion sub-machine gun got to his feet and ambled over, followed by another guy, a Latino, who was gripping a large .357 Magnum in his right hand.

This one said, 'Want me to kneecap him, boss?'

'No, I want you to shut up and listen,' Callaway said. 'Both of you go check behind these three buildings. If you see a parked vehicle anywhere, you come tell me, got it?'

Bishop sighed. *So much for Plan A.* 'I wouldn't do that,' he said.

All three turned to him. Callaway said, 'Why not?'

Bishop didn't say anything. Instead, he just slowly extended his right index finger and pointed at the ground five feet in front of him.

Callaway, Ramirez and Stack all looked down at the spot he was pointing at. Grass and weeds were growing through the cracks in the concrete. Callaway began to say, 'What—' when a bright red dot suddenly appeared on the ground, exactly where Bishop was pointing.

Bishop slowly raised his arm in the direction of the three men, and the red dot moved with him, following his finger. It travelled along the ground until it landed on Callaway's left shoe. Callaway looked down and watched it creep up his left leg, move past his belt, and continue up his waist until it stopped at the spot where his heart should be.

'That's why not,' Bishop said.

SEVENTY-SEVEN

Callaway looked up from the red dot and stared at Bishop. He was no longer smiling, but he still look pretty composed for a man a second away from death.

'For all I know this is coming from one of those dumb laser pens,' he said.

'You know better,' Bishop said.

Callaway sighed. 'I guess I do. I also know Strickland's not much good with a gun. So who is it up there?'

'Somebody who is good with a gun.'

Without warning, the black sniper crouching next to the sedan said, '*Got* him.' He quickly brought his rifle up at a thirty-degree angle with the butt tight against his shoulder, his left eye pressed against the sight.

Without turning, Callaway hissed, 'Radcliffe, don't even think about it. I told you—'

But Radcliffe was no longer listening. He was too caught up in the moment. Bishop saw his right index finger already squeezing the trigger.

Then the red dot instantly appeared in the centre of Radcliffe's forehead. There was a single crack from somewhere above and Radcliffe's head was obscured by a red mist as a 7.62 hollow-point entered his brain. The sniper was thrown back by the force of the shot, landing on his back with a large section of his skull missing, still holding the rifle.

It all happened in the space of a second. Bishop saw the red dot had already resumed its place over Callaway's heart. Radcliffe's right foot shuddered once and then was still. There was blood all over the ground.

A moment's silence. Then a babble of curses as the gunmen still out in the open quickly scrambled for cover behind the vehicles. Bishop now saw a dozen different weapons trained on him, and him alone.

'*Nobody else fires a shot without my permission,*' Callaway shouted, still standing in the same spot, both arms stretched wide. '*If I die, none of you get paid. Remember that.*'

Nobody else spoke. Everybody remained motionless. Finally, Callaway looked at Bishop and said, 'And just so you understand, Bishop. If I die, so does the boy. That's guaranteed.'

'I know that,' Bishop said.

'Good. So who is it up there, squinting down his sights at me?'

'A friend. That's all you need to know.'

It was true. Up till now, Nelson Daly had merely been one of a large number of ex-comrades-in-arms from his time in the Corps. But by his actions today Nelson had now elevated himself to the status of a true friend.

Last night when they'd stopped at Valley Park to pick up the GPS unit, Bishop had phoned one of the numbers on the card Nelson had given him when he'd delivered the fibreglass plates three days before, hoping he'd get more than just an endless ringing tone. Fortunately Nelson had finished whatever shady business deals he'd been working on in Mexico and answered on the second ring. And once he understood the full situation, he'd immediately offered to help Bishop in any way he could.

Any way he could. No questions asked.

Bishop had outlined his plan, that he was going to try and manoeuvre Callaway into changing the location for the exchange to the old Lima site, and that he wanted Nelson to make use of his private company jet to get there before everybody else. Bishop told him to bring along his M24A2 Sniper Weapon System with laser sight, and a few other bits and pieces, and then to find himself a good spot on one of the upper floors of the central building. He was to be used primarily as backup, but he also needed to be ready to act if required.

Nelson had told him he'd be at the site waiting for them and, as usual, he'd kept his word. He'd set down at Drayton airport and driven a rental car the rest of the way. He'd parked it about a mile away from the site and come the rest of the way by foot, lugging his huge gym bag full of lethal goodies along with him. The text messages between them had merely been Nelson confirming his position. *Penthouse* meant he'd found a good spot on the second floor of one of the structures, and *360* simply meant he had a complete panoramic view of the immediate area.

Upon Bishop's and Strickland's arrival thirty minutes ago, the three of them had carefully discussed what needed to happen. Bishop had quickly outlined a number of simple contingency plans should things go wrong, as things invariably did in these situations. Afterwards, Strickland had gone through Nelson's gym bag himself and when he saw the two rectangular blocks wrapped in olive-coloured Mylar film, he made one further suggestion. Bishop immediately gave his okay, and ten minutes later they were ready at their respective positions, waiting for the enemy to arrive.

Callaway said, 'Your friend's a pretty good shot.'

'He should be,' Bishop said. 'He's a military-trained scout sniper. We worked together before and I can't recall him ever missing a shot.'

'Figures.' He tilted his head at Bishop, then said, 'You corralled me into picking this place as the backup site.'

'I hoped you would. When Strickland described it to me I knew it'd be perfect, but only if we got here first. But I couldn't suggest it myself. You had to pick it. Fortunately, you did.'

'Looks like I underestimated you.'

'You're not the first, and you won't be the last.'

'And Strickland's really back there in that building behind you?'

Bishop nodded.

'So what now?'

'Now I've equalized the odds a little we can make the exchange. But first you show me Barney's still okay.'

'I'm sensing a real lack of trust here, Bishop. You honestly think I'd be dumb enough to waste the kid before we completed our deal?'

'Why not? Isn't that your specialty?'

'What are you talking about?'

'Killing kids. Isn't that what you do best?'

Callaway's eyes became hooded. 'I assume you got a particular someone in mind?'

'I do. A boy named Andrew Truman. That name mean anything to you?'

Callaway thought for a few moments, then he said, 'The Mechner job, back in Arkansas.' He slowly nodded to himself. 'Yeah, I remember now. So, what, you telling me you were part of that asshole's protection crew?'

'I was in charge of it, which means I got to witness the results of your handiwork up close. I was there when the boy blew himself into small pieces, and I was also the one who discovered his parents next door with both their throats slit. You've got a real talent for wiping out families, don't you? Men, women, children, they're all the same to you.'

Callaway smiled. 'I'm just a professional who does what he's paid to do. And I do it well.'

'So that's how a real-life serial killer justifies his crimes. I've always wondered.'

The smile disappeared from Callaway's face. 'Got through your security easily enough, though, didn't I?'

'And you *still* failed to hit your designated target. Brilliant. You must have been real proud of yourself that day.'

'Nobody's got a perfect record, and at least I made up for it a few months later. Thanks to a little inside help I managed to get my guy in the end. But then, I always do.'

'So do I.'

'You implying I should start looking over my shoulder from now on?'

'If you want. Not that it'll make any difference.'

'Now you really got me shaking in my boots. But if we could return to the real world for a moment, maybe you can tell your pal up there to remove this glowing bull's-eye from my chest. It's starting to irritate me. Then I'll let you see the kid.'

Bishop had no problem with that. He slowly reached a hand into the side pocket of his jacket and pulled out a slim Cobra walkie-talkie and raised it to his mouth. Pressing the transmit button, he said, 'Lights off.'

Almost immediately, the red dot vanished from Callaway's chest.

Bishop pocketed the walkie-talkie and said, 'But he's still tracking your every move, so I advise you not to make any sudden movements. Like trying to get out of range by diving into the back of that SUV, for example. My friend wouldn't like that.'

'The thought never even entered my mind.' Callaway turned towards the large vehicle and called out, 'Okay, Simons, bring the kid out now. But do it slow.'

After a short pause the rear door clicked open and Bishop saw a pair of sneakers push it open the rest of the way. Bishop recognized them as the same ones Barney had been wearing two days ago.

A boy's hand grabbed the inner door handle, and Barney slowly slid himself across the seat until he was half in and half out of the vehicle. Bishop saw the thirteenth man, Simons, was right behind him with an arm clamped tightly round his neck. His other hand held a semi-automatic to Barney's temple. As the boy very carefully stepped out of the car, Simons – a stocky young man with a shaved head and intricate tattoos crawling up the side of his neck – got out right behind him, matching his every move. Barney was still wearing the same jeans and the same sweatshirt. He looked a lot paler than before, but he didn't seem any the worse for wear, at least physically. Although Bishop saw he was shivering a little.

With the gun still pressed against his head, Barney gave Bishop a strained smile and said, 'Hey.'

'Hey,' Bishop said. 'How are you doing, or is that a dumb question?'

The boy gave a facsimile of a smile and said, 'I'm okay. I was worried for a while there, but I'm all right now you're here.'

'Good. Are you cold at all?'

'Little bit. Is Dad with you?'

'He's with me, and he's really looking forward to seeing you again. You've been on his mind constantly the last two days.'

'Yeah, I been thinking about him a lot too.'

'All right,' Callaway said, turning to Bishop again, 'that's enough yakking. You can see the kid's alive, just like I said he would be. Now what say we get this show on the road?'

'Ready when you are.'

'Glad to hear it. So how are we going to play this so we all come out happy?'

'I suggest we keep it simple,' Bishop said. 'I'll go back and talk to Strickland. When we're ready to go, you and I signal each other and set each of them on their way. Strickland walks towards you while Barney walks towards me. I figure father and son will want to spend a few private moments with each other once they reach the halfway mark, so I think it's only fair we give them some time together. A couple more minutes can't hurt. Agreed?'

Callaway shrugged. 'Sure, what the hell.'

'Fine. Then they'll part ways and continue the rest of their journey. Once we've got Barney and you've got Strickland, you go back the way you came, while we take off in the opposite direction. Simple.'

Callaway nodded slowly. 'Sounds reasonable.'

'But understand this,' Bishop said. 'You're my hole card, which means you stay out in the open at all times. And anything happens that I don't like, you'll be the first to go down.'

'That goes both ways,' Callaway said. 'That kid will have half a dozen guns on him every step of the way, so whatever happens to me happens to him a second later. You got that?'

'I understand.' Bishop smiled at Barney and said, 'See you soon.' Then he turned and began the long walk back to the old office building.

SEVENTY-EIGHT

Bishop was very conscious of the arsenal aimed at the back of his head, but he kept his pace deliberately steady and casual like it was just another day at the office. As though this kind of thing happened all the time. Be damned if he'd give Callaway the satisfaction.

He finally reached the large triangular gap in the front wall he'd exited by, and stepped through and immediately took cover behind a still-complete section of the wall. He waited for his eyes to adjust to the darkness of the room.

'Is Barn okay?' Strickland asked from somewhere in front of him.

'He's fine,' Bishop said. 'Shivering a little from the cold, but that's all. Fortunately, we came prepared.'

As his eyes adjusted, Bishop saw Strickland was only a few feet away, standing by the stone pillar Bishop had been standing next to before. In his left hand he held the small flight jacket that Nelson had brought along with him. It was Barney's size, or close to it.

'It's time,' Bishop said. 'Are you ready?'

Strickland exhaled loudly. 'As I'll ever be. It's weird. I feel pretty calm now, not jittery at all. It's like my whole life's been leading up to this moment, you know?'

'I can understand that.' In a slightly louder voice, he said, 'Nels?'

'Right here,' another voice said above them. Bishop glanced up at the huge ragged hole in the ceiling and saw Nelson's face peering down at them. He was dressed all in black, with a black beanie covering the top half of his head.

'Perfect shot,' Bishop said. 'I couldn't have asked for a better demonstration.'

Nelson smiled. 'Nice to know I still got it. What next?'

'Just stay in position and be ready to move fast when the time comes.'

'I'll be ready,' Nelson said, and immediately disappeared from view.

'Okay,' Bishop said, turning back to Strickland, 'this is what'll happen. You and Barney will walk towards each other then continue on until you reach your respective goals. Now when you meet in the middle I realize you'll each have things to say to each other, but try and keep it as short as you can. I know it'll be hard, but the sooner we can get Barney out of the danger zone, the better.'

'I'll try.'

'Also, emphasize to Barney how important it is that he keep walking at the same pace. As he gets closer to me his natural inclination will be to speed up, and the last thing we want is Callaway panicking and putting one in his back. Slow and steady at all times.'

'I'll convince him.'

'I know you will.' Bishop paused. 'Well, that's it. I can't think of anything else.'

'Me either.'

Bishop studied Strickland for a few moments, then extended his right hand. He hadn't planned to. It just happened. And it felt right after everything they'd both been through. Strickland looked down at the hand for a second, then clasped it in his own. They shook once. Bishop gave a single nod of respect, and Strickland nodded back, smiling a little. They each released their grip at the same time.

Further talk was unnecessary. They each knew what had to be done.

Bishop turned and went over to Nelson's large gym bag, still lying on the floor a few feet away. He crouched down, unzipped the bag and opened it up. He knew that, in addition to the wealth of extra ammo inside, the bag also contained various useful items such as M67 grenades, M84 flash bangs, a Mossberg 12-gauge pump, night-vision sights, reflex sights, thermal sights, sound suppressors, and more besides. Much more.

He rifled around inside until he found a matt-black Leupold telescope sight and pulled it out. He knew Nelson would have packed a spare. He always did. Maybe that's why he and Bishop had always gotten along so well.

Hope for the best, prepare for the worst. Words to live by.

Bishop walked back to the triangular gap in the wall and stepped outside again. He checked the Glock was still in his rear waistband where it should be. It was. If things went to hell it wouldn't be much good at this distance, but it was still better than the shotgun.

Two hundred feet away, Callaway was standing in the same position, more or less. He was watching the building and talking on his cell, no doubt updating his lord and master on the whole situation. Next to him stood Simons, still with his gun at Barney's temple. The others had spread out a little, although at least half of them were still using the two vehicles for cover. Bishop raised the rifle sight and panned around. He saw one of the two remaining snipers was using the hood of the SUV to support his rifle, which was currently aimed right at him, but he couldn't find the other one.

He pulled the walkie-talkie from his pocket and pressed the transmit button. 'I don't see sniper number two.'

There was an electronic beep, and Nelson's voice came back, 'He's there. I saw him position himself under the sedan earlier.'

Bishop repositioned the scope until he was looking at the car's underside, but all he saw was darkness. 'I'll take your word for it,' he said. He lowered the walkie-talkie and called out, 'All right, Strickland, you can come on out.'

After a few moments, Strickland's head emerged from the opening and he stepped out of the building. He stood a few inches to Bishop's right, still holding onto the flight jacket as he stared straight ahead at his boy. Bishop looked down and saw his knuckles were almost white with tension.

Strickland noticed him noticing and gave an embarrassed shrug. But as far as Bishop was concerned the guy had nothing to be embarrassed about. Nothing at all. He was doing just fine.

Bishop raised his right arm straight up in the air. A hundred feet away, Callaway turned to Simons and said something before raising his own arm.

They were ready. Bishop dropped his arm, and Callaway lowered his. Simons removed the gun from the boy's head and Barney started walking slowly towards them.

'Good luck,' Bishop said.

Strickland's gaze was focused entirely on his son. 'Goodbye,' he said, and began walking.

SEVENTY-NINE

Bishop kept his eyes on the man's back as he walked towards his fate. It was a hell of a thing knowing you were heading towards almost certain death, but Strickland was managing to hold it together somehow. He kept his pace slow and deliberate like he'd been told. So did Barney across the way. No doubt he'd been given strict warnings by Callaway not to run under any circumstances. But Barney was a smart kid. He knew what was at stake better than anyone.

Strickland had covered about twenty feet when the walkie-talkie in Bishop's hand emitted another electronic beep. Nelson's voice: 'He isn't exactly what I expected.'

Bishop pressed the transmit button, said. 'I know what you mean.'

'Man's got a lot of intestinal fortitude. Rare for a civvy.'

Bishop said nothing, but Nelson was right. The guy had guts in spades. More than he realized. The seconds ticked by as Strickland and Barney continued walking towards each other, each keeping to the same regular pace. Bishop felt his heart beating with each step they took, while overshadowing everything was the constant, pulsating sound of heavy machinery at work in the far distance. He saw Callaway hadn't moved from his position. None of them over there had moved.

The gap between father and son had now been reduced to a hundred feet. Less.

'You still think they'll try a cross?' Nelson asked over the radio.

Bishop pressed Transmit and said, 'I know they will. It's part of Callaway's MO. We just have to be ready for it when it comes.'

'I hear you. Just like that gig in Somalia, huh?'

'Christ, I hope not,' Bishop said. He preferred not to think about that particular episode from his past. Especially not now.

353

He raised the scope to his left eye. He estimated Strickland and Barney had each covered about seventy feet now, leaving about fifty feet still between them.

The seconds ticked away in Bishop's mind. The gap between them was reduced to forty feet. Thirty. Twenty. Then father and son just decided enough was enough and rushed towards each other, closing the distance in less than a second. As they made contact, Strickland dropped the jacket and wrapped his arms around his son, while Barney clasped his father tightly around the waist. After a few moments, Strickland carefully backed away and pried the boy's arms away from him as he spoke. Bishop couldn't hear anything from this distance, but he could see they were both pretty emotional.

He watched Strickland pick up the jacket he'd dropped and hand it to Barney, still talking to the boy. Barney started crying as he slipped his arms through the sleeves and zipped the jacket up. Then he hugged his old man again, around the chest this time, and Strickland hugged him back. They stood that way for a few moments, then Strickland gently pushed Barney away and held him by the shoulders and spoke to him some more. Barney, no longer crying, just listened while nodding occasionally, sometimes shaking his head.

Bishop began to wish he'd taken the time to learn how to lip-read, but quickly brushed the thought aside. Whatever they were saying was really none of his business anyway. It was nobody's business but their own.

He estimated they'd been together for about sixty seconds already. The conversation continued for a little longer, then Strickland and Barney hugged each other again, the boy burying his face in the man's chest. Bishop had a feeling this was the final farewell. After about twenty seconds of this, Strickland gently removed the boy's arms, ruffled his hair, then placed a palm against his cheek. He was trying to smile and not making a very good job of it. He took his hand away. Barney wiped his own eyes with the crook of his arm and watched as his father slowly turned away from him.

Then, without a backward glance, Strickland began walking towards Callaway at the same pace as before. To Bishop's dismay, Barney just stood there and watched him go.

'*Move*,' Bishop said under his breath, gripping the scope tightly. 'Come on, *move*.'

Finally, after three more painful seconds of inaction, Barney turned in Bishop's direction and resumed walking. Bishop breathed out again.

'Strickland's closer to them than the boy is to us,' Nelson said over the line.

Bishop pressed Transmit. 'I know.'

'Unless he slows down he'll reach them a few seconds before Barney gets to us. Might make all the difference.'

'I know.'

Pocketing the walkie-talkie, Bishop lowered the scope as the boy continued walking towards him, his eyes now locked onto his. He was still keeping to the same pace as before and Bishop couldn't very well motion for him to speed up a little. Not yet. He'd only get the wrong idea and start running, which would be the absolute worst thing he could do. He'd just have to wait until Barney was within hearing distance, that's all.

Both parties continued walking towards their respective goals. Bishop's senses were on high alert now. He was waiting for the double cross. Expecting it. He knew it was coming, but from where?

He estimated the boy was still about fifty feet away when he saw Callaway pull an automatic from a holster under his jacket and aim it at Strickland. He said something Bishop didn't catch, and Strickland, still walking, raised his arms in the air.

The hairs at the back of Bishop's neck stood on end. This was it. The start of whatever little scheme Callaway had in mind. Bishop had known the bastard wouldn't be satisfied with just having Strickland in his hands. He wanted the boy too. And if he couldn't have the boy, he'd make sure nobody else could have him either. At this moment Bishop felt worse than helpless. All those guns over there aimed at Barney's back and he was currently powerless to do anything about it.

Barney, unaware of what was happening behind him, just kept on walking. He was almost home. Not far now. He closed the distance to forty feet. Then thirty-five feet. Thirty.

Then it happened.

Without any kind of warning, Callaway suddenly dropped his shoulders and ran straight for Strickland, who immediately halted mid-step and began lowering his arms.

Bishop had no choice now. It was on. And Barney was still too far away. Tossing the scope, Bishop grabbed the Glock in his waistband and shouted, '*Run, Barney! Fast as you can. Don't think. Run!*'

The boy didn't even hesitate. He simply lowered his head and began running towards Bishop, arms and legs pumping away in unison. In his peripheral vision, Bishop could see Callaway already had an arm round the struggling Strickland's neck and was using him as a shield as he dragged him back towards the SUV.

Bishop heard the crack of a rifle shot, the one sound he didn't want to hear. And it sounded close. Nelson? Possibly. He didn't know. All his attention was on Barney, who'd already halved the distance and was still running full pelt towards him. He could actually hear the boy's rapid breathing as he got closer.

'*Keep going,*' Bishop shouted. '*You're almost home.*'

Barney was still only ten feet away when there was another shot, and the boy arched his back and his face went slack, all power in his legs suddenly gone.

Bishop watched in horror as the boy quickly sagged to his knees. The boy had enough time to give Bishop a look of complete astonishment, and then with his arms outstretched he pitched forward, face down, onto the ground.

Unmoving.

EIGHTY

As Bishop raced towards the fallen boy the sounds of distant gunfire started up all around him, but he was barely conscious of it. All that mattered was reaching the boy. Nothing else.

He covered the distance in no time at all and crouched down and grabbed the collar of the boy's flight jacket. He noticed the large ragged bullet-hole in the boy's back, around the lower spine area, but paid it no mind. Get the boy out of the crossfire first, worry about the rest later. Keeping as low as possible, Bishop began dragging the boy along the ground, back to the safety of the building behind them.

Something ricocheted on the ground a few feet to his right. Bishop ignored it. Then came another to his left, inches from his foot. And another. Stray bullets were whizzing all around them like mosquitoes, but none of them hit Barney. Or Bishop. He wasn't worried too much about small arms fire, not from two hundred feet away. It was practically impossible to get any kind of accuracy from that distance. Even the sub-machine guns would be useless at that range. The real danger came from the two snipers still left. He was sure it was one of them who'd got Barney.

Without slowing his pace, Bishop raised the Glock, aimed in the direction of the two vehicles in the distance and fired off a dozen shots. Purely as a distraction. He had no idea if he hit anything.

Sounds of rifle shots were also coming from above. Nelson was doing his thing up there, laying down what little cover he could. Knocking the enemy down whenever he could. Nelson was a good man. One of the best.

Bishop kept backing up, dragging the boy with him. Then, before he knew it, he felt the wall of the office building at his back. He turned and saw that beautiful triangular gap was just to his right.

Reaching down, he quickly hefted Barney up into his arms and jumped with him through the gap and into the safety of the shadows. He moved a few feet to the left, away from the light, then dropped to his knees and laid Barney gently down onto the ground.

The boy's eyes were closed. Bishop unzipped the heavy flight jacket and quickly reached round the boy's waist and carefully moved his fingers along his lower back. He felt no wetness. No blood. Removing his hand, he turned the boy over and inspected the bullet hole in the jacket. He saw the glint of something metallic and inserted a finger and enlarged the hole.

Bishop breathed a sigh of relief at the sight of the .223 slug embedded in the thick body armour.

The bulletproof jacket had done its job perfectly. Nelson had assured him the thirty layers of Gold Flex ballistic fibre sewn into the lining would be enough to stop most high-calibre rounds, and he'd been right as usual. The man knew his equipment.

Barney was all right. The poor kid would have some lower back pain for a while, but that would pass. He was alive, and that's what counted.

He turned the boy onto his back again and patted his cheek in an effort to bring him round. Outside, the sounds of gunfire had already died down to almost nothing. Bishop kept on patting the boy's cheeks until Barney's eyelids started flickering.

From upstairs, Nelson shouted, '*Bishop, give me a sit-rep.*'

'*We're both okay,*' he shouted back. '*What's happening out there?*'

Barney's eyes opened at that point, and he looked up at Bishop, blinking rapidly.

'*They're getting ready to take off,*' Nelson shouted back. There was the sharp crack of a rifle shot from upstairs. Then another. '*Managed to drop some of 'em and I killed the car, but Callaway's just gotten in the SUV with Strickland. I shot out two tyres on the sucker, but that won't stop 'em.*'

Bishop turned back to Barney, who was blinking as he took in his surroundings.

'You're in the old office building,' Bishop said.

'Yeah, I recognize it,' Barney said, staring up at the ceiling, or what was left of it. 'What happened? Something hit me in the back, but I don't—'

'You got shot,' Bishop said. 'The jacket stopped the bullet, though. You're all right now. You're safe.'

Barney just stared at him for a moment, and then his eyes got wide. He shouted, '*Dad!*' and struggled to get up, wincing at the sudden pain in his back. Bishop quickly got to his own feet and pulled Barney up with him. But before Bishop could stop him, Barney slipped from his grip and ran over to the gap in the wall and looked out. Bishop ran over and grabbed his arm, ready to pull him back out of harm's way, but paused when he realized nobody was shooting at them.

Standing next to the boy, Bishop studied the distant scene. There was a small column of smoke rising from the hood of the sedan, so Nelson had clearly made a mess of something in there. He saw three bodies lying on the ground around the car. They weren't moving. The SUV was, though. Lop-sided from the two flat tyres on the driver's side, it had just completed a U-turn and was now pointing away from them. Then the vehicle began to slowly move off, making jerky movements each time the wheel rims hit a bump. Further back, the two remaining vehicles were already facing the other way, apparently waiting for the SUV to reach them before taking off.

'Dad,' Barney said in a forlorn voice, with one hand pressed to his lower back. He turned to Bishop. 'Where is he? Did you see?'

'He's in the SUV,' Bishop said, then swivelled his body at the sound of movement behind him. He raised the Glock, finger already on the trigger.

But it was just Nelson. He was carrying his M24 rifle in one hand and a small canvas ammo pouch in the other. He nodded at Bishop, who lowered the gun and turned back to the departing SUV. It was already about two hundred and fifty feet away. The other two vehicles were also in motion just ahead of it.

Nelson stood behind them, watching the vehicles recede. 'I don't know,' he said in a musing tone. 'Maybe Callaway cuffed him before he could get to his pocket. Or maybe he just knocked the guy out and then searched him.'

'Maybe,' Bishop agreed.

Barney turned to Bishop, looking as confused as ever. 'What? I don't understand. Search for what?'

Bishop was just opening his mouth to say, '*The detonator*,' when there was a brilliant flash of light, accompanied by a thunderous roar, as the SUV exploded in a huge ball of flame.

EIGHTY-ONE

Barney jumped at the sudden noise of the blast. They all did. It was that loud. Even from two hundred and fifty feet away it sounded like the end of the world. Bishop watched as the flames coming from the vehicle were immediately engulfed by an enormous ball of black smoke, which in turn blossomed out even further before rising into the sky.

The SUV was gone. All that was left was an undefined shape that could have been anything. Bishop saw the other two vehicles had caught a good part of the blast too. One was lying on its roof about twenty feet away. The other car was still upright, but the roof and window frames were now completely missing, as though somebody had sheared through it with a large horizontal scythe.

'*Dad!*' Barney screamed. He tried to jump through the gap in the wall, but Bishop grabbed hold of his arm and pulled him back in.

'*You blew him up, you blew him up,*' Barney cried, struggling to free himself and punching Bishop in the chest, in the stomach, in the neck. '*You killed my dad, you shithead.*'

Bishop took the punches for a while, letting the boy work off his anger and grief. He understood the kid needed to lash out at something. It was only natural. But when Barney got a good one in that almost flattened his windpipe, he grabbed the boy's fist and said calmly, 'Stop, Barney. I didn't do anything. It was your dad's choice.'

The punches stopped as suddenly as they started. Barney dropped his hands and looked up at him, his eyes full of tears. 'What are you talking about?'

'Your dad was many things, Barney, but he wasn't stupid. He knew what would happen once Hartnell got his hands on him, and that it wouldn't be pretty. You understand what I'm saying?'

The boy swallowed. 'You . . . you mean they'd torture him?'

'Maybe not torture, but they would have certainly drawn things out to maximize the pain. See, your dad had already come to terms with the fact that he wouldn't survive this, but what he was most concerned about – other than making sure you were safe – was the manner in which he went. He told me that when his time came he wanted it to be on his terms, and that's exactly what he did.'

'What happened?'

'You saw what happened. You don't need to hear the grisly details.'

The boy sniffed. 'I want to know everything. Tell me.'

Bishop studied the boy for a beat, then shrugged. He had the right to hear the truth, if that's what he wanted. 'Nelson here brought along a lot of extra stuff in that bag of his, including five pounds of C4. As soon as your dad saw the two blocks of plastic explosive he came up with the idea of strapping them to his stomach and setting them off once he was alone with Callaway. I agreed, and reshaped the plastique and taped it to his body, then ran the detonator leads through his jacket pocket. That's why he pulled your arms away when you hugged him round the waist. He must have been afraid the stuff might go off by accident, but plastique only ignites when you send a high energy shockwave into the blasting caps.'

Bishop looked out at the still-smoking wreck of the vehicle, imagining Strickland's last few seconds on this earth. With what he now knew of the man, he had no doubt that Strickland had been thinking of Barney at the very last moment as he pressed down on that button. He said, 'I also think your dad purposely waited for the SUV to catch up with the other two vehicles before pressing the button. He told me he wanted to take as many of the enemy with him as he possibly could. No doubt about it, your dad had real guts.'

Barney was silent for a moment. Then he said, 'Did it . . . did it hurt at all?'

'No, it would have been instantaneous, like a light being switched on. Believe me, he wouldn't have felt anything at all. And he went out a winner too, remember that.'

Sniffing back more tears, Barney said, 'A winner?'

'I'd say so. Wouldn't you?'

'I know *I* would,' Nelson said. He was crouched down in front of the gym bag as he carefully placed his rifle inside. He zipped the bag closed and added, 'Your old man had class, kid. When my turn comes I want to go out like that. Not that I will, of course.'

Bishop pulled out his cell phone and checked the display. It was still only 06.23. Astonishing. He'd thought it much later.

'So what happens now?' Nelson asked, rising to his feet.

'Now I call the feds to come bring the two of us in,' Bishop said. 'But there's no reason for anybody else to know of your involvement here, so you'd better take off.'

'You sure, man? I don't mind sticking around. Maybe I can help.'

'You already have, Nels. I won't forget what you did here today.'

Nelson offered Bishop a clenched fist. 'What buddies are for, right?'

'Right,' Bishop said. He bumped fists with his old comrade, and said, 'Now get lost. And take your crap with you.'

'I'm gone.' With a grin, Nelson hefted the gym bag over his shoulder and stepped through the gap in the wall. Then he gave Barney a salute, turned right and immediately disappeared from view.

Barney stared mutely out at the wreckage, which was still sending huge black smoke signals up into the sky, and wiped an arm across his eyes.

Bishop raised the cell phone and keyed in the number he'd memorized while he and Strickland had been waiting in this very spot before. After five rings, the phone was picked up and a male voice said, 'US Marshals Service, Columbus Office.'

'My name's Bishop. I'm here with the son of a missing witness of yours. I understand you've been looking for us . . .'

EIGHTY-TWO

They were both sitting on the ground in front of the main building, waiting for the marshals to arrive, when Barney finally raised his head from between his knees to stare at the wreckage before them. Bishop saw his eyes were red-rimmed, but dry. He wondered if the boy had simply cried himself out, just as Bishop had done all those years ago.

After thirty minutes of silence he was still waiting for Barney to speak, but he figured he'd talk when he was good and ready. That's how Bishop had been after his own personal apocalypse. And after everything he'd been through, the boy deserved his own space and to be able to proceed in his own time.

So Bishop just waited.

The SUV remains were still smoking, although nowhere near as much as before. Bishop had already checked the other vehicles half an hour ago. The one with its roof sheared off had contained nothing but body parts and blood, a real mess. The car lying on its roof had contained three more bodies. The two passengers were dead while the unconscious driver was bleeding badly from numerous wounds caused by the explosion. Bishop just left him there to bleed out. With any luck, the guy was dead by now.

Best thing for him, really.

Finally, Barney gave a long sigh and said, 'So I'm alone now. Mom's dead. Dad's dead. I might as well be dead too.'

'Actually, the exact opposite is true,' Bishop said. 'You have to remember that everything your father did, he did so that you'd come out of this alive and healthy. That's all he cared about, all he talked about these last two days. And while I never met your mother, I can pretty much guarantee she felt the same way. They both lived for you, Barney, and that means you now have to live for them.'

Barney snorted. 'Sure, just live. Piece of cake.'

'Oh, it's anything but. Death is easy, it's living that's hard. I know that. Especially when you've lost the people who mean the most to you. And while it feels as though the sky's falling in on you now, it isn't. You'll get through this. I know you will.'

Barney looked at him. 'Yeah? How d'you know that?'

'Because you're tough, a lot tougher than most kids your age. It's a quality you've clearly inherited from both your mother and your father, and it's something I saw in you the moment I first met you.'

Barney stared at the wreckage. 'So I'm tough. Big deal. I'm still alone, aren't I?'

'Not necessarily. I believe your mom had a sister named Marian Slocombe, who lives in West Vancouver, isn't that right?'

The boy turned to him, a puzzled look on his face. 'Yeah, that's right. How'd you know about her?'

'You dad brought her name up while we were waiting for you. Said she'd moved up there some time back and that she was married with her own kids. He also said that while she'd never had much time for him she'd always been real fond of you, and he made me promise I'd go up there afterwards and tell her everything that happened. He seemed certain that she'd be happy to have you and that she'd do a good job of bringing you up right.'

'Aunt Marian,' Barney said quietly to himself. 'I forgot about her. Yeah, she didn't like Dad *at all*, but, you know, she always loved me. And she always treated me like one of the family too.'

'That's because you are. So maybe you're not quite as alone as you first thought.'

Barney gave a small frown, as though considering the possibility that there was some hope left for him. Then Bishop turned his head as he heard something that sounded like helicopter rotors in the distance. Looking up, he spotted two small specks approaching from the south-east and watched as the two specks gradually morphed into two helicopters. The larger one looked like a Sikorsky Black Hawk. He recognized the familiar bulky shape immediately. The other one was smaller and looked like a standard police Airbus.

'Looks like our ride's here,' he said.

Barney followed his gaze up to the two approaching choppers.

Thirty seconds later the Black Hawk reached the square and began to descend. It was black with a gold stripe running around the main body. The side door had already been slid into the open position and half a dozen armed agents were sitting inside, all watching Bishop. The harsh air currents from the rotors tore at his face as the chopper got closer to the ground.

Over the noise of the rotors, Bishop yelled, '*Better move away from me, Barn.*'

Barney didn't ask why. He just got up and moved ten feet to Bishop's right. The moment the helicopter's landing gear made contact with the ground, everybody poured out of the side door. Two men immediately crouched down close to the skid and covered the immediate area with automatic weapons as the other four ran towards Bishop and Barney.

Bishop knew what was coming next. He raised both hands and watched them approach.

Three males, one female, all carrying Glocks. The female and two of the men wore navy-blue caps, and navy-blue windbreakers with US MARSHALS printed in large white letters down the sleeves. The third man was in plain clothes.

When they were still only twenty feet away all four slowed to a trot and spread out. The male marshal in front yelled, '*On your knees, Bishop. Hands behind your head. Hands behind your head. Move.*'

Bishop obeyed. He raised himself up until he was on his knees and then clasped both hands behind his head. Behind the approaching figures, he saw the smaller chopper gently touch down about a hundred feet behind the Black Hawk. More figures exited this second chopper and moved towards the wrecked vehicles beyond.

The first marshal stopped in front of Bishop, his Glock still aimed at Bishop's head, and said, 'Don't move an inch. Just remain perfectly still.'

The other two marshals had already moved behind Bishop, and he felt himself being body-searched. He was no longer armed anyway. After wiping his prints off Trooper Steve's Glock 22, he'd placed the gun next to the dying gunman in the overturned car. He already had enough problems without adding possession of a stolen firearm to the list.

One of the marshals behind Bishop pulled his left hand down and snapped a flex cuff around the wrist. Then the other one. Bishop saw that the plain-clothes guy had holstered his weapon and was now showing Barney his ID while he spoke to somebody on his cell.

'What the hell went down here?' the first marshal asked. He was a burly, bearded, black guy of about Bishop's age, with small eyes and linebacker's shoulders. Bishop figured he had to be the senior marshal here.

Bishop said, 'Am I under arrest?'

'We'll call it protective custody for now,' the marshal said, and holstered his gun. 'Now what happened here, and where's that boy's father?'

'He's dead.'

'Dead? How?'

Bishop briefly explained how the man had blown himself up along with a large contingent of bad guys. When the marshal pressed for more details, he quickly went over the main events of the past two days: the escape from the safe house with Strickland and Barney; the firefight that resulted in the deaths of the two state troopers and Barney's kidnapping; Callaway's ultimatum and the deadline; their race across the country to get to Ohio in time. Bishop was just getting to the exchange itself when another marshal from the other chopper approached the black marshal and began speaking to him in a low voice.

The plain-clothes man also walked over to their group with Barney in tow. The boy was chewing his cheek and staring at everybody in turn.

Once the two marshals had finished their mini conference, the black deputy turned to Bishop and said, 'Seems some of the hostiles were taken out by rifle fire originating from this building behind you. Would that be the same person who supplied the plastic explosive?'

'It would.'

'So who is he?'

'A friend of mine. You just missed him.'

'Uh-huh. And this friend of yours, does he have a name?'

'Everybody's got a name.'

The marshal was about to say something else, but the plain-clothes man cut in with, 'Deputy Yeaton, I need to speak with you.'

The black marshal turned to him. 'What about?'

'I've talked to District Attorney Raines and he wants to talk to the boy here without delay. I'm to fly back to the courthouse immediately with him.'

'So go. You can take the Airbus back.'

'I would, except he refuses to go anywhere unless Bishop here goes with him.'

Yeaton looked at Barney. 'And why's that, son?'

'I'm not your son,' Barney said, his expression hard and unyielding. 'I don't know you and I don't know any of these people. But I know Bishop, and I trust him. And I want him with me.'

'Well, you can see we've got a lot of bodies here and the police will want some answers when they get here. And it's important that this man give them to us while it's still fresh in his mind. You do understand that, right?'

'I don't care,' Barney said. 'I'm not talking to anybody unless Bishop's with me, and that's that.'

Bishop silently applauded the boy. Only twelve years old and already refusing to take crap from anyone. But then it wasn't exactly surprising. Barney had had to grow up fast over the last couple of days, and he'd been pretty mature to begin with.

'See what I mean?' the plain-clothes guy said. 'Now you can call your superior if you want, but he'll only tell you what you already know, which is that the DA's directives take full priority here. Anyone who wants to interview Bishop can do it back at the courthouse, but we have to leave now.'

Yeaton gave a loud sigh. 'Fine. Williamson, Palmer, you stay here with the others and wait for the sheriff's department to get here. Tell them Golinski and me are flying back with the two witnesses and Mr Goodwin here. Got it?'

The marshal who'd spoken with Yeaton said, 'Yes, sir,' and trotted back towards the others. One of the other marshals behind Bishop helped him to his feet and then the five of them began walking towards the two choppers. He noticed the smaller one, the Airbus, was already powering up again. When they reached the chopper Yeaton helped Bishop aboard, placing him on the rear bench seat next to Golinski. Goodwin, Yeaton and Barney took the seats opposite. Nobody bothered trying to talk over the noise of the rotors, which rose steadily in pitch until it became almost deafening. The pilot completed his instrument checks, then took them up and headed back in the direction from which he'd come.

While everybody else stared out the windows, Bishop spent the journey looking at his shoes, thinking. There were still a number of other problem areas that nagged at him. More than a few, in fact. There was his own legal situation, of course, which was shaky at best, but he felt confident that would work itself out. Mrs Lomax could probably help in that regard, along with that footage on her husband's hard drive. But he could worry about all that later.

Right now he was going through every conversation he'd had with John Strickland over the past two days, paying extra special attention to the pauses, since it was often during those moments of hesitation that you got the real story. Back when they were in Clea's Explorer, for example, he'd asked Strickland, '*You saw him do it?*' in reference to Hartnell. And Strickland had hesitated for a moment before confirming that he had. Just a small thing, but that little pause had puzzled Bishop at the time. And it still puzzled him.

Then there were those phone calls between Strickland and Barney. In particular, that moment when Barney had said he was sorry. At the time Bishop had assumed he was apologizing for putting pressure on his father to testify, but now he wasn't quite so sure. So he went through everything again, slowly, methodically, piece by piece, missing out nothing.

Thirty minutes later they were flying over the outer suburbs of Columbus and heading towards the city centre when the clouds thinned out and the sun made a belated appearance. Which matched Bishop's state of mind perfectly. He'd gone through a wealth of possibilities regarding the night of the murder and was now left with just one. He sensed it was the right one. Slowly, it had all begun to take shape in Bishop's mind, with all the disparate pieces of the puzzle gradually coalescing to form a cohesive whole.

He still found it hard to believe. Yet while he recognized he could be completely off the mark, he didn't think he was. The whole scenario made too much sense, especially when you considered where they were all headed.

Bishop felt a sudden shift in altitude and looked out the window as they descended. He saw they were currently passing over a bend in the Scioto River and approaching the downtown business district. The pilot was taking them towards a modern, seven-storey building that took up an entire square block. The county courthouse, if that's what it was, looked as though it had just been completed yesterday. It was all very twenty-first century. The north side was broken up by a series of horizontal windows, while the west side was almost entirely made up of glass. Bishop couldn't see the other sides, but he figured they were probably heavy on the glass too.

The pilot took the helicopter down.

As soon as the skids touched the roof surface Yeaton slid the door open and got out, and the others followed. He led them all towards a small square building where Bishop saw another marshal already waiting, next to an open door. Through the door they all went, into an enclosed concrete stairwell. They descended the fire stairs in single file, Bishop and Barney in the middle, Yeaton in the lead, talking in low tones on his cell phone. Yeaton brought them to a halt on the seventh-floor landing, then opened the fire door and stepped through. Bishop and the others followed him into a short, naturally lit, high-ceilinged corridor with a right turn at the end.

After the turn they entered a much longer and much wider corridor with administrative offices running down the right-hand side. Natural light poured in from the exterior glass walls on the left-hand side. The floor was polished concrete. It seemed to be a fairly quiet little corner of the building, with not much pedestrian traffic. Or maybe it was just a quiet part of the day. Bishop spotted two men in suits standing outside a set of double doors thirty feet away. Even from a distance Bishop was able to recognize one of them. He'd seen him being questioned on the news two days before, Deputy Director Whitaker of the US Marshals Service. And he assumed the other one was District Attorney Raines. He was a thin man in his fifties, and wore rimless glasses that failed to hide the heavy bags under his eyes.

Once they reached the two men Yeaton immediately spoke in low tones with Whitaker, while Raines came over to Barney and placed a hand on his shoulder, moving him away from the others as he talked to the boy. Bishop noticed one of the double doors behind Whitaker was partly ajar. Through the thin gap he saw what looked like a large, spacious meeting room. Two harried-looking men in shirtsleeves were sitting at a conference table covered with paperwork and legal pads, talking amongst themselves.

Whitaker left Yeaton and came over to Bishop. He looked him up and down, and said, 'You have any idea of the grief you've caused my office these last two days, Bishop? And not just us, either. Just about every sheriff's office and police department from here to the West Coast has had men on the streets looking for you, and at the end of it our witness is still dead. So tell me, was it worth it?'

'No question about it,' Bishop said, glancing over at Barney, 'and I'd do it all again if I had to. Look, am I under arrest or what? Yeaton was kind of vague on the subject.'

Whitaker sighed. 'No, you're not, at least not yet. However, you'll remain in our custody until you've undergone a thorough debriefing by the relevant authorities, and I do mean *thorough*. Later we'll take you over to our offices at the federal courthouse a couple of blocks from here and get started, but you can expect to write off the next two days, at least. And possibly longer.'

'And I'm going to be in chains all that time?'

Whitaker studied him for a moment, then said, 'I think we can probably lose the cuffs for now. Deputy?'

'Sir.' Yeaton came over, pulled a small pair of wire cutters from his utility belt and turned Bishop round.

'Just so you know,' Whitaker said, 'at least two of my people will be with you at all times while you're in this building, so don't get any funny ideas.'

'All I want is a quiet life,' Bishop said. The cuffs were removed and he brought his hands round. 'I'm curious, though. I got the impression from the news that I was Public Enemy Number One. How come we're friends all of a sudden?'

'The news media don't know everything, Bishop. But we do. And over the last twenty-four hours we've been busy interviewing a number of people who were able to fill in a lot of blanks for us. There was a store owner named Clea Buchanan for one, and a pilot named Charles Hooper for another. Oh, and an old couple named Roger and Eleanor Souza. You remember them?'

'Yeah, nice couple. I liked them. I like them even more now. So tell me, is the man himself here yet?'

'If you mean Hartnell, he and his army of lawyers are due to arrive sometime within the hour. Although without the key witness I imagine it'll only be a brief appearance.'

Raines came over and said, 'Whitaker, I need to confer with Barney in private and he's demanding that Bishop be present with him.' He looked down at his wristwatch. 'Time is of the essence, so if you don't mind . . .'

'Fine,' Whitaker said. 'I'll be down on the second floor. Yeaton, you and Golinski remain at this door. Bishop doesn't leave this room without you both accompanying him.'

'If you'll follow me,' Raines said to Bishop, and entered the conference room with Barney. Bishop followed.

Inside, he saw five males and two females sitting around the conference table, all smartly dressed. A third woman was standing next to a water cooler, sipping from a paper cup. Bishop assumed they were all part of Raines' staff. They all stopped what they were doing to stare at the newcomers. Bishop turned away from them and saw there was another door set into the left-hand wall. Raines had already opened it and stood there waiting.

Bishop went over and followed him into a small, spartan, windowless office. Lights hidden in recesses in the ceiling gave the illusion of natural daylight. The room contained a large desk with a phone, four chairs, and three steel filing cabinets set against the opposite wall. There were no decorations.

After shutting the door, Raines marched over and sat in the chair behind the desk with a heavy sigh. 'Not much to look at, I know,' he said, gesturing them to sit. 'Our normal day-to-day offices are in the municipal court building across the way, but it's convenient to have a couple of rooms set aside for us here for major cases.'

Barney took the middle chair while Bishop took the one on the left. He sat down, looked at Raines and said, 'I have to say I'm impressed, Raines. I really am.'

The DA frowned at the spare office. 'I'm afraid you've lost me. Impressed with what?'

'At how you've managed to keep it a secret all this time. It's pretty remarkable, actually. I only realized the truth a short while ago myself, although I admit the clues were there from the beginning. I guess I just didn't pay them enough attention at the time.'

Barney was watching Bishop. Raines leaned forward and made a steeple of his hands. 'And what have you learned, exactly?'

'That John Strickland was nothing but a decoy,' Bishop said, 'used to divert attention away from the real witness.'

He turned to the boy. 'His son, Barney.'

EIGHTY-THREE

Barney gave an apologetic shrug. 'Sorry, Bishop. I would have told you before now, but I never got the chance.'

Bishop smiled. 'No, I guess you didn't. Not that it would have made any difference. So you were actually right there when Hartnell pulled the trigger? You were the one who saw it all first hand?'

'Yeah, I saw everything.'

'From your vantage point on the second floor of that old building we just left, right?'

The boy's eyes widened a little. 'How'd you know that?'

'When you regained consciousness in that same building earlier you said you recognized it, but since from the inside it could have been anywhere I don't see how you could have. Unless you *had* actually been in that building before, like on the night of the murder perhaps. So you want to tell me about it?'

The boy gave a small sigh. 'It was all just bad luck, really. See, that night I was sleeping over at a friend's house, which was kind of a regular thing with us. One week I'd stay at his and then the week after he'd stay with me. You know, watching movies and playing video games and stuff. Except this time he woke me up in the middle of the night and told me they'd got an emergency call a few minutes before. He said his grandfather over in Washington State had had a heart attack and he was in hospital and he wasn't expected to live. He told me they were already packing for the next flight out, and that his mom had already called Dad . . . called Dad to come get me.'

Barney closed his eyes for a moment, no doubt thinking about his father. Then he opened them and went on, 'So when Dad showed up I was still pretty groggy, but he told me he was already late for an important appointment and that I could just sleep in the back of the

374

car while he drove there. So that's what I did. When I woke up again, I saw I was wrapped up in a thick sheet and the car had stopped moving. It was still pretty dark out, but the sky was getting a bit lighter so I knew it was almost dawn, and I saw we were parked behind this old wreck of a building. I couldn't see Dad anywhere, but I knew he'd be around somewhere so I got out the car and started exploring. It felt exciting at the time, you know? I could hear these weird machinery noises in the distance and I imagined I was the last man on earth and the robots had taken over. You know, like in the movies.'

'I know,' Bishop said. Sometimes it was easy to forget Barney was just a twelve-year-old boy, with a boy's occasional need for make-believe.

Staring at the desk in front of him, Barney continued, 'So I was doing my recon of the building and found some stairs and went up to the second floor, and then I started hearing voices from outside. I went to one of the front rooms and looked down and saw this limo with its lights on and five men stood around it. I could see 'em all clearly. There was Hartnell, and that guy from today, and some guy in a raincoat and baseball cap, and the undercover cop guy, and my dad. After a few seconds Dad started walking back to the car. I figured he'd freak if he didn't find me there, so I was about to head back myself when I heard the voices getting louder and I stopped and went back to the open window.

'Hartnell and this cop were arguing about something, then this guy in the raincoat pointed at Ferrera and said something. Then Hartnell turned to him and said, "Are you sure?" I remember that even now. And this guy in raincoat nodded back and said something else. Then Hartnell pulled a gun and just shot the guy right there, and he just kept pulling the trigger until the gun was empty.'

'You must have been terrified,' Bishop said.

'Oh, yeah, I was. But I knew I had to be cool and stay quiet or I'd be next, so I made my way downstairs without making a single sound and then went back to the car. Except the car wasn't there anymore, which totally freaked me out. See, Dad had just sped off thinking I was still under that sheet. I spotted the car about a hundred feet away, though, and ran after it, but I knew I couldn't shout for him to stop or they might hear too. But luckily he spotted me in the mirror and braked and then reversed the car until I caught up. Then he drove us away and I told him what I'd seen and he got real mad and said I should just forget I saw anything. But I couldn't forget it. Some people can forget things easily, but I can't. And when I told Mom about it, she just laid right into Dad and told him enough was enough, and that . . .' Barney paused and raised a hand to his eyes. He sniffed, clearly close to tears, and said, 'Sorry, it's just . . .'

Bishop placed a hand on the boy's shoulder and gave it a gentle press. 'I know.'

'I can fill in the rest,' Raines said, looking quickly at his watch. 'To cut a long story short, Barney's conscience kept nagging at him and he felt more and more compelled to report what he'd seen to the authorities. His mother, aware that getting them into witness protection would finally get them all out of the life she hated so much, took his side and together they pressured his father until he finally gave in. He was willing to finally leave the business to hold onto his family, but there was one proviso he insisted on.'

'He'd assume the role of witness instead of Barney,' Bishop said.

Raines tapped the table with a palm. 'Correct. John knew that once Hartnell was charged with murder he'd do everything in his power to track down the witness and silence him permanently. So John knowingly set himself up as the focal target, knowing that if anything did happen he'd get the full brunt of it and Barney would be left unharmed. Unfortunately, Barney's mother . . . well, you know what happened there.'

Bishop just nodded.

Raines shook his head and sighed. 'Of course, when the FBI originally turned the case over to me I told them they didn't have a chance in hell of getting a conviction against Hartnell. I certainly admired John's courage in coming forward, but I also knew I couldn't possibly put him before a jury. With his arrest history I knew the defence would tear his credibility apart in minutes, the trial would be over before it had even begun and I'd end up as the laughing stock of the entire city. So I told them they had to either bring me more evidence or just forget the whole thing.'

Raines turned in his seat and looked at the shut door. 'Soon after, the family requested a private meeting with me in my office, just the four of us. And that's when they finally admitted to me that it was the son who'd actually witnessed the murder, not the father, and that's the moment I knew I was sitting on a gold mine. Even after a few minutes I could see Barney possessed all those qualities I look for in a key witness. He's intelligent, well spoken, quick-witted, forthright and, best of all, earnest. And I knew with him on the stand I'd have a real chance at finally putting Hartnell away for good. The only drawback was that both mother and father insisted that Barney's true role in this remain a secret until the trial date itself.'

Bishop said, 'What about the full disclosure rule? I thought all prosecution witnesses have to be listed by their full names.'

'Ordinarily, yes, but I found a precedent in an obscure attempted murder case from 1997, *United States v. Murdoch*. In that case the prosecution was concerned about religiously motivated reprisals against his key witness before the trial date and so he managed to have the court records amended so that the witness was listed by his surname only, since it was a fairly common name anyway. After conferring with Judge Koteas in his chambers where I explained the whole situation in full, he finally agreed that Barney could be granted the same protection as the witness in the Murdoch case. Just surname only.'

'Okay.' Bishop scratched under his chin. 'I've got one more question, though. Marshal Delaney told me the first trial date was postponed because John suddenly got cold feet, but that clearly wasn't the case. So what was the real reason?'

'That *was* the reason,' Raines said. 'It was just applied to the wrong person.'

'I got a panic attack that first time,' Barney said in a soft voice.

Bishop looked at him. '*You?* I don't believe it.'

'Oh, yeah, and it was a bad one too. That morning I suddenly realized what I was doing and I guess I just folded from all the pressure. I was shivering and everything, a total mess. Mom and Dad took care of me and somehow managed to keep it from the marshals, then Dad called Mr Raines here and told him everything and Mr Raines went to the judge and got him to put the date back. The next day I was fine, though, and I promised Mr Raines it wouldn't happen again. And it won't. I'm gonna tell my side now. Hartnell took Mom and Dad from me and I'm ready to make him pay.'

'That's why we're here, Barney,' Raines said. He checked his watch again. 'Now we've got just over an hour to get you prepared before the trial begins, so first we'll need to get you some presentable clothes. Nothing too ostentatious, a plain white button-down shirt, some smart chinos and a pair of black shoes should be sufficient. I'll get an assistant to take care of that in a moment, right after I introduce you to the rest of my staff in the next room. Then once I've brought them all up to date on the situation we'll do a couple of run-throughs to give you an idea of what to expect in the courtroom. It's just a formality. Believe me, you'll have nothing to worry about.'

'I'm not worried,' Barney said.

Raines smiled. 'Just a figure of speech. I know you'll be fine. Now before we get started, I just want to give you a few words of advice—'

'Which courtroom will it be?' Bishop interrupted.

'Courtroom 2A,' Raines said, turning to him. 'On the second floor.'

Bishop stood up to leave.

'Where you going?' Barney asked.

'I'm surplus to requirements here, Barney. This is your show now and I'll just get in the way. Besides, I'll still be in the building. Just make sure you stay with Raines and his people at all times and I'll catch up with you later.' He looked down at the boy. 'Okay?'

Barney looked up at Bishop for a moment, then nodded. 'Okay.'

Bishop turned to Raines and said, 'Nail the bastard to the wall.'

'We'll do our best,' Raines said.

Bishop patted Barney's shoulder and left them both.

EIGHTY-FOUR

Bishop passed through the conference room and opened the outer door. Yeaton and Golinski were standing on the other side of the hallway with the light at their backs.

'Going somewhere?' Yeaton asked.

'Thought we might take a trip to the second floor,' Bishop said, pulling the door shut behind him. 'Shall we take the elevator or stairs?'

Yeaton's eyes narrowed. 'I don't know about this . . .'

'I do. Look, your deputy director said I've got the freedom of the building as long as you're with me, and I want to see Hartnell in person. So let's go.'

Yeaton called Whitaker on his cell, who confirmed it was okay, then the three of them took the fire stairs down to the second floor. Yeaton led them to the main central corridor, which was already bustling with people, all walking with purpose towards their individual destinations. Bishop noted the various courtrooms were on the left-hand side, while more conference rooms took up the right-hand side, along with meeting rooms and some jury assembly rooms. A constant stream of people entered and exited the rooms on this side. Finally, they reached a large open mezzanine section on the right, with glass railings for spectators to see below. In the centre of this section was a long staircase made of glass and concrete. Thanks to the natural light, it actually seemed to float up from the ground floor.

Bishop leaned against the railing and gazed down at the foyer while the two marshals stood a couple of feet away. And he waited.

Felix Hartnell entered the building at 08.42.

He was hard to miss. He was accompanied by half a dozen very smartly dressed lawyer types, all of whom carried large briefcases and laptop bags, as well as two dozen reporters who were throwing questions at him as he walked. Even from a distance, he appeared calm and unruffled, as though this first-degree murder charge was nothing more than a minor misunderstanding. He passed through the security checkpoint with his team of lawyers, leaving the reporters and the TV cameras on the other side. He and his team then began climbing the stairs to the second floor.

Bishop noticed Whitaker had joined them at some point. He was standing alongside Golinski and Yeaton, watching Hartnell and his people without expression. A few other people on this floor had also stopped what they were doing and had come to the railings to see the source of the commotion below.

Hartnell finally reached the second-floor landing, still talking to one of his lawyers. As he turned, his pale grey eyes found Bishop and he stopped speaking and began walking towards Bishop with a ghost of a smile on his lips. Bishop knew Hartnell was supposed to be in his mid-fifties, but he looked at least a decade younger, even close up. His stern face was almost without a wrinkle and there wasn't a hair out of place on his head. It seemed there was no limit to what plastic surgery could do nowadays. His dark suit looked as though it had been moulded to his six-foot frame. He looked like the king of the world.

As he came closer he gazed briefly at Yeaton, then Golinski, before his eyes locked onto Bishop's again. Whitaker he ignored entirely. Purposely, it seemed. It was as though the man didn't exist. Still smiling, Hartnell passed within a couple of feet of Bishop and kept on walking down the corridor, his lapdogs still surrounding him.

Bishop, still leaning against the railing, watched him go.

Twenty feet further on, one of the lawyers opened a door to one of the meeting rooms on the left, then stepped inside. Hartnell came to a stop and turned back to Bishop. The other lawyers also entered the room until Hartnell was left on his own. One guy came out again and said something to him. Without turning his head, Hartnell snapped something back at him and the lawyer quickly ducked back inside. Hartnell just stood there, watching Bishop.

It seemed like an invitation, so Bishop pushed off from the railing and walked over to him.

Once he'd closed the distance, Hartnell said, 'So you're this Bishop I've been hearing about these last couple of days.'

'Been causing you problems, have I?'

'More a minor annoyance than anything. Kind of like an angry mosquito buzzing around my head. Nothing more than that.'

'Mosquitos kill over a million people a year. Other than man, they're the most lethal species on the planet.'

'Maybe so, but they also have a very short shelf life. Once second they're there, the next second they're gone – *poof* – like they never existed. Life's very fleeting for some creatures.' Hartnell gave Bishop a lazy smile, and said, 'It seems our paths crossed in an indirect way a few years back, in regards to an accountant who left my employ.'

'Depends on your definition of "indirect", but you're essentially correct.'

'Small world.'

Bishop nodded. 'Small world.'

'And I also hear that you took a big loss this morning. That's a real shame.'

'Seems we both took a loss this morning.'

'You mean Dominic?' Hartnell shrugged. 'Well, it's an inconvenience, I admit, but sometimes you have to make sacrifices for the greater good.'

'That's one thing we agree on then.'

Hartnell's smile dimmed. 'And what does that mean?'

Bishop fought the temptation to tell him he'd actually had the real witness in his hands for the last two days and had let him go. And that even if his lawyers somehow pulled a miracle in the courtroom today and got him off, he still had Rafael Guzman to look forward to. But the very last thing Bishop wanted to do was ruin the surprise, so he just said, 'You're a smart guy, Hartnell. You'll figure it out soon enough. Incidentally, I don't suppose the name Andrew Truman means anything to you at all?'

Hartnell gave another shrug. 'Can't say it does. Why? Who is he?'

'Maybe it'll come to you over the coming weeks, maybe not. Either way, I know you've got a big day ahead of you so I won't waste any more of your precious time.'

Hartnell's smile returned. 'Very understanding of you. Well, until we meet again, Bishop. Because I've got a feeling we will.'

Bishop smiled too. 'Don't count on it,' he said, then walked away.

EPILOGUE

It was 23.34 on a cold, drizzly Tuesday evening in mid-December, and Bishop was sitting in a rented Infiniti parked directly across from a three-storey townhouse on Chapin Street NW, in the Columbia Heights section of Washington, DC. The affluent, well-lit street was lined with similar houses, but 1209 had been converted into three separate apartments, one per floor, some time back. Bishop also knew that the tenant on the second floor was named Miss Veronica Knapp, that she was an adjustment clerk for a small IT consultancy in town, and that she'd signed a long lease agreement two years earlier.

But since Miss Knapp's salary didn't come close to covering the rent, the rental agency had required a guarantor at the signing stage to ensure she met her future obligations. In this case, the guarantor had been the company director of Hyacinth Inc., which, as it turned out, was an umbrella company registered in the Cayman Islands ten years previously.

Bishop was currently waiting for the company director to emerge from 1209's front door. The man generally spent two or three evenings a week in Miss Knapp's company, and this was one of those evenings. Bishop had seen him arrive at 20.34, and once he'd parked his Audi on the street he used his own key to let himself into the house. He'd been up with Miss Knapp for three hours already, so Bishop felt sure it wouldn't be long now. The small street was still empty of pedestrians, just like it had been for the last hour or so. It seemed nobody was willing to endure this grim weather unless absolutely necessary.

As Bishop waited, he once again cast his mind back to the events of the last four weeks. A lot had happened since that first day of the trial.

Barney had wowed them in the courtroom, of course, as Bishop had known he would. After he'd finished giving his testimony Hartnell's chief attorney had tried his damnedest to break him down, but the boy remained steadfast and refused to budge a single inch. It seemed he'd developed nerves of steel over a very short space of time. And Raines had been spot on. The jury loved him. The following Tuesday they proved it with a unanimous guilty verdict. Hartnell was handed a straight thirty-to-life, no parole.

Or so he thought.

Ten days later, the so-called King of Coke was found dead in his Ohio State Penitentiary cell with barely a square inch of skin left on his body. And Bishop knew he'd probably been alive while it happened. Nobody saw anybody go in the cell, and nobody saw anybody come out. Nobody heard a thing. Nobody knew anything. But as soon as Bishop read about it in the paper, he knew Guzman had been behind it. Skinning his enemies alive was exactly his style. It must have taken a small fortune to arrange, but he'd finally gotten his revenge on the man who'd killed his sister.

Bishop was also released without charge, as he'd suspected he would be. It helped that his version of events also matched up with those of Clea Buchanan, Charlie Hooper, Roger and Emily Souza, Karen Lomax, and Barney himself. And Nelson Daly's name never came up at any time during the countless interrogations either, which was all to the good.

As for Barney, shortly after Hartnell's death Bishop had driven him up to Vancouver and delivered him into the care of his mom's sister, Marian Slocombe, just as he'd promised. Bishop had visited the woman – an attractive, cheerful forty-something with an easy smile – earlier to sound her out and she'd been understandably devastated at the news of her sister's death as well as that of her brother-in-law. But she'd been the one who'd suggested filing the necessary papers to become Barney's legal guardian from now on. Bishop hadn't even had to ask. He thought that was a good omen. On Bishop's advice, once it was all finalized Barney was going to adopt the Slocombe name too. After all, you could never be too careful.

Barney looked almost happy when Bishop finally left him. Or at least, as happy as a boy who'd suddenly lost both his parents could be.

Bishop still found himself thinking about Angela Delaney, though, especially these past few days, which wasn't all that surprising. She was the main reason he was here in Washington, DC, after all. She was the last loose end. Bishop and she had been intimate once, yet he'd never really known her all that well. But he'd liked her a lot. And he would like to have gotten to know her a whole lot better, but that was no longer possible. She was dead. And the man indirectly responsible was currently inside the house across the street, enjoying himself with his mistress.

Well, that was okay. After tonight, he wouldn't be enjoying much of anything again.

At 23.42 the front door to 1209 opened and a man in a dark raincoat exited the house.

Bishop watched Lawrence Whitaker pull up his coat collar, then close the door behind him and begin walking down the long path towards the sidewalk and his parked Audi.

After checking the street was still empty of pedestrians, Bishop immediately got out of the Infiniti and shut the door and crossed the street towards the Audi. He was wearing a tan raincoat and kept both hands in his pockets and his head lowered as he closed in on his quarry. As Whitaker reached the driver's side of his vehicle, Bishop stepped onto the sidewalk and, still with his head down, walked towards him. There was an electronic beep as Whitaker unlocked the vehicle and, as he was opening the driver's door, the interior light came on and Bishop stepped up behind him and pulled the gun from his pocket and jammed the barrel into his lower back.

'Hello, Whitaker,' Bishop said. 'Now get in and slide on over to the passenger side. You and I are going to have a little talk. And make sure you keep your hands in plain sight.'

Whitaker stood stock still. Without turning, he said, 'Bishop? Is that you? What the hell is this?'

'It's me. Now stop talking and get in. Don't make me ask twice.'

Whitaker looked ready to say something else, but Bishop added pressure to the barrel and he raised his hands instead. Then he carefully ducked down and slid into the Audi's front seat. As he clambered over to the passenger side, Bishop got in the driver's seat in one fluid motion and shut the door, instantly killing the interior light.

Whitaker looked at the gun pointed at his stomach, then at the black leather gloves Bishop was wearing. He said, 'You've just crossed the line, Bishop. I hope you realize that.'

'Funny, I was just about to say the same thing to you. Keep those hands up.' Bishop then patted him down and when he felt the telltale bulge around the waist, he opened the man's raincoat and pulled the Glock from the belt holster. Using one hand, he quickly ejected the magazine and tossed the gun on the floor in the back. The magazine he pocketed.

'All right,' Bishop said, 'you can lower them now.'

Whitaker pulled his hands down to his lap, and said, 'So now what? I assume you've got a reason for threatening me like this?'

With his free hand, Bishop reached into his own raincoat and pulled out a large manila envelope and dropped it on Whitaker's lap.

Whitaker looked down at the unmarked envelope, then up at Bishop again.

'Go ahead,' Bishop said, 'open it up. You know you want to.'

Whitaker opened the top flap and pulled out a sheaf of paperwork with a cardboard DVD wallet on top. Using the light coming in from the streetlamps to read by, he began to slowly flick through the paperwork silently. And the photos too, of course.

The thin package had taken a lot of time and effort to compile, and Bishop hadn't been able to do it all on his own. Scott Muro had played a large part in the gathering of information, for example, as had Rafael Guzman, who'd surprised Bishop no end by sticking to his end of the deal. Quite simply, the man had contacts and informants *every*where.

Contained within the package on Whitaker's lap were half a dozen screenshots of Whitaker and Veronica Knapp involved in various intimate bedroom activities. The full footage was on the DVD, and the audio-visual quality was excellent. Bishop himself had installed the tiny camera in Miss Knapp's bedroom ceiling light one morning when she was out at work.

In addition, there were copies of Miss Knapp's rental agreement, including Lawrence Whitaker's signature as guarantor. There were also copies of overseas registration documents proving that Whitaker was the company director and sole employee of Hyacinth Inc., and there were also copies of electronic bank statements showing Hyacinth's deposits into Miss Knapp's account on the first of every month.

But that was all pretty tame compared to the rest of the contents. To begin with there were photos of Whitaker meeting with Hartnell and accepting a briefcase from the man, courtesy of Mr Guzman. There were also a number of financial documents taken from Hartnell's offices, again courtesy of Guzman, that showed large deposits made by one of Hartnell's shell companies into the same Caymans account as the one that paid Miss Knapp's rent.

Then there were the official documents relating to Whitaker's history within the US Marshals Service. They were the real cream topping.

Bishop had begun to seriously suspect Whitaker as being the source of the leak when Hartnell passed the four of them in the courthouse hallway on that first day of the trial. It was only a very small thing, but he'd acknowledged Bishop and the two deputies, yet for some reason completely ignored Whitaker even though he had to know who the guy was. It had seemed pretty odd at the time, and Bishop suspected the simple reason was that he already knew Whitaker very well and overcompensated by pretending the guy didn't exist at all. It was an amateurish mistake, but a mistake nevertheless.

Bishop also recalled something interesting Callaway had said at the exchange, about his finally getting to Mechner '*thanks to a little inside help.*'

Once the trial was over Bishop visited Scott Muro's Brooklyn office to settle his debts, then hired him to find out everything he could about Whitaker, including his history with the Marshals Service, as well as details of his increasingly unsatisfying, not to mention child-less, marriage. One week later Muro came back with the goodies. It turned out that Whitaker's rise to the deputy-directorship had been a slow but steady one through the ranks. He'd actually spent over fifteen years in the field, with seven of those as a supervisory deputy marshal.

And one of his final assignments in that role had been to head the team that looked after Paul Mechner and his wife, ten years ago.

Small world, all right.

In addition, one of those bank statements showed that his company had received a fat two-hundred-thousand dollar payment from one of Hartnell's shell companies the day after Mechner's murder. More recently, his company had received a million-dollar payment from the same shell company the day after Strickland blew himself up.

There was more, and Bishop watched as Whitaker slowly turned the pages and took it all in. It was too dark to really tell, but Bishop imagined his face had lost a lot of its colour in the last few minutes.

Finally, he looked up, his eyes hard, his face grim. 'Where did you get all this?'

'I have my sources.'

'It's all circumstantial. None of it would stand up in a court of law.'

'I'm not interested in the law,' Bishop said. 'But I am interested in settling accounts. You've been in Hartnell's pocket all along, and I know you were the one responsible for the leak of the safe house location that started all this. That leak resulted in the murder of Marshal Angela Delaney. You have to answer for her.'

'Delaney? So you *did* have something going with her then.' When Bishop didn't reply, he said, 'What are you planning to do now? Kill me? In cold blood?'

Bishop shook his head. 'I considered it, but then I realized that for some people there are fates worse than death. Like loss of position and career, for instance. Or public humiliation. Or the break-up of a long marriage. That one can often lead to financial ruin, too, especially if the wife has definite proof that the husband was cheating on her.'

Whitaker looked at him. 'You'd actually send these photos to my wife? So is that what this is about? Blackmail?'

'You're not listening, are you?' Bishop said. 'I'm not interested in anything you can offer me, Whitaker. All I want is to make you pay. And I have.'

'What are you talking about? What have you done?'

'A couple of hours ago an associate of mine went to your nice house and handed your wife another manila envelope containing those same photos of you and Miss Knapp, and that same DVD, which contains explicit footage from which those shots were taken, along with copies of that rental agreement of hers. My sources tell me you and your wife haven't been getting along for a while, so I wouldn't be at all surprised if she's beginning divorce proceedings as we speak. At the very least I expect she'll get that nice house of yours, along with everything in it.'

Whitaker looked at him.

'And by now Director Christiansen has probably already taken possession of an identical package to the one on your lap, minus the stuff concerning Miss Knapp, so I think it's safe to say your career's history too. Similar envelopes have also been delivered to the *New York Times*, the *Washington Post*, the *Huffington Post*, and a few other outlets. Also, the Internal Revenue. I couldn't really leave them out. They love hearing about secret overseas accounts full of undeclared income.'

Whitaker was glaring at him now, his eyes filled with hate. 'You bastard.'

'Takes one to know one,' Bishop said. 'And like you said, it's all circumstantial. Not nearly enough for a conviction, but there's more than enough in there to ruin you. I've got a feeling tomorrow's going to be a very interesting day for you, in all kinds of ways.'

Whitaker was silent as he looked down at the documents and photos that constituted the end of his life as he now knew it.

Bishop was done here. Now he'd said his piece he just wanted to drive back to New York. Pocketing the plastic gun replica he'd been threatening Whitaker with, he opened the door and got out. Leaning down, he said, 'Just so you know, I tossed your Glock in the back with a round still left in the chamber. Personally, I think the easiest thing for everybody would be to simply stick the barrel in your mouth and pull the trigger, but it's up to you.'

Then Bishop shut the car door with a clunk and kept an eye on the man as he crossed the street towards his car. But Whitaker barely paid any attention to him at all. He was still staring down at the contents of the envelope.

Once inside the rental, Bishop turned the key in the ignition and released the handbrake and stuck the gearstick into Drive. He took a long, deep breath and let it out. *That was for you, Angela Delaney. Rest in peace.*

As he pulled away, he glanced over at the Audi and saw Whitaker was half turned in his seat. He looked as though he was searching for something on the floor in the back.

Bishop just smiled to himself and drove on.